Rise From the Ashes

Book one

JD Grace

Cover design by: Bethany Faye Photography

Editing of second edition: Brittney Anderson

For Alyse and Isabella, I love you both to the moon and back! XOXO

Chapter 1

MOTIONLESS, SHE LAID as still as she could, thinking, *how did I get here, and better yet, how do I escape this never-ending Hell?* His arms smothered her, wrapping so tightly to control her every move, even as he slept; she did her best to keep her breaths shallow. Reese knew she couldn't live like this forever, with every breath she drew in she hated herself for not being able to get up in that exact moment, and run.

Reese Landon was as tough as they came, and just as stubborn too. Her bright blue, doe-like eyes, fair skin, and dark brown wavy hair noticeably turned heads everywhere she went. Despite her unyielding disposition, she was compassionate and truly cared for others the way most have forgotten how to in recent years. She laid there wondering how—of all the women out there—she was the one stuck being controlled by the exact type of man she despised.

There had always been red flags that she adamantly ignored, overlooked, or forgave his countless transgressions. Kyra, her partner at work and best friend, tried to warn her, but Reese maintained the idea that things would somehow be different for her. After all, she was never the girl to be pushed around, or so Reese believed. What she had yet to realize was beneath her hard exterior there was a brokenness that often crept in and lingered, giving way to brief moments of insecurity and frailty. It was a growing desperation to simply be loved. It was the kind of desperation a man like Alex enjoyed feeding on, landing her smack-dab in the middle of the kind of relationship she swore she'd never have.

Arrogance oozed from every pore of his impeccable physique and coordinated attire. His skin was beautifully tan with eyes that were hypnotizing green, pairing beautifully with his sculpted muscles. Reese knew that she could never stand a chance against him physically; too often he overpowered her in confrontations. Alex was not the type of man you could pick a fight with and win. He was a natural born hunter who preyed on the weak and vulnerable, his prey of choice being women. With Reese, he knew how to find the cracks in her armor, manipulate, and emotionally damage her. He exploited her weaknesses, took an injured woman, and broke her beyond recognition. Alex Cunningham was a sociopath, at best.

Reese had known Alex for about four years; both were paramedics at the local Fire Department before Alex got transferred from the ambulance, to the truck at Station 35. Reese laid there remembering how different her life was before she had agreed to go on a date with him; one date that became the catalyst to her unforgiving future.

Reese had always been told she was the life of the party, there was never a shortage of love and attention by her peers. She had an unexplainable magic touch with people; full of charisma, tenderness, and an unbeatable finesse. She could talk to just about anyone and often would; she found so much joy in being around others. These qualities were some of the things she thought Alex loved and found endearing about her, but in fact he openly despised her personality and would do everything he could to break her of her nature.

Kyra would get both annoyed and considerably amused by Reese being such a social butterfly, crinkling her freckled nose every time Reese fluttered off to talk to someone else, procrastinating on leaving. Kyra's long strawberry blonde hair would gracefully weave through her thin fingers while she patiently waited for Reese's wings to stop flapping. Reese thought of all the fun times her and Kyra had working together. They were the dynamic duo, everyone's favorite crew—Reese missed that. She missed talking to everyone, being able to tell Kyra everything, but most of all, she missed the person Alex took from her.

Alex was the jealous type, to put it lightly. He spied on her more and more as their two-and-a-half year relationship progressed. He would follow her and Kyra around from call to call, breeding his jealousy with every encounter Reese had with men. Job or not, to Alex, it was inappropriate and he made damn sure his feelings were known. Like a snake, Alex began to slowly constrict Reese squeezing her quietly so she wouldn't notice. He flexed his control over her and soon she was unable to breathe, allowing him to sink in his venom. He first began in subtle ways with snide comments to change her outfits. Initially she thought, oh, he just wants me to look good when we go out. Even when he began monitoring calls and texts, she justified it by thinking, *how can we build trust if I don't let him check? I've got nothing to hide.* Later came full-on explosions of him screaming at her for no good reason. All of their problems became her fault, every bruise from him was warranted, and she brought on the punishment herself by simply not following his rules. Unbeknownst to her, he was able to take her over completely, and he used every opportunity to isolate her from everyone she cared about. He had successfully driven a wedge between Reese and Kyra to where now they barely even spoke. Reese was alone. No one was going to come and save her from this monster she so loved. A part of her didn't want to be saved, she let this happen and now she would have to live with her decision. *I deserve him.*

She glanced at the clock: 3:14 am, still two hours left before she could wiggle from his grasp to get ready for work. Not only did Reese love being a paramedic but, she was good at it too. It was currently the only place she felt at home—in the back of her ambulance, attempting to save lives. On her bus, it was her rules. No one was there to scream in her face and call her a whore, no one to slap her in the face, and no one making her feel worthless like Alex did. In the back of her bus, she was free to be herself, to be the person she loved to be. Alex had chipped away at that joy, eventually, she began to question the way she spoke and treated male patients and even male coworkers. *What if Alex sees me? How do I explain to him that I was just doing my job? How many times will he hit me if I can't convince him?* These thoughts left Reese feeling lost and out of control. Her life had become a constant struggle of emotions. On one hand, she was counting down the minutes before the alarm would go off and she could finally break free of Alex, on the other hand, she dreaded the idea of the alarm stirring him, leaving her to deal with the monster that lay beside her.

After every exhausting shift, she would come home to be interrogated. It was an inquisition—she was forced to prove that her apparent whorish ways didn't bleed out into her work-life. Desperately she tried to prove her innocence with inconclusive evidence hoping her word was enough to convince him otherwise.

Alex had become worse with each passing day; Reese struggled to remember why she fell in love with him in the first place. *Oh, right, his charm.* He made her laugh and made her feel loved. He made her so very dependent on him, feeling desperate for his affection. He wasn't always terrible. In the beginning, he would buy her a bouquet of her favorite flowers for no reason at all. She would beam with adoration, and the biggest smile would spread across her face. He would go out of his way for no particular reason—all just for her. Most of all, he made her body feel things that she didn't know she could feel. Reese fell in love with Alex so hard and fast that she began falling before she knew who he really was. By the time he showed her, it was too late, and now his words from last night's fight rolled around in her head.

"You're a worthless whore! You'll never find another man that'll put up with you like I do! You'll never be anything better than a stupid bitch."

Those words should have made her angry. They should have sparked that fiery attitude to come alive again and rise up within her to leave once and for all, but instead, she believed him. Every word he screamed in her face broke her soul, words she just couldn't shake, and she believed every one of them. Those words crept into the crevices of her heart and brought all the insecurities she ever had to the forefront of her mind. His lies became half-truths which became reality in her head. She was a worthless whore.

Excuse me... just two simple words that sent Alex over the edge. Those words she had said to a random stranger in the grocery store when she had accidentally run into him. That morning everything began peacefully. Alex placed a cup of coffee on the nightstand before he gently moved her hair away from her face and softly kissed her lips.

"Wake up, sleepy head," Alex whispered in her ear.

Coming out of her slumber she smiled before opening her eyes, "Is that coffee?" she mumbled.

"Yes it is, come on babe, get up. I made you breakfast." He sincerely smiled and kissed her forehead.

"Mmm... breakfast and coffee, what did I do to get so lucky?"

"Get outta bed and I will show you just how lucky you are."

With a wink and another kiss, he walked out of the bedroom, leaving Reese to pull herself out of bed. The aroma of coffee was enough to nudge her up. She sat on the edge of the bed for a few short moments, and enjoyed her first sips, taking in the beautiful morning that shined brightly through the curtains. She smiled to herself with delight when she heard Alex rustling around in the kitchen.

She came down the hallway in her yoga pants and tank top finding the table set and holding two incredible omelets, more coffee, toast, and hash browns. Alex made his way around the table in nothing but his boxer briefs. Reese lovingly gazed at him, *what a perfect morning,* she thought as she sat down at the chair he pulled out for her.

"Babe, everything looks amazing! Thank you so much for makin' all of this!" Reese said as she leaned over and deeply kissed him.

"You're welcome, Sweetheart," he replied.

They both began to eat their breakfast and enjoyed the simplicity of each other's company. There was an ease to their conversation with the occasional chuckle, smiles on both their faces. This morning, like so many others, started out so perfect, and Reese began her day with Alex on cloud nine.

"Later today do you wanna go to the store with me? We could get the groceries we need for the week and I need more mouthwash." He asked.

"Sure, I actually need to get a few things for work tomorrow, so that works out good."

The day moved along effortlessly as Reese and Alex portrayed the ultimate loving relationship. They worked quickly as a team to get chores done, and after they fiercely made love as their reward. Reese couldn't be any happier at that moment even if she had tried.

Pulling clothes from the closet to get dressed for the store, Reese pulled a shirt from the hanger in the closet, holding it up awaiting Alex's approval.

"Wear this one instead, that one is too tight." He told her.

"Oh, okay." She agreed and mindlessly changed her shirt.

When they arrived at the store they picked out items they would need for the next couple weeks, making plans for dinner that night, and ensuring they had food for work. Reese was so busy trying to keep her focus on the ground and not on the world around her that she didn't realize she was walking right into a man's path. The man and Reese ran into each other, bumping their shoulders together, causing Reese to spin around and frantically register what had happened.

"Excuse me, sorry," she blurted out nervously before she could stop the accidental interaction. It had all happened within a few short seconds— a split second, one wrong decision, one wrong response was all it took to deviate from their course of happiness into Round 1 of her nightmare. It began as it always did, with him making an innocent situation about something that it wasn't.

"What the hell? Why'd you say excuse me to that guy?" His voice was stern and demanding.

In that instance, Reese was glad they were in public, she was confident that he wouldn't lay a hand on her with witnesses around.

"What are you talkin' 'bout? I ran into him... so, I said 'Excuse Me'." He glared at her. "Pretty sure that's just proper etiquette." She muttered under her breath, instantly regretting that her response was audible to him. She knew her tone, the underlying sarcasm in her words, and her "you're being unreasonable," body language would backfire, and she was right.

When they made it to the car a short time later, she had hoped he had enough time to calm down. Once the doors were shut, like the loose cannon that he was, he began screaming at her just inches away from her face.

"How dare you embarrass me like that, who the fuck do you think you are?" He grabbed her face palming her jaw into a death grip. Her lips were caught tightly between his thumb and fingers. He squeezed so hard that Reese almost couldn't focus on anything Alex was saying. She knew that focusing on the undeniable pain was pointless, so she began to pray it wouldn't bruise like last time. "Do you wanna be with that guy, huh?" He pulled her closer until they were nose to nose. She could feel the spit that flung from his mouth with every word like a rabid dog. "Do you? Why don't you go back inside, find him, and suck his dick, because that's what whores like you do! Is that what you want?" He finally released his grasp on her face as if he was repulsed by her, pushing her head back so hard she hit the window. He lowered his voice in disgust, "Why am I even still with you? All you do is disrespect me! I've lost count of how many times I've told you not to act like such a slut, but you continue to have inappropriate encounters with men! Are you even sorry? Do you even care about what you're doing to me, Reese; to us?"

Reese didn't respond out of fear of saying the wrong thing again. She found a small part of herself hoping Alex would just end their relationship and free her from this prison. She thought, *I didn't do anything wrong, did I? Did I sound flirty when I said excuse me? Did I give a hint of anything other than remorse? Did I do anything truly inappropriate? Ugh, inappropriate.* Reese had grown to despise that word. Alex constantly used it to describe her behavior and she cringed every time she heard it now. Reese looked up to meet his raging gaze, his green eyes wild with fury. *Oh no,* Reese thought, her silence was not the suitable reply Alex wanted, and Round 2 would soon start.

Reese laid there replaying Round 2 in her head. Every slap, every clump of hair he pulled from her head, every time he threw her like a rag doll. The savage look Alex had as he grabbed her by her hair still shook her, it didn't matter how many tears that fell from her cheeks or her screams begging for mercy, he was cruel and he liked it. There was still an overwhelming sense of fear yet to come when she was forced to see the devastation he had left when she looked in the mirror.

BEEP, BEEP, BEEP, BEEP, BEEP.

Reese snapped back to the present when the alarm clock sounded, quickly turning it off, wishing she could slip away unnoticed. Beside her, Alex began to move around with grunts and grumbles as he pulled her toward him, pressing her aching body into his. He held her so tightly that she winced and lost her breath.

"I love you, Reese, I love you so much."

"I love you too, baby," Reese whispered trying to sound convincing, but even she didn't believe it anymore.

She got up out of bed and suddenly he grabbed her wrist. Reese let out a faint whimper of pain as he pulled her back into bed and on top of him. He ran his hand roughly through her hair to the back of her head and she fought tears of pain as he did so. He then pulled her in and firmly pressed his lips against hers, kissing her and forcing his tongue into her mouth. He released his grasp and she scrambled off the bed ensuring she was out of his reach before he could push things any further.

Reese reached for the bathroom door and noticed the huge dent and crack down the middle. *How the...oh right, she thought,* as images of Alex heaving her into the door played in her mind. She lowered her head and wiped the single tear that trickled down her cheek as she prepared herself to look at the damage he had done to her body. She shoved open the bathroom door and switched on the light, revealing the reality of what the night before had left.

Reese immediately noticed the bruising to her right wrist and forearm. She softly ran her hand down her neck as faint bruising became more noticeable, luckily it was nothing her make up couldn't easily fix. She lifted her tank top, horrified that her entire left flank was covered in on giant deep purple bruise; the reason why she could barely breathe. She turned on the shower and pulled out her first aid kit from under the sink as she waited for the water to get hot. *Ace bandage,* she thought knowing she would definitely need that today. As she continued to thumb through her self-made kit she noticed she was getting significantly low on supplies and made herself a mental note to get more at work that day.

She looked up and noticed the steam that was rapidly filling the bathroom now blurring the reflection in the mirror. The shower was nice and hot and felt good running down her sore and bruised body. Thankfully, Alex hadn't been angry like that in several weeks; her body had been able to heal, however, now she was back at square one— long sleeves and heavy make-up. She tilted her head back and as the hot water ran over her head, she sucked air in through her teeth as it burned where he had pulled out her hair. Reese had to suck it up, for the last eighteen months since the abuse began, she had simply powered through the pain every time Alex had gotten like this— as if it was some cruel reward for her forgiveness.

Reese would never forget the first time Alex crossed that line, how scared she was the first time he put his hands around her neck, the first time she begged him to stop fearing for her life, and the first time she looked at herself in the mirror the next morning. That was also the first time she felt an earth shattering disappointment in herself for allowing him to apologize and justify his actions and, worst of all, her forgiving him for everything. That first night, he had choked her so hard that her voice was raspy for three days after, and she was forced to wear a turtleneck in public to hide the substantial bruises he had left. Reese was left with no choice but to take the entire week off work so no one would ask questions about the bruises she couldn't make excuses for. That was one of the worst days of her life and she wanted so badly to believe him when he promised her that it wouldn't happen again. Her gut tried to warn her of the future she had in store for herself by staying, if only she had listened to it. Alex deserved to rot in a prison cell for the rest of his life for what he had done to her, and undoubtedly many others before her.

Reese stood in the shower as that same feeling of self-loathing came over her like a wave. *How can I keep letting this happen? I hate him!* A rush of bravery to leave hit her like a ton of bricks but, within seconds of feeling that courage to walk away, she heard his voice in her head, "No one will ever love you Reese, and you should thank me every day for staying with you. Remember, I can replace you with a snap of my fingers." And it felt as if the water washed her fearlessness down the drain. *I don't want to be alone forever. I don't want to die without love in my life. I just need to learn to follow his rules better so I can avoid this.* Tears flowed from her eyes. *Is this really what love is? Is this really how I am supposed to spend the rest of my life?* Turning off the water she stepped out of the shower and stared at her uniform that hung off the closet door. It was pressed and ready for anything the day would hold. She struggled to get her uniform shirt on. The blinding pain in her side, despite the Ace bandage she had wrapped tightly around her body, made it difficult to raise her arms and she had to catch her breath once she was done. When she finished her final touches she took one last look at herself in the mirror.

She whispered to the battered girl in the mirror, "Everything's gonna be fine, Reese, you're okay, no one can know. Now wipe your tears, beautiful, and put your game face on, it's time to go."

Chapter 2

THE STEAM FROM Reese's coffee cup billowed out of the lid and into the crisp air. She was happy she had chosen to put on her Fire Department sweatshirt, the morning was cold and her oversized sweater made her feel cozy. The engine of the car sat and idled, waiting for Reese to organize her things and, more importantly, her thoughts. She had always had a handful of things she was OCD about, it was important to her to be able to shuffle everything in neat piles and plans; nothing out of place. Even as a kid her mother always loved to tell the story about how Reese had to have all of her shoes and stuffed animals lined up in just the right order, ironically, while the rest of her room was a disaster. The thought of her mother telling that story made Reese giggle under her breath.

Since she moved in with Alex four months into their relationship, she noticed her OCD began to get worse. She became obsessed with everything being in just the right spot and doing things more than once to make sure everything was where it needed to be. The cups had to be spaced evenly in the cabinet, and the cans stacked labels facing out and organized by product in the pantry. Her shoes still had to be lined to perfection just as when she was a kid, but now she had branched out to her clothes being hung up in a specific order and color-coded as well. Her life with Alex was so out of control, she focused hard on the things she could control, obsessing over meaningless tasks.

She sat in her car and placed her travel mug in the cup holder. *Turn it to the left... perfect.* Purse in the passenger seat for easy access, she noticed the air freshener in the vent was not centered and she spent a solid two minutes fixing it. She caught a glimpse of the clock out of the corner of her eye: 735.

"Oh crap, I'm late!"

She pulled out of the driveway and drove down their street, the car grinding, warming up enough to shake off the last bit of cold. When she turned out onto the main road she saw her favorite sight, the sun glistening against the mountain range. Reese lived in a fairly large town just south of Seattle in Auburn. She loved living in Auburn, not too big yet, not too small of a town either. Just like where she grew up in Northern Texas. The closest store to her childhood home was twenty minutes away and yet, everyone knew everything about each other. Gossip in a small town travels fast, like the day Reese and her sister Sophie stole their parents' car. It had spread like wildfire, two teens stealing their folks' car, out for a joy-ride.

Sophie was fourteen years old at the time, most would assume fourteen going on twenty-five with the way she acted, and Reese was only eleven. That night they decided they really wanted some candy and it was worth the risk to get some and Sophie knew which keys to take that were hanging on the key rack by the back door. That night their parents happened to be out on a date and that's when they decided to take their dad's old truck and go to the store. They would have gotten away with it too had the truck not broke down halfway home. They were forced to call their Uncle Trevor to rescue them.

Trevor Landon was Reese's favorite uncle, he was fun and carefree. He stood just shy of six-feet tall with tan skin, light brown hair, and piercing blue eyes. He wore a cowboy hat better than most men could and women fell for Trevor rather easily. They would whisper to each other about how good his butt looked in his wranglers and every time Reese would overhear them she would cringe and wrinkle her nose at the thought of her uncle in that way, yuck, boys have cooties! His all-time favorite saying was "Rules were meant to be broken." Sophie and Reese thought that by calling "Uncle T" they would be safe with their secret. However, Trever loved those girls more than words could express and he gave them an ultimatum instead.

"You girls have a choice to make, either you can tell your parents, or I will. I love you both too much to let this slide. Y'all could've been killed!"

"Please don't do this, Uncle T!" Sophie begged. "Mom and dad are gonna be so mad! We're gonna be grounded FOREVER!"

"Well, Soph, you should've thought about that before you stole the truck."

Reese remembered crying and not saying much the entire ride home, dreading the disappointment in her parents' eyes, but Uncle T didn't leave them much of a choice. When they got home Reese was the one to spill the beans to their parents. She tried to hold it in as Sophie instructed her to, but she blurted it out amongst the tears and fear of hearing it from Uncle T instead.

"We took the truck and drove to the store! I am so sorry! I wanted to get out of the truck! I told Sophie it was a bad idea but she told me I couldn't leave!" Reese began to divulge everything while Sophie sat there and stunned and glaring at her with horror and disbelief. "Sophie said she had done it before when we were all at the football game last week!"

"Reese! How could you?! I can't believe you told them that!" Sophie screamed.

Reese chuckled to herself thinking about how mad Sophie had been at her for that. She didn't speak to Reese for weeks. Reese thought about how it had been the best weeks of her childhood because Sophie avoided her like the plague, and she burst out with a full-on laugh as she turned onto the street where her station was located.

She pulled into the parking lot and saw Engineer West from engine 23 standing with Kyra. Louie West was the only African American they had at the station. He was tall, slightly plump and his bald head glistened in the sunlight. His voice was deep and booming, his eyes were large and chocolate brown and his cheeks round and puffy. He and Reese used to be close. He had told her several times how something wasn't right about Alex and he was worried about her. The day Louie begged her to leave Alex happened to walk up and he overheard the whole thing. The next day, Reese wore long sleeves to cover the bruises Alex had left on her arms, and then effectively terminated her friendship with Louie. Every time Reese saw him after that her heart broke all over again and she felt ashamed. They had been friends longer than she had known Alex. Louie was like a brother to her, and she wanted to tell him that she not only did it for her own safety but for his as well. Reese locked eyes with Louie with nothing but a blank look on her face, attempting to say "Hi" with her weary eyes. She immediately shot her focus back to the ground and then at Kyra.

"Good morning," her eyes darted to Kyra with desperation then quickly back on the ground again.

Reese always hoped that one of these days Kyra would go back to the way things used to be and throw her arms around her. However, Kyra just stood there, her thin body in defiance as she folded her arms. She shot Reese a glance of irritation and a crooked half smile before she turned back to Louie and continued talking.

"So, anyway, like I was saying..." Kyra looked back at Reese, waiting for her to leave.

Reese turned and walked away, she fought back the sting of tears she could feel building in her eyes. Keeping her head down, she looked at the ground to avoid any further unwanted conversation with her other coworkers.

The station was a large brick building with three large bay doors for the truck, engine, and ambulance. She entered through the open bay doors and like she always did, she admired the large red fire truck as she walked by it. She loved her job and she cherished the men and women she worked with. There was a part of her that didn't care about the rules Alex enforced. She secretly adored these people and he could never take that admiration from her. Reese worked with the best of the best. Everyone in her line of business thought they were better than the others, but with her crew, she knew by their humility and drive, they really were the best.

The Chief in her Battalion was Mark Gibbs. He was a legend amongst the emergency services world. His name was well known, even in neighboring cities like Seattle and Olympia, for saving two of his crew members and a four-year-old boy from an apartment fire. The two firefighters had gotten trapped by falling debris while clearing the building. Chief Gibbs went in and cleared a path through a wall to get them out, he happened to find the little boy in the process. Reese stopped and stared at the newspaper article that was framed in the hallway. You could see two firefighters in full turnouts behind Chief Gibbs who was running out of the apartment building holding the young boy. Reese stopped and thought for a moment, *it's a good thing those two guys were behind him or they would have never seen Chief.*

Chief Gibbs was a small but very muscular man with light skin and mousey brown hair that he kept short with a buzz cut. Reese swore he had negative 5% body fat on him. He was always clean shaven and his uniform pristine. Although Chief Gibbs was not the largest man in the Department the way he carried himself demanded respect, and very rarely did he go without it. He was an excellent Chief who deeply cared for his crew, they were all family.

He had called Reese in his office several times over the last two years to ask her if everything at home and in her personal life was okay. The pain on the Chief's face was obvious to Reese, he even told her how she reminded him of his own daughter, and every time they talked they both knew Reese was covering something up. She felt ashamed knowing that she was the cause of the pain behind his concerned eyes. She desperately wanted to be the woman she once was, but that woman was gone now, or so she thought.

"Mornin', Ms. Landon."

She turned to see Chief Gibbs standing behind her holding a hot cup of coffee. *Mmm, coffee,* Reese thought.

"Good Mornin,' Chief." Reese tried to sound as upbeat as she could and she prayed that she had pulled it off.

"Is everything okay, Reese?"

"Yes sir, just need a refill on coffee."

"I just made a fresh pot. See you at the morning briefing." He said with worry spread across his face, he stared into her eyes. Reese flashed a quick smile of reassurance before putting her head down as Chief walked away briskly back to his office.

She kept her head down as the crew went about their morning routine around her, as if she no longer existed, just the way Alex wanted. Reese hated feeling excluded from her work family, especially her brothers that she could no longer talk to. She poured her coffee in silence, stirred in the cream with her thoughts swirling in the cup with it, her night had been terrifying, and now she hoped the hot coffee would wash down the lump in her throat and the persistent fear. She felt a small hand on her shoulder and was startled by the gesture interrupting her thoughts.

"Hey, Reese! Did you get Coffee already?"

Reese smiled when she heard the voice of Jess Atwood, the single most amazing female firefighter she ever knew. This girl was fearless. She held her own against men twice her size even with her medium build and still managed to maintain her femininity; Reese thought Jess was stunning. She had that ever-coveted exotic look, olive skin tone, natural dark mocha beach waves that swayed just below her waist, combined with her gorgeous green eyes, she was absolutely beautiful. She looked like she belonged in a magazine, not turnouts. Despite her out-of-this-world beauty, she was a damn good firefighter and was just about the only friend Reese had left.

"Yeah, I'm already filled and ready to go." Reese managed to muster up a smile.

"You should come out to Charlie's with us tonight and get a drink."

Charlie's was a local dive bar a few blocks away from the station. The whole crew typically went there after night shifts and had a few drinks together. Reese hadn't been there for well over a year since Alex began to forbid her to go. She felt like the whole room stopped and stared at her, waiting for her answer, hoping she had finally come to her senses and was free from her shackles.

"Oh girl, you know, I, um, would love to but I, uh, have dinner thing tonight with Alex and his, um, his parents. Maybe we can another time, yeah?"

Jess looked at her with disappointment in her eyes. She must have known Reese was lying through her teeth, as usual.

"Uh, yeah, maybe next time, no worries."

Reese lowered her head as the side conversations continued once again in the station. She thought about how much fun she used to have at Charlie's with everyone, she even had fun with Alex there at first. He would meet her at the bar when he was off work and initially won most of her crew over with his charm. That was until the night Louie put his arm around Reese when he was drunk. She laughed and helped him to his seat before taking his car keys, and telling him he would be leaving with her so he could get home safely. Once Reese left to take Louie home, she found out that Alex made snide comments of his distaste for guys who get so sloshed in public and what kind of woman would leave with a guy like that, Reese's crew were loyal and easily started to dislike and distrust Alex from then on.

Reese got Louie home and he thanked her several times while they stumbled into his house. She left him on the couch with a puke bucket next to him, just in case. The whole thing was innocent to Reese, to Louie, and the crew. Neither Reese nor Louie realized that would be the beginning of the end for their friendship. Over the next several trips to Charlie's, Alex made his jealousy more known and to avoid any further fights between the guys and Alex, Reese began to slowly pull herself away, declining offers to go out and flat out not talking to the guys anymore.

She turned around to see everyone conversing. She saw Cole Higgins, tall and lean, who was the engineer for the truck. He used to run cross country in high school and still ran in 10K races and even long distance marathons. He was a handsome man all around physically, well except for that awful creeper mustache he grew out last year. Everyone in the station has been begging him to shave it. Cole was roommates with Ray Martinelli, the firefighter on the truck. Ray was your typical Italian, dark brown slicked back hair with a voice and temper that was effortlessly getting him into trouble. His stocky build helped him easily carry his protruding belly. In all the years Reese had known him he was always pudgy, so to speak. Reese continually found Cole and Ray's friendship odd. They fought a lot. Well, Ray fought with Cole and typically Cole ignored him, as per usual, that's what was happening this morning.

"Cole, are you even listening to me about this?" Ray's voice always seemed to carry throughout the station.

Cole continued to read the paper with a half-smile on his face because he knew it frustrated Ray.

Reese drifted her eyes to Kurt Long, captain of the engine. He always sat there in the same chair at the table, drinking his coffee and reading the morning paper. Kurt was short and stocky. His face was slightly weathered from years of experience. He had light brown eyes and sandy-blonde hair that hid his gray hairs quite well. He had bushy eyebrows and unlike Cole, he had an immaculate mustache that framed around his thin lips. Everyone referred to Kurt as "Stump." Reese never knew exactly where the nickname came from but it was certainly catchy, calling him Kurt or Captain Long just didn't seem to fit him. She glanced over and saw Kyra and Louie now sitting on the couch watching the news. Reese held a longing gaze at Kyra wishing things could be different.

A sudden burst of laughter pulled Reese's attention to notice that Jess had moved on to talking to Nathan Pearson, or Nate as everyone called him. Nate was the Captain on the truck and he is tall, dark, and incredibly handsome. He was dark brown, buzz-cut hair, piercing blue eyes, face cleanly shaven with looks that made women weak in the knees.

Nate was kind of the whole package and an all-around good 'ole boy that would bend over backward to make the people that mattered to him happy. Jess has been denying for weeks that she and Nate had something going on but Reese didn't believe for one second. Jess must have assumed she was being discreet but the one thing about being a girl that goes unnoticed, Reese had a front row seat to their giddy body language and the constant exchange of glances from across the room. *Jess is a lucky girl,* Reese thought.

"Morning briefing!" a stern voice interrupted her thought. It was Chief Gibbs.

Chapter 3

EVERYONE GOT UP and made their way into the training room where they held their morning briefings. Reese quietly found a chair where she sat down. Her mind had been so many places that morning she had forgotten all about the blinding pain in her side, a pain that harshly reminded her of what she really needed to focus on, *Alex.* Reese wrapped her arms around her battered body, gasping for the air that rapidly escaped her lungs.

"What's wrong?" Stump asked placing a hand between her shoulders blades and kneeling beside her.

Stump had become Reese's guardian angel when she moved to Auburn. She was just a young kid in a big city, lost in the fast-paced life. Stump took her under his wing and looked after her like she was his baby sister. Reese always loved how protective he was over her, and even now as she was isolated from the world, Stump was still concerned about her well-being.

"I'm good." Reese had to force the words out of her mouth with no breath. "Just went too hard at the gym last night. Leg day, it'll getcha every time," she said, followed by nervous laughter.

Crap, was that inappropriate? She thought remembering that no matter how far her thoughts traveled, Alex's voice in her head always rang the loudest. Stump just stared at her in disbelief, almost as if he was deciding whether to call her out on her lie or not. Reese sheepishly turned away from him in her seat.

"Good morning, folks. I just wanted to remind you guys; Fill the Boot is this Saturday, and you are all expected to attend and to do your civic duty in helping raise money for MDA. You have four days to cancel any plans you might have, no excuses will be tolerated. Okay, moving on, your nominations for Firefighter of the year are due on my desk by Thursday. The top two most nominated will be put to a ballot for you to vote. In other news, last week, Company 64 had one of their firefighters get injured, Tommy Garrison. Doctors say he will make a full recovery but still, if you are able to donate to help his wife pay for medical bills, they would appreciate it. Remember, ladies and gentlemen, stay safe out there, make smart and quick decisions, work as a team, and God willing, we can all make it home tonight. Let's get out there, get those check-offs done and our rigs washed. Let's GET IT! Chief Gibbs growled deep in his throat.

There was a roar of whistles, clapping, and the sound of Louie and Ray mimicking the Chief:

"Get it! Get it!"

"Let's get some!"

Reese walked out to the ambulance. Her wrist was throbbing and her flank felt like someone had put a branding iron on her— the brand 'Alex was here and angry'. She took out 800mg of Ibuprofen, 1000mg of Tylenol, and 150mg of Zantac or as she more commonly referred to it as, "The Pain-Dulling Cocktail." Every time she was forced to take her cocktail she wished the drugs were instant. *Okay, Reese, pull it together.* Her teeth clinched together rounding the back of the ambulance and found Kyra checking the oxygen tanks.

"I've got these if you wanna check backboards and c-spine equipment and then we can tackle the cabinets in the back together," Kyra said, not making eye contact.

"Yeah, sure, sounds good."

They both worked through their morning check-off in silence. Reese and Kyra had been partnered together shortly after Reese came to this station seven years ago. They've been full-time partners since then, and moved like a well-oiled machine. No matter how bad the call, they worked in perfect harmony. In fact, their communication was so strong together that they rarely needed to say what they were thinking out loud. Reese worried that their friendship would never be the same and even worse, she was afraid she had lost Kyra forever. Alex never cared for Kyra and though he never outwardly said anything to her, he made sure there was tension between them.

"If she cannot accept our relationship, then screw her! *I'm* your number one now, not her. She can go cry about that to someone else. We're together, you're mine, and you can tell that selfish bitch I'm done sharing with her."

Reese never told Kyra what Alex would say about her, but she never really had to, Kyra knew exactly how Alex felt.

Kyra used to work down at Station 16 where she and Alex worked a handful of shifts together. Kyra knew how Alex's rude comments and short temper really was and she had tried repeatedly to warn Reese that Alex wasn't the right guy to be around. Sadly, Reese used to think everyone was just blowing it out proportion and he just wanted to have a "tough guy" persona.

It had been a long time since Reese had met someone as captivating as Alex, he was the most charming, sweet, and loveable guy she had ever met. He bought her flowers for no reason and made her feel like the most beautiful woman in the world. They went on adventurous dates and laughed so much their sides would hurt. Now her side hurt for many different reasons. Reese shouldn't have blown off all the warnings she was given but, unfortunately, she did and now she would always be tormented by her choice to stay.

Oh no, Where's my phone? She internally panicked. She never went anywhere without it. If Alex texted her and she didn't respond right away, he would get angry. Reese's body couldn't handle another night of angry. She frantically searched her pockets. *Ugh, EMS pants, why do they have so many damn pockets?* She wore dark blue 5.11 tactical pants, which had regular pockets, a side pocket on each thigh with smaller pockets on the inside of them, back pockets and even side calf pockets. *Your phone would never fit in that pocket, ah screw it, and check anyway. Nope, not there either. Oh crap, it's already 9:38, he's gonna be pissed.* She got out of the back of the ambulance and went to check her purse. *Oh, thank God! There it is.* She hesitated for just a moment, not wanting to be confronted by the inevitable. Her phone screen animated to life, displaying a little envelope and the words: Text Messages (6) next to it. *Oh, Crap!*

ALEX: Good morning beautiful. 8:10 am

ALEX: Babe? 8:34 am

ALEX: Where the hell are you? 8:42 am

ALEX: REESE! WHY ARE YOU IGNORING ME? 8:50 am

ALEX: Is this how you are going to be? Really? 9:03 am

The next few texts were filled with horrifically vulgar words and accusations, Reese knew this was not going to be easy but, it was possibly salvageable. She started to type a response when it went off in her hands. It was Alex.

"Hey, babe!" She said, forcing a cheery tone into her voice, "I was just textin' you back."

"I'm sure you were, Reese. What the hell have you been doing all morning? Who've you been talking to?"

"No one, I swear." Reese walked out of the bay door into the parking lot so no one could hear her beg for his forgiveness. "Baby, I'm so sorry, I left my phone in my purse on accident and it's been in the rig this whole time. I wasn't ignoring you. I came in and got coffee, then the Chief did his mornin' briefing and now Kyra and me are checkin' out the rig. Nothing happened, it was just an honest mistake, babe, I swear." Silence was all she heard. "Alex?" her hands and her heart trembled.

"I'm here," his voice was sullen, sheer disgust in his tone. "I'm just sitting here trying to decide if I can truly believe a whore like you to be honest. You've lied to me so many times that it makes it hard for me to trust you."

You can't trust me? Are you freaking kidding me? Thoughts tore through Reese's head. *I'm the one you can't trust? I'm the problem? BULLSHIT!* There was that spark, that fire. She could feel it boiling inside her boosting her confidence. A flash from last night entered her thoughts. The sting of his enormous hand smacking her across the face and at that exact moment she became very aware of the pain on her side, and that fire fizzled out instantly. *I have to fix this.*

"Baby, I told you that I wouldn't lie to you anymore, and I haven't. I love you, Alex, with everythin' I am. I'm so lucky to have you in my life and I know my behavior this mornin' hasn't shown you that, but I am very lucky. I made an honest mistake and I will try really hard to not ever make that mistake again. You are amazin' and I love hearin' from you, I would never ignore you on purpose, please believe me." She pleaded. *Please work, please work.*

"Do you realize how lucky you are to have me?" Alex boasted.

"Yes baby, of course, I know."

"Don't let it happen again." His voice was stern and terrified Reese to her core.

"I won't."

Reese hung up the phone, disgusted with her begging pleas. *Is this really my life now?* She looked up and saw Kyra standing at the front of the ambulance watching her.

"Is everything okay?" Kyra asked. She seemed genuinely interested which was out of character for her lately.

"Um..." Reese wanted to scream, *no it's not!* Instead she said, "Yeah, oh yeah, all good. You ready to wash the beast?" As she walked past, Kyra placed a hand on her shoulder to pause Reese.

"You know you can talk to me about anything, right?" Kyra was the most sincere and concerned Reese had ever seen her. "I know I've been distant lately," Kyra said shyly, "but I love you and I'm here if you need me."

So many thoughts tumbled around Reese's head as Kyra stared compassionately into her eyes, so many secrets jumbled behind her closed lips ready to spill out but, in the end, she couldn't face reality with Kyra, not yet.

"I love you too." Reese broke free from Kyra and continued to walk toward the bucket and brushes to wash the ambulance.

Chapter 4

AFTER THE AMBULANCE was washed and ready to go, Reese retreated to her station duties. Once she wiped down the kitchen and cleaned up the coffee area she headed out back to dump the trash. Reese was entirely lost in her own world replaying her phone conversation with Alex earlier. *Is this really what you want, Reese? Nothin' you do is ever good enough for him.* She lifted the lid to the dumpster slowly trying her best to hoist the trash bag into the bin despite the pain. The second attempt she had to strain and tense her side, holding her breath she managed to get the bag high enough to flop inside.

"Reese."

She jumped and turned around to see Stump standing behind her. His brow was furrowed and his mustache wrapped tightly around his pursed lips.

"You scared me... Are you okay, Stump?"

Reese knew that if Alex learned of it, this conversation would send him into a fury but, at this moment she did not care, something was clearly wrong.

"Leg day?" he ran his fingers over his thick mustache. "You know, some of the other guys might believe you, but I don't. I haven't said anything. I've let you live your life how you've chosen to, but I can't sit back any longer."

Stump reached out and gently grabbed her wrist. Reese tried to hide her discomfort but by the horrified look on Stump's face, she knew she hadn't been successful. He reached over and pulled up her sleeve to reveal the bruising around her wrist and forearm. *Crap, how do I explain this?* She looked up and met Stump's sorrow-filled eyes. Reese could see his heart breaking as his brain wrapped around the idea of the abuse going on in her life; the truth she had kept secret for eighteen months. He tightly closed his eyes and dropped his head while her brain spiraled trying to find an explanation, but Stump was already putting things together.

"Oh Reese," his voice trembled, "how long?"

"It's not what you think it is." Reese knew her efforts were pointless but she had to try.

They heard a door slam shut inside the station. Reese practically jumped out of her own skin and she quickly ripped her arm from his hand. Her mind and body so hardwired to fear Alex and the fact that she was engaging in a conversation that could get her killed had every nerve in her body was on high alert.

"Reese, you're terrified of him, aren't you?"

She couldn't look Stump in the eyes, and tears trickled down her cheeks. She didn't answer. Instead she just stared at the ground.

"No woman should ever fear the man she's with, Reese. On some level, you have to know that. I know that girl you used to be is still in there and somewhere inside you lives the strength you've been looking for to leave. This isn't you, Reese. He's changed you, and not for the better." He gently placed his hands on the side of her shoulders slowly pulled her closer to him. Tears beginning to brim his eyes, his voice lowered to just above a whisper, he said, "Reese, you deserve better than a life filled with fear. You deserve a life of happiness and love, a life full of laughter and content. You're an incredible woman, but he's stripped you of all your joy, and it kills me to see you like this and now knowing what he's been doing to you." Stump paused, "You're not alone, Reese. We all love you and we're here for you if you would just let us be."

Reese wiped the tears falling from her cheeks searching for the right words to say. She slowly inhaled trying to sort out the river of emotions she felt when that voice crept back inside her head. *You can never leave him or he'll find you and kill you.* Reese dropped her head in defeat.

"I can't leave," she said, her voice a whisper.

She pushed her way past Stump with her head hung low and went back inside the station, pulling down her sleeve and wiping her tears. *Deep breaths; pull it together.* She made her way to the bathroom and built up a dam around her heart to contain the river of emotions that had spilt over. She paced back and forth in the bathroom and was internally pleading with God, that Stump wouldn't tell anyone her secret. There was a part of her that wanted to hide out in the bathroom the rest of the shift. She dreaded walking out and facing everyone.

The loudspeaker called out, "Ambulance twenty-three, we got a call for a victim of a fall at two-three-four-six, twenty-three forty-six West Cobble Street, an elderly female, possible hip injury." With a sigh, Reese emerged from the bathroom.

"You ready to see Millie?" Kyra asked with a smile.

Millie Henderson was a regular patient for them and she was their absolute favorite. Millie was the sweetest woman Reese had ever met. She was very short with a petite frame. Millie always saw the good in every situation, even when she lay to rest the love of her life and husband of sixty-four years. She was just happy that William was no longer in pain. He had passed away of heart failure five years ago. Millie always hated using her walker, but William used to make sure she used it, and every time they went out to pick her up she would tell them, "I should have listened to William."

Reese put a smile on her face and ran the call as she had hundreds of times before. She was on autopilot, going through all the motions, except her mind was a million miles away thinking about what Stump had said. *What am I going to do if Stump tells everyone? I mean, in all fairness, Stump is probably right, but what am I supposed to do? I can't leave, can I?*

"Reese dear, is everything okay?" Millie broke through her thoughts with warranted concern.

"Oh yes, Millie, I'm fine. Sorry, I just have a lot going on and my brain is going a hundred miles an hour. Enough about me, love, how are you? Is your pain okay? I know the bumps while we drive to the hospital can be brutal."

"I'm fine, dear. Do you really think going all the way to the hospital is necessary?"

"Hon, you know it's better to be safe than sorry, you have quite the bruise on your hip, plus it hurts you to walk. You need to be checked, love, you know that." Reese softly looked at Millie on her gurney and grabbed her hand.

"You know, sweetie, if I had just listened to my William I wouldn't be here." Millie looked up at Reese. "Did you know I met William when I was fourteen? I knew the moment I met him that I was going to marry him. He gave me sixty-four incredible years, so many laughs, so many happy memories. We raised four children who have all grown up and now have families of their own. Most of our children are even grandparents now." Millie shifted her eyes up toward the ceiling. "We did well, my love." An enormous smile emerged on Millie's face as she returned her gaze to Reese. "That man loved me more than I'm sure I deserved. We would dance in the kitchen together and he always put my needs and desires above his own. He was the type of man every woman deserves. Like you, Reese do you have a man like that?"

Reese froze with her eyes wide and locked on Millie, terrified to say the wrong thing.

"Oh Millie, I don't know that men like your William truly exist anymore," she said finally.

Millie released her grasp on Reese and placed her frail cold hand on Reese's face pulling her slightly toward her.

"God has someone for you, sweetie. An amazing man that'll love you with everything he is. You just have to have faith, dear, and patience."

Reese smiled as Kyra opened the back doors of the ambulance.

"We're here, how was the ride Millie?"

"Oh, Kyra dear, you are just the best driver." Millie had a sincere smile on her face.

Later as Reese was gathering her things to leave the hospital Millie stopped her.

"Reesey-Piecey, come here honey."

Reese turned to look at Millie with a bewildered look on her face—that's what her dad always called her.

"Yes, Millie?"

"Come here, dear." Millie reached out her hand and motioned Reese to move closer to her. When Reese did, Millie grabbed her hand and looked deep into her eyes. "God wants you to know, He hasn't forgotten about you, Reese. Where you are now is not what He has for you. He knows your fears, but he will protect you."

Reese kept her eyes locked on Millie while building her internal dam even higher. "Thank you, Millie. You feel better, okay?"

Reese walked out of the room, speechless. *What the hell, how'd she know?*

Chapter 5

DRIVING BACK TO the station Reese had her window down. It had warmed up outside and the chill in the air was gone; all that remained was the sun shining and the wind on her face. *Is there some sort of divine intervention happenin' here?* Even though she had walked away from her faith shortly after leaving home seven years ago, she couldn't help but let out a faint chuckle under her breath. *Yeah right.*

The wind continued to blow on her, Reese felt the warmth of the sun on her face and she was reminded of her home; Texas. She couldn't wait to leave when she was younger, but recently she missed every part of it. Crazy enough, she even missed the heat in the summer, the kind of heat that made you sweaty even if you were sitting in the shade with a fan and ice water. She missed the backroad bonfires with friends and taking their four-wheel drive trucks off-road on the weekends. She loved the way her beer tasted sitting on the tailgate of her truck and the feel of a good pair of worn-in boots. She even missed getting up and feeding the chickens at the crack of dawn just before school. Reese surprisingly missed church as well, which was the one thing she never imagined would happen.

Growing up in Texas, the church was unquestionably a rite of passage and was most certainly not optional. During her rebellious teenage years, church felt more like a prison than a place of God. Her parents never gave Reese a choice, she and Sophie were expected to be there, depressed appropriately, and on time. Reese initially felt a sense of freedom when she left. A freedom she would never dare to share with her parents. Recently though she missed it. She missed singing hymns and worship songs, and even the way her bible smelled like leather and ink. She even missed listening to her dad talking about God. She remembered that her intention had been to find a church in Auburn, but she never did. Reese could almost smell the fresh-cut flowers, leather, and the communion grape juice that filled the church back home. She took a deep breath in. *Home*, she exhaled. It seemed so much further away now, more than it ever had before. Reese's mind wandered back to Millie and what she and William had. That was the kind of love Reese always dreamed of finding. It was the kind of love she grew up with.

Her mother was Maggie Landon who always wore her long blonde hair in a French braid. She was a stay-at-home mom who raised Sophie and Reese while tending to the chickens and her garden. Maggie always liked to stay busy. Reese was astonished some days wondering how her mother truly did it all—PTA meetings, driving her and her sister to their sporting events and was always there to help them the best she could with their homework and extracurricular activities. She did all of this, plus take care of eight chickens, three dogs, two barn cats, and the four fish Reese and Sophie always forgot to feed. Maggie had leathery tan skin from working outside and crystal blue eyes.

She was beautiful in every way. Not only did she have physical beauty, but she was also the most giving person Reese ever knew. Maggie also cooked, cleaned, and made her husband Rusty's lunch every day.

Rusty Landon was Reese's father. Rusty was what they would call a "man's man," and was tough as nails. He was very tall and relatively thin except for his small gut that stuck out. He joked around that he traded his six-pack in for a small keg years ago. His hair once was dark brown but was now speckled with grey, and a nicely trimmed mustache that was more grey than brown.

Rusty and Maggie were high school sweethearts. They quickly fell in love shortly after going on their first date midway through their junior year, and they haven't been apart since. Rusty was never the overly affectionate type, but he had his own way of showing Maggie exactly how much she meant to him. Sunflowers were Maggie's favorite flower, and Rusty would bring her back one every time he had to go into town. Even on the hottest days of summer he would come through the door after a hard day's work and kiss Maggie on the forehead before whispering "I love you" in her ear and insisted on hearing all about her day after he showered.

Rusty was a cattle rancher. His work was long and grueling, physically demanding, and even dangerous. Rusty had landed himself in the emergency room a time or two, having to be stitched up and x-rayed after overzealous steers got ahold of him. Reese always remembered that no matter how tired Rusty was, he would always make the time and effort for Maggie. Maggie and his two girls were his life and the three of them made Rusty the richest man in the world. There were several times Reese would catch her parents dancing in the kitchen, just like how Millie described her and William used to do. Rusty would tell Maggie she was beautiful, even on her worst day. And Maggie would find a way to render him speechless on the occasional date night when she wore her fancy clothes. Reese knew in her soul that Alex would never love her the way she wanted him to. He would never be "her Alex," but she was just too scared to admit that to herself.

Kyra backed the rig into the station, and Reese immediately became very aware of the nervous knot twisting in her stomach. *I hope Stump didn't say anything to anyone*, she thought. Reese felt terrified to face her co-workers. *What should I say to them? How could I possibly handle them being mad at me all at once?* She reluctantly stepped out of the ambulance and toward the loud chatter from inside.

She came into the station with her hands shoved deep into her pockets and her head down. The dull roar of talking was getting closer, *keep it together, Reese.* All the noise ceased to exist as she rounded the corner to the common room, and as every eye shifted toward her, her stomach twisted. It was even worse than when she had a solo in her 7th grade Christmas program. After the longest two seconds in history, the room returned to conversation and laughter. A sense of total relief came over Reese like a warm blanket. That feeling instantly vanished as she locked eyes with Stump. *Damage control time.* She intensely stared at Stump and nodded her head in the direction of the barracks where they all slept when they worked overnight. Stump continued to sit at the table as if contemplating whether to go and listen to Reese and her lies. Perhaps out of loyalty and love he stood up and followed her.

"Hey, Stump, I think we need to talk."

"Okay, Reese, but first I have a question. Do you really want to talk, or do you wanna just make up more excuses?"

Reese just stared at him, defeated. No words came to mind. Her brain was like a desert; dry, cracked, and nothing for as far as the eye could see. She stood there; still and unable to wiggle her way out from this.

"Look, Reese," he continued, "I love you like a sister, which is why I can't sit here and listen to your excuses and lies anymore. Are you ready to be honest with me? Or better yet, yourself?"

"No, it's...just that..." Reese hung her head as the words tried to escape her mouth. "I was just hoping... no... I'm begging you to please not tell anyone, please Stump."

Stump looked at her with such disappointment and betrayal. "Fine," he said with a hint of condescension in his voice. "But this isn't over, Reese. As your brother, it's my job to protect you."

"You can't save me, Stump," her voice cracked trying to hold in the tears, "no one can."

Reese didn't even pause to look him in the eye. She turned and walked back to the bathroom.

She paced back and forth in front of the mirrors, trying to figure out how to salvage this situation with Stump. Just as she was about to become completely unhinged there was a vibration coming from her pocket. It was Alex.

Reese answered as fast as she could, "Hey babe."

"Hey beautiful, what are you doing?"

Looking around the bathroom she thought; *I'm hiding in the bathroom from my co-workers.* But she decided to go with, "Oh nothing, love, I was just washing my hands in the bathroom, what are you doin'?"

"Well, I went to Starbucks and got you some coffee. Wanna meet me outside in a few minutes?"

"Mmm... You're amazing! See you in a minute, love you."

"Love you more." Alex seemed to be in a good mood, and Reese felt relieved.

She left the bathroom and went unnoticed through the common room. She didn't dare make eye contact with Stump as she passed by. She continuously looked over her shoulder to make sure he wasn't following her outside. Passing the guys from the truck doing training in front of the bay doors, Reese kept her eyes locked on Alex. *Don't screw up, Reese. Stay focused on him; don't let him see you notice them. Eyes forward.* Reese always gave herself mandatory internal pep talks in hopes to avoid another beating.

"Hey, babe," Reese put a huge smile on her face.

She felt almost excited Alex was there, simply ecstatic that he obviously wasn't mad anymore and she could finally talk to someone without feeling remorse, and yet, she felt worried that she would slip up or make him mad any second.

Alex stood leaned up against his 1968 custom coupe Chevelle. Alex and his dad had rebuilt the Chevelle together over the last year, and he drove that car everywhere. It was charcoal grey with two thick silver stripes stretching from the hood of the car to the trunk. He mesmerized her standing there looking like a hunk, wearing blue jeans and a plain white t-shirt. He was even wearing the Ray-Ban aviators Reese had gotten him for his birthday a few months ago.

"Hey there, handsome," Reese said as she grabbed his shirt and pulled him into her, giving him a kiss.

Reese loved the giddy feeling she got when she kissed Alex in their good moments, and she loved him when he was like this.

She always wished that the good moments would last longer. A part of her wondered how, after everything he had done to her, she could still be so attracted to him? Nevertheless, she was powerless against her lust for him to simply love her, and maybe, if she could be the woman he demanded her to be, then he finally would.

"Mmm, hey beautiful," Alex said, licking his lips after their kiss. His eyes then glanced past Reese over to Nate, Ray, and Cole doing their drills. Alex grabbed Reese, pulled her into his rock-hard body and deeply kissed her again. His tongue swiftly whirled around hers and she felt a rush of excitement come over her. Alex moved his hand down her back and squeezed her butt, and with a nice firm smack to the same butt cheek, he pulled her whole body into his. As their lips parted Reese was left feeling tingles through her entire body and yearned for more. Alex had a way of making all of the bad just melt away when he passionately kissed her. Reese shamefully lived for those moments.

"Wha... um... wow," Reese was left unable to focus on anything but her deep desires. "What was that for, baby?" She stood there completely elated, feeling the stir between her legs.

"Just because I love you," Alex said as his eyes shifted back to Nate, Ray, and Cole.

Reese quickly lost her excitement when she realized that the public display of affection was for the guys, and not for her. Alex may as well have lifted his leg and marked his territory like a dog would have. Reese stood there, fighting an escalating irritation with Alex, despite her better judgment; she forced herself to choke down her feelings. It was not worth the bruising or torment from a fight later. Her feeling never mattered much to Alex anyway.

"You're so sweet, what's the plan for tonight?" Reese forced a smile.

"I have a plan; you will see when you get home. What time are you off work tonight?"

"I should be off around six tonight. So you have a surprise for me, huh?" Reese's face lit up with false excitement.

She knew exactly what her so-called surprise would be. Alex always did something special after a night like last night, *could he possibly have a guilty conscience? I think that would require actually having one*, she thought. Alex left Reese with bruises and then would give her flowers, as if they could make up for what he had done.

"I better get going and get the stuff done I need to do." Alex leaned over and kissed her gently.

"See you in a bit, my love." He winked at her as he got into his car and drove off. Reese stood there on the curb and watched as he drove out of sight. As soon as he was gone she exhaled a sigh of relief.

Chapter 6

AS THE REST of her shift drug on, Reese spent her down time lounging in the barracks hoping no one would barge in and force her into light conversation sprinkled with fake smiles.

Hiding in the barracks was just another way for her to continue avoiding Stump and to ensure she wouldn't make a mistake and wreck Alex's apology. Her mind wondered what exactly Alex was planning for his grand admission of guilt and what would happen if she accidentally ruined the surprise somehow before her shift was through. *I can't mess up this up, I won't ruin this surprise like I did last time, not if I can help it,* she thought.

Last year in late April, Alex had beaten her senseless and shoved her down a flight of stairs. Afterwards, he was forced to nurse his battered masterpiece back to health, going as far as to relocate her shoulder that night at home, in order to avoid questions in a hospital setting. Reese was unable to walk for nearly a week and was confined to their either the bed or the couch. Once Reese was able to function on her own without the help of Alex, he conveniently pulled out all the stops; two sprained ankles and a dislocated shoulder warranted a trip to Las Vegas for a few days. Perhaps, the trip could have been fun had it not been a ploy for her to forgive and forget, under the constant scrutiny of Alex. Vegas should have been a place where Reese could escape the shackles of her life in Auburn, no one in Vegas would know who she was or how violent her travel companion could be.

The flight to Vegas was hard on her sore body and as soon as the plane landed Reese swallowed a dry, bitter pill-cocktail, which caught in her throat leaving a taste of resentment. *Drinks, I will be needing lots of drinks*, she thought, knowing if she kept Alex heavily intoxicated it *might* be easier to keep him happy, though deep down she knew this plan wasn't full proof. She had to keep her focus on Alex.

As their first night out in Vegas began, they were approached by an eccentric man named Eric. He promised the couple VIP access at Studio 54 in exchange for their company and of course, only if they pay for his drinks for the rest of the night. Eric was just as tall as Reese and had a slender build. He wore black slacks that had a black sequin stripe down each side and his shirt was a bright array of colors spread over an intricate paisley print. His skin was as dark as a moonless night, and his hair was a perfectly shaped afro with a pic comb stuck in it. Reese analyzed Eric from her peripheral vision. She admired his confidence and charm but, was dubious of the expeditious friendship. Nevertheless, the deal was struck and the three of them paraded into Studio 54 as if no one would recognize the counterfeit couple behind their spurious new companion. Reese walked timidly behind Alex, keeping her focus on him and not the crowd of people around her, a formidable task that was more daunting than she expected. Alex remained close behind Eric, there seemed to be a gravitational pull between the two, as the three of them sauntered upstairs. Everyone around them seemed to know and love Eric, there was no shortage of secret handshakes and kisses on various cheeks while they weaved through the crowd to the VIP bar.

Reese recalled how awestruck she was throughout the night watching the performers of the acrobatic show, it was the only time she allowed herself to let her guard down and take her focus completely off of Alex. She was filled with delight watching them twirl and swing from the high-rise ceilings with extraordinary agility and balance; she had never seen anything like it, she would be lucky to see these stunts on a semi-decent action television show.

Alex and Eric went shot for shot while Reese just sat there quietly and slowly sipped her Strawberry Long Island allowing her gaze to follow the strategic moves of the graceful acrobats. As the night carried on the three of them glided to the dancefloor, Reese couldn't help but succumb to the intoxicating feeling of being wanted by Alex. Reese seductively danced against Alex's body, his arm hung around her hips possessively, his breath caressing her neck, and what seemed like an infinite amount of drinks making their dancing more carnal. After what seemed like hours of dancing they finally moved back to their VIP table, waitresses immediately began taking another round of drink orders. It wasn't long after sitting down with drinks in hand before Eric began to get serious, talking loudly over the club music, he began seducing Alex with a pitch about a luxurious lifestyle and how Eric would get Alex in nice with the people he did business with. He began telling Alex about how he would be greatly compensated for just a small amount of work. Alex, who was completely drunk, was mesmerized by the idea of money and power being spun by this charlatan. Alex was practically ready to sign his life away before Reese finally stepped in, she wouldn't let this snake oil salesmen take advantage of Alex, drunk or otherwise.

"Alex, baby," she put her hands on each side of his face and pulled him close until he finally managed to lock eyes with her. She kissed him softly on the lips, then the cheek, and finally on the upper neck before whispering in his ear. "Take me to our hotel... I want you inside me right now..." she took one of his hands and placed it on the inside of her thigh, higher than what would normally be acceptable in a public setting.

She kissed him again more deeply, gently parting his lips with her tongue. Grabbing his shirt, she pulled him into her body while her tongue continued to dance around his. She prayed her distraction would work before Alex signed both of their lives away to what sounded like con-artists or hard-drug dealers.

"Okay, baby, let's go," Alex whispered in her ear. "Sorry, man," he briefly turned his attention back to Eric. "We will talk more another time, but right now I need to go and take care of her." Alex looked back at Reese, gently running the tips of his fingers from her collarbone down to her breast and around her nipples, and biting his bottom lip. He looked back over at Eric, giving him a wink. "If you know what I mean." Although Reese was embarrassed, she sat there quietly forcing herself to tolerate the degrading situation.

"No worries, man, just call me when you guys get back home." As Eric reached over to shake Alex's hand, he slid his business card across the table.

Reese picked up the card and placed it in her purse before Alex could collect it and take Eric up on his offer at a later time. "I'll keep it so it doesn't get lost, babe." Alex simply nodded his with attention quickly back on Reese and her sexy black dress.

She didn't think she had consumed enough alcohol to feel as drunk as she did, as the patterned floors spun she quickly realized the difficulty in attempting to help Alex down the stairs and stumble out of the club. His level of intoxication seemed to increase with every passing minute while outside on the crowded streets. She released her grip on him letting him flop all his dead weight onto a bus bench and helped prop him up against a pole in the hopes he wouldn't fall to the ground and be completely uncooperative.

"I love that you take such good care of me, Reese." Alex drunkenly blurted out words just coherent enough for Reese to understand.

"You had better," Reese joked, trying to make light of her irritation and doing her best to flag down a taxi.

"Do you know what we should get? We should get one of those underage hookers to come back to the hotel with us." His words slurred but as he let out a little chuckle, Reese knew she couldn't have misheard him.

"What the hell did you just say? Are you kidding me?" Reese felt disgusted.

"Kidding about what?" he slurred, a half smile creeping across his face.

He must be so messed up he doesn't know what he's actually saying, she thought as anger and revulsion slowly started to build inside her. Reaching into her purse she grabbed out Eric's business card and threw it into the trash can, not letting Alex notice her sleight of hand. There was no way she was going to allow Alex to drag her into anything illegal and ruin both their lives.

Luckily, she was able to hail a taxi cab driving down the street before Alex became determined to let his drunken words reach fruition. She opened the sliding door of the taxi van and poured Alex into the back seat. The taxi maneuvered around the congested traffic, finally making it to their hotel on the other side of the strip. Reese paid the driver and thanked him, struggling to pull a half-asleep Alex from the taxi, forcing her to bear most of his weight. She heaved the two of them to the elevators and down the hall to their room, thankful they had actually made it back unscathed.

She removed his shirt periodically catching him before he swayed too far backward. She unbuttoned his pants. Alex took it as the invitation to her earlier advance to get him out of the club. Although Reese was not in the mood for sex after basically carrying Alex back to the hotel, she did not resist. She knew better than to turn down Alex when he wanted her, whether she wanted him sexually or not was not relevant.

She could still feel the sting of his slap on her face when she told him no for the first time and how she gasped for air as he choked her to the point of almost passing out. Remembering most vividly how powerless she felt as he held her down and forced himself inside her, no love or passion, he was angry and wanted to show her it was not about sex but, about power and control. The tears that ran down her face and her begging him to stop seemed to feed his rage as he raped her. After that night, she never dared to reject him again.

Reese remembered how quiet the hotel room was that night; she didn't feel good about being with Alex in the moment as he roughly pulled her dress over her head. His breath was heavy and reeked of whiskey, Reese avoided his mouth the best she could. He grabbed her hair at the base of her skull and slightly pulled while he drunkenly kissed her lips and moved clumsily down her neck. Reese prayed he would be done quickly, she didn't know how long she would be able to fake her enthusiasm. She typically enjoyed sex with Alex, but when Alex was this drunk, he was sloppy, making Reese less than turned on.

He finished undressing and pushed her onto the bed. Trying to crawl on top of her he careened his way across the bed, fumbling to get himself out of his boxers, and falling twice before finally making it to her. He leaned over her naked body and kissed her. Faster than he could even get his clothes off, Alex abruptly pushed himself up and shifted his upper body over the side of the bed and vomited onto the floor, heaving several times before finally collapsing on top of Reese. He hit the bed like a rock falling from the sky, the majority of his body pinning her between himself and the bed, making her feel as though she was suffocating under his weight. Alex was now completely comatose. Reese struggled to get out from underneath him so she could get towels and clean up his mess, but she was stuck. She struggled for almost fifteen minutes giving it her all to push him away. She kicked out her legs using all her might to get him off of her. Finally, she was able to catch her breath, long enough to break free rolling him to one side of the bed. In a huff she quickly grabbed some towels from the bathroom and placed them over the vomit and cleaned it up the best she could. Her fun apology trip had turned into a vomit-filled nightmare.

Reese stared up to the ceiling as she lay quietly in the barracks not really sure why she even bothered to revisit the memory of Vegas. She remembered what a letdown that Vegas trip was. *Some apology.* With a roll of her eyes she wondered what surprise was awaiting her at home. *Of course, it wouldn't be an apology without flowers.*

He probably made reservations at Verrazano's, the Italian restaurant where they had their first date. That's what he always did. They went on these apology dates so often the waiting staff and hostess knew them on a first name basis. They also knew to only address Alex for orders and light conversation and not Reese, and knew not only their food order but, knew to immediately place Reese's favorite bottle of Moscato on the table before they sat. Despite wanting to glance at a menu, Reese got use to Alex always ordered her the same thing, eggplant parmesan. Unfortunately for Reese, she hated eggplant, but she was forced to choke it down. As her mind developed into a blizzard of thoughts, her face became sullen and discouraged. Then Reese heard footsteps in the barracks.

"Hey, girl, are you going to hide out in here all day?" Jess said as she plopped herself down on Reese's bed.

"You know how Alex gets jealous. It's just easier to be in here." As the words came out of her mouth she couldn't believe she was saying them. Reese was never this honest with anyone. She pulled herself up and sat upright on the bed with her legs crossed.

"Reese." Jess' look turned uneasy. "Why are you wasting your time on someone like Alex anyway? He's taken the best parts of who you are and locked them away." Jess placed her hand on Reese's thigh. "Look, all I'm saying is that it's typically the jealous one that's being untrustworthy."

Reese dropped her head and Jess placed her fingers under her chin gently forcing Reese to stare into her vibrant green eyes. "Reese, you are an amazing woman, and the right guy will love you for exactly who you are."

"What if I am just not 'marriage material' because of who I am?" Reese said defeated as she recalled her total devastation when her ex-boyfriend broke up with her. She loved him very much, but after almost three years he didn't feel the same way. Rather than a proposal, he dumped her, leaving her to question if she will ever be good enough.

"Babe, you are perfect just the way you are. How Alex doesn't see that is beyond me. I'm serious." Jess paused for a moment, as if trying to figure out how to be encouraging. "Maybe you should start checking his social media accounts. If he's so paranoid about you cheating, I would be willing to bet he's the one actually doing the cheating, or at the very least, talking to other girls behind your back."

"Do you really think so? I mean, what kind of reasoning would he have to cheat on me?"

Reese felt like she couldn't breathe. She had bent over backwards for him, trying to be what he wanted her to be. *What if he is cheating?*

"Well, my buddy Gabe from the fire academy works the engine out at Station thirty-four on Alex's shift. Has he told you about the new medic they hired for Ambulance thirty-four?"

"No, why would he tell me about that? It's kind of hard to talk about anyone to Alex for that matter."

"Well I don't want to cause any problems but, the medic is young and all the guys seem to think she's really hot, and her name is Vanessa... And you should know that, Vanessa and Alex are supposedly getting to be very chummy together, if you know what I mean."

"How do you know all of this?" Reese said, hurt and in disbelief.

"Gabe called and asked me if you and Alex were still together."

"Well, you know how rumors are spread around in these stations, I am sure there's a good explanation for it, Jess. I really believe Alex wouldn't do that to me." Reese felt like the room was spinning.

"Reese, babe..." Jess put her hands on each side of Reese's face. "Ask yourself one thing: what would Alex do if he found out you were being chummy with a new male recruit?" Reese didn't answer, her brain drifted a million miles away. "Just think about that before you dismiss anything."

Jess got up and walked out of the barracks, leaving Reese with nothing but questions that demanded explanations, and no way of getting them. Reese refused to see that this could be her way out of this horrific relationship; this could very well be her saving grace. Instead, she sat in the barracks alone and feeling like her soul had been ripped out of her body.

Reese stared intensely at the floor as flashes of all the familiar slaps across her face came to mind. She felt a tinge of pain to her head while she vividly relived him dragging her down the hallway by her hair last night. Cringing at these memories, she thought, *how the hell am I supposed to confront him about Vanessa? He'll kill me.*

Chapter 7

THE DRIVE HOME from work was nerve-racking. Reese felt like she was losing her mind. She didn't know what to believe and the overwhelming feeling that her life with Alex had been one big lie weighed heavily on her, her heart felt as though it was being crushed and she could barely focus behind the blur of tears brimming her eyes. The words Jess said bounced around in her head destructively as she staggered her way through an array of memories. She was so lost in her thoughts that she almost missed the turn onto her street. *Shit, get it together Reese*, she told herself. *He can't see you like this.* As she pulled into her driveway, she continued to talk herself down, afraid of what Alex might do if he could read her thoughts.

"Deep breaths, Reese, deep breaths, in through your nose and out through your mouth. It's apology night..." She said, checking herself in the rearview mirror, "you won't survive messing it up again."

A grimace came over her face, the pain from her ribs throbbed like a beating drum, as she reached into her purse for another dose of painkillers.

One final slow breath before she opened the door to her car. *Oh great, he's gonna meet me outside*, she forced a smile as she saw Alex standing in the doorway. *He's dramatically overdressed.* Her eyes narrowed as she looked him up and down. He had on slacks, a white long-sleeve dress shirt with the sleeves rolled up, and a solid crimson-colored tie. Reese could tell he had been cooking by the way he had the hand towel from the kitchen thrown over his shoulder. Basking in the realization of what stood in front of her, a real smile began to emerge.

"Hey there, stud." She leaned in and gently kissed his cheek.

"Good evening, Ms. Landon, your table is ready for you once you shower and change."

He extended his arm out to his side, gesturing Reese to come inside.

Stepping through the door she saw the table to her right, it was set up like an upscale restaurant with three tall candles in the center and the biggest attraction being the incredible flower arrangement. Two dozen long-stem red roses garnished with baby's breath were beautifully arranged in a crystal vase that shimmered in the candlelight.

"Oh honey, these are beautiful!" Reese exclaimed, grinning from ear to ear. "I'm gonna go rinse off. I'll be quick, I promise."

"There's another surprise hanging up in the bathroom, please put it on when you get out." Alex said with a devilish grin on his face, as if he knew his gifts would make her forget about everything he had put her through.

And just as Alex thought, Reese became eager with anticipation. *What could he have gotten for me?*

In the bathroom she saw the most amazing dress: crimson-colored satin, form fitting, and knee length; in other words, it was the perfect dress. It had one-inch straps and a plunging sweetheart neckline. Reese was overcome with delight getting undressed and forgetting in that moment about the bruises that were now deeper colors of blue and brown that encircled her arms. After she got out of the shower, she plugged in her curling iron. *This dress deserves curls,* examining every detail of it. She slipped the dress on. It was exquisite. Her curves were accentuated in all the right places and the plunging neckline hugged her breasts. She had the perfect pair of plain black peep-toe heels to go with it. Quickly she curled her hair and added a black smoky eye.

She lined her lips with a deep red lip liner and giggled to herself when she recalled what her momma used to tell her.

"With red lipstick, sis, promise me you'll always use lip liner. Always! It's the difference between classy women and whores, for God's sake."

Reese was astonished that her mom would say such a thing, but the one time she tried it without lip liner she thought, *Damn, Momma was right. This doesn't look classy at all.* Reese loved to tell people that story because it was the most risqué thing her mom had ever said to her.

Now that her lips were perfectly lined and colored a deep red to match the dress, it was time for the final touch; the solitaire two karat diamond necklace Alex gave her for their two-year anniversary. In the midst of her anticipation for the night ahead of her, the worries from the day became a distant thought. *See, he does love me. Jess has to be wrong, he would never cheat on me; I mean, look at what he is doing right now!* She checked her make-up one last time.

Reese emerged from the bathroom feeling like royalty. She did her best cat walk down the hallway and through the living room. The house was her runway and she flaunted her curves like a model for Alex. A smile beamed across his face while he watched her with sheer delight and lust.

"Babe, this dress is amazing!" Reese ran her hands all over the silky material. "It's just perfect! I love it baby, thank you!" She walked over and gave Alex a huge hug, and softly pressed her lips against his. "I love you beyond words, babe." To her it wasn't just another dress; it was him truly trying to make her happy.

"I love you too, sweetheart," he said examining every inch of her with his eyes and biting his lower lip. His hand held firmly on the side of her face as he slowly swept it into her hair. In that moment Reese didn't notice the pain; she became putty in his hands. "You look so incredibly beautiful," he whispered as he lightly touched his lips to hers.

Reese threw all thoughts out of her head except one. She wanted Alex, right here, right now. Her hand swiftly made its way to the back of his head and she passionately gazed into his eyes; her breath quickening. Pulling him toward her, their lips met more passionately this time. Her tongue danced around his like a well-choreographed routine. Every nerve in her pulsing body was tingling, yearning for more. She reached up and removed his tie, and next the buttons on his shirt were undone with ease. Reese hoped that he wouldn't stop her.

She knew if she stopped, even for a second, all of those thoughts from earlier that day would come rushing back and ruin her desire for him. Alex gradually reached his hand up her back and to her zipper. As he slowly unzipped her dress, he kissed her jawline and down her neck, strategically biting as he went down to her collarbone and back up her neck again. Her body felt electrified as her dress fell to the floor and Reese reached over to unbuckle his pants. She drifted her hand down his well-defined body to his boxer briefs to stroke him. Alex moaned with pleasure before unhooking her bra, her breasts overflowing in his hands. His kiss traveled down her chest until his tongue swirled around her nipples. Reese could feel an explosion of excitement. She could feel the silk forming between her legs. She went to move her hand inside his underwear when he stopped her.

"Tonight isn't about me, it's about you." He smiled. He grabbed her by the butt and hoisted her up into his arms and she wrapped her legs around him, and he carried her to their bed where he sensually and graciously pleasured her for hours.

They laid there, hearts pounding, and out of breath while wrapped up in each other's arms, naked, sweaty, and both completely satisfied. Reese refused to ruin her euphoria with accusations and worries from earlier that day. He had successfully taken all of her doubt and fear of losing him, and drenched it with her overwhelming hunger for his touch. She turned her head and softly kissed his lips.

"Mmm, I love you, Reese." Alex pulled her body closer to his.

"I love you too, babe."

"I made dinner for us. Are you hungry?"

"I'm starving!"

With another soft kiss they leisurely pulled themselves out of bed. Reese put on her best matching Victoria's Secret set, cream color with intricate black lace; her push-up bra allowed for her 38D breasts to spill gently over the top and her matching boy shorts with a satin bow on the back accentuated her hour-glass figure. Alex pulled out her chair and motioned for her to sit. She couldn't help but admire his great physique in his black boxer briefs.

"Well thank you, sir." She slightly dipped her head in a bowing motion.

"You're welcome, my love."

Reese sat there lovingly gazing at Alex while he methodically made his way around the kitchen setting things back up and warming up the dinner that was now cold, stopping only for a moment to pour her a glass of chilled Moscato. She quietly sat there, sipping her wine, blissfully remembering all the reasons she loved him.

The candles were lit, wine was flowing, and dinner smelled amazing. Garlic butter salmon filets with roasted asparagus. *Mm, my favorite!* She thought relishing in the moment.

"This looks incredible, babe," Reese said as she enjoyed a sizable deep breath in, ignoring the pain.

After dinner they enjoyed more sips of wine in between several long kisses and soft giggles. It had been ages since they had a night filled with romance like this one. *I don't know what has gotten into him, but I hope it stays this way all night,* she thought.

Melted wax poured down the sides of the candles as they shared a piece of strawberry cheesecake, another one of her favorites. *Just when I began to think he doesn't pay attention to little details, he goes and surprises me to no end. What a perfect night.* Reese thought, flirtatiously licked strawberry sauce from her finger. She longed for more, desire filled her body and in that moment she only wanted Alex. Tonight, he had successfully swept her off her feet in the same way he use to in the beginning of their relationship. Reese knew that all of this didn't vindicate or justify his abuse; however, tonight she just wanted to enjoy him and the way he used to be. This was the Alex she had fallen so hard for and she never knew how long these breathtaking moments would last. Reese chose to bask in their sexual chemistry and worry about everything else tomorrow.

They cleared the table and seductively washed the dishes together with playful sexual taunting and deep kissing. Reese leaned over the sink while washing their plates and strategically stuck her tail out to catch his attention. Alex placed his hand firmly on her lower back as he turned her around. His hand traveled down to massage her butt while he ran his tongue from her collarbone to her ear. He sucked in her earlobe and gently bit down before slowly pulling away, letting it go. That was her favorite move that he made and every nerve in her body danced with excitement.

His kiss reemerged back at her collarbone and down to her breast. Reese anticipated his tantalizing nipple play as he continued down her stomach, running his lips and tongue down to her panties. He grabbed her hips and began to nibble at her inner thighs. *Oh my!* She moaned with pleasure. Alex stood up lifting her onto the kitchen island and removed her panties. She leaned back, feeling the tinge of cold from the granite countertop on her back. Her fingers curled around the edge of the counter as Alex began the best kind of Round 2.

Reese felt pure ecstasy as he swirled his tongue in multiple directions around her sweet spot. Her toes curled as she grabbed his head and pulled him into her harder, moaning with pure satisfaction until she climaxed with an explosion she felt through her whole body. Looking down at Alex she saw him licking his lips with an alluring smile.

"Did you like that, baby?" he asked as he stood up.

"Mmm..." Reese bit her bottom lip. "God you're good at that," she said as she leaned back and enjoyed the intoxication of her orgasm.

Alex pulled her up and removed her bra, and then his boxer briefs. He brought her body to the edge of the counter as he slid inside of her. Reese moaned with delight when he thrust himself back and forth. She loved every part of sex with Alex. Her body fluttered with exhilaration, digging her nails into his back as they both climaxed.

"God, you turn me on," Alex uttered amidst his heavy breathing.

"You have no idea what you do to me, babe." Reese tried to catch her breath while he helped her off the counter. "I can finish cleaning this all up in the morning. It's getting late. You have to work tomorrow. Let's get some sleep."

"Okay, babe," He said, looking completely satiated.

They walked down the hall wrapped up in each other's arms, and went to bed.

Chapter 8

REESE SLEPT CONTENTLY in his arms that night. She didn't feel suffocated, she felt loved. For the first time in a very long time she wasn't counting down the minutes until she could break free. That night it was replaced with dread that the alarm would sound, and she wouldn't be ready to let him go. These moments had become a rarity for Reese, and she forced herself to enjoy them when they manifested.

Alex roughly moved his body around amidst their sleep. He grabbed her, effortlessly forcing her hips and backside into him. He ran his hand along her thigh up to her hip. Reese woke up, *Round 3 already?* He swiftly brought his hand to her lower abdomen and down in between her legs. He aggressively moved his fingers around her moist lips and back up to her sweet spot. Reese was caught off guard, but was once again beaming with desire and she felt her world become whole as she began to let go.

"Oh yeah, baby. Tell me how bad you want it, Nessa." Alex mumbled under his breath.

Reese suddenly realized Alex was not completely awake and he was ready for Round 3 but, apparently not with her. He was asleep and dreaming about being with some girl named Nessa. *Who the hell is Nessa?* Reese thought. Her pleasure was now displaced. Jealousy and anger crept to the surface as she put it all together.

Vanessa! She thought angrily to herself with a sense of revelation and clarity.

She felt betrayed, furious, and once again it was hard to breathe. Her perfect night was ruined. Not ruined by her for once, but ruined entirely by him. No way was she going to give him the satisfaction of pleasuring her while dreaming of Vanessa or let him get away with a blatant disregard for respect. She wiggled her hips as hard as she could to break free of his hand that was steadily at work. She then began moving her body and shaking her foot in an attempt to wake him up.

"Reese! What the fuck are you doing?" he snapped.

Alex was not happy about being woken up from his fantasy.

Success, Reese thought as she smiled.

"Sorry, my foot and leg are numb and tingling." She concealed her rage with seemingly pure innocence. "I'm just going to go to the living room and walk around until it stops. Go back to sleep, honey, I didn't mean to wake you."

Alex grumbled unrecognizable words under his breath before his head hit the pillow. By the time she had made it to the bedroom door, there was a faint snoring that slowly developed and filled the room.

"Good," she whispered to herself before walking out of the room.

The dryer door was cold as she opened it and grabbed out her robe. Reese untangled the robe and her brain became a hurricane of emotions when she began to pace. *Was Jess right? I mean, obviously he wants to bone her, but I wonder if he has already, or if he's just dreaming about it.* She bit her nails, noticing the table and flowers that beautifully sat there taunting her. *Why bother with this whole amazing night to just ruin it... can I even be mad at a dream... this had to come from somewhere, right?* She mumbled out loud to herself.

"You made me this whole amazing dinner and planned this whole night which was basically a night of my favorites, and yet you go to sleep and dream of another girl in our bed? Ugh!" She grunted. *I have bent over backwards to try and be perfect for you, and yet you scream at me and tell me how I am such a whore. Look at you!* "Are you really some innocent bystander I should be thankful for?" She rubbed her hand across her forehead and stopped pacing. *I need black and white proof if I'm going to take him down.* "Tomorrow it starts." She took the bottle of Tennessee whiskey out of the cabinet and downed three shots to help calm her down. "I'm callin' Jess tomorrow," she said as she tossed back her last shot.

She walked down the hall and stopped. Standing there frozen like a statue, seething, *I don't want to sleep in his arms tonight, damn it.*

When she got back into the room the whiskey began to hit her. A warm feeling trickled over her body, and she was able to get back into bed without reservations. That night was the first time they slept on opposite sides of the bed. Alex would typically roll over and find her no matter what. He insisted on holding her tightly even in his sleep. This was something Reese despised. She always thought there was a time and place for cuddling— like on the couch watching a movie or after they made love— but she wanted to be left alone while she slept. It had been a little over two years since Alex gave her that freedom, until tonight. Reese snuggled herself under the blankets and enjoyed her peaceful solitary sleep.

BEEP, BEEP, BEEP, BEEP...

The alarm sounded for Alex to get up and head to work. Reese didn't budge until she felt his smothering arms around her.

"Morning, babe," Alex pulled her close and softly kissed her cheek.

Reese grumbled and eventually got the words out, "Mornin', love."

At this point Reese had become so good about suppressing her true feelings, that putting on a happy face was something she did effortlessly. Alex got up and into the shower as she snuggled back under the blankets and fell back to sleep, she hadn't slept this solid in a long time. She fell deeper into her sleep although she felt like someone was watching her. Her inner voice tried to warn her to wake up, Reese knew she was expected to get out of bed and see Alex off to work, but she was so comfortable lying there in the bed alone. She was jolted from her peaceful sleep when she felt Alex kick the bed shaking her awake, and then she felt his hot breath next to her ear.

"Wake up, Reese! I'm leaving," he viciously yelled in her ear.

Reese jumped as she opened her eyes.

"Geez, Alex, you scared me." She sat up holding her ear.

She wiped the sleep from her eyes, when out of nowhere she felt a sudden sting as his hand connected with her face. Reese was caught off guard. "Shit!" she cried out and her hands now held her face. "Why did you do that?" She tried her best to sound remorseful and not angry, but she was confused. "What was that for? What did I do?"

"I went all out for you last night and you can't even get your worthless ass out of bed to see me off to work? You are the most selfish person I've ever known!" he snapped. "You deserve more than that, but I don't have time to properly punish you." His body moved in a threatening manner toward her when he reached out and grabbed her face, her lips once again trapped between his thumb and fingers. Nose to nose he continued to talk to her with such revulsion. "This house better be clean by tomorrow when I get home." His spit flung onto her face. "You better get your shit together."

"I'm sorry." Her words came out garbled from his hand squeezing her mouth. Tears began to steadily stream down her cheeks. He squeezed even harder while lowering his voice; his look became terrifying.

"I will consider forgiving you."

He released his grasp from her face and then turned on his heel and walked out of the bedroom. Reese pushed down the anger and embarrassment she felt creeping up within her before she got up and went after Alex.

"Alex! Wait! Please!" she yelled as she ran down the hallway wiping her tears.

With his hand on the handle of the front door, he stopped and looked at her. His eyes were filled with rage. Treading lightly with her words, she began to grovel, "I am so sorry, babe, please don't leave angry. I was so tired after our wonderful night. I didn't even realize you were out of the shower. I must've fallen back to sleep. You're right, I should've been up and ready to see you off to work. Please forgive me." As much as she despised him when he was like this she couldn't bring herself to leave. She loved him, even when she wished she didn't.

The fury dissipated on his face as she pleaded with him, and a smirk slowly appeared.

"I wore you out last night huh?"

The emotional roller coaster of Alex was overwhelming, but she knew this was her only chance to smooth things over.

"Oh yes, babe, my inner thighs are so sore. I didn't mean to disrespect you. It's more of a compliment actually, if you think about it."

"I guess you're right." He chuckled before kissing her on the cheek where he had slapped her just minutes ago. "I love you, doll face, I gotta go."

"I love you too, handsome. Stay safe out there today."

Alex walked out the door and Reese softly closed it behind him as she exhaled a sigh of relief. She locked the deadbolt as more tears began to trickle down her face. Wiping it away, *that hurt so damn bad.* She stood there rubbing her cheek lost in her chaotic emotions battling inside her.

Chapter 9

ONCE HER COFFEE was the perfect balance of coffee and creamer she grabbed a blanket and sat on the couch. With the blanket wrapped tightly around her body and hands on the hot mug, she sat and stared off replaying what Alex had said in his sleep. A cataclysm of tears formed into dark spots on her blanket as she pictured Alex with another woman. *Maybe if I was a better girlfriend this wouldn't be happening. I try so hard to be what he wants me to be.* Her thoughts weren't her own anymore; they were her thoughts but Alex's words. She reached over and grabbed her phone and as if on autopilot, unlocking the screen to text Alex. She didn't want to make this morning any worse than it already had been.

REESE: I miss you already babe. 7:55 am

Selecting Alex's name she sent it off. Then she pulled up Jess Atwood's name before wiping away the water from her eyes.

REESE: Hey! 7:56 am

It was early, Reese knew she wouldn't be awake yet but she sent it anyway.

Determination found its way to the surface of her emotions as she got up and put on her running clothes. Thoughts continued to race through her head as she took off down the driveway and onto the sidewalk. There was an array of music that filled her workout playlist. She started out feeling sluggish, letting her negative thoughts affect her body. Until of course, the fast-paced rock songs came on; Linkin Park, Godsmack, and Metallica began to play and she felt herself gradually pick up speed. Her blood pumped harder through her veins, and her lungs burned from the cool air. She became angry thinking about Alex. *Who the hell does he think he is? I do everything he asks and yet I'm never good enough. Last night was amazing! We are talking off-the-charts amazing, and then this morning happens?*

She turned the corner as memories began to once again flood her mind, flashes of his abuse over the last eighteen months. Bruise after bruise that he had given her. The look on the faces of the men and women she worked with as she changed. The disappointment Stump had for her. Before she knew it more tears seeped out without any effort when she thought of how she had even lost Kyra because of him. The tears that now fell were no longer filled with sorrow but with anger and disappointment. She had sacrificed everything for him; her friends, her personality, and he almost cost her job about six months ago.

Alex hated Reese working at Station 23 because he knew that everyone on her shift were very close, they all hung out outside of work and, what Alex seemed to hate the most, they all had each other's backs no matter what. Reese had grown tired of the constant interrogation she received after every shift from him, so she called in sick often. Although she hated calling in and deserting her crew, she felt trapped between a rock and a hard place. Chief Gibbs had pulled her into his office and gave her what they call "a come to Jesus talk."

"I don't know what has been going on with you lately, Reese, but calling in sick as much as you have been, will no longer be tolerated. If you call in sick without a doctor's note again, you will leave me no choice but to fire you. Am I clear?"

Reese recalled how embarrassed she was to put Chief Gibbs in that position. This was the first time she had a boss mad at her. That day she felt the tears build up in her eyes and tried with all her might not to cry. Crying in front of people was a personal no-no for her. She put her head down to conceal the tears forming in her eyes.

"I'm sorry, Chief Gibbs, it won't happen again."

"Are you okay, Reese? You haven't been yourself lately, and now this?"

"I'm fine, sir."

He looked at her as though trying to identify if she was being truthful or not and after a long pause he finally spoke.

"I know I'm your Chief but if you ever need anything, I want you to know I'm here."

Reese nodded her head as he spoke. "You're dismissed..."

"Thank you, sir," she said before hastily leaving his office and making her way back to her bed in the barracks.

On her run, Reese now came around the corner to the final stretch of her three-mile run. *Push through, strong finish.* She picked up her speed to a sprint. Her heart pounded against her aching chest and lungs burned, she pictured the slap Alex had given her just an hour ago. She ran even faster as she discovered more anger to push her further. She pushed harder and faster only slowing down as she crossed the invisible finish line, and then proceeded to slowly jog down to the other end of the street and back. She was completely out of breath and her legs felt like jelly. *Haven't run like that in a while,* she thought, walking around her front yard with her hands on her head.

It felt good outside, her body radiated heat in the cool morning air and when she walked into the house, it felt like a sauna. After pouring a glass of ice water she made her way to the backyard and sat at their outdoor table. Phone in hand, she drew her knee up and got comfortable in her recliner. Text Messages (1), her phone read.

Reese sat there staring at the phone contemplating whether to check it or not. *Maybe it's Jess, but it might be Alex.* She took a deep breath, unsure if she really wanted to hear from Alex, but she decided to check it anyway.

ALEX: What are you doing? 8:50 am

The thought popped in her mind, *Well, I was enjoying my morning until now.* The anger she used to push through her run still boiled beneath the surface. Anytime he texted her, she didn't have to hide her true feelings. With a loud sigh she leaned back in her chair and rolled her eyes.

REESE: Just got back from a run... 3 miles! 8:52 am
ALEX: Cool, I did 5 yesterday. Don't forget to clean the kitchen. 8:53 am

Reese rolled her eyes again, tired of him always having to one-up her with everything.

"No shit! I'm not incompetent, asshole!" she said out loud with heavy irritation.

REESE: Yes, I will. Gonna do it here in a few minutes. How's your shift so far? 8:53 am
ALEX: It's going. Gonna go do drills, talk to you later. 8:55 am
REESE: OK babe. Love you. 8:55 am

ALEX: Love you too. 8:57 am

Reese sat there staring at her phone. *Maybe a drop-by visit this afternoon is in order. Make sure Vanessa knows Alex is taken.* She figured if he could come to her station and mark his territory randomly and whenever he pleases, than she could do the same. A soft giggle escaped her lips as she devised her drop-by plan. Her brain daydreamed about what she would say to them if she caught Alex and Vanessa in the act. A smile grew on her face as the world of possibilities came to mind, and she decided she wasn't going to hold anything back and let him have it. All the feelings she had bottled up for almost two years would break free and the fantasy of releasing her anger flourished, she felt the power to leave rise up inside her but, Alex's pull was stronger, she felt the sting on her face from his enormous hand that morning.

Normally Reese had time to brace herself, or even move out of the way and dodge it, but not that morning. *Letting everything out in front of Alex will end badly for me,* she thought. Her hands were trembling while fear swarmed over her, extinguishing any trace of anger she had. She jumped when the phone went off unexpectedly in her hands with another text message, but thankfully this time it was Jess.

Chapter 10

REESE TOLD JESS about what Alex said and did in his sleep, she held nothing back as she vented to her via text for about twenty minutes. Afterward, Jess said she wanted to come over and talk in person. Reese welcomed Jess' self-invitation, happy that someone on her crew wanted to hang-out with her despite her recent personality changes.

She started cleaning the kitchen and glanced over at the computer screensaver bouncy idly from corner to corner. She stopped and stared remembering last week Alex made her do something she ended up completely being appalled by and regretted entertaining Alex's perversion for even a second. Reese decided to go over and erase the search history on the computer just in case Jess decided to try and find evidence of cheating through Alex's social media. She didn't want to be forced to tell Jess how Alex made her watch porn with him and in the midst he decided to pull up videos of young girls said to be early teens being sexually assaulted and raped by older men.

Reese remembered feeling completely heartbroken as she tried to stare past the videos in a feeble attempt to not directly see the heinous acts performed on poor young girls. Just minutes after the first video started Reese had to turn her head away desperate to un-see the horrific scenes. She glanced up to Alex hovering next to her smiling with pleasure. She remembered feeling so confused at how he could possibly be finding pleasure out of the video but, she wouldn't dare say anything simply out of fear. When he caught the abhorred look on her face he offered what seemed to be rehearsed explanation.

"I stumbled onto these videos by *accident*. I thought they were funny, that's all."

Funny, Reese shuttered, feeling unsure of how he could possibly think that. She remembered not wanting to care why he made her watch the videos but, desperately wanting him to stop and never look at something like that again. She hid behind the dam around her emotions to keep the tears from seeping out while he played video after video. Reese picked a spot on the bottom of the screen to stare at with a blank expression because she was unable to muster up fake enjoyment just to make him happy, not with this. That night after watching several videos, Alex took her to bed, held her down, and forced himself inside of her. Reese remembered how rough he was and the aggression in which he took her, and how much physical damage it caused.

When they woke up the next morning he apologized for making her watch those videos, and then promised to never do that to her again. Reese let the whole thing go but, she didn't want Jess to see it and cause her to have to figure out an explanation, without hesitation, she deleted the history.

Reese returned to the kitchen and began scrubbing the dishes with severe anguish as her emotions morphed from anger into sadness and self-loathing. She was scrubbing everything around her as she zoned out on what her life had become. She made her final touches in her clean-up feeling remorseful. *What if he is innocent and I have this whole thing wrong? Maybe I am the problem. If I was a better girlfriend this wouldn't be happening.* Alex had manipulated and mentally broke Reese past the point of reason. She constantly blamed herself, believing that she deserved the abuse and all of the torment he gave her. He had her convinced that she was undesirable and that she should be thankful he was willing to put up with her. *He's right; no one will ever love me the way he does. Maybe I should just let this whole thing go and just be thankful I have him.* Just as those thoughts entered her brain, there was a knock at the door. Reese wiped her hands dry and cracked open the door to see Jess standing there with two coffees in hand.

"Hey girl, I thought you could use one!" Jess held up one of the cups.

"Oh man, you have no idea." Reese took the cup and removed the lid, taking in the tantalizing aroma. "Mm, white chocolate mocha is my favorite! Thank you so much!" Reese stood to her side and allowed Jess to walk in, both pausing to lean in for a quick hug.

"No problem." Jess came in, dropped her purse at the door and got straight to business. "Okay, Reese, what's the plan here?"

Reese moved towards the kitchen and turned on the light. She really hadn't devised a plan. She didn't know how to do any of this worked, let alone, how to spy on someone or hack into social media accounts.

"A plan... yeah, I should probably have one of those?" Reese and Jess both burst out with laughter as Reese turned to face Jess.

"Reese! Oh my God, what happened to your face?" Jess blurted out in horror, stopping all laughter, the mood becoming instantly serious.

"My face, what's wrong with it?" Reese played it off like she didn't just get slapped a few hours ago. She jumped up and looked in the mirror hanging up on the wall by the door. "Oh gosh, it's all red!" Reese ran her hand over her face as her heart broke. "I went running earlier. Maybe my cheek got chapped in the cool air? I honestly have no idea where it came from... that's so weird. It wasn't there this mornin',"

"That is weird, maybe it's just chapped." Jess looked at her skeptically.

"It's fine." Reese reassured her as she waved her hand. "So, let's plan, I honestly don't really know how to do this part. I've never felt the need to spy on a boyfriend before." She shrugged her shoulders. "I thought about doing a surprise drop-by today."

"That's a good idea but more than likely you won't catch him doing something at the station. Although, I could always be wrong, that could be prime opportunity. I would be lying if I said Nate and I hadn't taken advantage of the opportunity a time or two." Jess must have realized what she had said once the words left her mouth. "Um... uh, what I meant to–" Jess' eyes widened as she scrambled to find the words to say but all she could get out were fragments while Reese roared with laughter.

"Girl, you honestly think I don't already know? C'mon now, give me more credit than that."

"You can't tell anyone! Please, Reese! We agreed to keep it a secret for now. No one can know!" Jess begged.

Reese smiled and winked her eye at Jess, "You know I got you."

Jess let out a sigh of relief, hoping that her secret remained safe. "Even though you aren't supposed to know, I am so glad you do! Finally I can talk to someone about all of this!" Jess grinned from ear to ear. "But we will talk about that later. Do you know any of his passwords to anything? We can try hacking into his Facebook and Twitter accounts."

The girls gathered around the computer and Jess suggested they start by pulling up the computer history and Reese felt relieved that she had decided to clear it. When there was nothing there to see, they moved on to Facebook, and once again nothing to find. Twitter was next, still nothing. The final account was his email but when she pulled up Yahoo Mail she found an unfamiliar email address already placed in the sign-in.

"One of his friends must've checked their email here, or maybe his brother," Reese said, immediately trying to disregard the potential of secrets.

Jess snapped a quick photo of the unfamiliar address before Reese erased it and put in his info. All they found was a few pornographic pictures that Alex emailed to his brother Lance.

"Well, Jess, maybe I was wrong." Reese initially felt disappointed but, soon it turned into relief.

"Maybe, but I honestly don't think you are... let's just call it a gut feeling." Jess bit her nails as she stared at the screen. "I would still drop by the station if I were you."

"Yeah, I think I will. Lately though, Alex doesn't like it when I show up unannounced. I mean, is it worth the potential fight?"

"He started getting mad when you show up without warning?" Jess, like a hound hot on a trail, scrutinized the comment.

"Sometimes, but it's not all the time. Why do you look so intrigued about that?"

"People who have nothing to hide don't get mad about being caught off guard, Reese."

"True." Reese bit her lower lip, trying to suppress the suspicious feelings creeping up inside her.

"Okay, girl, I have to go. I'm meeting Nate for lunch." Jess got up, grabbed her purse, and stopped to examine herself in the mirror. "Just drop by," she said, fixing her hair, "...and then let me know how it goes, okay?"

"Of course, thanks so much for coming over."

"Any time," Jess said with a smile.

They hugged before Jess fluttered out the door, obviously giddy about her hunky lunch date. Reese leaned up against the doorway and watched her bounce all the way to her car. Less than twelve hours ago, Reese felt that way and now she was hacking accounts and planning a surprise visit. She smiled in spite of her pain and gave a friendly wave at Jess before closing the door.

The house was spotless so Reese decided to take a long and hot shower. In the bathroom she examined her face in the mirror while waiting for the water to warm up. *Man! He hit me harder than I thought.* Her fingertips ran over the redness he left on her face. *I hope he doesn't get too mad when I drop by later,* Reese worried. She had just smoothed over her morning mishap with him. *Maybe I should wait on it. Ugh, I don't know what to do. I mean, he is on all night so if he gets mad then at least he has time to cool off before he comes home. Plus I work tomorrow... screw it, Jess is right, I'm doing it.* She got into the shower, her heart filled with boldness. The hot water felt amazing running down her body and she leisurely stood there exulting in the heat as her worries seemed to wash away down the drain. Her anxiety about everything began to fade, and she relished in the simplicity of the hot shower as she washed herself.

Wrapped in a towel she stood in front of her neatly hung clothes, unsure of what to wear. *What does one wear to go mark their territory?* A mischievous giggle came from her mouth and then she saw just the right thing hanging there. It was a black shirt with a low scoop neckline that had three small buttons down the center in a straight line that unbuttoned to reveal more cleavage. It fit tightly around her body with small cap sleeves, and it was just short enough to sit about half an inch above her pants, showing off her lean stomach. The jeans she chose to wear were skinny jeans that hugged her curves in all the right places, with slight destruction down the legs, and Alex couldn't resist her when she wore them. She chose to pair this outfit with her low-top black and white Chucks— Converse shoes were her favorite shoes and she owned just about every color. She put back on the necklace Alex had given her and moved on to her hair and makeup. Her hair was blow dried and then straightened. Only minimal makeup was applied. Reese stood in the bathroom, staring at herself in the mirror and she gave herself a pep talk.

"You can do this, Reese," she said out loud. "Yes, he'll probably be mad, but you have recovered from worse. It's time to get to the bottom of this and that homewrecker needs to be put in her place, and so does he. Don't you dare chicken out now!" With a deep breath she grabbed her keys, gathered up her purse, and walked out the door.

Ginger Teriyaki was Alex's favorite place. He loved their teriyaki with General Tso's chicken and Reese thought, *what a perfect way to surprise him.* When she pulled up to the station with his food in hand, butterflies formed in her stomach. *Here goes nothing.* Putting on her happiest face, she walked toward the station and noticed a woman standing next to ambulance 34 on her phone; Reese overheard her for a brief moment.

"Oh he's amazing, I can't wait for all you guys to meet—" The woman abruptly stopped when she noticed Reese. Through her black Ray-Ban sunglasses Reese watched the woman, not having to second guess who this new girl was, *and this must be Vanessa,* she could feel her feathers ruffle. She was much shorter than Reese with beautifully light brown skin that appeared to be flawless. Her hair was slightly below the shoulders and was layered with bangs that swooped to the left side, framing her young face and deep brown eyes. She stood leaning on the hood of the ambulance and Reese couldn't help but noticed how her uniform fit tightly around her full-figured frame.

"Oh honey, I think you missed a button," Reese said with a condescending tone, pointing to the woman's shirt that was unbuttoned to expose her cleavage, *Desperate much?* The woman just stared at Reese with a look of disbelief on her face while Reese sauntered by and into the station to find Alex.

Reese concealed a giggle when she looked down at her own protruding breasts and thought, *Yeah, like you have room to talk.* Reese made one last adjustment to her shirt and bra to make sure everything was in prime position when she turned the corner into the common room where Alex was sitting and reading the paper.

"Hey, babe," Reese said as she walked toward him. Alex began to form a smile on his face while his eyes grazed over a last sentence, when he looked up and saw it was Reese, his smile quickly faltered. She could see the confusion swirling inside his head. "I decided to surprise you with your favorite for lunch." She sat the bag of food down in front of him on the table, and kissed him on the cheek.

"Hey, Reese, um, uh... what are you doing here?" The concern in his voice was noticeable when she sat down in the chair next to him and leaned forward, resting her elbow on the table. With her other hand on his upper thigh she ran her fingertips in a swirling motion in an attempt to be flirtatious.

She leaned in and lowered her voice, "Well, you did so much for me last night that I wanted to do something for you in return."

Alex shifted in his chair, noticeably uncomfortable, so she casually removed her hand from his thigh. He leaned over with a smirk on his face and kissed her on the cheek.

"Thank you, baby, this smells amazing."

"It's your favorite."

"You got me teriyaki chicken from Ginger Teriyaki?" Alex couldn't contain his increasing excitement.

"Yes, sir," Reese grinned.

"Mm," he said pulling the food from the bag and handing her a fork and all the napkins.

They started to eat when Reese looked up and saw the woman from outside walking into the common room. Reese turned to Alex and placed her hand back on his thigh and slowly ran her fingers toward the inner thigh when he grabbed her hand to stop her.

"Hey, Nessa, come here for a sec," Alex blurted out. Reese tried very hard to conceal her irritation, *Nessa,* anger bubbled up inside of her. "Reese, I want you to meet Vanessa, she's the new medic for Ambulance 34."

Reese turned to look at Vanessa. *Of course it's the pretty girl from outside.* She put on an obviously fake smile and looked straight at her.

"Hey." She waved her hand slightly annoyed, as if meeting Vanessa was the last thing on earth she wanted to do, mainly because it was. "You know, I bet if you tell your Chief, I'm sure they could get you a new shirt, one that buttons correctly," Reese said with a belittling tone as she turned back toward Alex. "How's your lunch, my love?"

Alex appeared horrified and significantly displeased with Reese and her behavior. Reese didn't really care what Alex thought at the moment but then she saw the irritation on his face. Alex leaned toward Reese and with a low growl he whispered in her ear, "What the hell is wrong with you?"

"Me?" Reese whispered, placing her hand over her chest with dramatized disbelief. She shifted her body away from Alex and began to talk louder to ensure Vanessa would hear her. "I just wanted to bring my amazing boyfriend his favorite food for lunch. I thought after the romantic night you planned for us last night that was the least I could do. I'm here, for you right now, are you here with me right now? Or should I just go?" He looked infuriated sitting there staring at her. *Shit, too far Reese, too far!* She put her head down remorsefully. "I'm sorry, babe. I'm bein' rude." Reese turned toward Vanessa, swallowing every ounce of anger she felt before extending her hand out. "Hi, I'm Reese, Alex's girlfriend."

Vanessa shifted her eyes toward Alex as if to get permission to proceed. *What was that?* Reese thought.

"Hi, I'm Vanessa." Vanessa placed her hand in Reese's and firmly grasped for an awkward shake.

"How long have you been a medic?" Reese made a shallow attempt of being friendly.

"Only for a few months now, Alex told me that you started out young as well."

Vanessa seemed suddenly overzealous to get Reese to like her.

"Uh yeah, I was probably no older than you are. What are you? Twenty?"

"I turn twenty-two next week actually," Vanessa said proudly

Twenty-two!!! Seriously, she's a baby? Reese thought.

"Oh, well... happy early birthday."

"Oh thanks! I'm not sure what I'm going do yet," Vanessa said with desperation in her voice.

"Well, I'm sure you will figure it out," Reese said before turning back to Alex. "What time are you off in the morning again, babe?" She tried her best to detach the conversation away from Vanessa. Seeming startled Alex spoke in fragmented words as he was caught off guard, staring at Vanessa.

"Uh– oh– I'm, uh–" Alex stammered.

"We're off at eight in the morning," Vanessa chimed in.

Reese turned and shot her a look of irritation.

"Oh, you're still here?" Turning back to Alex, she continued, "Well, I guess I won't get to see you in the mornin' then. I have to be at the station by eight." Reese stuck out her bottom lip to pout.

"Aw babe, I'll miss you too." Alex kissed her on the forehead as he stood up.

He walked to the trash can and threw away his container from lunch. Reese didn't have much of an appetite, but sat there pushing her rice around in the bowl feeling like she wanted to leave but yet didn't want to go just yet. Her suspicions of Alex and Vanessa magnified as she watched them dance around each other with long lasting glances and soft giggles. *If I acted that way with one of the guys at my station in front of him he would literally kick my ass, and yet it's okay for him?* Reese stewed.

"I'm gonna get goin', babe," Reese interrupted their awkward attempt at avoidance. "Walk me out?"

"Sure." He said, gesturing Reese to walk in front of him out of the station.

I wonder, Reese turned to the guys sitting on the couch in the common room.

"See y'all later, have a good shift!" she said with a smile on her face.

"Thanks, Reese!" one of the guys said.

"See ya later!" another said.

Alex shifted his violent gaze at her, grabbed the back of her upper arm and dug his fingers into her skin, pulling her out of the station.

"Would you care to explain yourself? What was that?" He demanded as they reached the parking lot, his fingers pushed harder into her skin.

"Ouch!" Reese exclaimed as she jerked her arm free. "Explain myself, for what? For conversing with the men at your station the way you converse with Vanessa? Pretty sure she is a beautiful girl and it seems to me that you are more than just professional colleagues. Am I wrong, Alex?"

"I talked to her about you!" His voice was deep and growling, filled with fury.

"Why? Why talk to her at all? It's rather inappropriate if you ask me." Reese was proud of herself, thinking she finally had the upper hand.

"Well, because she has a rough home life and she's young. I thought maybe you could take her under your wing and help her."

"Me? I don't even like her and yet you think because you laid some groundwork, I'm supposed to jump at being BFFs with her? No!"

"Reese." His voice was stern.

"No!" She folded her arms and held her ground. *No freakin' way, I am not doing that,* she thought.

"Well, you better find a way to get over it because she's coming to our house for dinner tomorrow night."

"I'm sorry, what!?" Her hands flew into the air. "Are you kiddin' me?" In shifting her body she saw Vanessa standing out by the ambulance watching them. "Well, at least she's subtle," she said under her breath, anger oozing from every pore.

Alex grabbed her and spun her around to face him, his voice low and horrifying when he spoke.

"I don't know what your fucking problem is, but unless you want to be punished later I would shut your damn mouth. You better think before you speak to me like that again." He grabbed her face and tilted it, examining the red mark he left earlier that morning. "I will make this red mark look like a fairy tale. Know your place. I said she was coming to dinner, so then she is coming to dinner." He released her face. "You *will* be nice, and you *will* build a friendship with her." He got in her face, forcing her head back to look up at him. "Do you understand me?"

Reese was petrified. "Yes, I understand."

"Now go. You've made a complete fool of yourself." Alex walked away from her.

Although she couldn't see his face when he walked away, she saw Vanessa look directly at Alex and smirk. *I just screwed up,* Reese thought. *Tomorrow at dinner I have to fix this.*

Reese got into her car, overwhelmed with disappointment in herself. *I took it too far.* Her soul ached as she went over how she acted in her head. This was not who she was, she was not the jealous type. In every relationship she had in the past jealousy was never a part of it. Carefree and go with the flow were two of her best personality traits. *Who is this person I've become?* She had a hard time recognizing herself anymore and she suddenly realized that she needed a break from all of this, from everyone, including the person she had become. She flipped a U-turn at the next stoplight and headed toward her Chief's house.

Chapter 11

CHIEF GIBBS LIVED in a beautiful WWII era cottage-style home. It was tan with white trim lining the roof and the windows with a chimney that stood tall off the front of the house which was also white. Mike Gibbs and his wife had bought that home about six years ago, when they had their first child. Chief Gibbs always wanted a place where his kids could run around and play, complete with a backyard and a jungle gym.

Reese remembered that the entire crew came together to help them paint and move in. Gibbs' wife, Audrey, was seven months pregnant at the time and no one would allow her to lift a finger, she was charged with telling everyone else what to do and where to put things. Mike would joke around by saying how he thought she enjoyed her new position a little too much at times, but he was always happy to oblige and do whatever she asked.

Anxiety crept up within Reese as she put her 4Runner in park. *Maybe this was a bad idea.* Out of the corner of her eye she saw a man standing on the front lawn. Chief Gibbs was standing there wearing jeans and a dark blue Auburn Fire Department shirt, the AFD logo on the upper right side of the chest. *Well, too late to change my mind now.* She exited her car and walked toward her Chief, with her hands in her pockets.

"Hey, how's it going, Chief." Her head was down and her voice timid. "I'm sorry for dropping by like this but I need to talk to you if that's okay... or, uh, I can come back another time, just wait until we work again, if you prefer?"

"Oh, there's no trouble, Reese, I'm here for you no matter what, what's up?" He shifted his weight and looked concerned.

"I need to ask a favor... I'm having some serious personal problems. I know I've called out of work way too much lately but, I really need to take a day to figure some things out. I just don't want anyone to know about it. I'm not even going to tell Alex I want to take off work. I just really need to be alone with just myself; I need to figure things out, figure my life out really... I know I'm probably not making much sense, and I'm sorry but, I just don't really want to talk about it in large detail. I promise this is not me trying to screw you over, or leave you shorthanded. I just feel like I can't breathe." Her voice cracked. "I can't breathe, like all the time. I just need... I just– honestly, I have no freaking clue what I need." She felt the dam she'd built up around her emotions crack. An unbroken trickle of tears rushed down her cheeks.

"Reese, slow down. It's okay, take tomorrow off and clear your head. I'll tell the crew that you were moved to another station for the shift. But, if Alex shows up at the station what do I tell him?"

Reese knew it wasn't like Chief Gibbs to go along with a lie especially, lying to everyone at the station. He must have known how much she needed this to happen. Despite his hard exterior, Reese figured Chief Gibbs softer side was hoping this personal day would be the first step in bringing back the old Reese everyone really missed at the station.

"If he shows up unannounced, maybe tell him I'm out on a call? Or that I've had back-to-back calls and haven't been there all day. Do you think that would work?"

"I can do that for you." Gibbs placed his hand on her shoulder. "Reese, I'm going to tell you something as your friend and not as your boss. I don't know what exactly has been going on at home for you but, I do know what I've seen at work. You don't seem happy, Reese, you seem hurt and withdrawn. I wish I could fix it all for you but, I think this is probably one of those things you have to fix on your own. I miss you Reese, we all do because you're not the same girl that became a part of our Station 23 family. You've changed a lot and, I hate to say it but, not for the better. We've all been worried about you for a while now. I'm just hoping you can make the best of your time to sort things out." Chief Gibbs looked at her with concern and support before he pulled her close to him and hugged her tight. "We are all here for you, Dear."

"Thank you." Reese sniffled into Chief Gibbs shoulder, she pulled away from the embrace, wiped her tears and left.

Millions of thoughts raced through her head while she made the drive home. She didn't know how she was going to pull this off yet, but she knew it was necessary. If she was going to survive dinner tomorrow and be a better woman than she was earlier, she had to clear her head. Just then, her phone vibrated. Jess was calling her. *What am I supposed to say to her? I can't deal with this right now.* Hitting ignore, she continued driving in silence.

Tonight she planned on mapping out the county roads outside of the city. She needed to take a drive and get away from the people in Auburn. That's what she used to do in Texas when she felt overwhelmed. Once again her thoughts were interrupted by her phone and a short vibration: New Text Message (1).

JESS: Hey girl! How'd it go today?! I need details!!! Call me back. 1:18 pm

Reese read the text, locked her phone, and set it back down. She was out of things to say and she sat there thinking about what Chief Gibbs had said to her. 'You've changed— We all miss you–You seem hurt and withdrawn–' those words rang the loudest in her head. Those were the same words her mother told her when she went home to visit a few months ago.

Reese and her parents had always had a close relationship and they talked just about every day on a regular basis. Even though the distance between them was hard, they managed to always make time for each other. When Reese left Texas, it was one of the hardest decisions she ever made. It was so hard in fact that she initially decided to turn down the job in Auburn and stay, but he mother Maggie was the one who told her to go.

"Sis," her mother started, a nickname her mother always called Reese and Sophie. Reese never knew why her mother called them that but, she liked that it was different and felt like their own. "I know this is gonna be hard, but it's time for you to spread your wings and build your own life. Don't just stay here because you'll miss us. This is your time to shine, my sweet girl. Experience life, make mistakes, and then make some great memories along the way. Maybe Washington will be where you find your forever, maybe it won't. You know Daddy and I will always be here for you, no matter what. Accept the job with Auburn Fire Department, because that's really what you truly want. And if you hate it, we'll just come get you and bring ya back here." Her mother kissed her on the forehead looking back at her with a smile as she walked out of her room.

Later on the same day, Reese accepted the job and three weeks later they moved her roughly two-thousand miles north. She recalled the way her dad was during the drive. Every few hours he would call her while they drove tandem in two cars to constantly double check with her that she still wanted to go. The last call was as they reached the city limits of Auburn.

"Are you sure this is what you want, Reesey Piecey?" Reese knew he would have a crooked smile on his face when she heard a giggle under his breath.

Reese knew he was joking, but also that there was a part of him that wasn't. Rusty was such a mellow and a fairly passive man, but he had no problem protecting his family in spite of his easygoing attitude. Reese was always told growing up that she was just like her daddy. They both were always the life of the party, making jokes about anything and everything they could, and sarcasm was like a second language for them. Maggie always said Reese and her father were 'Otters', they liked to play and swim carefree rather than get the work done. Rusty and Reese referred to Maggie and Sophie as the 'Lions,' always barking orders like they were the boss of everything, and always ready to crouch in on the fun. It became a longstanding joke in their family, otters against the lions and lions against the otters. Reese smiled.

When they arrived in Auburn at Reese's first apartment, the mood quickly became somber. As they unloaded the truck, the jokes became less frequent with each box that made its way inside. That night, when all the boxes were stacked and the air mattresses were made, there was a deafening silence that enveloped the room. Rusty was the first to break the impending sadness that had begun to take over.

"Hey kiddo, I saw a gas station up the road, wanna come with me to get a soda?"

"Yes, of course, sure thing, Dad."

Reese put on her shoes and they headed to the store. Rusty must have wanted a moment alone with Reese, just the two of them. He pulled into a parking spot and placed the car in park, but when Reese went to get out of the car she noticed her dad was still sitting there, facing forward with his hands firmly planted on the wheel staring straight ahead.

"Dad, you comin' in... or?"

"Reese." He paused and gripped the steering wheel tightly. "I know we joke around a lot and poke fun of each other, but I want you to know that I'm proud of you, kiddo." Reese turned in her seat to face her dad. "I love you more than I know how to express and I just want you to know that I have no doubt in my mind that you will be successful here. You, my sweet girl, are one of the most precious things God has blessed me with and I am goin' to miss you so darn much, baby girl." A single tear ran down his cheek, and Reese fought back her own wave of emotions as her eyes began to well up. "I just– I need you to know how incredibly proud I am of you."

"Thank you, Dad," she whispered as several tears broke free and streaked her down her face.

Rusty was still facing forward when Reese wrapped her arms around him and they just sat there in each other's arms for several minutes enjoying the last time they would be together for a while.

"I love you, Dad, I'm gonna miss you so much."

"I love you too, baby."

Over the next four days Reese's mother and father stayed around to help unpack boxes and get Reese everything she would need for a while. Six trips to the store later her apartment finally began to feel like home. The dreaded day her parents were set to leave for home was much harder for her than she was prepared for. Tears effortlessly flooded her eyes, watching them pull away, and she suspected that her parents had the same stream coming from their eyes.

Her first year in Auburn was the hardest, but once she got to know the people at work, it became easier being away from her family over time. Eventually, Reese began to build her very own "Auburn family." Now in the midst of her isolation, she felt as lonely as she did when she first moved there and didn't know anyone. She had pushed everyone she loved away, even her parents. Although she hadn't pushed them away to the same extent as she had with her work family, she still avoided talking to them more than she ever did before and kept conversations light and as short as possible.

When she went back home for a week, a few months ago, her mother began to question all the changes she noticed in her daughter. She commented that Reese didn't look like herself, she was withdrawn and unusually quiet, which was something Reese, had never been in her entire life. Both Maggie and Rusty seemed worried about their daughter, the concern was written all over their faces, and it wasn't long until they let Reese know they knew something was wrong. Reese hadn't been home no more than two days when Maggie just couldn't keep her opinion to herself any longer, and that night at the dinner table she made an attempt to get to the bottom of the situation. She set her fork down, took a long dramatic drink of her chardonnay, and bluntly asked Reese, "Sis, your father and I know somethin' is up, seriously, is everythin' okay, you're not acting like yourself and it's scaring us?"

"Um, yeah, everything is fine, why are y'all worried?" Reese continued eating trying to avoid the deeper conversation that she didn't want to have.

"You just don't– um, you just don't seem yourself these days." Maggie shifted in her chair her as her nerves became more obvious. "You seem lost, sweetheart, and completely withdrawn. Today, when we saw Uncle T and his friend Robert at the store, you basically ignored them both by starin' at your feet. Robert's been Uncle Trevor's best friend since they were kids and you haven't seen your uncle in, damn near forever, and you acted as if you didn't know either one of them. That's not like you, Reese. What's goin' on, dear?" Once Maggie began it was hard for her to stop. She no longer felt nervous to be honest with Reese, and she began spilling everything she had apparently been holding in for months now. "Is this because of Alex? Ever since y'all been together it seems like he has changed you, and clearly, it hasn't been for the better. I know you think you love him, sis, but I just can't help but think he's not a good person." Maggie's level of stress was clearly being elevated, her bottom lip began to quiver, seemingly to herself she said, "What has he done to my little girl?"

Reese became angry and defensive, slamming her fork down on the table, and startling her parents.

"Mom, that's enough! Alex hasn't done anything! He's a great man who loves me. I'm sorry you can't see that, or be happy for me, but I will tell you this, I don't think I love him, Mother, I know I love him! He's hands down the best thing that has ever happened to me and I don't care if you like him or not! He's a part of my life and that's not changin' any time soon!"

She pushed her chair back, threw her napkin on her plate, and stormed off down the hallway to her old room. Reese overheard Rusty immediately whispering condolences to Maggie who was clearly afraid she had lost her daughter for good. Alex had successfully transformed their vibrant daughter into a shell of a human being.

Fortunately, Reese and Maggie were able to smooth things out the next morning, at least enough to be on speaking terms, over a cup of coffee. However, things between them hadn't been the same since that night. Although she would never admit this to her mom, that night was the start of Reese examining things in her life that didn't make sense. Avoiding Maggie's calls didn't exactly send the right message, but Reese wasn't sure how to deal with her mother anymore. She certainly didn't want to be left defending her relationship, a relationship she wasn't sure why she was in anymore and couldn't explain entirely why she was choosing to stay.

Chapter 12

THE HOUSE WAS dark except for the light from the television that flickered with each passing scene of a sitcom television show. Reese sat on the couch with her knees drawn up to her chest, and a blanket wrapped around her, staring off in the distance with a blank look on her face. The television was nothing but noise to cut the silence in the house. Jess had texted her several more times since she had been home, but she continued to ignore her. She successfully closed herself off from everyone, and now she sat alone wondering how she was going to make Alex happy and become the woman he demanded her to be.

She pulled up the county roads on her phone and mapped out her impromptu trip for tomorrow, she decided that Vashon Island would be the place to clear her head. She got up and went to the closet where she had a secret envelope of money stashed back behind her mountain of shoes. Alex was in charge of the finances because Reese was never very good with money, and after only three months of dating he'd convinced her that it would be easier to get a joint checking account. He paid all the bills and told her constantly how they didn't have any extra money. When they merged their money together, thankfully, Reese decided to set up her check to keep a percentage separate from her direct deposit. It was a small amount of one-hundred dollars a month that she would cash and hide in the envelope for their emergency fund. She had saved roughly twenty-four hundred dollars over the last two years. Thumbing through the cash she thought, *I better take it all just in case something happens, I can pay cash and not leave a trail.*

With the envelope of money shoved in her purse she turned off the television and headed to get ready for bed. She took a quick shower and laid out her uniform for tomorrow, because even though she wasn't going to work she had to stage the house to look like she was. Standing with her pajamas on and hair wet she examined everything making sure she hadn't forgotten something vital that Alex would notice. Reese genuinely did not want to know the punishment for this magnitude of a lie. With one last final check she set her alarm and went to bed.

Tossing and turning most of the night, she was unable to sleep due to the lump she felt in her throat and the sick feeling rising in her stomach. *I'm betraying him. If he finds out about this he is going to kill me... actually, kill me.* She started questioning if any of this was a good idea. Every hour she woke up with the same feeling in the pit of her stomach, like her gut was trying to warn her that he would find out. Even her subconscious was filled with horrific dreams of torture at the hands of Alex.

She tossed and turned with, visions of Alex tying her to a chair while she screamed out for help. No one came to save her, only Alex was there grinning an ungodly grin and hysterically laughing as he tortured her. Her body was drenched in sweat from the pain as she struggled to escape. Her hair stuck to her blood-soaked face, blood sprayed from her mouth as Alex punched her as hard as he could making her eyes swell shut from the trauma. Reese restlessly slept. It was as though she could actually feel every blow dealt by Alex even from her sleep. She was startled awake once Alex began sending shocks of electricity through her body like a prisoner in an electrocution chair being sentenced to death for his crimes. Alex had never taken her punishments to that extreme before, but Reese also had never significantly broken the rules like this before either.

It was now 4:50 am and she reached over to shut off the alarm set to go off at 5:30 before she got up out of bed. With her robe wrapped around her she sluggishly walked into the kitchen and made herself a cup of coffee. While the coffee brewed she stood at the counter and began constructing a new plan. *Maybe driving that far off grid isn't the best idea.* The thoughts raced in her mind of how to not waste the opportunity Chief Gibbs had given her but, also how to keep Alex from finding out. She poured the flavored creamer into her coffee before heading over to sit on the couch, her hands wrapped tightly around the steaming cup. She slowly took small sips from her coffee. Once she began to wake up her brain was able to devise a better plan. She went to her purse, pulled two-hundred dollars from the envelope and stashed it into her wallet before returning the rest of the money back in her hiding place at the back of the closet.

Her phone was next to the bed on her nightstand. She grabbed it and decided to send Alex a text so there would be no cause for suspicion.

REESE: Good morning babe. I love you, can't wait to see you tonight. 5:15 am

She put on her uniform and began getting herself ready as if she was going to work. *I really hope he doesn't just show up at the station today.* Reese was worried. *He doesn't usually do that, but with my luck, today would be the day that he does. What if he stops by in retaliation for me going to see him at his station? What if he talks to one of my co-workers on shift today and they tell him I didn't come in?* Looking at herself in the mirror she decided to put the negative thoughts behind her and go forward with her new plan. Time away from everyone to think was exactly what she needed, and nothing was going to take that from her, not even the fear of Alex.

She cast one last look around the house, double checking she didn't leave anything important behind and as luck would have it, her boots caught her attention out of the corner of her eye.

"That could've been the death of me," she said out loud to herself.

With boots now in hand, she walked out the door and made her way to her car. Sitting in the driveway she made small adjustments to her purse, air vents, and stereo. Once she pulled out of the driveway and headed down her street she thought, *Screw it,* and cranked her music up as loud as she could stand it.

The songs blared through the speakers and she sang at the top of her lungs allowing the music to drown out all of her paranoid thoughts. Even Alex and the thought of his potential torture began to fade away, and her worry about Vanessa was now a distant memory. Her music was upbeat and she enjoyed her one-woman car concert. While she gave the performance of a lifetime, her music began to shuffle in a less upbeat direction and she felt undertones of anger rise up inside her. Reese felt her caged anger chugging through her, singing the songs as if she was saying the words straight to Alex straight to his face. She flooded with desire, wanting to see him standing there in front of her, petrified, while droplets of her spit landing on his face. Resentment seeped from her whole body and she was no longer paying attention to where she was, or how fast she was driving.

Approximately fifteen miles out of town she noticed the Auburn Police car as she flew by it, leaving it in the dust. Glancing down at the speedometer, reality came into focus seeing she was doing one-hundred and ten miles per hour. *OH Shit!* The police car flipped around and came after her with red and blue lights flashing.

Reese pulled her car to the side of the road before the officer had reached her. *Please be someone I know, please,* she thought over and over as the uniformed officer approached the car to find that her window was already rolled down.

"License and registration, ma'am," the officer said in a monotone voice.

"Chad?" Hope rose up within her.

The officer bent down to get a better look into the car and Reese exhaled as his face come into focus.

"Reese? Is that you?" His chocolate brown eyes intensely looked at Reese over the brim of his sunglasses.

"Oh my gosh, it's been forever! How's it going?"

Reese got out of her car and gave Chad a hug without even realizing what she was doing.

Chad Platt was one of her all-time favorite officers in her district. Not only was he easy on the eyes, but he was a genuinely nice guy. He was a little taller than Reese with dark brown hair, and olive complexion. He was one of those men that would shave every morning and yet by three in the afternoon he had an undeniable five o'clock shadow on his face. His body was lean and defined, with broad shoulders and from what Reese could see, very strong arms. Chad was a light hearted man that easily brought laughter to those around him and had an undeniable sense of calm with his large smile, like the one he was currently giving Reese.

"Reese, what the hell are you doing out here? I clocked you at one-hundred and ten miles per hour!" Chad's voice was authoritative and his incredible smile was gone and replaced with an uneasy look as he furrowed his bushy eyebrows.

"I'm so sorry, Chad! Seriously, I didn't even realize how fast I was goin'! My boyfriend and I had a fight and I wasn't payin' any attention to what I was doing. Please don't give me a ticket, Chad!" In a desperate attempt, she flashed a smile and slightly nudged him in the arm. "C'mon, for old time sake, please!" Reese begged. She knew if she got a ticket Alex would put it all together and seal her fate.

Chad looked around and placed his hand on his gun belt before mindlessly drumming his fingers on the grip of his holstered gun. His internal struggle was palpable but, luckily, he always adored Reese and wanted to help her out.

"Ugh, of course I'm going to let you go with a warning. But, you have to slow down! If another cop would have pulled you over that's an automatic suspension on you license and a fat ticket, and if you get pulled over again I can't help you."

"I promise! I will slow down! I seriously owe you one! Thank you so much, you're amazing!"

Chad looked at her and suddenly that beautiful smile was back. "Yes you do! I hope you know I will cash in on that one day!"

He leaned in and hugged her one last time before getting back into his car and driving away.

Reese stood next to her car, *that was close.* Her heart was pounding when she looked down the road and saw a sign that read, *Lake Holms 2 miles ahead.* Swiftly getting back into her car she drove off toward the lake. This wasn't a part of her plan, but what would be better than a lake to help gather her thoughts, just the way her Gran used to do. When she pulled away Reese did not allow her mind to wander. She stayed very aware of the speedometer over the next two miles, until she arrived at the turnout she was looking for.

Pulling up to the lake, all of the beauty it held surrounded her and she smiled. *It's perfect.* As the car door shut she took a deep breath, taking in the fresh air around her. It was incredibly serene and completely wonderful. Reese climbed up on the hood of her 4Runner and laid back, basking in her solitude. Her back pressed against the windshield as her eyes gazed at the puffy clouds surrounded by the bright blue sky. She closed her eyes taking slow, deep breaths. She lay on her car for almost an hour before she allowed for thoughts about Alex to fill her head.

"What am I doing?" she spoke out loud to herself. "The real question here, Reese, is do you really love Alex?" She paused briefly, and then shook her head. *I mean, of course I love him! I just don't understand why I feel so conflicted about all of this. If I love him, I should fight for him. If he is cheating on me, it's probably my fault. I know I haven't been the best girlfriend. I've done plenty of inappropriate things.* She sat up, putting her head into her hands and sat there silently, taking deep breaths, in and out. "Ugh!" She let out a groan filled with dissatisfaction. "How am I going to fix this?" She paused for a brief moment and exhaled. *Do I even want to fix it?* She stared off at the horizon.

Yes, yes I want to fix this. No, I need to fix this! She sat upright, *But how?* Her brain was working double time trying to figure out a solution. *I don't know why everything I do is always wrong. How can I make him happy if I can't do anything the way he wants?* She ran her hands through her hair and clinched her fingers at the top of her head before releasing her hands back down to her sides. *Well, I'm just going to have to figure out how to be better. He is all that matters to me, and I will do whatever it takes to keep him. I can't lose him! No one will ever love me the way he does...*

With one last look toward the horizon and a substantial breath in despite the pain that still ached in her side, she slid down off the hood of her car. Her phone went off with a text from Alex.

ALEX: Hey babe, how's your morning going? 11:15 am

Reese responded in line with the story her and Chief Gibbs had planned.

REESE: Busy!! Haven't stopped all freakin' morning! 11:16 am

ALEX: I'm sorry babe. I love you. Don't forget about tonight. Xoxo 11:17 am

REESE: I know babe, I'm excited about tonight! Should be fun! I gotta go, text you later. Xoxo 11:17am

She locked her phone and tossed it into the cup holder.

Dirt and rocks kicked up as she hit the gas and pulled away from the turnout where she had parked. Her mind finally felt at ease although she had no idea how she was going to fix her relationship with Alex but, she left the small lake behind her, along with all of her doubts.

Chapter 13

THE WIND TWIRLED through her hair driving along the county road outside of Auburn with her windows down. A smile illuminated Reese as she set aside her conflict about Alex and decided to fight tooth-and-nail to save their relationship. Her mind swirled around with ideas of how to become the woman he always wanted. *You can do this, Reese. Remember, all good things are worth fighting for.* She truly believed Alex was the best thing to have ever happened to her, despite his horrifying downfalls. He'd convinced her that she would never find anyone better than him. Alex made her body feel things it had never felt and he made her heart skip a beat on a regular basis. She lusted after his touch and more importantly his undeniable affection in the good moments they had together.

Driving along the road she felt free. The storm that had built up inside of her was finally calm, and then her phone rang. Reese's dad, Rusty, was calling her. Surprised by the random call, initially worry popped into her head but subsided quickly, he's probably calling to check in, she reasoned.

"Hey, Pop!"

"Reese?"

"Yeah, Dad, it's me. What's up? Is everything okay?"

"Um, yeah, yeah everything is fine here. I was callin' to talk to you." He cleared his throat several times while he spoke.

"Okay, what's up?"

"It's about Alex."

"Okay..." Reese's tone changed immediately, she could already feel her defenses going up.

"Well, I just— Oh man, how do I put this? I can't shake these changes in you. You're not you, Reese! I don't know what Alex has done to you, but he has taken my little girl from me."

"Daddy, it is really not—"

"Yes, it is!" Rusty cut her off and raised his voice. "Stop making excuses for him! This isn't you, Reese!"

"Dad, please!" Reese felt her voice crack. Her father had never raised his voice that she could recall. "Please stop, I've just—"

"No, Reese!" Rusty was now screaming at her, his voice coarse in his anguish. It sounded to Reese like he was crying. "He is using you, Reese! Why do you refuse to see that? You are being taken for the fool! Why won't you pull your damn head out of your ass so you can see what he is doing to you?"

Reese was not able to fight back the tears that now ran down her face. Water fell from her eyes like a raging river, and suddenly her happiness vanished and she was crying so hard she could no longer see, so she pulled over to the side of the road and tried to catch her breath.

"Why are you screaming at me?" she cried out.

"I have tried talkin' to you, but ya won't listen." His voice was still loud and stern. "So maybe I need to scream at you to get your attention! I can't shake this feeling, that man is destroying you! Please! I'm beggin' you, run! Just run! Don't make me drive up there! I will drag your ass out of that house kickin' and screamin' if I have to. I just want my daughter back!"

There were no words spoken for over a minute, just sobs from both ends of the phone. Reese was unable to speak or catch her breath. She felt devastated and broken. She could handle Alex screaming at her, hell she even expected it most of the time, but not her dad.

Even as a kid, Rusty never rose his voice or yelled at Reese. Not even at sixteen years old when he found marijuana hidden in her car. Maggie on the other hand, she screamed at Reese about how irresponsible she was, and several other things Reese had tuned out. But, not her dad, Rusty had been so ashamed of her poor choices that he wouldn't even look at her. He said no words, but the disappointment on his face spoke loud and clear. That look, it changed Reese's life forever. She turned her life around and stopped partying, and she vowed to never be a disappointment to her father again, and until today, she had kept that promise.

Rusty broke the exchange of sobs with a whisper.

"I love you, Reesey."

"I love you too, Daddy." Reese forced the words out through the tears gushing down her face.

"Please come back to me, Reese, come back to us." And before Reese could respond, Rusty hung up the phone.

She sat on the side of the road alone, surrounded by her inability to breathe and uncontrolled tears. The sound of his voice echoed through her mind, his tone as he pleaded with her shattered her heart, she was left with a gut-wrenching ache in her chest. Her father ripped through her soul like a tornado. There was no warning, and no time to take cover. Rusty bared his heart to his daughter that afternoon, and it left her feeling vacant and drained.

She slowly found her breath. The stream that escaped her eyes began to dry, but the void left in her soul was ever present. She sat staring straight ahead not focusing on anything as her mind replayed the conversation with her dad over and over again. *Is he right?* She contemplated. Unsure of what to do or where to go, Reese felt more lost than ever. *Just stick with your plan, pull yourself together. Put this out of your mind, take some deep breaths, and drive back into town.* She began taking slow deep breaths as she slowly started letting go of the things her dad had said to her. *Alex can never find out about this.*

By continuing slow calculated respirations, in and out, she was able to pull her emotions into perspective. She placed the car into drive and headed back to the city.

Chapter 14

SHE DROVE AIMLESSLY down the road while the silence in the car was deafening. Her mind was filled with her feeble attempt at dismissing her father's words. Rusty pierced her soul and left Reese in a daze. She looked around not knowing how she had made it back into town already; she continued to drive, drifting through the streets of Auburn like a lost puppy. A park caught her attention out of the corner of her eye, and without thinking, she turned in.

She pulled into a parking spot that faced the park. Everything was green and bouncing with life, laughter, and happiness. Kids running around, water slowly moving through the stream where geese swam, and dogs happily trotting on leashes with their owners. Although she was surrounded by joy, emptiness was all she felt. She watched the children run and play with laughter. *Such innocence,* she thought to herself. She replayed all of the wonderful memories she had as a kid. How she and Sophie would play on their old metal swing set for hours on end. They would play princesses who were in need of saving by their handsome prince.

A flash of riding on her dad's back like a horse entered her mind. Knowing now, as an adult, just how exhausted he must have been coming home from work, and yet he would crawl around on the floor with them on his back. No complaints, no feeling of obligation from pleading little girls, just pure and simple joy. Reese remembered wearing her father's cowboy boots and hat around the house. The boots would swallow her entire legs and the oversized hat covered her tiny face. She admired her father in ways she never told him, and they always had a connection that was noticeable to anyone around them. When she cried as a teen because some boy broke her heart, he was there. When she came clean to him when she lost her virginity, he held her, wiped her tears, and told her he loved her no matter what. When she made mistakes she never felt judged or belittled by him, and he always seemed to handle her shortcomings with poise and nobility. Tears seeped from her eyes and trickled down her face as she sat in her car feeling overwhelmed by all of these memories. The one man who had been a constant in her life, who has always been there no matter what just drove a spear of words through her heart, leaving Reese unsure of where their relationship stood. The fear of losing him was important in her mind, but sadly, her fear of losing Alex was paramount.

The activity in the park continued as she grabbed slices of bread from the passenger seat, bread she had brought with her as faux lunch items. She opened her car door and stepped out of her car. Clutching the bread in one hand, and wiping her tears with the other, she looked forward and made her way toward the stream. There was an empty bench next to the water where she decided to sit down and laid the bread in her lap. While she tore up pieces of bread to throw out for the geese, she told herself, *you gotta pull it together. It's time to fake it 'til you make it. Pretend Dad never called, you felt happy before that.* With a final deep breath she dried her face one last time and put a smile on. She thought of things that made her happy. *My job and Jess... the laughter of these kids... the stream... feeding these geese... the sunshine... the lake... music.* Before she knew it she felt at ease an emotional Band-Aid that she knew wouldn't last forever but it would suffice for the time being.

Tossing pieces of bread into the water she let out small chuckles of laughter while watching the geese fight over it. It reminded her of kids swarming a piñata as the candy dropped to the ground at birthday parties. She and Sophie had several of those, "fight-to-the-death," moments as kids. Sophie used Reese's age and smaller stature against her often when they were young, it worked well for Sophie until the day she stopped growing and Reese surpassed her. Sophie eventually regretted how mean she was to her little sister the day Reese snapped.

Reese couldn't find her lip gloss one morning and knowing Sophie took it, she confronted her. Before this, things always ended with Reese yelling for their mom and Maggie handling it, but unfortunately for Sophie, that's not how things went that morning. As Sophie walked back toward her room with a towel wrapped around her head, the way she always did after a shower, Reese began her interrogation.

"Where's my lip gloss, Soph?"

"I didn't take your stupid lip gloss," Sophie replied back, almost as if she was mocking Reese.

Reese quickly scanned the room and noticed the long slender tube of pink sparkle lip gloss sitting right there in plain sight on Sophie's desk.

"Oh you mean this lip gloss?" Reese barged her way into Sophie's room. "It's sitting right here, Soph!"

"That's mine, Reese! Don't touch it!"

"It is not yours! It was in my room, on my dresser, and now it's here in your room! Care to explain yourself, thief?!" Reese was surprised by the amount of anger she felt brewing inside of her.

"God, you are so dramatic! I didn't take your stupid lip gloss, I have my own." Sophie scowled before reaching over and grabbing the tube out of her hands.

Something came over Reese as she had had enough of her sister pushing her around. She went after Sophie with animalistic inclination ripping the towel off Sophie's head in the midst of slapping her. Reese shoved her to the ground and began whipping her with the towel, and all Sophie could do was scream for help.

"Stop it Reese, Mom, Help!"

Maggie ran down the hallway and pulled Reese off of her sister, having to physically hold her back. Reese decided right then and there that she was done being a doormat for her sister, or anyone else, from that day forward. Over the next couple of years Reese perfected that attitude, or so she thought. She still had moments of struggling with her undeniable need to please people and even now her desire to please Alex overwhelmed her life.

Reese chuckled to herself as she re-lived the event from her memories. She continued to feed the geese and she slowly let what happened between her and Rusty earlier allowing it to become another distant memory. She threw out the last piece of bread into the stream and with one last look around she smiled at the children playing as they caught her eye. She glanced at her watch, 2:17 pm, it was time to leave and make her way closer to home. When she got up, she placed a smile on her face and headed out to her car. Once she got in, she immediately turned on her 'Dance Party' mix on her iPod before heading in the direction of her favorite coffee shop.

The music filled the car, filling all the nooks and crannies of her mind once again singing out at the top of her lungs, feeling lighter. Carefree, she danced around as if no one was watching her, while shoving down her true emotions one dance move at a time until she pulled up to her next stop.

Chapter 15

ZOLA'S CAFE WAS small and quaint; there was something about that small town charm Reese adored. She had found this shop one day while she was out exploring her new surroundings shortly after arriving in Auburn. The hustle and bustle of busy people with busy lives filled the café as she walked in, realizing in that moment just how much she had missed this place. When she moved in with Alex, his house was a good distance from Zola's, so she eventually stopped making the drive. Plus, Alex didn't like when she made unnecessary trips from the house.

The aroma of coffee was alluring, pairing nicely with the friendly smiles from the busy baristas. Reese got herself a white chocolate mocha and a bear claw before finding a lounging chair, a prime seat for people watching, which was something she very much liked doing but couldn't with Alex around. With headphones in her ears she flipped through magazines left on a coffee table for customers to enjoy, glancing up often from the pictures so her eyes could scan the room. Many different people in business suits came and went, while she imagined they were flittering off to their afternoon meetings filled with others in their business attire. She imagined they were simple people, who enjoyed their 9-5 jobs and their happy ordinary lives. Reese fantasized about how easy their lives must be. They come, they go, and they live a life filled with data analysis in a cubicle, never having to deal with death and potential mayhem like in her job. None of them has had to tell a wife, that her husband of forty years is dead. Those people will never know the horrifying feeling of holding a lifeless child in their arms while the parents are screaming with fear and denial, begging you to save their baby. They will never feel the hopelessness Reese and others like her have felt. They will never battle the demons she hides within the walls she has built around her heart, all because they chose a career that fit into a cubical. Their lives were tidy, simple, and presumably boring. Although those people in their fancy suits will never know the despair, they will also never know the satisfaction of her job; feelings that overwhelm a person when they know they literally saved someone's life, and that indescribable joy that takes over, causing a person to walk a little taller.

As much as Reese envied those people in their suits with their simple lives, she also pitied them. A life as a paramedic wasn't for everyone, but those who do it live an astounding and exciting life. There are tragic stories, but there are also victorious stories, and Reese sat there thinking, *I wouldn't trade places with any of you, not even for a second.* Medicine was in her blood, it was a part of who she was, and she knew that a cubical would never satisfy her.

The time seemed to tick away slowly as she continuously thumbed through the few magazines left out. She felt unaccomplished and bored, and then the bell at the door rang out and the next customers entered the cafe. One of the customers was a tall thin man with dark bushy hair streaked with grays and what seemed to be deep furrowed lines from years of disapproval on his aged face. Next to that man stood a much shorter woman who was thin and frail looking wearing clothes that looked two sizes too big. The man walked up to the counter and ordered their coffee while the woman stood silent, staring at nothing in particular on the floor, looking as though she was emotionally drained and entirely disconnected with the world around her. Reese stared at this woman piecing the information together, and she sat in horror as the picture became crystal clear. The look of fear in the woman's eyes was a familiar one, the broken spirit, and the unnecessary long sleeves. *Oh, that poor woman,* Reese thought. *I know Alex is not perfect, but at least I don't look that pathetic, do I? No, no way do I look that sad all the time.* She shook off the image of her and Alex resembling that couple. *Besides, Alex is delicious, while that man looks like a piece of asparagus.* She chuckled to herself.

The couple got their coffee and off they went out the door. Reese stared, watching them intently as they headed out the door and to the parking lot, all while continuing to try and convince herself that she was nothing like that woman. They got into their car and she watched as the man began speaking to the woman. His body language started to escalate into obvious anger as the woman sat quietly in the passenger seat, staring at the ground, and trembling with fear. Reese sat there as the similarities became more obvious. She knew those gestures, and she watched the woman just sit in terror as the man grabbed her face and pulled her close. Reese hastily stood up and continued to watch, thoughts racing through her mind. *What do I do? Do I go over there? I mean, what am I going to do? What if Alex finds out somehow? I can't, I shouldn't get involved. Ugh, but that poor woman. I know what comes next. What if I see she was murdered by him on the news tomorrow?* Reese stood frozen with fear as she tried to sort out her internal conflict when suddenly the car drove away. Defeated, she sat back down and picked up her magazine.

Reese sat. The coffee shop faded away, her music in her ears drowning out the noise, and she became so wrapped up in her own head she didn't even notice the hustle and bustle of the shop anymore. She just sat, as flashes of Alex grabbing her face in the parking lot just a few days ago came to mind. She continued to try and convince herself she had not become that frail and broken woman. *There's no way that woman would last a day in my shoes, I bet she wouldn't even be able to lift my work boots up, let alone extricate a grown man from a vehicle. Sure there are similarities with our relationships, but I wouldn't have put up with that oversized vegetable like that. No freakin' way.* The memory of the night Alex taught her how to throw a punch came to mind.

Alex had been drinking one night when Reese came home from work. Her hair was a mess and she was obviously angry about something.

"Babe, what's wrong?" Alex asked, taken aback by her demeanor.

"Ugh, I hate crazy people!" Reese shouted.

She told Alex about this psychiatric patient she had, just before the end of her shift. This man was at least three times her size and not happy. They were told by the police department that he had not been taking his medications for his bipolar disorder and was in a manic state. The man was amped up and angry as some bipolar patients can be when they are not taking the proper meds. She went on to tell Alex how it took her, Kyra, the three guys from the engine, and three officers to get this guy onto the gurney and into restraints. Alex decided right then and there that Reese needed to be prepared to defend herself for the next time this happened.

"Okay, babe," he explained to her, "you want to step into the punch to give it more power, and follow it all the way through. Don't stop once you hit their face, you got to swing it all the way through kind of like when you hit a baseball with a bat."

"Like this?" Reese made a fist, stepped into her swing, and finished it all the way through.

"Perfect! Have you ever punched someone before?"

"Um, like a person? No."

\Reese was a tough girl, but she always had a way of resolving conflicts with minimal violence.

"I want you to punch me," Alex said as he stood across from her.

"What? No! I'm not punching you! That's crazy! No way!" Reese was surprised by his request.

"Yes, babe, do it! Punch me! You need to know what it feels like. That way you're not scared if the day comes you have to punch someone. Let's go!"

"You're crazy!"

"Maybe, but if you can punch me now I'll know that you'll be able to do it later if you have to." He grabbed her hand. "Babe, this is about your safety. It's okay, seriously, do it!" Alex psyched himself up. Once he was ready for the punch, he motioned Reese toward him. "Come on. Just do a light one to start."

"Okay." Reese walked up to Alex and at half strength punched him in the face.

"Good babe! That was real good!" He said, his hand rubbing on his jaw for a brief moment.

"Are you okay?" Reese examined his face as he urged her to hit him again but at full strength.

"Yes, babe, I'm fine. Again, but don't hold back. Give it everything you got." Reese squared back up to him, stepped into her swing and followed through beautifully. She didn't hold back, she swung as hard as she could and Alex stood there dumbfounded after her fist connected with his jaw.

"Damn, Reese!"

"Babe! Are you okay? Please don't make me do that again! Let me see your face!"

Alex rubbed his jaw again as he smiled with delight. "You will be just fine out there, baby. You have one hell of a right hook."

Reese smiled sitting in the coffee shop thinking, *that man of mine is crazy!* Glancing at her watch she realized it was time to go, so she enjoyed the last gulp of her coffee and grabbed what was left of her bear claw and headed for her car. It was time to head home, put on a smile, and be the best damn girlfriend Alex has ever had.

Chapter 16

PULLING INTO HER driveway Reese noticed an unfamiliar car parked in front of the house. *She's already here? How long has she been here?* Reese wondered. She reached up to grab the door handle, *Show time.* With a long and drawn out exhale she grabbed the handle, opened the door, and walked through to see Alex standing in the dining room dressed once again in black slacks, a crisp white button-down shirt, and a solid black satin tie. *Damn, he looks good.* A seductive smile emerged across her face.

"Hey there, handsome!"

"Hey you," Alex said with a half-smile.

"Why you dressed all fancy?"

Reese's mind filled with images of the things she wanted to do to him. Her fantasy was short lived and interrupted by a voice in the hallway.

"We are going out for my birthday!" Vanessa squealed like a schoolgirl.

She threw her hands in the air in celebration fluttering down the hallway in her five inch stilettos. Reese stood in horror as Vanessa came into the light.

Her round face was framed by large flowing curls that made her hair bounce when she walked. Makeup covered her face with a smoky eye look that was dark and sultry, and her lips were smothered in pale pink lipstick. She was wearing a tight black dress. It was barely long enough to cover below her butt and it had a neckline that plunged down below her breast, with a string that zigzagged back and forth down the plunging neckline. Form-fitting was an understatement for this dress. Even the long sleeves hugged her arms so tightly Reese checked to see if her fingers were purple.

Reese stood motionless as her eyes scanned Vanessa up and down. A smile remained on her face as her thoughts ragged. *Seriously, where exactly does she plan on going, the strip club? She looks like a freaking hooker! What kind of a woman would wear that dress in public? A freaking slut! That's what kind!* Her downward spiral into her own thoughts was interrupted by Alex.

"Nessa told me that her family was refusing to do anything for her birthday, so I thought we could take her out to celebrate. Go take a shower and get dressed. We need to leave here in an hour."

Nodding her head Reese walked off down the hallway without a word.

The water streamed down her soapy body as she tried to distract her thoughts, but with all of her emotions bubbling up within her, she tried with everything she had to seal the cracked dam around them. The bathroom door opened unexpectedly. Startled, she jumped.

"Hey babe, how was work today? I barely heard from you!" Alex said as he poked his head into the shower.

"I know, love, it was crazy busy. All my spare time was filled with reports and the occasional bathroom break. Hell, most of the bathroom breaks were even interrupted! I barely ate today. It sucked."

"I figured you were busy. I'm sorry your day was shitty. You're home now. I'll leave you be to shower and get ready. Love you."

"Love you too."

Alex closed the door behind him as he left. *That was odd,* Reese thought. Alex rarely came in while she was showering and didn't join her, plus he was being overly understanding of her being too busy for him. It didn't make sense to her because Alex was the least understanding man she had ever known, however, she decided to take advantage and enjoy the hot water for a few more minutes before reaching over and shutting off the water.

Wrapped in a towel, she stood in front of her clothes scanning for a dress to wear. *Not that I have anything that remotely competes with the wardrobe of that whore out there,* she internally grumbled as she riffled through her dresses. A deep purple lace caught her eye and she removed the hanger from the rod. *I think we found a winner.* With a bite of her bottom lip and a soft smile she hung it on the door. She had worn this dress to a wedding she and Alex attended about six months into their relationship. It was classy and sassy all rolled into one. Reese remembered that Alex couldn't keep his hands off of her that night.

She quickly did her hair with loose curls and swept it to the side in a loose and low ponytail. She strategically pulled curls out to frame around her face, and added a touch of hair spray to lock it in place. Then she moved on to her makeup, using her deep purple eye shadow to create a smoky and captivating look. She finished the look with plum blush and a deep mauve lip color. She looked classy, fresh, and not over processed. *Vanessa will look like trash next to me.* Reese zipped her dress and slipped into her shoes. Taking one last look in the mirror she gazed at herself with a smile, examining the final product. The dress was a deep purple, and it had thick tank top straps with a deep V neckline that accentuated her breasts without putting them on display for the world. It hugged her body and slightly flowed out in an A-line skirt that stopped just above the knee. She wore her black peep toe heels, large diamond hoop earrings and her necklace from Alex. With two carats of sparkle around her neck and one carat in each ear she was finally ready to go.

Reese walked down the hallway expecting to see Alex anxiously waiting to see her, but he was not. Her eyes scanned the living room when she reached the end of the hall.

"Alex?"

"There you are, hey, babe!" Alex popped out from around the corner. He seemed taken by surprise while he fixed his shirt and tie. "You look stunning, my love."

"Thank you, so do you babe." Reese smiled with delight. "Where's the birthday girl?" Her head swiveled from side to side looking for Vanessa.

"I'm right here. Sorry I had to fix my, uh, makeup." Vanessa spoke out of breath when she pointed to the bathroom. "Wow Reese! You look stunning!"

I know I do, she thought before answering, "Thank you, so do you." Reese felt like she choked on the words as they left her mouth.

"Are we ready, ladies?" Alex said with a smile.

The three of them walked out the door and headed for Reese's car.

As they drove toward the restaurant, Reese tuned out Vanessa while she talked non-stop. Reese looked over at Alex to find him intently listening to every word she said. *Seriously, how can he possibly want to keep up with this teeny-bopper? I mean does she ever shut up? And he hangs on her every word!* She reached over and gently grabbed his hand, then leaned over and kissed him on the cheek. Vanessa stopped talking mid-sentence.

"I love you, babe, you look so handsome."

Reese ran her hand up his arm, to the hair on the back of his head, gently running her fingers in his hair and down the back of his neck. Alex looked at her with a smile on his face.

"I love you too, baby."

Vanessa sat in silence as Reese subtlety marked her territory.

"Aren't you two just adorable?" she said with a hint of sarcasm in her voice when the car came to a stop.

"We're here!" Alex said. Reese looked out the window to see they had arrived at Verrazano's. *You've got to be fuckin' kidding me! Verrazano's is our place! We had our first date here! This is where he takes me to apologize! Now he's sharing it with her?* The anger boiled inside of her as she turned around to look at Alex. Their eyes met and Alex must have noticed the anger within her because he leaned over and whispered in her ear, "Remember, I'll make that slap yesterday feel like child's play."

"But Alex, this is our–"

"Knock it off right now." Alex cut her off, his voice inflexible and grim. Reese lowered her head, and she took a deep breath before swallowing the hurt she felt. Grabbing her black clutch purse she stepped out of the car with fake happiness on her face.

Walking in Reese kept her head down, making sure to only make eye contact with the women working. The hostess greeted them as they walked in, "Alex! Reese! Hey guys! Are you the reservation for three at seven-thirty?"

"Yes, we are" Alex answered matter of fact.

"Excellent! Follow me to your table."

They walked into the softly lit dining area and were led to a round table that sat four. It had a maroon table cloth with a white overlay, a solitary candle flickered at the center of the table. Alex pulled out Reese's chair for her as the hostess laid the menus at the table.

"Reese, you look stunning! Are we celebrating something special today?"

"Thank you, Sarah!" Reese said delighted. "We're actually celebrating Vanessa's birthday tonight."

"Fantastic! Happy birthday! I'll pass that along. Daren will be your server tonight, enjoy your evening." Sarah said before walking away.

The three of them sat down and began to situate themselves when Daren started walking over to them.

Daren was around twenty-five years old. He was short but muscular with shoulders similar to Alex. He wore a well-groomed scruffy beard, and a smile swept across his face when he arrived at their table. Reese sat staring at Daren out of her peripheral vision.

"Hey, guys! I have waters on the way for you, but in the meantime, can I get you all something else to drink? Ms. Landon, would you like your usual?"

Reese kept her head down and shifted her eyes to Alex waiting for him to answer Daren.

"Yes, she'll have a glass of Moscato, I'll have a Vodka Tonic, and Vanessa will have a glass of the Moscato as well," Alex said with testosterone pouring out of him.

"Actually," Vanessa interrupted, "I don't like wine, so I will have a vodka cranberry, please."

Alex quickly jolted his eyes at Vanessa with his intimidating gaze unwavering. Reese recognized that look. He shifted his weight in the chair before he broke his stare at Vanessa. *What the hell was that?* Reese looked over at Vanessa as she sat frozen. The look on her face was all too familiar. Reese put the pieces together. All of the suspicion she had vowed to let go came back like a flood when the cracks in her emotional dam became giant gaping holes. She knew in that moment all of these emotions would eventually consume her, but then Alex interrupted her brewing jealousy and rage.

"Well, I was going to wait until after dinner to say this, but I might as well tell you."

He directed his attention toward Vanessa, and just then Reese felt her stomach turn with nerves. *Is he going to confess?* She was caught off guard by her own thought. "Reese and I," Alex continued, "planned an after-dinner gathering at our house for you." Vanessa's entire face lit up with excitement. "I invited some of the people from 34 to help us celebrate, it's nothing major, but we felt you deserved to have at least a small party." Alex smiled at Vanessa.

We, what the hell? Reese thought. *You got a mouse in your pocket?* The anger within her began to grow. *He's not even trying to hide it anymore!* Before she could stop herself in the midst of Vanessa's squeals and laughter with happiness, Reese looked at Alex, furious.

"We...we thought that, really?" she whispered.

Alex snapped a look at Reese that would normally put her in her place, but not tonight, it was too late for that, anger raged in her veins and she no longer cared about the consequences of her actions when she looked up and motioned Daren over to the table.

"Are you guys ready to order?" Daren said with a smile.

Reese smiled back at him, looking him directly in the eyes, and cut Alex off before he could speak.

"I believe we are, honey. First things first, I'm going to need a bottle of wine to start, this glass just ain't cuttin' it." She lightly laughed at her own joke before continuing. "I know that I'm gonna have the beef Bolognese lasagna, and I would like salad with the house dressing, please." Reese flashed another smile as she handed Daren the menu. The look Alex had on his face was pure wrath. He stared at Reese as if he was trying to stare into her soul and crush it, but Reese stood her ground and looked right at Alex and said, "Are you ready to order, dear?" Her tone was condescending.

He sat in silence. Reese continued to look at him without breaking her gaze. Alex finally broke eye contact and began to order.

"Well, I'm going to have the spaghetti with meatballs." He shifted his eyes to Vanessa, and with a point of his finger he continued. "She will have the eggplant parm, both of us will have salad with the house dressing." His eyes locked on Vanessa as she put her head down.

"Okay, I'll go put that in, and I'll be right back with that bottle of wine for you, Ms. Landon."

"Thank you, Daren." Reese smiled as he walked away.

A tinge of pain hit her thigh as Alex wrapped his hand around the top of her leg and he dug his fingertips in, but instead of conceding, Reese reached down grabbing his hand and pulled with everything she had until he released her leg.

"Don't touch me." She leaned over toward Alex and spoke with a low but stern voice.

Her look was serious, demanding, and steadfast. Reese was furious and she refused to hide it any longer. She moved her chair away from Alex when Daren came back with her bottle of wine, and she filled her wine glass to the brim before throwing her reservations out the window and began drinking.

The remainder of dinner was uneventful. Reese enjoyed every bite of the dinner she had wanted to try for over a year, and she also relished in every drop of her wine; carefree and buzzed. She made it through dinner and was happily without worry of her impending fate, the wine significantly helped with her newfound attitude. Alex was typically an angry drunk, Reese, on the other hand was the exact opposite. She felt exhilarated and confident, and the more she drank, the friendlier she became.

The buzz from the wine pleasantly settled within Reese as the plates were cleared and the check came. Vanessa and Alex had exchanged friendly glances throughout dinner, glances they probably thought Reese didn't notice, but she did. Alex paid the bill and the three of them walked out to the car.

"Can you give us a minute?" Alex turned to Vanessa.

He unlocked the doors, and Vanessa nodded before she obediently got into the car. Once the door was shut, Alex turned his focus back toward Reese. His level of anger was enough to make even the car uncomfortable without even saying a word. The tension between the two of them would have been obvious to anyone, if only there had been another person in the parking lot. Alex stepped towards Reese. Normally she would step back out of fear, but that night she planted her feet firmly on the ground. However, as soon as he came nose to nose with her, his eyes blazing, that fear she had shut out was back in an instant. She trembled within as Alex stood over her, silent, daunting, and resentful.

"Who in the actual fuck do you think you are?" His voice was at a growl. "You acted like the true whore we both know you are tonight and I hate myself for loving you. You took a wonderful night and ruined it with your actions. You are the worst damn girlfriend I've ever had. I wish I could find a way to stop loving you for my own sake. You have some real problems, Reese. Apparently no matter how much I love you I can't keep you faithful to me."

Reese stood there in disbelief.

"Me? I ruined tonight? You might as well take Vanessa, pull down her panties and screw her right here in front of me! You didn't discuss a party at our house? It's our house, Alex! You planned a whole night for some girl and we both know that if I planned a night like this for Stump, Nate, Louie, Chief Gibbs, any of the men I work with you would lose your shit. But I guess because it's you doing it that makes it okay, right? I'm supposed to be a good little girl and just sit there quietly and not say a word? How is that fair?"

Alex grabbed her face up under her jaw and pulled her so close. Her face felt moist from his breath. His eyes were crazed as he squeezed her jaw so hard she began to taste blood in her mouth from her teeth cutting her cheek. His voice demanded her attention.

"Don't you dare try to turn this around on me, you fucking worthless bitch. You will straighten your shit out before we get home. You will put a fucking smile on your god damn face and conduct yourself much better than you did at dinner. Do you understand me?"

Reese did everything she could to hold back the water seeping from her eyes, and she tried so hard to not focus on the pain. Her fear expanded throughout her body, overwhelming any anger or resentment she felt only moments earlier.

"Yes," she whispered.

"Good. It would do you good to remember your place." He released her face and walked off to the driver side of the 4Runner.

Reese leaned forward trying to catch her breath as she rubbed her jaw that now ached. Several tears trickled down her face. She stood upright, and wiped her face dry before getting in the passenger side of the car. She sat there, head down, once again trapped in the world of staring at the floor.

"I'm sorry, Alex." Her voice was sullen and overflowing with regret.

"You should be," he snapped back at her.

She sat quietly for a minute, gathering her emotions before she turned her attention to the back seat where Vanessa was.

"How did you like Verrazano's?" Reese asked through the sniffles with a smile on her face.

Vanessa seemingly startled, looked at her in bewilderment.

"Oh, it was really good! Thank you both for everything. First, we had an amazing dinner and now a party? I really appreciate it."

"Of course, you're very welcome," Reese said.

Alex looked at Reese, pleased with her change of attitude.

He reached over and held her hand while they gradually made their way to the house where they were greeted by some of the Station 34 crew and Alex's brother.

Chapter 17

BETWEEN ALEX AND Reese, the tension in the car was inescapable. He held her hand as an empty gesture—force of habit while being in the car. Despite being home now and in front of guests, Alex made sure Reese knew he could get away with hurting her without anyone paying any mind to his perverse games. After a night out he would typically open her car door and treat her like a princess; that was not the case for tonight. Tonight, Alex opened Vanessa's door and treated her like the princess, all while burning angry daggers into Reese almost triumphantly. Vanessa was his shiny new toy and he had no intension of getting rid of her. *What was I thinking tonight?* He opened the front door and motioned for Vanessa to come in first and she graciously smiled up at Alex, both exchanging looks of desire as he followed behind her into the house.

"Happy birthday!" the crowd shouted as Vanessa walked through the door.

Alex followed close behind Vanessa, not bothering to hold the door open for Reese, practically letting the door hit her as she walked in.

I can fix this, I know if I just behave and don't do anything inappropriate, it's going to be okay, she plastered a fake smile on her face and mindlessly drifted through the crowd. She made sure to keep her eyes shifted down and, more importantly, her mouth shut. She felt defeated on every level and while her face told the world everything was fine, inside she was broken. *I'm not worth saving,* she hopelessly thought as she heard laughter and playful banter from all the happy party goers. She walked down the hallway and once she reached her bathroom, she quickly closed the door before a few tears escaped her. Her anger helped her not care what Alex thought during dinner but now, she felt sad and empty. He managed to break her within seconds with the greatest of ease. Her overwhelming fear of him took over. Reese couldn't help but feel incredibly disappointed that she still feared losing him.

Light filled the bathroom as she flipped the light switch on, and when the lock clicked, she felt comfortable to let herself break. The last twenty-four hours had been filled with a plethora of emotions. She ignored all the red flags, advice from her family and friends, and her instincts, in an attempt to save her relationship with Alex—only for things to come crashing down. *He planned an entire night around the woman he is probably cheating on me with,* her thoughts were unbearable. A down pour of tears uncontrollably fell from her eyes, it was as if her fear was wrapping around her so tightly that it pushed her tears out in buckets. In an effort to catch her breath she couldn't help but to cry even harder. Now in the midst of her break, her father's words rang the loudest in her head. She lifted her body upright and saw a reflection of a woman she no longer recognized in the mirror.

What the hell happened to you? Look at you, you look pathetic. You changed everything, for a man! Only weak women do that! You have turned into the kind of woman you used to pity. Take a look around, Reese; do you even know what you are doing here anymore?

This can't be it for me, this isn't fair! Her tears relinquished as she did her best to dig deep to find that anger that she lost amongst the fear. That girl she used to be was still within her, hiding. Her star shined clearly, and that spark within her burned brightest until the day she allowed Alex to suck the air from her—the spark grew dimmer with each slap. She stared at the woman she barely knew in the mirror and she didn't fight her anger, she refused to shove it back in the closet. Her eyes fixed on the eyes staring back at her, the pathetic eyes of a defeated person that were her own, and she spoke to her directly.

"When will enough be enough, Reese? I can't even believe what you have become! Is this really what you want out of life?"

She stood up straight and wiped her tears. With a tissue she cleaned up her face before touching up her makeup with color and mascara. The click of the door unlocking seemed louder as she left the bathroom, she quietly moved across her room, with her hand on the doorknob. For the briefest moment she hesitated but, the anger simmering in the pit of her stomach wasn't going away, she opened the bedroom door and walked back out toward the crowd ready for a fight.

Weaving around guests she found herself in the kitchen pouring a shot of whiskey, shooting it quickly enjoying the burn. She immediately poured another, looking forward to the warmth that was going to hit her stomach soon, and just before she swallowed away her fears she spotted Lance, Alex's brother, walking over to her. Anyone could tell even from a distance that Alex and Lance were brothers. Their features were so close many made the mistake that they were twins. In reality, Alex was only a year and a half older than Lance.

"Hey, Reese," Lance said with a friendly smile. "Are you okay?"

"Yeah, I'm good." Reese replied as convincing as she could muster up. "How are you? Is Helen with you?"

"I'm doing pretty well, actually. Helen's at home with the kids, the babysitter canceled on us last minute, unfortunately, she had to stay with them tonight."

"Oh, man that's a bummer! It would've been good to see her, in fact it would be good to see all y'all sometime soon! We haven't seen the kids in over a month! How is Miss Harper doing? And my favorite nephew, Oliver, how is he?"

Reese loved these kids as if they were her own and would do anything to make them happy. She threw back another shot as she waited for Lance to reply. The burn from the whiskey was beginning to warm her from the inside out, cinnamon whiskey was her favorite, but in all fairness, any whiskey was fine by her.

"They are doing great! Harper is so smart. She just amazes us all day, every day! She won the seventh grade spelling bee last week and is moving on to compete in the regional competition." Lance beamed from ear to ear and his whole face lit up with pride.

"Oh my goodness, that's incredible! That little girl is just too darn smart!"

"Tell me about it! She's been asking when she and Oliver can come over for another sleep over. I told her I would have to talk to you both about it soon." He smiled.

"She is welcome any time as far as I'm concerned, but you would have to run that by your brother." Reese's face told Lance all he needed to know and he chose to not pry. Reese quickly changed the subject, "...and Oliver?"

"He's doing great too, just running around being a crazy six year old. Most days we can hardly keep up with him."

"Oh, to have just an ounce of that boy's energy for the day, the things I could accomplish." Reese winked jokingly at Lance as she fantasized, taking another shot.

Reese saw Alex staring at her in the kitchen with Lance holding an empty shot glass in her hand.

"Babe, slow down." He demanded in a low tone.

"What's the problem Alex?" The heat from the whiskey was fueling her anger allowing for hostility to rise up. "I'm just enjoying my whiskey and your brother's company. Can I not do that anymore either, any other rules you want me to follow for tonight?" She was condescending, looking at him with complete disdain.

Lance knew this was a good time to slip out of the conversation and give them a minute alone. Reese could see the rage building in Alex's face, she began an internal struggle between the woman she used to be and the woman she had become. Before she knew what was happening, Alex grabbed her arm and muscled her through the crowd toward the hallway. *What's he gonna do? Beat me right here in front of all these people?* His fingers dug into her arm as she delicately began to resist him as to not draw attention from the crowd.

They made it halfway down the hall when she finally broke free from his grasp, pulling hard and stopping in the hallway. Placing herself in between him and the bedroom door, she stood there looking at him with a level of determination she had missed.

"Reese!" His voice was rigid. "Get your ass in the fucking room, right now."

"No!" Reese was smoldering on the inside. Alex flashed a look toward the people in the living room and back at her, almost as if he was weighing his options. He stepped toward her grabbing her wrist so tight the bruise he left a few days ago burned, but Reese stood her ground refusing to budge. *I won't let him win!*

"You better get your ass out of my way, and into that fucking room" he said, centimeters away from her face, "or else."

Reese stepped over her fear and into him closing the gap between their faces.

"Or else what?" she inquired, she was crossing a very thin line.

Alex became enraged at her defiance and he wasn't able to hold back his demons any longer. He shoved his hand firmly into her neck, knocking her breath away immediately, his fingers formed a vice grip squeezing tighter with every struggled breath Reese tried to take in. Her eyes locked on Alex, his face was red with relentless hostility as he thrusted her back against the door with all his strength, splitting the door with a loud crack. Reese continued to fight for air as she tried to focus on pulling Alex's arm away from her throat. His face sucked into a tunnel of blackness as her world closed in around her. The noise from the party and chatter from their guests became nonexistent. In the midst of his rage, Alex must have noticed the party had gone silent, he released her throat but, his anger was still consuming him, and he wanted to keep punishing her, his hand moved to her jaw. His classic move that has always put her back in her place, he pulled her into him scolding her.

"Look what you made me fucking do!" He spoke through his teeth while he visibly wrestled his anger down.

Releasing her entirely, he turned to walk away toward the group of people who were now staring, alarmed and concerned by this graphic show. He began to smile gingerly at the crowd, looking apologetic to presumably ease their minds, and of course, make it seem like this was just an isolated drunken event. While he took a few steps away from her, the fire from within ignited and she felt that woman she used to be rise from the ashes in her soul. The take-no-shit attitude had found its way to the surface and without thinking, she decided enough was enough. Lunging after him she grabbed the back of his shirt and flung him back down the hallway. Alex hit the cabinet at the end of the hall. Bewildered, he looked up to meet Reese's furious stare. She stepped into him grabbing his jaw the way he did to her countless times before, and she brought herself to his ear. She was filled with a rage that she didn't know she possessed.

"You're never going to touch me like that again, asshole! Do you hear me? No more!" She was screaming in his face. "Never again! I'm not your punching bag! I'm fucking done!" The party stood silent as all eyes had shifted to the two of them while Reese continued. "You hit me ever again, and I promise I will fucking kill you!" She released his face and stormed off down the hallway. Alex stood there dazed in disbelief, because no one had ever stood up to him like that before. When Reese made it to the living room she saw the horrified looks on people's faces, she immediately apologized to the crowd. "I am so sorry y'all had to witness all of that. Please stay, have another drink, enjoy your time. I promise that will not happen again." Her voice was hoarse from being choked and shaky from adrenaline but, she had never felt more confident and satisfied.

She walked out to the garage, grabbed the pack of cigarettes and lighter she hid, and headed outside to the backyard.

Chapter 18

HER HANDS WERE still shaking as she struggled to light her cigarette, flicking the lighter over and over. Unsuccessful, she stopped. With the cigarette in her mouth she dropped her head, braced herself on the patio table, and took a deep breath. She couldn't stop the regret she felt for her actions and became overwhelmed with worry before that voice inside rose up to remind her that the fire remained strong and burned brightly within her. *If he even tries to hurt you, leave.* Reese was pushed to her limit with him.

She was unsure if maybe it was the alcohol talking but she felt an undeniable shift within her. *If he wants to be with me, then he needs to be with the real person I am or this relationship won't work, and he needs to change.* Her hands began to shake less and she stood herself up straight. *If he can't love me for me now, then he'll never truly love me ever.* She picked up the lighter, flicked it and got a steady flame. As she enjoyed the first inhale of nicotine, her phone went off.

"Hey Jess," she answered with ease, "I'm sorry I haven't called you back, I've had a lot going on."

"Reese!" Jess's voice sounded terrified. "Are you okay? My friend that works at 34 called me and told me what happened!"

"Oh, yeah girl, I'm okay, promise."

"Do you need a place to stay tonight?"

Reese stood in silence thinking about whether she should leave tonight or not, but having let go of the fear Alex controlled over her, she decided against leaving. She felt leaving would lose her the upper hand she just gained. "Um, I honestly think I'm goin' to be okay, Jess. I'm not sure what I'm goin' to do yet, but I don't think leaving is the right choice."

"What do you mean you're not sure, Reese?" Her voice quickly changed, becoming filled with frustration. "How could you possibly be unsure? What the hell is wrong with you?"

"Jess," Reese remained calm, "I know you probably think I'm an idiot, but I have to do this my way. You gotta trust me, girl, I got this. Plus I think Lance is staying the night here so I won't be alone here with Alex."

Jess gave Reese her opinion of how ridiculous she was being, but Reese tuned her out and began thinking about Alex and Vanessa. *There has to be a way to catch them red-handed.* Reese was trying to devise a plan when out of nowhere the lightbulb clicked.

"Do you still have the picture of that random email address?" she interrupted Jess.

Taken off guard, Jess stumbled over her words.

"Um, the wha–, oh, wait, from the other day? Yeah, I do. Why?"

"What if that email is a secret account that Alex has?"

"That's what I wanted to talk to you about. I thought about that after I left your house. I'll send it to you right now."

"Thank you, Jess."

"Are you coming to work tomorrow?" Jess asked.

"Yes ma'am, I will be there, bright-eyed and bushy-tailed!" Jess sighed. Reese could hear her hoping for the best.

"Okay girl, if you don't show, I'm calling Nate's brother who will bring the police department down to find you!"

"Jess, I love you, girl, you seriously gotta relax. Everythin' will be okay. I'm not gonna be here alone with him, Lance is staying the night and I don't think he'll do anythin' more while he is here. Plus, he revealed to a room full of people he was ready to kill me, so if I end up hurt or dead they'll know who did it. Maybe I am too intoxicated to see the reality of it all but; I truly think everythin' will be okay. I will see you tomorrow, try not to worry."

"If you say so Reese, but still. If you need a place to go even in the middle of the night, my door is open."

"Thank you."

The girls said their good-byes and hung up the phone. Reese enjoyed the final drag of her cigarette before she put it out in the ashtray. With a deep breath, she nodded her head to herself and went inside.

All eyes were on her as she came back through the door. She looked around and noticed several people left, and those that remained seemed fearful to leave. Not afraid that they would be the new focus of Alex's anger, but afraid to leave Reese alone with him.

"Who needs a shot? I know I do!" Reese shouted with a smile, a feeble attempt at putting everyone at ease.

Everyone nervously chuckled under their breath while the tension in the room remained thick. Only a handful of them raised their hands and came into the kitchen with her.

"Who wants whiskey?"

Those who came with her nodded their heads in agreement causing her to turn on her heel and grab the bottle off the counter before filling the shot glasses all the way up and passing them around. She lifted her glass to the center of the group for an impromptu dedication.

"Here's to unexpected drama!" She laughed at her attempt to lighten the tension in the house. "Cheers!"

The glasses clinked and the whiskey left a trail of warmth as it made its way down her throat. All of the people dispersed back to their previous conversations, except one.

The man that remained with her in the kitchen had a husky and muscular build. His hair was dark brown and spiked up with gel. He had caramel colored Latino skin, and Reese had no idea who this man standing with her was.

"Want another shot?" she offered as she poured herself another, she was already feeling rather buzzed and decided that tonight was a good night to allow the alcohol to take away any remaining fears that still lingered.

"Sure." He looked at her. "Do you know who I am?"

"Um, I'm really sorry, but in all honesty, no, I don't."

"I figured as much. It was pretty obvious that when you came to the station you weren't allowed to talk to any of us."

"Oh, you work at thirty-four? Well, I will say this, those days are over. So officially, I'm Reese Landon, I work out at twenty-three." She stuck out her hand.

The man reached over and firmly shook her hand.

"I'm Gabe, Jess's friend."

"Oh! Wow! Yeah, hi! It's extra nice to meet you then. Jess is my girl, she's amazing!"

"Yeah, she's pretty great."

Reese handed him an overfilled shot glass that spilled out the sides before raising her glass once more.

"Here's to, Jess!" She laughed.

A smile swept his face. "To, Jess."

Once again the glasses clinked and the whiskey warmed her throat. Reese looked up to only meet Alex's glare, but instead of cowering down she simply smiled, and raised her empty glass toward him before setting it back down for a refill. In the midst of her haze she hadn't realize that all the guests had slowly left the party.

"Reese," Alex scoffed.

"Yes?" She turned to face him.

"I'm going to bed." He seemed to hint for her to join him.

Once again she raised her glass, over-filled with whiskey, and motioned it toward him.

"Good night," she boldly said before she downed the shot.

"Are you coming?" The irritation in his voice was apparent.

"Nope," Reese didn't even turn to look at him as she sat her glass down to refill it. Alex shifted his weight as she caught a glimpse of him glaring at Gabe.

"So you're going to just stay out here and drink with another man? Do you seriously think that's appropriate behavior, Reese?" His face was dark and grim.

Reese turned to face Alex. "I don't remember asking for your opinion. Good night, Alex."

Alex looked at Gabe, sternness in his eyes. "Get the hell out of my house." He pointed his finger to the door.

"Alex!" Reese snapped. "Knock it off." She turned her attention to Gabe. "You don't have to go unless you want to."

Gabe looked uncomfortable yet torn over what the right thing to do was. He turned to look at Reese. "Are you going to be okay?"

"Yes, I'm fine, you can leave if you'd like. Oh, can you please tell Jess that I'm fine as well?"

Gabe nodded his head in agreement before walking past Alex, grabbed his jacket and left the house. Reese looked around, they were the only two left.

"Where'd Lance and Vanessa go?" Reese kept swiveling her head around wondering at what point everyone had left. In the midst of her countless shots they must have snuck out. Her eyes met Alex's glare, a glare that would usually strike fear into her, but instead she refused to crumble to her fears. She realized in the midst of her anger just how done she was with him pushing her around. Alex threw a hand up at her.

"He's passed out in the guest room and she is on the couch in the office, not that any of that is your concern. Are you coming to bed?" Although he asked a question, Reese knew what he really meant was, 'We are going to bed.'

Reese shifted her weight with overwhelming irritation and just stood there, staring at him. She refused to answer him for the second time. Alex began to huff and puff, pacing back and forth a few times until he threw his hands up and walked off down the hall to the bedroom exuding frustrated rage. Reese laughed under her breath and with a huge smile on her face feeling extremely proud of herself. She took one final victory shot in celebration.

That night she slept on the couch. She refused to feel suffocated by his arms wrapped around her. She could feel the person she had locked away coming back and the thought crossed her mind, *the truth will come out in the midst of this crap.* She decided to pack up her laptop in the morning to take to work, determined to hack the mysterious email account. The decision was also made to be the person she wanted to be, and not the person Alex has been forcing her to be. Reese was tired of hiding her true self, and promised to never feel inadequate at the hands of another person ever again. *If he truly loves me, he will accept me for who I am.* She rolled over with a smile on her face, placing her fear of Alex completely aside. She decided to put her faith in the protection of Lance, who was sleeping in their spare room, trusting if Lance heard any commotion, he would immediately come out and help Reese. She hoped Alex wouldn't encourage anything further with Vanessa, fearing they were sleeping in the same bed at that very moment in spite of her. She was a little too drunk at this point to do anything about it if that were really the case. Regardless, Reese was happy and finally felt an overwhelming serenity envelop her, despite knowing, surely, there would be consequences she'll have to endure for her behavior towards Alex that night.

The alarm sounded from her phone and she jolted awake—frantically she reached to turn it off—a habit she had become accustomed to because of Alex and never wanting to disturb his sleep when she had to work. As she silenced her phone and realized she was still in the living room, memories of last night flooded her mind. Despite the alcohol being worn off, the confidence she felt hours before seemed to increase each time she replayed standing up to Alex after he attacked her in front of everyone. Even though she had a slight headache from the one too many shots she took last night and getting her head banged against the door by Alex, she had never felt better. She quietly tip-toed her way through the bedroom where Alex slept, he was alone. Fortunately, there was no sign of Vanessa anywhere in the room, *I don't think I would have had the strength to deal with that kind of Vanessa-drama this early in the morning,* she thought. She crept through the master bedroom quietly and collected her uniform hanging in the closet, laying it over one arm, she began assembling the necessities. She closed the dresser drawer gently as she held a fresh pair of socks and underwear and silently made her way over to the shoe rack, she gathered up her work boots before making her way into the bathroom.

She carefully placed her clothes on the bathroom counter, lightly set her boots on the linoleum, and closed the door smoothly behind her. Once the door was closed, she let out the breath she didn't realize she was holding. She couldn't help but glance up and notice herself in the mirror, she didn't have to examine any new bruises, worry about covering anything with make-up, or pull out her stash of medical supplies to tend to any fresh wounds. She stared closer into her eyes, she saw the happiness she had feared, up until that point, and would forever be a distant memory. A soft smile spread across her face as she began to feel a something she hadn't felt in a very long time, peace. The tables had presumably turned in their relationship, and she finally felt as if she had the upper hand.

She showered and threw her wet hair into a messy bun. The bruises on her ribs had had already started to fade and the pain now was barely a dull ache. Her uniform went on with ease and she couldn't help but feel the same excitement she use to feel when she was a brand new employee just starting out. There was no fear, no dread of talking to someone and believing she would get into trouble, and no worry of making a stupid mistake, it was all replaced with exhilaration. After placing her boots on her feet she took one last look in the mirror staring at this glowing woman, satisfied and confident, she turned and left the bathroom ready to tell Alex of the new changes that would be happening.

She eased herself on to the edge of the bed and with butterflies in her stomach she almost let her nerves get the best of her. She had to remind herself that it would be important to keep the momentum going with this new found strength, making it necessary to wake Alex up. She was more determined than ever, fear was something that would not control her life any longer. *No more fear, he can't hurt me unless I let him, and that's never gonna happen again.* Reaching up she placed her hand on Alex's waist and gave a couple gentle shoves until he woke up. He rolled over with a grumble and a moan and looked at her almost immediately with irritation on his face.

"What do you want?" his voice was unsteady yet, demanding. Clearly, he was displeased with being woken up and growing more irritated as last night flooded his memories as well.

"I've been doin' some thinkin,' and I wanted to let you know my new terms of this relationship. You physically hurt me again, ever, and I'm gone for good. From this point forward, I will talk to whoever I want, hang out with whomever I choose, and you will not say a word. Relationships are built on trust, and you are gonna have to learn to trust me. I'm still here because despite the way you've hurt me, I do love you. Now it's your turn to truly love me, Alex. I am goin' to be the person I choose to be and you'll no longer control every move I make. If you decide you still want to be with me after all this, than great! If not, that's fine too. But I'm done sacrificin' my integrity for you. Do you understand how this is gonna go?" Reese felt so good putting her foot down. *This is it, the new start we both need,* she thought, feeling empowered.

Alex laid there obviously trying to thwart off his anger.

"Fine, Reese, whatever." His tone was filled with resentment.

He rolled back over in bed, he didn't say good-bye, he didn't kiss her, and he didn't even smile; she had hoped for a better reaction.

"I love you." She said, hoping the conversation wouldn't die on a sour note but, there was no response from Alex.

She got up, feeling like she had just got punched in the gut. *How can he not see this will be good for both of us, I can't stand the thought of losing him.* She wasn't sure how she managed to convince herself to care for a man that would treat her like a punching bag, belittling her at every chance he got, and making it a point to control every aspect of her life. She just couldn't help but feel like if their relationship was going to reach its demise. It would be her fault and hers alone. She destroyed something that has the potential to be good or even great. Alex brainwashed her into believing she deserved every drop of spit slung on her face, every violent act of aggression was justified, and every bruise, broken bone, and slap to her body was warranted. *I made him do it,* the thought had been engrained in her, and it would take a lot for her to be able to etch out his influence from her mind.

First step: admitting you have a problem, Reese thought to herself as she looked up and decided no more. She grabbed her stuff and left out the door, shaking off the empty feelings and mixed emotions he left her with, and drove down the road to work.

Chapter 19

THE DRIVE TO work that morning seemed different. The closer to the station Reese got, she felt her heart lighten, happiness was bubbling inside her, and like she could finally breathe. It was as though the sun was beaming brighter and even the colors around her seemed more vivid. The morning discussion with Alex that had made her feel incomplete was now a far off fog in her mind that had finally lifted out of sight. *Free,* she thought as she looked around in aw, finally seeing the world around her as if it were the first time in her life doing so. *Funny the things you realize you've taken for granted after they've been taken and finally given back,* she relished. Reese pulled up to Station 23 feeling like a weight had been lifted off her shoulders, and with a smile on her face she got out of her car and headed inside.

"Hey, it's good to see you, Louie!" Her voice was pleasant and full of life.

Louie looked over to meet her bright eyes and as if having an epiphany a smile emerged on his round face. At first, no words came from his mouth, but he immediately walked over and hugged Reese tightly.

"I've missed you, kid!" He said with excitement.

Happiness gushed from both of them as they stood in a long-overdue embrace.

"I've missed you too, Louie... hey, look... I'm, um... I am so sorry, for everything, I just—"

"Hey," he said, his eyes shown with understanding, "It's water under the bridge... welcome back."

He released his grasp on her, placed his hands on each side of her face, and smiled. After a sweet moment, Reese headed inside, ready to personify the love she had always felt for her Station 23 family.

She hadn't been this happy to come to work in a very long time. She wanted so desperately to just hold everyone and catch up on their lives, regretting the magnitude she had missed out on. She kept Alex's voice in her head at bay. She wouldn't let the fear of him permeate her mind anymore, especially because of how good the feeling was to reunite with her work family. She was finally able to ignore the guilt she was forced to feel every time she spoke with men or tried to make friends, the guilt that had become such a horrible habit that was instilled inside her by Alex. The scrutiny she was kept under would no longer play a role in her everyday life, but she knew it would take time to adjust. Most of all, in her heart, she knew an apology was owed to each and every one of her brothers and sisters.

Rounding the corner into the common room she felt a rush of nerves in the pit of her stomach. *I've been the worst. I really hope they will forgive me.* With a smile and a light heart she entered the room.

"Good morning, guys!"

All eyes quickly shifted to her. For the briefest moment she saw micro-expressions of bewildered stares, quickly fading to smiles and sporadic morning greetings. Jess briskly made her way over to Reese and pulled her aside into the barracks where they could speak privately.

"Girl, are you okay?" Jess asked concerned as scanned Reese's body.

Reese let out a chuckle. "Jess, I'm fine. I really put my foot down last night, and I'm not backing down." She reached out and grabbed Jess's hand. "I promise, everything is good now, look at me, I'm great!"

"Do you promise?" Jess' eyebrows furrowed, not sure if she should trust the entire situation.

Reese smiled and squeezed her hand. "I promise."

Reese reached into her pocket to check her phone after it went off with a text.

ALEX: Well, I don't know what has gotten into you, but I hope you understand, this "Do what I want attitude" goes both ways. 8:52 am

A smile parted her lips, she felt a rush of bravery and a little disbelief that he felt as though he had any ground to stand on for making demands, the guilt and fear she had felt that morning had completely dissipated.

REESE: How is this any different for you? You befriended some random girl from work, set up an entire birthday dinner and party (at OUR house) all for her all because you supposedly want me to be friends with her? I guess you think I'm an idiot. All I did was make things even. If you're going to do "whatever you want," then I will too. You can go ahead and blame me all day long, whatever makes you feel better darling but, just know you only have yourself to blame. 8:58am

"Damn, girl!" Jess said as she read her response over her shoulder. "Gloves are coming off!"

Reese smiled at her and they both laughed as they walked arm in arm back to the common room.

Stump caught her attention when they came back into the room. Reese knew she needed to talk to him next, let him know everything was going to be okay. She reluctantly walked across the room, nerves twisting in her stomach. All these guys were her brothers but, Stump was definitely the man that would ask, "How high?" if she said jump. He was the big brother she never had, and he was by far the most important to her. She was worried that her actions over the last two years had ruined that. *What if he hates me forever?* She worried.

Nervously, she stood right in front of where he was sitting, "Stump? Can I talk to you... please?" She asked with her voice soft.

He looked up at her, straight in her eyes making it easy for him to notice the change within her.

"Of course you can." He said with a raised brow and curiosity all over his face.

He got up from the table and followed Reese out back, where he, less than a week prior, had first confronted her about Alex. She turned to face him, and tension was high as she searched for the right words to start. In the midst of her racing thoughts, she became weary of stifling her emotions, and she almost couldn't control throwing her arms around Stump. Her voice was trembling and barely above a whisper.

"I am so sorry, Stump." She released her grasp and looked him in the eye. "I know I'm sorry doesn't cut it. I just wanted you to know that I took care of things... I won't be getting hurt anymore."

"You left him?" His was voice surprised and hopeful.

"No," she said, noticing the immediate disappointment on his face, "I put my foot down. I know it's not the answer you want but, trust me, I am going to be fine and I just... can't let him go just yet. I feel good about this and I am sure he can love me, for me."

His face now filled with sorrow. "I wish you didn't feel that way, Reese. He doesn't deserve you and you don't deserve to be treated like shit."

"Stump," she placed her hands on each side of his face. "Things are different now, you'll see. Look at me, I'm going to be okay, and this is the last chance I'm giving him, if it doesn't work out for any reason, I'm gone. I promise."

He forced a small and quick smile before reaching out and wrapping his arms around her. "I love ya, kid, I hope you know that, and you know my door is always open. If you need to run, you run to us and we'll take care of you, okay?"

Reese smiled. "I love you too, Stump. I promise, I will."

They released their embrace, dried their cheeks, and with smiles on their faces went back into the station.

Stump sat back down at his spot at the table, and as if she was on a divine mission, Reese headed off to Chief Gibbs' office. She felt as if even more weight had been lifted off of her shoulders talking to Stump, and she wanted the feeling to last forever. She reached her hand out and pulled the office door open, sticking just her head through.

"Chief, do you have a minute?" She was smiling up at him.

Chief Gibbs was sitting behind his desk shuffling through paperwork when he looked up to see Reese's head poking into his office. He probably didn't realized he had cocked his head to one side and was looking through squinted eyes as if trying to figure out if the free day she had truly brought the old Reese back.

"Sure, come on in, Ms. Landon. How are you?"

She moved inside the office with a bounce in her step, she answered. "I'm doing great, actually!" She sat herself down in one of the two empty chairs occupying the space in front of Gibbs' desk. "First, I wanted to say thank you so much for yesterday, it really helped me out so much and second thing, any chance during morning briefing I can have a minute to chat with everyone?"

Gibbs looked skeptical at her; his eyes scanned her for some hint as to why. "Uh... hmm... I mean, yeah, sure, why not?"

"Perfect! Thank you, sir!"

"Tell everyone, five minutes until the morning briefing." Gibbs gave her a half smile, not knowing why there was a sudden change in attitude from her but, seemingly grateful for it.

Reese popped up out of the chair and made her way to the door, ready to let everyone know she was back and ready to be her old self again. She turned to face him. "You got it, Chief." She walked back into the common room with her hands cupped around her mouth, announcing, "Morning briefing, five minutes!"

Everyone got up and gathered their things, including refills on coffee. Reese walked over to the coffee station and poured herself a cup and mixed in the creamer even though she felt elated and positively energetic. When she entered the briefing room it was filled with conversation and laughter. As she found a chair Louie stood up.

"Reese! Look who's back, everybody," he shouted.

He clapped his hands together and when everyone else joined in, a smile illuminated her face. She had been so scared they would all hate her for the way she had acted the last couple years but, just like a normal family, they welcomed her back with open arms. In the midst of the celebration Chief Gibbs entered the room. The celebration quickly fell to dull whispers and then to silence.

"Good morning!" Chief said. "This morning will be short and sweet. Don't forget the MDA fundraiser, again, I expect you all to attend! No excuses will be tolerated. Also, I need your votes for Firefighter of the Year. Remember to always stay alert and have each other's backs. Now, Ms. Landon has asked for the floor before we close, so I will turn it over to her... Ms. Landon," he gestured for Reese to stand in front of the briefing room behind the podium.

Reese stood up out of her chair and timidly walked to the front. She clasped her hands around the edge on the podium trying to calm the sudden nervousness she was feeling and with a deep breath she put a smile on her face, *here goes nothin'.*

"Hey everyone..." she began, a little uneasy, "look, I just wanted to take a moment and apologize to all y'all. I, uh, know for a little while now... shoot, more like the last couple years, I have been terrible, and I have been, well, for the lack of a better word, a bitch." She nervously cleared her throat. "I just wanted to tell y'all how deeply sorry I am for my behavior, I haven't been very good to all y'all and I've had a bad attitude in this station that I'm sure made everyone uncomfortable. I love each and every one of you like y'all are my own family. I really hope y'all can find it in your hearts to forgive me." She paused and looked into the eyes that were staring back at her, sincerity on all their faces. "So, yeah..." she sniffled, "that's all."

She released her hands from the podium and began to make her way back to her chair when Kyra stood up.

"I love you too, Reese! And as far as I am concerned, all is forgiven. I sure am glad you're back, girl!" She had a smile on her face. "I think it's safe to say we all understand and we're here for you, honey."

Kyra began clapping her hands as the others joined in with her. Sporadic whistles and cheers came from everyone, even Chief Gibbs. Reese looked over at the Chief and smiled, mouthing the words 'Thank you' and Gibbs nodded his head as if to say 'You're welcome'.

"Okay, everyone, you're dismissed! Let's all stay safe out there today!" Chief said.

Reese felt as if she was walking on clouds, like an overwhelming joy had taken over her heart. She felt light as she happily bounced out the door and over to the rig to start the morning check-off. Once she rounded the corner into the ambulance bay she was bombarded by arms around her. Reese was stunned when she saw Kyra was hugging her from behind.

"I've missed you, Reese." Kyra's eyes were reddened holding back tears of joy.

Reese's bottom lip quivered as a smile easily came to her. Kyra was her best friend, her person out of all the people, and she was finally back in her life.

"I've missed you more." Reese turned her body to face Kyra and held her in a long and heart-felt embrace.

Chapter 20

KYRA AND REESE went about their morning check-off, both talking non-stop, their male co-workers taking notice to the "chatty Kathy's", and they couldn't help but shake their heads and laugh. Their bus turned into the place where they caught up on each other's lives from the last two years, advice was given, gossip was spilled, tears were present, and laughter was exchanged. Once Jess was done with her check-off she joined them in their happy chitchat hour. Reese noticed Nate looking over at the ambulance as a roar of laughter came from the back and he smiled. The tension that was ever present in the station seemed to fade away as quickly as it came, and things seemed to flash back to two-and-a-half years ago, to a time before Alex. Life at Station 23 had returned to extraordinary and wonderful.

"Did you get my text of that email address last night?" Jess asked Reese.

"Oh! Yes I did, wanna go see what we can find?"

Kyra looked confused. "Someone care to fill me in?"

Reese and Jess looked at each other sighing in the idea of seeking out truth that could potentially be hurtful.

"Of course," Jess said, getting ready to explain the tedious efforts that would be required to see if Alex had been, in fact, cheating on Reese.

The three girls walked arm-in-arm with towards the barracks while Jess filled Kyra in about all the red flags that had been going on in Reese's relationship, including that of Vanessa.

"Geez, Reese!" Kyra shrieked. "I had no idea things were so bad! It was obvious that you weren't yourself anymore, but damn, girl! Why didn't you tell me?"

Reese hung her head as guilt crept its way back into the forefront of her heart. "I don't know Kyra. I thought you hated me. I didn't think you wanted to hear any of it, honestly. I mean, you have barely said anything to me in the last year or so, before now."

"I'm really sorry, Reese, I just knew Alex was bad news, and then you started changing so drastically, I–" Kyra put her head down. "I just couldn't be a part of something I knew was wrong, ya know?" She looked Reese in the eye and took her hand. "But now knowing all of this, girl, I should have been there for you, and I am sorry."

"It's okay. It's all in the past now. I honestly don't blame you for how you handled everything."

They both smiled at each other followed by another bear hug. Jess threw her arms around them both.

"I love you crazy girls!"

"We love you too, Jess!" Reese and Kyra said in unison.

A moment later, Reese grabbed her laptop out of her bag and sat down on one of the beds in the barracks with Kyra and Jess gathered on each side of her. Nerves fell over her like a blanket while the computer booted up and turned on. She pulled up the picture of the email and typed in the address. She paused. Her mind raced trying to think of a password.

"Does he have a password he uses frequently?" Jess asked.

"Yeah, I guess that's a good place to start." Reese said typing on the keys.

Reese typed in "Paramedic1," denied. She moved her fingers across the keyboard as she came up with three more passwords, all denied.

"What's his middle name?" Kyra asked.

"Um, it's Paul, why?" Reese asked.

"Try Paul and his birthday." Kyra replied

She typed in Paul3780, denied. Frustration began to build in a short amount of time.

"Ugh, what if I can't figure it out? Give me a minute you two, would ya?"

Reese hastily sat the computer down on the nightstand and stormed off to the bathroom, leaving the girls sitting on the bed.

Reese walked over to the sink and rested her hands on the counter. She looked at herself in the mirror. Fear once again came over her. *What if I do crack it and I don't like what I see?* The thought of losing Alex overwhelmed her, taking over any trace of confidence she had recently rediscovered. She knew he wasn't good for her yet, deep down she knew she didn't want to end up losing him. Cheating or not Alex would never allow her to be herself, and he would never love her the way she needed him to. *If he was going to love me for me, then he would already be doing that.* The fire within her once again engulfed her fear, swallowing it whole. *I refuse for this relationship to end being my fault. I have to catch him!* Her thoughts were interrupted by the door opening. It was Jess and Kyra.

"Girl, are you okay?" Kyra asked.

Reese stood up tall, determination radiating from her body.

"Yes, I'm good. I have an idea." She began to walk past them. "C'mon, girls, let's go catch us a cheater."

They sat back on the bed as Reese pulled the computer into her lap and typed in a couple inaccurate passwords, doubt began to linger as she brushed over keys, finally, with a stroke of genius Reese typed in "Nessamedic34." Bingo, Reese thought, as the computer flashed over to the email home screen, all while feeling a tinge of jealousy.

"We're in!" Reese told the girls.

"Nicely done, Reese," Jess proudly said.

The three of them leaned into each other so they could examine the computer screen more closely. Immediately the women came across several email threads exchanged between Alex and Vanessa. Reese scrolled down and found that the emails had started a little over six months ago, anger and disbelief consumed her as she scrolled to the most recent one dated that morning.

To: Alex Cunningham

From: Vanessa Alvarez

Date: February 17th, 2012 08:47:33PST

Subject: Hey Baby ;]

Babe, what are we going to do? Do you even still want to be with me? Alex, I love you so damn much. I just want us to be happy, just the 2 of us. I hated leaving you this morning after making love. It was wonderful sleeping in your arms last night. Reese clearly doesn't love you the way I can, and she never will! How much longer are you going to make me wait?

Alex responded:

My most beautiful Nessa, I'm sorry that I've put you through all of this. Reese will be gone soon, I promise. Every time I am lying next to her I dream of holding you, when I am inside her, I desperately imagine it's you. I love you more than I have ever loved anyone. We will be together soon my love.

Reese sat, frozen, her eyes reading as fast as they could. Over and over, reading the reality of her life, sitting there feeling like someone had ripped a gaping hole in her chest. Tears seeped from her eyes. She felt humiliated, angry, and heartbroken. Jess and Kyra placed their arms around her.

"I'm so sorry, Reese." Kyra squeezed her tightly.

"It's going to be okay, Reese." Jess began to rub her hand up and down her back.

Her voice barely audible, Reese spoke. "I'm so stupid." She sunk her head low.

"No, honey, you're not stupid," Jess said.

"Six months, Jess. How could I have not known this for six freaking months?" Blinding anger simmered within her.

"Because you love him, Reese," Kyra said.

"I guess it's true what they say, love is blind as hell," Reese scoffed. She sat her computer down and stood up. Trying to suck in a deep breath between her trembling lips, "I need some air," Reese said.

She left the barracks and stormed out the door into the bay. She rushed so quickly out of the bay she didn't even notice Nate and Ray standing next to the truck. Reese felt like she couldn't breathe, her world was spinning like a carousel that she didn't know how to stop. She looked lost standing in the parking lot, pulling at her uniform shirt trying to loosen it so she could breathe, but everything continued to spin while she struggled to grasp what was happening. Leaning over she placed her hands on her knees, and tried to take slow deep breaths as the chaos in her head settled. She felt a hand on her back.

"You okay, Reese?" Nate said, concern stirring in his eyes.

She looked up at Nate standing beside her and quickly stood upright, pulling away from him. She couldn't help but want to shy away from a man wanting to help, just as Alex had always liked it. To the left she saw Ray standing with obvious worry on his face, but still no words came out of her mouth. She just continued to breathe. *In and out, Reese,* she told herself. When she slowed her breathing, reality sunk in deeper, she dropped to her knees and tears free flowed down her face. Reese had reached her breaking point, and no amount of willpower could stop the tears that kept coming. Nate and Ray knelt down on each side of her, wrapping their arms around her, and they simply held her while she wept.

"I'm so sorry, guys." Reese forced the words out.

"Sorry for what?" Ray asked confused.

"I hate cryin' in front of people." The tears were intensely flowing, no signs of letting up.

Nate squeezed her tightly.

"Considering everything you're dealing with, it's okay. We're your brothers, Reese. We'll always have your back."

"No judgment here," Ray chimed in.

Reese caught her breath and was able to dry her soaked cheeks and neck. Nate pulled out a tissue from his pocket and handed it to her. He scooted his body around to be in front of her and grabbed her face, his eyes soft and loving.

"He doesn't deserve you, Reese. You're entitled to someone who'll treat you like a queen."

Reese smiled before she reached out and wrapped her arms tightly around both of them. "Thank you both for everything."

With a few last minute sniffles, Nate and Ray helped her up to her feet, she dusted off her pants, and with her head held high, the three of them walked back to the station.

Chapter 21

AS THE REST of the day wore on, everywhere Reese turned, she was surrounded by love and support. Word quickly spread throughout the station about Reese finding evidence that Alex had been cheating on her and every person at Station 23 offered to help her pack and move, including Chief Gibbs. Many of them even offered her a place to stay. She felt overwhelmed with affection from those she had treated so poorly for so long. *How could they just forgive me like that?* She wondered. In the midst of her unwarranted questions of their loyalty, she looked around at her family and thought, *Rather than overanalyze, I'm just going to be grateful for each and every one of them.* A smile developed watching them go about their afternoon. Before Reese could get too wrapped up into her thoughts the tones over the loudspeaker announced:

"Engine twenty-three, Truck twenty-three, Ambulance twenty-three, Battalion twenty-three, multi-vehicle accident at the corner of Central and Main, possible pin-in."

The crew dropped what they were doing, changed into their turn-out gear for extra protection, and swiftly made their way to their vehicles. Being on the ambulance Reese and Kyra only had turn-out jackets for fires, so they were able to get in their rig quicker and leave first.

The siren blared as they rapidly made their way to the accident, being delayed only slightly by a couple of cars that did not pull off to the side of the road like they were supposed to. Reese couldn't help but see the humor in Kyra and how she always got road rage while driving Code 3, with the lights and sirens blaring, Kyra would burst, "stupid cars in the damn way move!"

Today was no different and Kyra had pure disdain for bad drivers, "Pull to the right!" Kyra screamed. "The right, damn it, they gave you a license!?" Kyra's knuckles were white around the steering wheel, "Where did you learn to drive? Move, people! Come on!"

"You look like a woman with a bad attitude who just found out her boyfriend's been cheating on her," Reese giggled, choking back her heartache. She looked over to catch Kyra's glance of sarcasm, met with a roar of laughter between the two of them. "Feel better?" Reese asked, still laughing.

"Actually, yeah!" Kyra said with her middle finger sticking straight up in the air for Reese.

The laughter faded when they turned the corner and saw the accident they were responding to.

A semi-truck was parked against the curb and a four-door sedan had run into the back of it. The sedan was barely recognizable, the entire front end was smashed in, and the driver was clearly trapped inside the car. Reese grabbed the mic to the radio.

"Ambulance twenty-three, on scene, truck twenty-three, what's your ETA? There's at least one pin-in."

"Copy that, Ambulance twenty-three at scene." Dispatch acknowledged.

"Ambulance twenty-three, Truck twenty-three is about two out." Nate advised.

"Copy that," Reese said before jumping out of the rig to assess the damage.

Walking up to the scene she found a white female possibly in her early twenties in the driver seat. The steering wheel had been pushed toward her and it sat only inches from her chest, the dashboard was in her lap, pressing down into her legs. The girl was unresponsive and not moving. Reese reached her gloved hand in and checked for a pulse, placing two fingers on the woman's carotid artery in her neck.

"I've got a pulse on the driver," Reese yelled to Kyra.

The woman was startled awake by Reese calling over to Kyra, within seconds she screamed out in pain.

"My legs!" she hollered. "It hurts! Get me out of here, please!" the woman begged.

Just then the engine, Truck 23, and Chief Gibbs pulled up. The crew all jumped out of their vehicles and methodically began pulling equipment from side compartments and quickly ran over to the scene.

"Reese!" Nate yelled. "What's the damage?"

"Her legs are pinned. The dashboard's in her lap and steering wheel is pushed up to her chest." Reese replied.

Nate threw his thumb up in the air to reassure that he had copied what she said. He immediately barked out orders to his crew on what equipment they needed and delegated those who would be carrying out specific tasks. As the truck crew was busy following his commands, Nate and Chief Gibbs walked over to Reese. Leaving her hand on the woman's arm she turned around and was met by them waiting for information.

With a look of concern in her eyes she said, "I can't see for sure, but we have to error on the side of caution here. We might be lookin' at crush syndrome here. Will y'all be able to work around me in the car, so I can get at least one IV going? If she has toxic buildup in her blood from a crush injury, we'll only have seconds to get her sodium bicarb—she'll die if I don't get it administered in time."

Intensity built in the silence as Chief Gibbs considered her plea. Nothing was in Reese's mind except this girl and how to save her life.

Over the last two years Alex had slowly taken over her thoughts. Even in the most critical situations she would be left questioning if her plea was professional enough, or if she looked too long in Nate's eyes while she spoke. Today, in this moment, Reese was able to leave all thoughts of Alex at the station with the printed evidence of his betrayal.

"Grab your turnout jacket from the rig, Landon. You're going in the car." Chief Gibbs ordered.

Reese nodded her head to copy the orders and then she turned her attention back to the woman in the car. She was a thin woman with fair skin and mousey brown hair that clung to the sides of her face from sweat and tears, her light brown eyes were wide with fear and intense from the pain she was feeling.

"I have to go grab my gear. I'll be right back, okay? Nate here is going to stand with you."

The woman grabbed her arm, begging Reese not to go. "Please don't leave me! Get me out of here!"

Reese stopped and gently spoke to the woman. "What's your name, hon?"

"Stacey." Her nails dug into Reese's arm, panic clearly swelling inside her.

"Okay, Stacey, my name is Reese. Listen to me, I'm going to get in the car with you, but I need to get some stuff first, you need fluids and oxygen, and I have none of those things with me. We also need a blanket to cover you with, and I need my protective gear." Reese bent down and looked her straight in her frightened eyes, and she gently put her hand on top of Stacey's that dug deeper into her arm. "I'll be right back, I promise you."

The woman reluctantly released her grasp on Reese's arm and nodded her head with several quick nods. Nate replaced Reese standing next to the woman while he cut off her seat belt and airbag. Reese ran and got her gear, heady with adrenaline. Being inside the car while they extricated a patient was one of her favorite things to do. She loved the thrill and the challenge of being inside a crushed car, trying to work around the saws and "Jaws of Life." And more importantly, she loved being in the middle of the action to save someone.

With her turnout jacket and helmet on, she quickly made it back to the car. Her hand tightly gripped around the bag of IV supplies, a blanket secured under her arm, and the oxygen bag strap slung over her other arm. She wiggled her way into the car from the back seat of the passenger side. The guys from Truck 23 had forced the back of the passenger seat down so Reese could slide into the front seat and wedge herself next to the patient. A cervical collar was secured around her neck due to a possible spinal injury.

"You came back!" Stacey cried.

"Of course I did," Reese said calmly with a smile. "Okay, Stacey," Reese continued as she began to cover her with a blanket, "I'm going to cover you up with this blanket so you don't get any glass or sparks on you while they cut you out of here." Stacey nodded as the blanket came up over her head and Reese strategically positioned herself under the blanket with her. She grabbed an oxygen mask and placed it on the woman's face. "This is just oxygen, it'll help you breathe. Stacey, I know you're scared, but I'm right here with you. It's gonna get super loud as they start to cut, but it's very important for you to stay calm. Can you take a couple of deep breaths for me?" The woman followed her commands. Reese placed her stethoscope on her chest and listened to her lung sounds when she took several slow deep breaths. "Good job, hon, you're doing great! Next, I'm going to borrow your arm and place an IV."

"Is it going to hurt?"

With a tender smile Reese placed her hand on the woman's arm. "Compared to the pain you're already in this will be easy."

"Okay, okay, do it, don't warn me, just do it," Stacey said her eyes turned up to the roof of the car.

Reese moved quickly in setting up her supplies, she moved Stacey's arm into position and placed the tourniquet. Nate lifted up a corner of the blanket.

"We're ready."

"Okay," Reese acknowledged. "Stacey, it's about to get loud. Remember, deep breaths."

The noises from the machines blared in their ears, and the whole car vibrated as they began to cut and pry apart the door. They could hear small pieces of glass and metal bounce with light thuds off the blanket. Reese started the IV with no complication, and once it was secured in place she opened the line for the fluid to run in. Holding the bag on her shoulder with the side of her face holding it there, she squeezed Stacey's hand and over-exaggerated a breathing motion to remind her to keep taking slow deep breaths. Stacey turned her focus to Reese. They both were taking slow deep breaths. Suddenly the car shifted, it startled Stacey and her eyes grew wide with panic. Reese was struggling to regain control of Stacey's emotions but the noises from the machines were too loud.

Stacey cried out. Her breathing became erratic and her body language indicated that she was in full panic-mode. There was a loud pop as the driver door was opened. Reese continued trying to calm Stacey down, but her efforts were not much help. *Shit, this is bad,* Reese thought. The dashboard was moving up, giving Stacey more room to frantically wiggle around. Reese gave one final attempt at gaining control, a last-ditch effort she didn't use often: she yelled.

"Stacey!" She could barely hear herself over the machines and that's when Reese began screaming at her. "Stacey! You need to calm down! We can't help you if you freak out! Slow deep breaths! Stacey!"

Unfortunately, her efforts remained futile. One final jolt to the dashboard and Stacey was able to break free, and in one swift motion Stacey was up and out of the car. Reese yanked the blanket off the top of her while Jess and Kyra went after the woman, who now had blood running down her arm where she had ripped the IV out. Stacey was running from the car in circles when Stump finally grabbed her and Kyra was able to talk her down. Reese forced herself from the car as fast as she could and briskly walked over to Kyra and the patient.

"Just breathe, it's okay, we got you," Kyra repeated multiple times.

Jess rolled the gurney over with a backboard on it.

"Stacey!" Reese said sternly. "You need to pull it together."

"I know, I'm sorry, Reese, I just panicked." Stacey was beginning to slow her breathing by doing what Reese taught her.

"Come on, hon." Reese, Jess, and Kyra placed her on the backboard and began buckling the belts. "How the heck did you run from the car? Are you hurting anywhere?"

"I don't know. I just had to get out of there! My stomach feels sore and my head kind of hurts, but that's it."

Reese lifted the woman's shirt up and saw faint bruising to the lower abdominal area. She didn't know if the bruising was from the seat belt or dashboard—astonished her legs and pelvis were not shattered. Reese continued to perform a detailed exam of the woman's body during transport, searching for any major injuries. Bumps, bruising, and minor lacerations were all she found. No broken bones, no toxicity in her blood from being crushed, nothing.

"You are one lucky girl, Stacey." Reese said in shock. "Seriously, you should buy a lottery ticket because there is no way you should walk away from that."

"Was it that bad?"

"Well, you ran into the back of a semi-truck going at least forty miles per hour, yeah, it was that bad." Reese laughed.

Reese asked her all the basic information necessary for her report gathering: name, birthday, age, medical history, and other things pertaining to the accident. They chatted about how lucky she was to be alive. Reese replaced the IV Stacey had ripped out and did continuous checks on her blood pressure and pulse, just in case the bruising on her stomach was a sign of internal bleeding. Each time she reassessed her Reese was more and more amazed.

"Hey, Reese, could you tell me something about you, something to help get my mind off all of this." Stacey said shyly.

Reese sat trying to think of anything to say other than her news about Alex but, it was the loudest thought in the back of her mind.

"Hmm, let's see." Reese continued to search for anything at all to say. The only thought she had now was of Alex, so she went with it. "About an hour ago I found out my boyfriend of two-and-a-half years has been cheating on me, of course with some twenty-two-year-old skank, who very much knew he was involved with me, she even tried to be my friend." Reese flashed a fake smile down at Stacey who was lying flat on the backboard.

"Oh... my... God, no freaking way, that's horrible!?" Stacey shrieked.

"Yep, isn't that just the sweetest thing you ever did hear? He's so incredibly kind and thoughtful." Sarcasm poured out of her, it almost felt therapeutic to be letting it out with a stranger.

"How are you holding it together right now? Seriously, I would be a mess! And then you were there for me, you were calm and collected, levelheaded even! How could you do that? I would be a wreck!"

"It's a part of the job, hon. I have to be calm and levelheaded, for your sake. If I panic, then you panic even more! And let's face it, you bolted from your car and ran around like your hide was on fire. Imagine how you would've been had I not been calm." Reese smiled.

"Yeah, I did pretty much lose my shit back there, didn't I?" She laughed.

"Just a little, but in your defense you had the front end of your car on your lap so, I guess we'll let it slide this time." Reese winked at her in hopes that the subject could change from Alex, and back to the accident.

"Well, Reese," Stacey said as they pulled into the hospital, "all I know is you are one hell of a woman, that poor bastard doesn't even realize what he just lost. You don't need someone like that! You need a man that treats you like you're the only woman he'll ever love, besides his mama."

How sweet is this girl right now? Reese thought with a soft smile "Thank you, Stacey."

They took her inside the emergency room and transferred her care over to the trauma team that was eagerly awaiting their arrival.

During their drive back to the station Reese and Kyra began talking about how lucky Stacey was to walk away with possible minor injuries. It wasn't long before they burst out with laughter as they re-lived her jumping out of the car and running in circles.

"I've never seen anyone do that before!" Kyra exclaimed amidst the laughter.

"You should've seen Nate's face!" Reese was unable to control the side-splitting laughter. "He looked like a deer caught in the headlights. It was the best thing ever!"

"And I missed it! Damn it!"

"You certainly did!"

Reese enjoyed the moment of joy they shared before arriving back at the station. The shift was nearly over and Reese knew she had to confront Alex, so she devised a plan. She was going to go home and quickly pack an overnight bag while she confronts Alex that she knows all about Vanessa and their infidelity. She prayed it would be a civil split yet, she knew deep down she should prepare for the worst. Her hands trembled in her lap at the thought of what he might do to her. Kyra offered up her place for Reese to crash that night and she wouldn't take no for an answer. Reese hoped she would be able to figure out a place to stay within a month. Kyra had an extra room in her apartment that she would occupy until then. As Reese rehearsed the plan in her head she heard Kyra's voice.

"Reese, I've been thinking," Reese broke her concentration to look at Kyra, "why don't you just stay with me? No need to find a new place and spend your money. I figure, you need a place to live and I could use a roommate. What do you say?"

Reese looked at Kyra with joy and gratefulness in her eyes. "Are you sure?"

"Of course I'm sure! This way you're not alone. Plus, I could really use the help with bills, and I would love your company."

Reese jokingly hesitated for a moment "Okay!" Reese smiled. "Let's move in together!"

The girls jumped up and down as they hugged with excitement.

When the shift came to an end, little by little Reese gathered her things before walking out to her car. Fear started to take over her once again while loading up her bags. While battling to control her breathing, she tightly gripped the emails she had printed out earlier that day, when a voice startled her out of her downward spiral into dismay.

"Reese?"

She quickly spun around to see Stump standing there. She nervously rocked her body from side to side, unable to stand still.

"Hey, Stump."

"I was thinking, you must be terrified to confront him, but I'll go with you if you would like, in fact–" Stump looked behind him revealing her entire crew standing there. "We all will."

She felt their wonderful love encase her entire body standing there, unable to speak.

"Can I ask you somethin'?" Louie stepped forward.

"Sure," Reese wiped away her tears.

"What is the number one emotion you're feeling right now?"

"Well, to be honest... fear." Reese put her head down. "I'm incredibly terrified of what he is going to do. Between my behavior last night and now this," she held up the emails. "What if I can't bring myself to do it?"

Louie placed his hands on her shoulders. "You need to put the fear aside, Reese; you should be filled with anger. You bent over backwards to be perfect for him and he slaps you in the face by cheating on you! You need to go in that house angry, or he'll twist this so much you won't recognize it. Get angry, Reese."

She looked up to see Louie's intense stare. "You're right, Louie, I *am* angry. I should be furious!" The intensity in her eyes flourished with resentment. "That's how I found the strength to stand up to him in the first place, through anger and all the crazy shit he has put me through." She shifted her eyes to everyone. "Thank y'all for this amazing offer, but this is something I have to do on my own." She turned to Kyra. "I'll be at your house at some point. I wish I could tell ya when."

Kyra looked at Reese. "No worries, take all the time you need. I'll leave the key under the mat and blankets on the couch." Kyra's eyes gave away her concern. "I just have to tell you, Reese, I think you going alone may be a terrible idea."

"I know, but no matter how terrified I am or how stupid going alone is, I know this is just something I have to do by myself. How about this, I'll keep my phone in my hand and if he starts getting angry I'll call you while I'm walking out of the door."

"I guess that's better than nothing." Kyra shrugged, clearly unhappy about Reese's decision.

Reese smiled, and focused back on everyone standing there. "If all y'all are free tomorrow I could use some help moving my stuff out. Alex will be gone at work." Without hesitation they all nodded yes. "Thank y'all, so much! I don't know what I would do without each and every one of you!" She turned back to Louie. "Thank you for saying exactly what I needed to hear."

"Anytime, Reese," Louie hugged her before walking away.

Stump was still standing there as everyone parted ways. "I'm just a phone call away," he told her. "If you have to leave, make me your second call, okay?"

"I will, I promise." Reese smiled and hugged him tightly. "It'll be okay." She turned and got into her car, placing the emails on the passenger seat.

Pulling away from the station she began to pray, *God, I know we haven't talked in a really long time, and I am in no position to ask for any favors but, please, please keep me safe. I am beyond scared of him. Give me the strength to leave, please.* She trembled with fear as it crept back in. She fought the tears that built up in her eyes when she heard a voice within her speak. *Lay your fear down and replace it with confidence. Like Louie told you, get angry, Reese. That is the only way you will survive this.* She nodded her head in acceptance of what she needed to do, and with a long exhale she shoved her fear aside and found the anger that seemed to have always been brewing deep inside her. In an attempt to make her anger bigger and bolder she began talking out loud as if she was already talking to Alex.

"How could you do this to me? How could you do this to us? I tried so hard to be perfect for you, but I see now, no matter how perfect I was it would never be good enough! You have no idea what you just lost, you son of a bitch! Vanessa can have your worthless ass!" Her hands gripped the steering wheel so tightly her knuckles hurt. "I hate you!" She screamed.

The anger manifested into pure rage and she felt her breathing increase as her blood began to boil throughout her veins. There was no room in her heart for sympathy, no room for love, all she wanted was to walk through that door, rip off the Band-Aid, and shred the relationship she once thought she had. She pulled into the driveway of the house and to avoid any nerves or fear from coming back, she hastily got out of the car and made a b-line for the door.

Chapter 22

THE DOOR FLUNG open with ease to reveal Alex sitting on the couch watching television. Reese had no idea what she was going to say, or what she was going to do. Stopping to think about it and analyze the situation couldn't happen. She walked right over to the couch and slammed the printed emails down on the coffee table.

"Care to explain these?" She stood with her arms folded over him.

Alex seemed peeved that she had interrupted him as he sat up and riffled through the papers. A look of panic slightly exposed itself under the surface, just for an instant, and then it was gone. He would never give her the satisfaction of losing control in any way.

"Where did you get these? Did you hack someone's email account? What the hell has gotten into you?"

In typical Alex fashion he tried to turn it around and make this her fault.

"Don't change the subject! I know this is you and Vanessa." He kept fishing through the papers as if he was trying to buy himself time for an answer. "Well, while you try to figure out a believable lie to tell me, I'm gonna step outside."

Reese turned and headed toward the back patio. The idea came into her head. *I can probably break Vanessa before I break him.* She pulled out her phone and called Vanessa.

"Hello?" Vanessa answered.

"We need to talk about emails I found between you and Alex, care to explain?" Her voice was stern and unwavering.

"I—Um—I don't know what you're talking about."

The anxiety was palpable even through the phone.

"Don't play the stupid card, Vanessa, it's beneath even you! I read them all! I know that you've been sleeping with Alex, just admit it!" The sounds of sniffling and tears came through the phone, but no words from Vanessa. Reese began yelling. "Admit it! Fess up! You want to play around in an adult relationship then be a grown-up about it and tell me!"

"I didn't do anything." Vanessa's voice was cracking, forcing words through her tears.

"I have evidence in black and white, Vanessa! I am not an idiot so don't play this like I am. I know everything! It's time to come clean!" She was rigid and cold.

"I'm sorry, Reese," she said, her voice quivering.

"Sorry for what, Vanessa?" Her voice was now condescending. "You didn't do anything wrong, remember?" Sobbing was now coming from the other end of the phone. Vanessa was in shambles and Reese was only filled with anger. She knew Vanessa was about to break. "Tell me!" Reese demanded.

"I've been in a relationship with Alex for, I don't know, six months..." Vanessa blurted out in-between her unstoppable sobs.

"I know you have. What the hell is wrong with you? First of all bitch, you've been screwing him for six months—you weren't in a relationship. You can't have a relationship with a taken man, Vanessa! I knew, even before the emails, I freakin' knew it. You know what, princess, you can have him! Good luck with all of that!"

"I'm sor–"

"Save it!" Reese cut her off. "Have you screwed him in our bed?"

"Yes," Vanessa whispered.

Reese was astonished at how little respect Alex had had for her and their relationship. She choked back her devastation and her anger smoldered at the surface.

"Anything else you care to tell me?"

"Last night too, before my birthday dinner..." Reese stayed silent for a moment as her cheeks grew hot.

"When he went to talk to you while you were in the shower..."

"Yeah... what about it, Vanessa, get to it," Reese recalled how odd she thought that seemed at the time.

"Well, he went in there to make sure you were in the shower before he came out and we had sex on the couch. He said it might be the only opportunity he would have to give me birthday sex. We hooked up again after your guy's fight and you fell asleep on the couch."

Anger, rage, and fury didn't come close to describing what Reese was feeling as she listened to her.

"Seriously? I slept on that fucking couch!" Reese snapped, speaking through her teeth, her jaw clinched tightly.

"Reese, I didn't mean for you to get hurt, I'm so sorry."

"What did you think was going to happen, Vanessa? Did you think I would hold your hand and we could skip and sing lullabies together? Grow the fuck up! Life doesn't work that way! Do me a favor, and save your apologies for someone who gives a damn."

"Reese, I—"

Reese hung up the phone, unable to listen to another apology. She sat there staring at the ground as her world spun with agonizing hatred. The thought of the two of them together made her sick. Images of them on her couch while she was there in the next room rolled around her head. She shoved the broken pieces of her heart down below her anger, below her rational thinking, and below her tolerance for Alex and his lies. Her fist clinched so tightly that her hands ached.

Enraged, she marched back inside and came face to face with Alex. Her eyes filled with disgust, and she no longer feared him the way she had for so long. All she saw was red.

"What lie are you planning on telling me?"

"It's not a lie, Reese. I'll tell you the truth. This is my brother's email account, not mine. She's been sleeping with Lance." Reese just stared at him, so filled with anger she couldn't blink. "I swear, baby, I love you."

Alex reached out to grab her hand. Reese jerked away from him, bewildered at his feeble attempt to cover up the affair.

"It's in black and white, Alex, and you can twist it up or set it on fire for all I care, but its right here! It's all right here! She mentions your name, not Lance. She mentions me and asks when you are going to leave me! This is you and her!"

"No it's not! Reese, I swear, it's her and Lance, you have to believe me!" He exclaimed with anger in his voice as he stood up from the couch.

Reese clutched her phone and cracked a wicked smile. She knew she had him by the balls, and she refused to back down.

"Are you serious right now, Alex? Because I just broke your little girlfriend and she confessed everything to me, just now." Reese's tone turned vicious and foul. "I broke her in less than five minutes, actually, had her crying while she begged for my forgiveness." She walked toward Alex, fearless, and brought her face into his. "So how about you stop wasting both of our time and just admit it already. Stop trying to make excuses, because, sweetheart, I'm not some twenty-year-old and I'm certainly not a moron."

Then something happened that Reese never expected. Alex stood there, no longer wrestling his anger, but he was clearly fighting back tears. He fought with everything he had but he couldn't hold it in any longer. He fell to his knees as tears streamed from his eyes.

"You're right, okay? Yes, I have been cheating on you with Vanessa. I don't know what I was thinking, baby."

"Don't call me baby, I am not your fucking baby anymore!" Reese fought through the tears that now fell from her eyes.

"Reese, please don't do this! I need you! I love you! I can't lose you!" Alex begged.

"Guess you should have thought about that before you slept with someone else!" Her voice was monotone as she stared at the wall, a swirl of emotions battling inside her.

Alex reached up and grabbed her, pulling her numb body to the floor with him. His breathing was shallow and rapid, he continued to apologize and plead with her to not leave. Soon he was sobbing, unable to control his tears or his breathing, and as he found himself unable to speak, his sobbing turned to panic.

"I ca–I–can't–" A pause as his breathing increased. "...breathe...!" Alex reached for her and held her tightly. *You've got to be kidding me. A panic attack, really?* Alex forced words through his breaths. "Hand–numb–" He pulled her into him. "Help–me–"

There was a part of her that wanted to leave him on the floor to deal with his mess alone, but the paramedic in her couldn't do that. She took his hand and gently grabbed his face and in a calm voice she spoke to him.

"Look at me. It's going to be okay. Keep your eyes on me. We are going to focus on your breathing together. Remember, in through your nose, out through your mouth." She grabbed his hand. "In three seconds, out three seconds. Do it with me." Reese began to count as she inhaled. "Breathe in, one, two, three, and out one, two, and three." Alex began to breathe with her as she continued to count. "Good Alex, just like that. Breathe in one, two, three, and out, one, two, and three."

Alex finally relaxed and maintained control of his breathing as tears continued to escape his eyes. He kept trying to wrap his arms around Reese, but she blocked his attempts. She wasn't helping him because she planned on forgiving him, she helped him because she was compassionate and it was in her blood to help. She was hard-wired with a "fix it" mentality, even for those unworthy, like Alex. While he kept his breathing steady she got up off the floor.

"Please, Reese, please don't leave me! I am sorry, baby! I screwed up, please forgive me! Don't leave! Let me fix this, baby, please!"

Alex grabbed her pant leg like a toddler not wanting his mommy to leave. He begged her and pleaded while he sobbed. His breathing started to creep back into a rapid rate. Reese knelt down to be face to face with Alex.

"You better get a handle on yourself, Alex, because I ain't talkin' you down again. You can apologize 'til you're blue in the face, but *you* broke us, and there's no fixin' it."

She reached down and pried his fingers off her pants and walked down the hallway, leaving him on the floor.

Quickly she grabbed as many clothes as she could throw into her open suitcase. She raided the bathroom for necessities, fearing what she left behind would be ruined. *Everything is replaceable, Reese, you just gotta get out.* Frantically she stuffed the suitcase to the brim and forced the zipper shut. Reaching into the lower space behind her shoes in the closet, she grabbed her stash of secret money and shoved it into her inside jacket pocket. With a deep breath, not knowing what she was walking into, she opened the bedroom door and came back down the hallway. Alex was now standing, his eyes and face soaked with tears.

"You're just going to leave? You're going to throw us away, like trash, just like that?" He flung his arms out to the side in disbelief.

Reese stopped in her tracks, her mind spinning trying to find the right words. She decided to stop trying to think and just be brutally honest.

"Let's see, Alex, if I screwed someone else, would you still want me?" Her glare was unwavering. "Would you forgive me?" She put her hand up in front of her. "Before you answer, remember how you beat the shit out of me for simply talking to a man, because I do. I'm done. You never loved me, Alex." He stood frozen, seemingly unsure of how to process what she said. Reese began walking toward the door, when Alex reached for her arm. She whipped around jerking her arm out of reach. "Don't you fucking touch me!" she screamed at him. "Never, ever touch me again!"

She opened the door and quickly walked to her 4Runner. Throwing the suitcase into the back seat, she sped off, vowing to never look back.

Once she turned onto the main road, she found a place to pull over. Leaning over the steering wheel she cried. She felt as if a ton of bricks had been lifted off her shoulders and she could finally breathe again. The tears that ran down her face were a mix of joy and sadness. Although she hated Alex in this moment, it did not erase the love she felt for him deep in her heart. Minutes passed as she sat parked, feeling relieved and devastated all at the same time. When those feelings finally settled, she put the car into drive and continued toward Kyra's house.

Chapter 23

REESE PULLED UP to Kyra's feeling like someone had punched her in the gut, and then gave her the best news of her life. It was an odd feeling, to be brokenhearted and yet, feel happy all at the same time. In her car she sat there staring into the darkness of the night, lost in thought, she didn't notice that the parking lot had several familiar cars that surrounded her.

A piece of her missed him already, but she knew this was the right move. Leaving on her terms and not his, the relationship ended due to his shortcomings, not hers. A tap at her window startled her.

"Hey, girl, why are you sitting out here?" Reese looked up to see Kyra's face and a sense of relief came over her. "I have drinks ready inside, c'mon." Kyra was noticeably pleased to see Reese.

Reese smiled, thankful to be pulled out of her mixed emotions and jumbled thoughts. "Yea, I could use some of those!"

She got out of her car, grabbed her suitcase and unhurriedly went toward the apartment. Walking through the door she saw everyone from Station 23 waiting for her inside.

"Wow! What are all y'all doin' here?" Reese was dumbfounded. She really wasn't expecting everyone to be here waiting for her.

Jess stood up and wrapped her arms around her. "We just wanted to be here to support you." She held Reese at arm's length. "We know how hard this was."

Reese couldn't sit still, she felt awkward and put on the spot. This was the last thing she really wanted to talk about. She fought the tears as she felt her strength begin to crumble, Reese hated crying in public, but she felt so broken it became increasingly harder for her to hold back. She despised being the center of attention in such a devastating way, and all she wanted was to not think about any of this for just a little while.

"You know, let's not talk about it! Who's up for a shot of whiskey?" Reese shouted dropping her suitcase to the ground she walked to the kitchen, without another word.

"A shot of tequila for me, please!" Jess yelled, following Reese.

Turning around Reese saw Jess, Kyra, Louie, and Stump standing there.

"Alright, so that's whiskey for everyone except Jess of, course!" Reese said, getting everyone to chuckle from of the inside joke.

Reese poured all five shots and passed them out as her crew all stood around waiting for a toast. At first she felt as if they were watching her, waiting for her to break, or maybe they were waiting for her to say something profound in some way. Instead, she raised her glass and shouted a simple cheer.

"Here is to my freedom!"

Everyone repeated after her with just as much enthusiasm. "To freedom!"

The night continued with multiple rounds of shots and countless fits of laughter. Reese noticed that her feelings of sorrow were barely noticeable, surrounded by so much love, there was hardly any room left for despair. In this moment, with the people who mattered most to her, she knew that everything was going to be okay. Looking at everyone, she felt an immense sense of gratitude and she stopped to thank God, *thank you for surrounding me with such amazing people, and thank you for keeping me safe.* A soft smile spread on her face.

One by one her crew members trickled out and headed home, the place became quieter with each person that left. Reese felt her body that was now warm and delightfully numb begin to relax as she said her good-byes and thank you to everyone for being there. Louie stood in front of her before they embraced each other and he whispered in her ear, "I am so incredibly proud of you." He released her and they both smiled.

"Thank you, but I couldn't have done this without you. Seriously, you helped me find the anger, the strength, really, that I needed to be able to leave for good." She placed her hand on his shoulder. "And without your wise words I would've buckled and given into him, like I always did before. I'll never be able to express to you the gratitude that I feel."

"I'll always have your back, Reese." He gave her a peck on the cheek before walking out the door.

"What time are we moving you tomorrow?" Ray asked.

"I was thinking eleven, sound good?"

"Eleven's good," Ray said before giving her a hug.

Next was Cole who just smiled and gave her a quick hug before heading out the door. Then Jess pulled herself away from the chatter around the room saving the last good bye for Reese.

"Hey," Jess smiled affectionately as they stood hand in hand, "are you going to be okay now?

"You know me; I'm tougher than I look." Finally, Reese was starting to believe her own words.

"Good, I am going to head out now but, you text or call anytime you need me, okay!?" Jess pulled Reese into a deep hug.

"I will, I promise, thank you Jess, I love you, girl!" Reese stared into Jess' glossed eyes, stifling back tears.

"Love you," Jess slipped out the door, briefly she looked back to give Reese a wink, letting her know she knew everything was going to be okay from then on.

Reese turned and looked over to see Stump standing by. He walked over to her and grabbed her tightly.

"Proud of you, kiddo," he said.

"Thank you." She smiled.

Their embrace lasted a long time. He fought tears while hers soaked into his shirt.

"I love ya, kid, you're my little sister and I'm so happy I can finally stop worrying about you now. You deserve the world, and one day, mark my words, one day you will have it."

"Oh well, I don't know about all that." She shifted, wiping her wet face once they pulled away. "But, I do know a happier life begins now, and I wanted to tell you, thank you for never giving up on me. I love you too, brother."

One last quick hug and Stump was gone. Soon Reese and Kyra were all that was left. They sat on the couch facing each other, sipping the last of their beers. They sat in silence for a bit, enjoying their inebriated state of mind.

"Are you doin' okay?" Kyra asked.

"Well," Reese cracked a slight smile, "I'm not great, but I will be."

They let their beer bottles clink together and finished off the last swigs. Kyra looked around at the empty bottles and chip bowls that had taken over their living room.

"Do you want to just crash and take care of this tomorrow?" Kyra asked.

"Yes! Thank God, sounds like a good plan."

Reese got up and stumbled to her new bedroom. Kyra had set up an air mattress in the room for her. Reese stood there realizing she had nothing but the contents of her overstuffed suitcase.

"Chief let us borrow the air mattress so you don't have to sleep on the couch," Kyra said over Reese's shoulder.

"I can't believe all of the things everyone has done for me." She turned to face Kyra. "I was such a bitch to everyone." Tears sporadically streamed down her face. "And they just forgave me, just like that! I mean, even you! I'm so sorry for everything I did and I hope you know how grateful I am that you opened up your place for me."

Kyra wiped the tears from Reese's face.

"We will always have your back. Plus, you genuinely apologized. A simple and real apology can go a long way, Reese."

"Yeah, I guess you're right." She drew air in deeply before forcing it all out trying to relax her weary nerves.

Reese hugged Kyra before walking into her room. She fumbled to put on her yoga pants but managed to slide into them before crawling into bed. With a hard thud she plopped herself down.

She laid face down on the bed, the silence allowing her to finally touch the thoughts she was avoiding. *I don't have a bed, a dresser, or any furniture for a house actually. Except my sofa and table, that's if Alex hasn't destroyed it yet.* In the midst of the quiet her mind raced further down and tears once again began to fall. She had lost Alex and now she had nothing else because of him. Her sobs seeped out and into her pillow. Reese tried to conceal the noise of her breakdown, but she must have been unsuccessful because just then, the door to her room opened and Kyra poked her head in. She found Reese burying her head in the pillow. She didn't have to say anything, she knew. Kyra pulled back the blankets and crawled into bed with Reese.

"Come here, girl," Kyra said. Although Reese hated the attention she could no longer do it alone, she rolled over and into Kyra's arms. "Just let it all out, girl, it's okay to cry."

Reese let go of every oppressed emotion. Tears flowed from her eyes like a river, she cried harder than ever before. So many emotions rolled around within her, she felt overwhelmed and exhausted.

After around twenty minutes of hard crying she was finally able to pull herself together.

"I'm sorry, Kyra." She wiped her tears. "I don't even know why I'm crying. He's not worth this."

Kyra held her tightly. "I know, girl, but you still loved him. No judgment, I promise. I just want you to know that you are not alone."

"Thank you, for everything. I've been shoving my feelings down for so long. I guess they finally caught up with me."

Kyra continued to hold her tightly as a fresh flow of tears poured out.

Once Reese had calmed down Kyra slithered off the air mattress and out the door. Deep down Reese knew Kyra wished she could relate to what she was going through so she could better know how to be there for her.

Reese didn't want to show the world how truly broken she was inside. Alex may have left physical marks on her body, but those bruises and breaks healed. Her soul on the other hand would take much longer to truly heal; the damage ran deeper than any bruise he left on her body. Reese had become too good at shoving down her true feelings, and she feared that she would keep her anger at the surface for too long. Reese knew, deep in her heart, that this moment was the beginning of a very long journey for her

Chapter 24

REESE WOKE UP the next morning with a splitting headache but, today was moving day, and there was no time for a hangover. In the bathroom she splashed cold water on her face and brushed her teeth. She threw her hair up in a messy bun and then headed to her room to get dressed. She put on her moving clothes; yoga pants and an old ratty t-shirt from high school, *go Bronco's,* she thought. After adjusting her shirt she was ready to go.

Last night she had worried about not being ready for moving all her things out even though she was sure that she couldn't give Alex another chance. This morning she still felt a plethora of mixed emotions, for some reason, every part of her felt as if she was betraying Alex in some way. Flashes of his gut-wrenching apology raced in her mind, from the tears to the tug on her pant leg as he begged her to stay, she had never seen him like that before. Reese worried if she was making a mistake, and yet, simultaneously she felt that she wasn't. *How can he have this hold on me? I mean, should I stay and give him one last chance, he seemed like he was really willing to change?* She sat down on her bed and called her mom.

"Hello," Maggie's voice rang.

"Hey, Mom, how are you." Guilt washed over Reese, it had been a while since they last spoke and she started to resent the fact that she let a man stand between her and her family.

"Reese! Hi, my love, how are you?"

"Hey, I'm doin' okay, mom."

Reese wanted to tell her mom everything but, she couldn't help but hold back. She knew that her parents would be happy about her breaking up with Alex, but Reese wasn't really ready to talk about it in detail with them so suddenly. Instead, they exchanged the typical small talk for several minutes while Reese looked for her opportunity to casually slip the break-up into the conversation.

"Hey, baby," Maggie said, sounding as though she was talking to someone else. "Reesey, your dad just walked in, do you want to say hi?" Reese paused, unsure of how she felt about talking to her dad. Their last conversation had ended with yelling and a fountain of tears. "Reese?" Maggie asked.

"Yeah, Mom, I'm here. I actually need to go, though. Today is movin' day for me and my crew from 23 is going to help me. Love you, talk to you soon."

Reese quickly hung up the phone before Maggie could offer up any questions. She sat with her phone in her hands, tossing it around in anticipation for a few minutes expecting Maggie to call back demanding answers, but her phone remained silent.

She pulled up her contacts, selected Alex's name and began to type.

REESE: I wanted to let you know the Station 23 crew and I will be heading to the house today at 11 to move out my things, I will take only what's mine and leave your key under the mat out front. 8:45am

She immediately got a response from him.

ALEX: Fine, I'm at work. I can't bear to watch the love of my life just up and leave and give up on what we have. Why won't you even let me try to fix this? 8:45am

Reese didn't know how to respond. *Should I let him try? Will I regret it if I don't?* She didn't trust herself to answer those questions yet and after a brief moment, she decided that distance was going to be a good thing. She quickly responded, ignoring Alex's plea of what she was sure to be an empty promise.

REESE: Thank you. I will let you know when we leave. 8:47am

Alex responded:

ALEX: Okay. I'm sorry Reese. I love you. 8:47am

She didn't respond to his last text and went about her morning. She came out of her room ready for the long day ahead of her.

The living room and kitchen were a mess, empty beer bottles and glasses everywhere, chips and dip were left all over the table. Kyra hadn't come out of her room just yet, so Reese started cleaning alone. She grabbed a thirty-gallon black bag and aimlessly went to work throwing away all the trash. Before she knew it, the trash bag was filled with empty bottles and paper plates. Next she tossed out all the chip fragments that were all over the table and threw out the mostly gone chip dips. The apartment was getting back to normal. Grabbing cleaning wipes from under the kitchen sink she wiped down the counters and tables that had spilled whiskey from her sloppy pours into the tiny shot glasses. Before she knew it, she had moved on to the dishes, mainly shot glasses and silverware. In the midst of her cleaning, she didn't notice Kyra come up behind her, she practically jumped out of her own skin when she felt a tap on her shoulder.

"Good morning, busy bee!" Kyra had a smirk on her face.

"God, you scared the shit outta me!" Reese declared with her hand on her chest trying to conceal her rapid breathing.

"I'm sorry," Kyra giggled, "I said your name like twelve times, but you couldn't hear me. Looks like I woke up at the perfect time!" She playfully changed the subject.

"Yeah you did, slacker!" Reese joked.

They both giggled as Kyra made coffee.

"Do you want some, Reese?"

"Yes, please! How could I possibly say no?"

The girls blended creamer into their coffee and sat down at the freshly cleaned dining room table. Reese stared out the window, bracing her cup of coffee and recalling last night's breakdown, embarrassment took over her. Despite her feelings about it, every break down felt unstoppable. She hated feeling broken, like some charity case. Swallowing her pride she continued to stare out the window.

"Thank you for last night, Kyra." Reese couldn't bring herself to make eye contact with her.

"Of course, girl, I got you." She placed her hand on top of Reese's.

Reese looked down at her coffee before quickly glancing at Kyra, flashing an awkward smile then quickly shifting her eyes back out the window. Reese wasn't sure why she feared that Kyra would judge her, but there was a part of her that thought Kyra would never understand how she truly felt on the inside.

They both sipped their coffee and went over the plan for moving her stuff out. Reese felt relieved that the subject had changed from her emotional turmoil to something a little easier for her to talk about—staying busy.

"So, I sent a text to Alex earlier to let him know we would be over in a few hours. He's at work until tonight so we should be good. I also told him I would let him know when we left."

"At least he won't be there to cause any problems... are you okay after having to talk to him?" Kyra's eyes narrowed as she examined her.

"I'm doin' okay." She insisted, ignoring the knots in her stomach. "Oh!" Reese exclaimed. "Don't let me forget to leave his key."

Kyra softly smiled at Reese. "I got you."

Phone calls were made, and plans were set. The girls got in their cars and headed towards Alex's house. They decided to take both cars so they would have more room to pack her things and would avoid having to make multiple trips back and forth. Reese stopped at the store by the apartment and grabbed boxes and newspapers.

The drive to the house was sullen while Reese drove in silence, there was no music that was going to calm her or help with what she was feeling now. The closer they got to the house the harder her stomach turned. Anxiety built up within her. *What if I'm making a mistake?* Her hands gripped tighter around the steering wheel. Pulling in the driveway the knots in her stomach multiplied. She sat in her car for a few extra seconds staring at the house. Her hands still gripped the steering wheel so tightly that she lost feeling in her fingers. Kyra walked in front of her car pulling Reese out of her panic. With her stomach still in knots she got out of the car, keys in hand, and got the boxes out of the back. Using the packaging tape Stump had brought they put the boxes together in the driveway.

Once the boxes were done she walked up to the door. Turning the key in the lock she choked back the vomit that she felt creeping up at the back of her throat. She walked in to see that everything was in pristine order. Her couch seemed to be untouched and not harmed in any way. The anxiety magnified walking into the house, Reese felt like she couldn't breathe.

"Are you okay, Reese?" Kyra asked.

She wasn't okay, Reese couldn't speak. She stood immobile; the room felt like it was spinning out of control. She went running down the hall and into the front bathroom where she hit her knees and threw up in the toilet. Kyra was left outside pounding on the locked bathroom door while Reese draped her arms over the toilet, resting her forehead on her arm. The only thing she had in her stomach was coffee and her throat burned from the acid. She wiped her face with toilet paper before she stood up, rinsed out her mouth and washed her hands.

Kyra was still pounding at the door begging Reese to open it. "Reese! Are you okay? Open up!"

Reese slowly opened the door and stood face to face with Kyra. She stood there, frozen, unsure of what to say. Reese finally spoke, her voice at a whisper.

"I feel like I'm making a mistake, maybe I should give him the chance to fix this." Tears slowly fell from her eyes. "He apologized and begged me to give him a chance, maybe I should. I mean, he genuinely begged me to stay and I just dismissed him. What if I leave now and that's it?"

Kyra stared at Reese, the wheels visibly turning trying to find the right words to say. Reese knew on some level she, in fact, was making the right move but, she desperately needed some sort of a confirmation from Kyra, confirmation that everything was going to be better without Alex. Reese stared back with pleading eyes, and Kyra seemed to realize how much Alex had broken her down. He was still the loudest voice Reese could hear in her head, and she feared that he would always be there to haunt her thoughts.

"Reese, you're doing the right thing here. Are you forgetting about all the times that he hurt you? How he secluded you?" Kyra put her hands on Reese's shoulders. "Look, how about this, we move your stuff out, get some distance. If you still feel like you're making a mistake then try to mend it but, give it some time so you can think straight."

"What if I'm too late?" Reese began to wipe her tears.

"If he truly loves you, sweetheart, you won't be."

Kyra softly smiled at Reese, then wrapped her arms tightly around her. Reese knew Kyra had a point, but she couldn't convince herself to think rationally. She felt defeated and scared, which were the two feelings that Alex always made sure she felt. Being in his house and staring at what used to be their home was a reminder of the dull ache in her heart she had been feeling ever since she left Alex.

"I don't think I can do this."

Kyra let her go, lifted her face, and looked Reese in the eyes.

"Of course you can, you're the strongest person I know. I know this isn't easy, Reese, but the right choices rarely are. You need some distance. It's easy to look around this place and see the home you and Alex built together but, you need to stop seeing what you wanted it to be, and see what it was. He controlled you, he manipulated you, and he broke you down. Physically he hurt you, emotionally he destroyed you. Don't let him control you like that in this moment of triumph. He screwed another woman on your couch and in your bed all while you were home, remember that."

Reese stood up straight and nodded her head in agreement. "You're right. Distance wouldn't be such a bad thing." The thought of Alex and Vanessa left a bad taste in her mouth.

They came down the hallway. Kyra had one arm around her. They found Stump, Nate, and Jess standing in the living room. They all had looks of concern on their faces. Stump walked over to Reese, wrapping his arms around her.

"We got you." He held her tightly. "Kyra is right, let's move your stuff, get some distance."

Reese took a deep breath. "Y'all are right. Distance is good."

She smiled at them all, the knots in her stomach starting to ease up. She felt her body start to relax and the anxiety began to dim while she packed up the things that were hers.

Ray and Cole were the last to show up, and the guys took out the bigger items to the trailer that Cole brought. Reese closed up the boxes she marked 'kitchen' and stacked them next to the door. Jess came down the hallway, struggling to drag trash bags filled with clothes and hangers.

"Let's just take them straight out to my car. We can pile them into the back seat," Reese said, grabbing the bags from Jess.

"I'll go get the other bag and shoes. You got a lot of clothes, you know that?" Jess joked.

"Well, one day you just might look as good as I do and then you'll understand why," Reese joked as she stuck her tongue out in her direction.

Walking out to her car Reese chuckled at her comment to Jess. There was no doubt that in a beauty contest Jess would blow her out of the water.

After stuffing the bags into the backseat Reese came back inside and went into the bathroom to gather the things she left.

She dumped hair products and curling irons into a box without a second thought. It wasn't until she saw her two-karat diamond necklace hanging there that she stopped dead in her tracks. Pulling it from the necklace holder she held it up, admiring its classic and elegant beauty. She remembered the night he gave it to her.

He had sushi delivered to the house so they could have a private, romantic evening together for their anniversary. Reese recalled feeling a sense of relief that night knowing that it would be just the two of them and near impossible for her to mess up his plans. She spotted the small box giftwrapped in dark blue wrapping paper with a solid white satin ribbon that crossed over the box and into a beautiful bow at the top. She wondered if it was a ring, feeling hopeful and yet, extremely terrified at the possibility. After dinner in the candle light, she opened the box and to her delight, it was the most beautiful necklace she had ever seen.

"Oh, my goodness, baby!" she whispered. Her eyes fixated on the solitary two karat diamond and all of its glimmering beauty. "It's absolutely beautiful, my love!"

"I'm glad you like it." He smiled. "I saw it and said, that absolutely needs to be on my Reese! It's simple, elegant, timeless, and full of breathtaking beauty; just like you."

Reese held up the necklace and admired its sheer elegance, smiling to herself as she stood in the bathroom alone remembering one of the few good memories she had with Alex. She stood there struggling with whether to take it with her or not, but in the end she decided to leave the necklace there. She didn't want ghosts of those few good memories haunting her or biting her in the ass later.

Reese came down the hallway and stacked the box marked "bathroom" at the door with the others. Turning around she walked over to her couch and started to remove the cushions to prepare it for the guys to move. She pulled the last cushion off the couch and found a red bra with black lace that had been stuffed down into the couch. Using only two fingers she carefully picked it up trying to not let the stains of infidelity, surely that it had on it, rub off on her. Holding the bra out in front of her, she stared at it and with a disgusted look on her face, she slowly stood upright. Everyone stopped and stared at her. Her eyes were wide and unruly as she fiercely stared at the bra that was in her hand, clearly not her style or size. Reese felt infuriated, used, and the bra reminded her of the hatred that she harbored for Alex deep within her.

"Didn't cheat on me, my ass!" she snapped. Reese glared at the bra, a frenzy of anger boiling within her.

"I take it that's not yours," Nate innocently chimed in, breaking the silence.

The anger rapidly flowed throughout her body. She felt like she had become one of those cartoon characters from her childhood that had steam coming from their ears when their anger exploded. The sentimental feelings she had while packing her things and seeing her necklace were long gone now, and all she could see was red. Furious, she turned around and looked at Nate.

"Do you have a hammer and nails?"

Bewildered, he blankly looked at her. "Um, this was your house, Reese. I don't know where you kept that stuff."

"Right," she chuckled jokingly.

She stormed off, bra in hand, to grab the hammer and nails. Reese was so furious that she was no longer worried about touching the harlot's bra that was now clinched tightly in her balled up fist. The door of the storage cabinet at the end of the hall flung wide open, hitting the wall. Enraged, she sifted through the shelves until she found what she needed, leaving the once organized cabinet a mess. Slamming the cabinet door shut she stormed back down the hallway.

She spotted an empty wall in the living room. *Perfect!* Without saying a word she marched over while the crew watched in suspense. She held up one strap on the wall, placed the nail on top of the strap and began to hammer, once it was secured, she placed the other strap up on the wall and secured it with a second nail.

"Is that straight?" Reese asked as she turned to face everyone, her hand was up as if to showcase her masterpiece. She sarcastically smiled and everyone burst out with laughter. "He is such an asshole! Let's finish this."

"Girl, that's awesome!" Jess exclaimed while clapping her hands.

The last box was loaded and ready to go; everyone else had left the house and headed over to start unloading Reese's things at the apartment. Reese was all alone in the house that held so many memories she hoped would become distant memories sooner rather than later. She stopped by the door to take one last look around. She admired her handiwork with the new wall art. A giggle was muffled under her breath as she shook her head and walked out the door, all traces of guilt were gone. She confidently locked the deadbolt behind her, and then tossed the key under the mat.

"Good-bye, Alex," she quietly said with her hand on the door.

Chapter 25

THE NEXT DAY was Fill the Boot, the MDA fundraiser. The girls decided to carpool over to the station that morning and during the drive over they danced and lip-synced to their favorite songs. Some of the songs brought Reese back to a couple years ago, being awake in the middle of the night, the lack of sleep causing them to laugh and make jokes of everything around them, a delirious state of mind on which their friendship was built. Reese was the one who would always take the songs and change the words to fit the situation.

"I just wanna, take a nap! Take a nap! Yeah, yeah, take a nap! Take a nap!" Reese sang out to the song "Shake It Off."

Working a twenty-four-hour shift with someone is the best way to get to know a person. By two o'clock in the morning the real you will come out, whether you want it to or not. Reese and Kyra knew after their first shift together that they would be bonded for life, and although Alex caused a temporary bend in their friendship, even he couldn't entirely break them.

Those who worked on the engine and truck were dressed in their turnout pants with their company-issued Auburn Fire Department t-shirts and their rubber fire boots. Reese and Kyra, however, wore their uniform pants, Auburn Fire Department t-shirts, and work boots. They all poured into the common room, coffee in hand, waiting for their assignments.

The Fill the Boot fundraiser consisted of firefighters on local street corners, with rubber boots in hand, asking drivers and pedestrians on the street to donate toward research for muscular dystrophy. It was an annual event that all the firehouses within the department participated in and they intensely competed against each other for the grand prize. The house that brought in the most money won various prizes over the years. This year the prize was five-hundred dollars' worth of Harris Ranch steaks.

Chief Gibbs had a strategy, he would post their best-looking people on the busiest corners, and those teams always seemed to bring in more money than the rest of them. Reese always wondered if it was the fact that they were easy on the eyes or that they scored the busiest corner. It was hard to say, but Station 23 had won the contest three years in a row and they were all hoping to win again this year as well.

Jess and Nate were by far the two most attractive people on their shift. They were the team placed at the busiest intersection, two blocks from the station. Reese was paired with Louie at the second busiest intersection. The others were scattered in pairs at the other major intersections. Chief Gibbs way of thinking had paid off so far, *who am I to question it?* The entire house was hoping for those steaks; they planned on doing a station BBQ for everyone and their families to come to. Needless to say, a lot was riding on their efforts today.

Reese and Louie worked well as a team. They stood across from each other on opposite sides of the street, dancing and singing with smiles on their faces. She laughed more in those four hours than she had in the last two years. Alex had never allowed her to have fun on her own terms, only his. He abraded her carefree happiness, her smile, and even her genuine laughter. She felt those broken pieces of her soul beginning to heal that day, amidst the laughter and fun. Somehow the sun seemed brighter, and its warmth warmer. She worked not just to raise money for MDA, but to put a smile on every person's face that stopped, whether they donated or not.

Spreading joy helped her healing more than she realized in that instant. Reese had no idea that these events were just scratching the surface of her brokenness. They were merely the beginning of a process that would take her years to complete. Reese convinced herself that she was healing faster than she truly was.

"Hey!" A familiar voice interrupted her thoughts. She turned around to see Chad, the officer who had pulled her over a few days ago.

"Hey, what's up, Chad! How's it goin'?" As Chad got out of his car and walked toward Reese, she yelled at Louie, "I'm taking a quick break, okay?"

Louie waved his hand at her in acknowledgment. When Chad approached her he had a smile that revealed his perfectly straight white teeth.

"How's the fundraiser goin'?" he asked.

Reese felt butterflies and nerves rise up in her stomach. She was unsure if the nerves she felt were just her response to men because of Alex. Or if it was because she thought Chad was handsome.

"It's goin' good. I think Mr. West over there and I, well, we're killing it, goin' to bring in a decent amount this year. What are you out doin'?"

"Just driving around, saw you... I wanted to ask you somethin'."

"Yeah sure, what's up?"

"I heard that you are single now... is that true?" he bluntly asked.

"Oh! Um, yeah, actually, I moved out yesterday." Reese was stunned by the fact that Chad knew about her break-up.

"I'm really sorry. Are you doing okay?" He gently placed his hand on her shoulder.

"Uh, yeah, I guess. I'm dealing with it." She sheepishly tucked her hair behind her ear as she looked down at the ground.

"Sounds like you need to get your mind off things, are you free tonight?" Dazed Reese just stood there staring at him. *Did he just ask me out?* "Reese?"

"Oh! Yeah, actually tonight I'm not. We're all heading out to Charlie's either to celebrate our win, or drink our sorrows away, from our loss." She laughed nervously. "Um– You should totally come! It should be fun!"

"Uh, yeah, I would love to! What time?"

"Eight, I believe." She felt a sudden surge of excitement.

They exchanged numbers before Chad placed a twenty-dollar bill into her boot and left. Astonished by what had just happened Reese held up his number and examined it. At first she wasn't sure how she felt, she knew without a doubt that she wasn't ready for any of this. *Who's to say we can't just be friends?* She asked herself, not letting the underlying excitement fade.

Louie leisurely walked across the street to Reese. She looked up to see the look on Louie's face, a giddy smile that made his round cheeks puff out, and a look of 'big brother knows you have a crush' in his eyes. His final step toward her was a bounding leap, landing with his toes inches from hers.

"Hey! What was that all about?" He sounded exactly how a brother would.

Reese felt that her best option was to play it off like nothing.

"Oh, that? Chad?" she scoffed. "He's local PD, and just a friend... I don't know what you're thinkin'?"

Her futile efforts of trying to turn it around on Louie had failed.

"Oh no, don't you even try that shit with me! You over here grinnin' from ear to ear, so let me ask again. What was that all about?" He looked at her intensely.

Reese stared back, trying to hold her ground, but after a few seconds she caved.

"Ugh! Okay, fine! I used to have a crush on him before Alex and I got together. Please don't make a thing of this! I'm nowhere near ready for anything more than drinks, but it's nice to know the options might be there down the road. Shoot, Louie, I honestly don't even know if he's interested in me like that."

She knew that emotionally she was not healed and that would not be fair to Chad but, part of her was curious about him. So, she figured she would say something if he actually showed up that night.

"Yeah, I know Chad. He's good people, Reese. You need to be honest with him. And trust me, he's interested."

"I know I do, and I already planned on it. I promise. Wait, how do you know he's interested?"

"Because I'm a guy, I can see it," he said with a wink and a smile as he skipped back to the other side of the intersection. Once he reached his side of the street he yelled at the top of his lungs, "Reese has a date!"

Reese stopped, jaw dropped with her cheeks blushing bright red, *he did not just yell that out for anyone and everyone to hear!*

"You promised!" she yelled, mortified.

Louie just looked at her and smiled. "I know! I lied!" He yelled back, obnoxiously laughing.

She shook her head in disbelief before bursting out with laughter, laughing so hard it was difficult to catch her breath, and her cheeks ached.

"I hate you!" she yelled in between giggles.

"No you don't! You love me!" Louie smiled, blowing her a kiss.

"Yeah, yeah, whatever bro... I love you for now!" She waved her hand.

When their time collecting donations came to an end, Chief Gibbs was there to pick them up. Reese and Louie grabbed a few more last-minute donations, carefully weaving through the cars while they were stuck at the red light. The light turned green as Louie grabbed one last donation and he joined Reese and Chief Gibbs in the battalion vehicle.

"So, how do you guys think you did?" Gibbs asked.

"We killed it!" Louie announced before holding out a fist to Reese for a celebratory fist bump.

"Yeah we did!" she agreed, hitting her fist into Louie's.

"Good! Good!" Gibbs said.

When they got back to the station it was time to count the money in their boots. Each person was responsible for their own boot and money. They were all gathered in the training room which they used as a counting station. Reese dumped the money out of her boot onto the table and counted it. *Oh dang, there's way more in here than I thought.* She counted in her head, *sixty-seven, one hundred, one hundred-eighty, two hundred-forty, three hundred-fifty-six, four hundred-twenty-five, four hundred-eighty-seven dollars!* She re-counted it two more times just to be sure.

"How much did you make, Reese?" Stump inquired without looking up from his paper, he was in charge of writing down everyone's totals.

"I got four-hundred and eighty-seven dollars!" She was thrilled to have collected so much for a great cause.

Stump stopped and looked up at her in disbelief. "Are you sure?"

"I counted it three times." She held up the money and began flipping through it. "But you can count it again if you want."

"Nah, I'm good." He chuckled.

Everyone gathered around to see the final tally of what their station had earned. Reese looked at all the total amounts and noticed she was only behind Jess by forty-seven dollars and Nate she beat by seven dollars. Wow, she thought.

"Alright, everyone, gather around, I have the total," Stump announced. Everyone stood by Stump in a half circle around him, silence fell slowly over the room. It was so quiet all you could hear was the sharp breaths of a crew that sat in suspense as he double checked the numbers. "We earned a total of... two-thousand, nine-hundred, and ninety-six dollars! That's about a thousand dollars more than last year! Good job, everyone!" Cheers of celebrations briefly filled the room.

Stump pulled out his phone and called headquarters where they were holding the final tallies. Silence once again engulfed the room as they waited to see if they were in the number one spot. He hung up the phone and hung his head while letting out a deep sigh. Everyone began to lower their heads as they anticipated defeat.

"Well guys... next year we'll definitely have to do better... but, feels damn good to be... number one right now!" Stump shouted as he jumped up out of his chair.

The station filled with a relentless roar of celebration—hoops and hollering, clapping, and dancing—everyone was elated.

"Did they tell you who came in second?" Nate asked through the cheers.

The celebration promptly muffled, waiting for his response.

"Station sixty-seven is in second, with two-thousand and eighteen dollars!"

The cheering resumed louder this time knowing they wouldn't be beat. Station 67 was their biggest competition every year. Last year Station 23 beat Station 67 by forty-three dollars, and the year before by only nine dollars—significant improvement with each year. This year it was a landslide win. Confident no one would beat them; they changed out of their uniforms and headed off to Charlie's on cloud nine.

Reese was smiling ear to ear, excited about the victory and yet nervous about seeing Chad. *Take a breath, Reese. This isn't a date. He was just being nice.* She pulled out her phone and text him since they had finished earlier than she thought.

REESE: Hey Chad, its Reese. Just wanted to let you know, we are all heading over to Charlie's early. They serve food there, so you're welcome to join us in celebrating our VICTORY! 6:27pm

She sent it off, *that sounded casual, right?* Shaking off her insecurities, she grabbed her stuff and headed for the door.

"Are you ready, girl?" Kyra asked.

"Yup, let's do it!" She looked at Kyra, unable to hold anything back. "I saw Chad today."

Kyra stopped and flipped around. "Chad? As in, the hunky and delicious officer, the save me by giving me mouth-to-mouth, that Chad? Oh my God! Tell me everything!" She entangled her arm with Reese's.

"There's not much to tell. Well, except that I invited him to come to Charlie's later." Reese flashed Kyra a nervous grin.

"What? Holy shit, girl!"

"Look, we're just friends. I don't know, girl, I'm not over Alex and I'm certainly not ready for any of this." She lowered her head. "I have to tell him tonight. God, I wish I was ready. He's a great guy, but I just can't. I mean, I know I'm not with Alex anymore but it feels like I'm cheating on him. I know that sounds stupid, but I do."

Kyra squeezed tightly around Reese, "It's not stupid, Reese, but it is okay to let loose and have a good time."

"I know, but I also have to be honest with him."

"That's not a bad idea." She tugged on Reese's arm.

They started walking out to the car when Reese's phone went off, a text from Chad. She held up her phone and looked at Kyra.

"It's Chad." Her heart was pounding, not with excitement, but fear.

"Open it, silly."

CHAD: Oh nice! Congrats on the win! I'm just leaving the gym, be down there in a bit. Save me a spot! 6:30pm

Reese smiled with relief.

REESE: *Sounds good! I'll save you a seat! See you soon.6:31pm*

"Well played, girl, casual, smooth, I like it."

Reese rolled her eyes at Kyra before getting into her 4Runner and heading toward the bar.

The entire Station 23 crew took up several tables and Reese saved Chad a spot next to her, as promised. She slowly sipped her beer and ate her cheeseburger when the waitress brought out her order. She was picking at the fries left on the plate when she saw Chad walk in. He was dressed in straight-legged dark blue jeans and a black fitted thermal with the sleeves pushed up on his forearms. Once he spotted Reese he casually made his way over to her with the most genuine smile on his face.

"Hey," he said leaning in and hugging her. "How are you?"

His cologne was enticing and Reese inhaled, taking a deep breath in and soaking up the aroma.

"I'm good. How was the gym?" her heart began picking up speed as her nerves became ever present.

"Grueling." He laughed. "Want another?" he asked pointing at her beer.

"Sure."

"Be right back."

Chad headed to the bar and Reese watched him effortlessly move through the people. The bar was at a good pace, not too crowded but not desolate. He flashed Reese a smile when he caught her watching him. Reese panicked, quickly looking away before locking eyes with him and smiling back. *What are you doing, Reese? You need to stop this.*

Before she knew it Chad was back with their beers. She smiled and enjoyed the strong flavor of her IPA beer. They had a simple conversation about where they were from and how they got into their careers. Reese enjoyed listening to him talk about his past and his family and she realized that her nerves had dissipated. She told him all about Texas and what it was like to grow up there, but what she didn't tell him was how much she had been missing it over the last few months or so. She told him how she left Alex, slipping him into the conversation so when she told him why she had to push pause later, he wouldn't be shocked. He listened to her and hung on every word of her stories.

They both felt at ease with each other within a few minutes, something Reese was not used to. They were intimately leaning into each other, and when he placed his hand on her thigh she knew the time had come that she needed to come clean with him about where she stood.

"Can I talk to you outside? I need some fresh air," Reese said.

"Sure, absolutely," he immediately stood up pulling out her chair for her, when she stood up he took her hand in his and led her through the crowd and out of the bar. The crisp air hit her face when the door opened. She walked down the street a few steps to give them some privacy from the traffic in and out of the door of the bar. When she turned around she came face to face with Chad, who stood much closer to her than she anticipated.

"Hi! Sorry!" She nervously laughed.

Taking a step back she was stopped by his hands on her arms. He gently held her in place, inches from him. Her heart began to race. *He's not gonna let me do this, is he?*

He said, "Look, I know what you're going to say, and I respect that you just ended a long term relationship. I want you to know that I'm not going anywhere, and before you shut me down I just wanted to do this."

Leaning into her, he softly pressed his lips against hers. Reese felt a jolt of excitement. She hesitated to kiss him back and then decided to go for it because it didn't feel wrong. Leaning her body into his, she firmly had her lips on his. He wrapped his arms around her waist while he parted his mouth and waited for Reese to do the same. She parted her lips and their tongues danced around each other. Reese pulled away slowly, nibbling his lower lip.

They both stood there, inches from each other trying to catch their breath. He stared into her eyes with pure endearment and excitement. The only word Reese could get out was, "Wow."

Chad smiled. "I could say the same about you." He backed away reluctantly, as though fighting his urge to kiss her again.

"I wish the timing was different on this." She put her head down.

He placed his hand under her chin and gently lifted her head. "Don't ever apologize for needing to put your healing first. I wish things were different too, but it's okay. I'm a very patient man, Reese."

She loved the way he talked to her. He was gentle and understanding in a way Alex never was. The only difference was that when Alex touched her, when he kissed her, she became weak in the knees and every ounce of her body yearned for him. He turned her on like no one ever had before, and she missed his sexual touch more than anything else. *Will I ever feel that spark again, the kind of spark that could start a forest fire?* What Reese was unable to see was that her lust for Alex far surpassed any amount of love she had for him.

Chapter 26

DAYS SEEMED TO quickly pass as the girls took time to organize Reese's things in the apartment. Kyra wasn't big on cooking so Reese found lots of space throughout the kitchen for her things. She admired the new pots-and-pans set her parents bought her last year for Christmas; they were beautiful, all black with silver handles. They were sleek and classy, and made Reese feel more grown-up, it was a real adult gift. She had been admiring that set for months prior to Christmas. She always dreamt of having a top-of-the-line quality set of pots and pans, unlike the mismatched cheap Teflon she already owned.

Christmas morning last year she opened her gifts from her parents and shrieked with delight. The joy she felt opening the giant heavy box they came in surpassed anything she felt for Alex's gift he bought her. *You named a star after me... that's it?* She thought to herself while trying to seem enthused. As he tore through multiple gifts she bought him, like a few new power tools, shave kit, clothes and a shop-vac he could use while tinkering with his Chevelle. She had put so much time and effort into choosing each and every of his and with each present he tore open, she became more and more disappointed. Although, she truly thought that having a star named after you is pretty amazing, she was left feeling like he hadn't put much effort into getting her anything that she truly wanted. As usual, Alex never gave much thought into what Reese wanted, which was the real problem she struggled with that morning. Maybe Alex thought it was a romantic gesture, and with any other person giving it to her it would have been just that but, when she didn't dance with delight the way she did for her parents' gift, Alex tore her down and subtly made his resentment known.

She let go of that Christmas memory with Alex and went to put clothes away in her new room. One thing she was definitely missing about being with Alex at that moment was realizing her new closet space, or rather, the lack of. She stood analyzing the small enclosed space. *How the heck am I going to fit all my stuff in here?* After about an hour of strategically hanging her clothes up, organized by color and style, of course, she moved on to all of her shoes. *Oh man, this isn't going to be easy.* Carefully, she lined up her shoes in just the right way only to find not all of them would fit in her closet. Half-an-hour passed, she made several attempts with multiple different ways to get everything perfectly compacted into the closet but, nothing worked. With heightened emotions from the break-up, the whirlwind of being suddenly moved out, and being stuck in her many thoughts while trying to get organized, frustration set in and without a word, she grabbed her keys and headed for the door.

"Where are you going?" Kyra asked wiping down the counters in the kitchen.

"I'm headed to Target. I never thought I would say this, but I have too many shoes! I need to get a shoe rack. Wanna go with me?"

"Hell yeah, I wanna go!" Kyra exclaimed. She loved Target the way every woman across America did. It was the store you never got out of for under a hundred dollars. "Let me put some shoes on."

She practically skipped down the hall, giddy with excitement. Reese shook her head and ever so slightly laughed under her breath. She chose to put aside her frustration and enjoy their Target adventure.

The girls weaved through the isles spotting several things they did not need but, could not live without. By the time they made it to the isle of shoe racks the cart was half filled with various items, from decorative wall hangings to a new color scheme of dish towels. It was exactly what you would expect a typical cart of two unsupervised women at Target to be. Reese browsed through the shoe racks carefully looking at measurements and number of shelves. She did not want to buy one too small to fit all of her shoes, or too big to fit in the closet. She finally settled on a four-shelf rack that was forty-eight inches long.

"Two of these should be good, right?" she asked Kyra, anxiously waiting her approval.

Kyra examined the box and its dimensions for about a minute before finally answering. She bowed her head and clasped her hands together.

"Dear Lord baby Jesus, please let two of these shoe racks fit in her peasant-sized closet and still hold the mountain of shoes she owns. Amen." Kyra peeked up at Reese once her prayer was over and mischievously smiled.

"Ha, so funny I almost forgot to laugh!" Reese giggled sarcastically. "I'm being serious here."

"So am I! You have an unnatural amount of shoes!"

"I know, but I'm not throwing any out or giving any away, don't even ask." Reese's tone was more defensive than she intended.

"I'm just messing with you, girl."

"I know, I didn't mean to sound so... well, bitchy." She giggled.

"Forgiven. Now put the shoe racks in the cart and let's get the hell out of this place before I spend my entire pay check in here!" The girls checked out with both amounts, not surprisingly, over a hundred dollars.

Back at the apartment they gawked over their merchandise and picked out where to hang their new decorations. After she avoided the shoe crisis for as long as she could, Reese retreated back to her room and spent the next two hours assembling both racks. She confidentially placed them into the closet. It was a snug fit, but they were both uniform and in the closet, that's all that really mattered. She began placing her shoes in the racks one pair at a time. She got down to the last two pairs and very little room left. Squeezing all of the shoes together, she was able to get them to all fit and just like the racks themselves it was snug, but doable. Reese came down the hallway with a new sense of accomplishment in her stride.

"Finally, I'm all done!" She smiled at Kyra. "I mean, I can't buy any more shoes for a while, but they all fit! That's what truly matters." She overdramatically winked and threw her thumb in the air expecting some sort of applause for her accomplishment.

"Impressive, Ms. Landon," Kyra indulged her needs with a delicate clapping of her hands.

"Why thank you, Ms. Vaughn," she said with a bow.

Within no time at all, the girls overhauled the entire house. After disinfecting Reese's couch, they angled both couches just right to provide more seating space in their not so spacious living room, and swapped out Kyra's old wobbly dining room table for Reese's brand new one. It was a dark-stained high-top table that seated four with light brown faux suede seat covers on the chairs. This table was much different from the farmhouse style table she grew up with. As much as Reese loved the change she secretly yearned for the familiar. This table was actually Alex's choice, but was bought with her money. She took it with her when she left in hopes that Kyra and she could build new memories around it.

Over the next few days Reese had begun to embrace her newfound freedom and she was content with how things had turned out. All of her final bruises from Alex had healed and any physical trace of him in her life slowly disappeared. The moments of longing for his touch faded on the surface, but she knew that sexual desire for him was still there.

The Firefighter of the Year party was in just a few hours, it was something her crew did every year. They would decide where they could all get together and cast their votes to determine which crew member would be honored that night. Reese was happy to attend the celebration this time around, last year she was forbidden to even make an appearance, she felt a great deal of excitement for the upcoming festivities and not having to worry about an impending fight for going. The girls got ready for the party, neither one of them wanted to be late. Making an entrance by being late was more of a Jess thing than theirs.

The attire for the evening would be, of course, casual, the guys often joked that they didn't want to have to get dressed up after being in a uniform all day. Reese scanned her newly organized clothes in the closet, sifting through so many clothes she rarely wore. As much as Reese enjoyed getting all dolled up for special events and the occasional night-out on the town, at heart, she was a casual clothes kind of girl. Grabbing a pair of dark wash, slightly distressed jeans, and one of her favorite baseball tees, she was satisfied with her outfit. The body of the shirt was grey, it hugged her curves just tight enough to give her shape and the neckline was a V neck that made her breasts look nicely accentuated. The arms of the shirt were a deep crimson red. They gently hugged her arms, stopping just below the elbow. She put her light grey Converse shoes on before heading to the bathroom to fix her hair and makeup. While her curling iron warmed up she did her makeup quickly and with precision. Her face looked flawless and was illuminated with a glow after putting on foundation and powder. Once she curled her long eyelashes with her curling tool, she applied a thick coat of black mascara, and to ensure they were perfectly separated she ran her eyelash brush through them just once. To finish it off, she added a natural color blush and nude lips. Her soft curls fell around her face, giving her a natural yet polished look which she loved. She referred to it as her "go-to" look and it fit her personality perfectly, laid back with a little touch of class. She finished her last minute touches just in time.

Kyra was also ready to go. She wore black skinny jeans, a Caribbean blue loose off-the-shoulder t-shirt and her grey Vans. Kyra wasn't big on dolling herself up. She left her hair straight and lightly coated her lashes with mascara. They slipped their ID's and money into their back pockets and headed to Charlie's and despite their best efforts, they were still the last to arrive at the bar.

This was the first time Reese had gone out since the break up and truly felt free. She surged with excitement walking through the doors of the bar. The first night without Alex's voice in her head, scrutinizing her every move, she felt a rush of deliverance. For her, tonight was a celebration of her freedom, as well as, the Firefighter of the Year. She ordered herself a double shot of whiskey and two beers to start.

"Dang, Reese, you're starting off right!" Ray said with a laugh.

Ray was saturated in his cologne. His scent was strong, spreading out and reaching the noses of people at least three feet away. He wore straight-legged blue jeans and a black button-down dress shirt that was unbuttoned just enough to see several of his chest hairs protruding out. His hair was slicked back to perfection, not a single piece out of place. Reese wondered if she touched it if it would be crunchy or leave her with a palm full of grease.

"You know it!" Reese declared before downing her double shot of whiskey.

The heat of the whiskey coated her throat and she ordered another. She sipped her first beer and enjoyed the salty malt as it cooled the fire from the whiskey. Patiently she waited for her refill, lightly drumming her fingers on the bar.

She and Ray swiped their drinks and headed through the bar and to the back room that was reserved for them. Reese took her seat, which was snuggled in between Kyra and Jess. Shortly after sitting down she finished off her first beer. A warm feeling flowed through her body. She held up her second whiskey, toasting her newfound freedom to herself, and downed the double shot in one gulp. The burn she felt was something she had ironically grown to like. Everyone settled into their seats while Chief Gibbs started the party off with a speech announcing the winner of this year's coveted title.

"Welcome, everyone! It's nice to see that all of you made it out tonight to celebrate our in house Firefighter of the Year party. I just want to say what an honor it is to be the Chief of such an amazing crew. Each and every one of you goes out there and gives it your all, every shift. I couldn't ask for a better group of people to lead. We're a family; we have each other's backs, no matter what! We head into danger at full speed, never asking for recognition. We risk our lives for those whom we've never met all while holding the top-ranked firehouse title within the department." Everyone began cheering and clapping. "Okay, okay, settle down." Chief Gibbs put his hands up to gesture everyone to stop, even off duty, Gibbs held a command presence that everyone respected. "Let's get on with it, shall we? Now this year I had several votes turned in, but within the last few days I received many phone calls requesting to change their vote. This is the first time since we began this tradition ten years ago that this has happened so, I decided to allow it. This person has developed so much strength and integrity throughout their time here at 23. This person is also, without a doubt, a one-in-a-million, and this house wouldn't be the same without this person. I couldn't be more proud to announce that this year's Firefighter of the Year is... give me a drum roll, please..." Everyone pounded their hands on the tables in a quick and unified manner. Chief Gibbs took a quick pause to allow the drumming to quiet down. "Reese Landon!"

Everyone rose up out of their seats with excitement, cheering for her. Reese sat in disbelief that they would pick her, that they would go as far as calling to change their votes for her. She felt the sting in her eyes as she fought back tears. Pushing her chair back, she slowly stood up and made her way to Chief Gibbs, receiving hugs and high fives from her Firehouse 23 family. She felt honored they would chose her, and now a girl who felt unworthy suddenly became the most worthy. Chief Gibbs hugged her tightly before handing her a personalized stainless steel Yeti travel cup that was engraved with 'Firefighter of the Year' on one side and 'R. Landon' on the other.

Louie started the chanting, "Speech! Speech! Give us a speech!"

Reese stood smiling while covering her mouth in disbelief. The room silenced, giving her the floor to speak.

"Wow! Um– y'all," she gushed, "I don't even know what to say! First of all, thank y'all so much! I know this is an in-house thing we do, and not everyone cares about winnin' it, but I do. I'm so honored and overwhelmed at the same time." She continued to fight back the relentless sting in her eyes, a sting that had become all too familiar to her. "Thank you for takin' a chance on me when I was just a small town country girl from Texas seven years ago. All y'all have changed my life in more ways than I have time to list. I truly do not know what I would do without each and every one of you in my life. I vow to always strive for greatness every single day to honor this job, this city, and most importantly the best damn house in the department!" She raised her Yeti cup high in the air.

The room became overwhelmed with clapping and cheers, the noise was deafening for a few seconds. The bartender brought out a round of shots for everyone at the request of Chief Gibbs. Stump hastily climbed up and stood on a chair, shot in hand.

"Here's to Reese! The most incredibly badass medic I know!"
Everyone raised their shots and repeated, "To Reese!"

She smiled with delight, raised her glass high in the air then tossed back her whiskey.

The alcohol flowed heavily in the bar that night while they all celebrated Reese and her award. Her crew celebrated her, and she celebrated her freedom from Alex. She had lived the last two years of her life controlled, every movement, and every word, like a puppet forced to follow her puppet master. She wasn't even in charge of how much she could drink. Most nights with Alex she had to remain relatively sober because she had to take care of him. But this night, Reese drank freely and without inhibition, throwing back countless shots and enjoying celebratory beers.

Kyra put her hand on her shoulder with worry in her eyes. "You ready to head out?"

Reese was very much intoxicated more than she led on. She turned to look at Kyra, not ready to go home yet, so she declined.

"No, girl, but go ahead and head home. I'll call an Uber or whatever. I'm going to hang here with those girls I just met from Station thirteen." She pointed at the table across the bar that had two girls sitting at it. "I know you're ready to head out, and that's cool. I'm good here, I promise. I think I did training last year with Heather, the blonde, but I'm not sure."

Kyra looked over at the table where Heather and Gayle sat. "Okay, are you sure you're good?"

"Yeah, I'm good," her words slurred out of her mouth.

Kyra put her arm around Reese and walked her over to the table. Heather was a thin blonde with a relatively large nose. She was wearing jeans and a bright red blouse with lips that matched. Against her pale white skin the red seemed to pop. Gayle had more olive tone skin with mousey brown hair. Her make-up was neutral and she wore blue jeans with a deep purple V-neck. They both were sitting drinking their beers when Kyra and Reese walked up.

"Hey, ladies," Kyra said. "How's it goin'?"

"Hey, it's Kyra, right?" Heather said with a smile.

"Yes." Kyra smiled back. "So, I'm going to head out and Reese said she wants to stay. As her best friend and partner at twenty-three, I just wanted to ask if you guys could make sure she calls an Uber to get home. Maybe look after her? She's had quite a bit to drink already."

"Of course, we'll take care of her, don't worry!" Heather reassured her.

Kyra looked at Reese and gave her a hug.

"See you later, wild cat." Kyra giggled as she turned and walked away.

"See ya, girl!" Reese laughed. She turned to the girls at the table. "Alright ladies, who wants another shot?"

Reese, Heather, and Gayle spent the next hour drinking and laughing. They caught up on each other's lives and gossiped about what everyone was doing. Heather talked for a solid twenty minutes about Calvin, the engineer she had a crush on at Station 13. Gayle rolled her eyes listening to all of the things Heather has said a million times before. Reese listened, eager to hear more about someone else's love life other than hers. She hung on every word and displayed enthusiasm when she talked. Reese refused to bring up Alex. She liked the fact that these two girls didn't know a thing about her misery and vowed to keep it that way. They swapped stories about the thrilling and crazy medical aids and traumas they each have had over the last several years, when Gayle had an idea.

"Hey, why don't we head over to Jack's Tavern? They have dancing!"

"Dancing, hell yeah, I'm in!" Reese yelled out as she struck a pose.

After ordering a ride through Uber, the three girls laughed together while they gathered their things and eagerly headed off to Jack's.

They walked through the large wooden doors of Jack's Tavern confident and ready to dance their hearts out. They didn't stop at the bar or find a table. Instead they headed straight for the dance floor. They moved their bodies around each other to the beat of the music. While they danced, buoyant and carefree, Reese remembered how Maggie used to bring her and Sophie into the living room after a rough day and she would tell the girls to 'dance it out'.

"Dance away your problems! Dance away your bad moods! Just keep dancing until you feel free of all the negative things of the day," Maggie said while moving her body in various motions.

The girls would giggle, feeling self-conscious in front of each other until they found their own rhythm. Reese continued this long-standing tradition up until she met Alex. *Why haven't I done this yet?* She danced away all the bad memories with Alex. Other men tried to dance with the three of them, or pull one of them out of their group, but they blew them off. Tonight wasn't about men, or going home with anyone, it was about having fun.

Little did Reese know that Alex was walking through the doors of Jack's as she danced away her memories of him. The alcohol she consumed throughout the night significantly affected her, and she felt off balance while she danced.

"Let's take a break, get a drink?" Reese yelled over the music to her dancing buddies.

Both girls nodded. Gayle led them off the dance floor while they held hands. At the bar Reese got a shot of whiskey and an ice water. They found a table and sat down, sipping their waters and catching their breath from the dance session they finished. Reese downed her shot before realizing just how intoxicated she had become.

"I'm gonna run to the bathroom, be right back," Reese abruptly told the girls.

She stumbled her way through the crowd to the bathroom, feeling uneasy, she could swear someone was watching her. Alex sat, at the bar, his eyes locked on her. As Reese made it to the bathroom, wiping the sweat from her brow, she remembered how Alex had always loved her best when she was sweaty, whether it was after a workout or after sex. She thought about how he would tell her that he loved the way the sweat glistened on her skin. A faint smile came over her face about the pleasant memory that crossed her mind. She missed Alex. Once in the bathroom, Reese splashed some cold water on her face hoping it would help sober her up. She dried off her face with a paper towel and stared at herself in the mirror. *Pull it together.*

Emerging from the bathroom she found Alex leaned up against the wall. Her eyes scanned his muscular body as she stood there, craving him the way she always had. He seemed to always have this power over her, not in just the obvious physical way, but with just the right glance she would feel weak in the knees and it just so happened that he was giving her that glance as she looked up at his chiseled face.

"Hey, beautiful, what are you doing here?" Alex had a sexy smirk on his face.

Reese could feel her reservations with him begin to melt away. She missed his nicely sculpted physique and how he felt against her. Every part of her drunken body ached for him, his hands, his lips, she missed it all. In her inebriated state she forgot about all the terrible things he did to her, she didn't think about how he had cheated and devastated her. All she saw was an incredibly handsome man who was taking her breath away with that seductive look he was giving her. She did not care if he was still with Vanessa or not, she wanted nothing more than to go home with him.

"Hey, I'm just having fun with some of the girls I met from Station thirteen." She flirtatiously ran her hands through her hair putting her head down and then looking back up at Alex.

"Can I buy you a drink?" he asked as he reached his hand out to her.

"Sure," She said without hesitation and a smile on her face.

He firmly held her hand, leading her toward the bar. When they got there he ordered them both whiskey sours. After finding a table to sit at, they sat close, sipping their drinks and leaning into each other. Reese weaved her fingers into his while they laughed and snuggled close. He would lightly kiss her neck before innocently looking at her to see how far she would let him go, knowing damn well she wanted him. Reese danced in her seat when Alex grabbed her hand and pulled her to the dance floor.

"Dance with me," he said weaving through the crowd.

Their bodies danced in sync, Reese pulled him close and pressed herself into him. This was the Alex she fell so hard for, and she danced away any reservations she had about her tipsy decisions. She smiled as he ran his hand down her back, grabbing her butt and pulling her hips into him. In return, she brought her hands up his chest and neck to his hair. He smiled at her while she bit her bottom lip. Her body yearned for him, craving his lips on hers. Turning her body around, she pressed into him. Wrapping his arm around her waist he placed his hand on her stomach and slid it down toward her hips. A rush of tingles hit her body while she reached her hand up placing it behind his head. Their bodies grinded together, neither of them wanting it to end. Dancing the night away they flirted back and forth with their bodies. Neither of them made a move to kiss the other, the mere anticipation of his touch turned Reese on. Her body warm and her mind foggy she flurried with every touch. She wanted Alex. She needed his lips on hers. Stopping in her tracks, she stared deeply into his eyes, unable to hold out any longer.

"Reese, are you okay?" He brushed his hand gently against her cheek.

She bit her bottom lip as she grabbed his shirt and pulled him into her. When their lips touched, Reese felt a bolt of electricity explode throughout her body. Parting her lips she ran her tongue around his, deeply kissing him in the middle of the dance floor. She forced him into her tighter before slowly pulling away biting his lower lip. Her eyes connected with his when she pulled away and the rest of the bar faded away.

"Wanna get outta here?" she asked him tugging on his belt loop.

"Hell yes!"

He took her hand, once again leading her through the crowd. Reese spotted Heather and Gayle from Station 13, she waved and smiled, excited to indulge her craving for him. The girls gave her a thumbs-up as she was whisked away, not knowing who the mysterious handsome man was. Alex and Reese left the bar with their arms wrapped tightly around each other.

Chapter 27

REESE GROANED IN defiance of the morning sun. She reluctantly opened her eyes, unsure of her surroundings. *Where am I?* She was lost in a haze of last night and her now pounding headache. She blinked her eyes rapidly in an attempt to help them adjust, so she could see. Things seemed familiar, yet she still couldn't place them, until she felt his arms wrap around her. He held her so tightly she couldn't move, again. *Oh no, no, no. What did I do? How? I mean, why would I do this?* Her mind was racing and her world spun out of control. She felt his hot, moist breath in her ear.

"Good morning, baby."

"Alex, what happened last night?" Reese was internally panicking.

"You came back to me, baby!" He hugged her even tighter. "I have missed you so much, Reese. I love you!"

Breaking free from his grasp, she quickly sat up in bed. Covering her naked body with a sheet, she rapidly realized what had happened. She continuously ran her fingers through her hair, rubbing her head, trying to find the off switch to the merry-go-round she was stuck on.

"Alex, we're not back together. I need you to one-hundred percent know that. I– I don't–"

"Reese," he cut her off, "please, please just give me a chance. Will you let me make you breakfast? Or, how about I take you to somewhere? We can spend some time together, maybe even work things out."

Although Reese knew there was no "working things out," she felt guilty and caved, as she always had before.

"Fine, Alex but, breakfast only," she reluctantly said.

Alex took her to a small hole-in-the-wall diner they went to frequently when they first started dating. Reese remembered they had the best chocolate chip pancakes she ever had. The hostess sat the two of them in a booth. Reese sat on one side and motioned for Alex to sit on the other side. Her nerves built up within her. *How the hell am I going to get out of this?* She smiled through the dismay, once again forced to suppress her true feelings.

"I've missed you so damn much. I know it's only been less than a week, but it's been horrible without you." Alex intently began his plea.

Reese lowered her head. Somehow she felt ashamed because the last few days for her had been so wonderful and now, sitting in that booth she felt in some way that she has been betraying him the entire time. Her heart raced as the dread built up inside her, unsure of what to say.

"I'm sorry." Reese wasn't sure why she felt the overwhelming need to apologize, but she did anyway.

When the waitress came around they both ordered the chocolate chip pancakes, and in a surprising turn of events Alex actually let her order for herself. *Maybe he is different.* A small part of her became curious if this was in fact the new and improved Alex Cunningham, or if this was just another front. *Can someone like Alex really change?* He was always good at being charming, she knew that much to be true. He was charismatic, handsome, and had a smile that could melt your heart. His chiseled features only enhanced his attractive qualities. Her mind wandered off remembering how they began.

She looked back on their first date at Verrazano's and how he made her feel like a princess. He even showed up with lilies, they were her favorite. His focus and attention were both solely on her; she was, after all, his beautiful date that he noticeably felt proud to show off. She ordered for herself, they enjoyed their wine and their meal all while snuggled next to each other in a booth at the back of the restaurant. The rest of the world seemed to fade away that night. Every time she was with Alex in those first few months she wrapped herself up with him. No one and nothing else mattered. He even told her that he loved watching other men's heads turn as she walked by, because he had what they all wanted, her. Things were perfect, almost how they seemed now. That was until he started forcing her to be wrapped up in him every second of every day even if he wasn't around.

At first Reese liked how protective he was of her. The masculine 'don't touch my girl' or forcing people to apologize to her when they ran into her, she found it endearing and sexy. That was until the night Alex punched a guy in the face for accidently running into her at a bar. She tried to calm him down and reminded him she wasn't made of glass, which was when he first turned his anger on her. That wasn't the first night he hit her, but it was simply the beginning of the downward spiral of fear he instilled deep within her.

In an attempt to not think about the negative, her mind switched back to the night he first told her he loved her, before all the bad, before the bruises and all the pain. Reese had made a run to the drive-thru to get them lunch, and she had called him just to confirm what he wanted.

"Hey, babe, you want a number two, right?"

"Yeah, but can you get me the large soda?" Alex kindly asked.

"Of course, no worries, I'm pulling up to the speaker, see you in a few."

"Okay, babe, I love you! Uh– I mean–"

Alex stumbled over his words, realizing what he had said. Reese knew it was a mistake, and she giggled under her breath at his obvious panic.

"Bye, Alex."

She hung up the phone and ordered their food. As she pulled up, she paid and sat waiting for them to get her order together. She got a text:

ALEX: I'm really sorry. I don't know why I said that. Please don't judge me. 12:35pm

She smiled, amused with how vulnerable he seemed in the midst of his mistake. So, she replied in typical Reese fashion.

REESE: Too late, I already bought the dress and booked the venue for our wedding. You dropped the L bomb, no going back now. 12:38pm

She pulled up YouTube and sent him a link to the song "Going to the Chapel" by The Dixie-Cups. She laughed so hard that she nearly didn't notice the girl trying to hand her their food. Reese got a couple extra bags from the girl at the window, when she got to Alex's house she had ripped one of the bags up to make it longer. She used several bobby pins that she had in her car to place it just right on her head to make a paper bag veil. The other couple bags she made into "flowers," holding the food under her faux bouquet, she walked into his house as if she was walking down the aisle. The look on his face was absolutely priceless. Reese placed the food and drinks on the table and busted up laughing. Alex had a mischievous smirk on his face before he grabbed her in a playful way. They wrestled and he chased her around the living room before finally catching her. When he did he held her, kissing her lightly. He stood like a statue, out of breath. They both were breathing hard looking deep into each other's eyes.

"You know something, Reese, I really do love you. You are incredible." He grinned ear to ear. "I love you."

Reese felt butterflies in her stomach; Alex was everything she ever wanted in a man. Her entire face lit up and although she wasn't convinced it was exactly love yet she smiled and kissed him lightly.

"I love you too."

They passionately kissed and their desire for each other tripled in size within seconds.

Reese hid a smile under the surface of that memory. They used to have the type of relationship others envied, they were happy and carefree. Reese felt a pain in her side, as if her body was trying to remind her of why she left. Images of his rage and abuse flashed in her head like floodgates opening up. He put on a show for her, just long enough to dig his claws in, and once she was stuck in his trap that's when his true self came out.

"I can be a better man for you, Reese." Alex broke through her thoughts. "I've never loved anyone the way I love you."

She nervously smiled at him wondering how many women before her he had used that line on. Reese felt uncomfortable. *What am I supposed to say to that?* Unsure of how to respond, she finished the last of her chocolate chip pancakes. Alex continued to make extravagant promises to change, most of which went unheard.

She cupped her hands tightly around her hot coffee mug. The sting from the heat was a nice distraction from Alex. He remained solid with his plea for redemption. Reese politely listened to what he had to say, all while quietly planning her rejection in her head.

"I want you to know, I ended things with Vanessa." Alex leaned forward with a smile, as if he expected her to jump glee or have some sort of sigh of relief.

"Okay," Reese replied, unwilling to praise him for it. "...and?"

Alex became noticeably frustrated in an instant with Reese, he obviously was fighting back his resentment.

"And... now you can come home." He reached out for her hand. "I know I screwed up and I've learned my lesson. But, it's time for you to stop playing this game, and come home." He was clearly forcing himself to sound sincere.

Reese sat there astonished by his arrogance in the face of his mistake. Emotions swirled in her mind while she put the pieces together: he was telling her, not asking her. He wasn't begging for her forgiveness, he demanding it. He didn't make any relevant promises, he simply ordered her to come home. Not a care in the world for her wants, desires, or even her fundamental needs. Alex hadn't changed and he wasn't going to, he was the same son of a bitch he had always been. The only difference this time was Reese finally could see what he was trying to pull. She scooted herself to the edge of the booth and stood up.

"No." She looked him dead in the eyes. "You don't get to decide for me anymore. Last night was a mistake. I can't do this with you anymore. We're over, Alex. Don't call me. Don't talk to me. As a matter of fact, do me a favor and act as if I don't exist. If you want to be with Vanessa, go ahead! But don't for one second act like you are doing me some sort of favor by breaking it off with her. The real favor would have been you not screwing her in the first place! Leaving is not temporary, it's not me playing a game or teaching you a lesson for your wrong doing. I'm leaving forever. Good-bye, Alex." With her confidence at an all-time high, she left the diner.

After walking off some of her anger for few blocks, she stopped to call Kyra. No answer. *She must still be asleep, Uber it is.* During her ride home she smiled and enjoyed the view out the window. Reese knew that she and Alex were done for good this time, she had zero desire to mend things. She rolled the window down, closed her eyes, and savored the cool and crisp air on her face.

Chapter 28

OVER THE NEXT several weeks, Reese found a way to leave Alex in the past where he belonged. There was a new level of freedom she felt along with an overwhelming happiness. When she was with Alex everything was complicated and, more times than not, ended in a fight. Often she had found that while his hands were around her throat, he wasn't just trying to stifle her breathing, he was desperately trying to suffocate her spirit. It was a sense of smothering she didn't even realize was there until Alex was finally gone and she could open herself up and breathe again. There was a weight lifted off her shoulders and the essence of her true self was finally able to move freely. She enjoyed the nights at Charlie's with everyone, and she even fell in love with her job again. The old Reese began to resurface, the sweet, sassy, and sarcastic personality that everyone missed, including her.

Jess and Nate had gone public with their relationship and decided to move in together. To celebrate they hosted a BBQ and everyone from Station 23 was invited. Reese was specifically told she was not allowed to say no.

"I need you there, Reese." Jess sounded like she was about to panic. "This is the first time Nate and I are doing anything like this as a couple, and everyone from the house will be there. What if it's a disaster? What if we get into a fight?" Jess covered her mouth as she gasped, "What if no one shows up?"

Reese intently listened to Jess and watched her become frantic with worry. She tried her best to suppress the laughter building up as she watched this beautiful woman making a mountain out of a mole hill.

"Hey, Jess!" Reese cut her off mid rant and placed her hands on her shoulders. "It's going to be just fine. You know we all love you and are always here for you. Breathe, girl, I will be there, and so will Kyra. Hell, you know we'll all be there, Jess, but ya have to relax before you have an aneurysm!" Reese joked.

"You're right, of course you're right." Jess took several slow deep breaths.

The BBQ went exactly as planned, they had an excellent turnout from their families, and of course, as Reese said, each person from Station 23 was there. Stump and Chief Gibbs brought their wives, Louie brought his new girlfriend, and Cole brought Ray while Reese brought Kyra. Reese thought about texting Chad Platt, the officer she kissed after leaving Alex but, her gut told her she still wasn't ready. She was kind of enjoying being single, not having to answer to anyone or feel obligated to put effort into someone new, it felt good. She knew Chad was a good man but, she also knew that a new relationship sounded like a lot of work to her, *it's hard to start over... more like exhausting,* she let out a heavy sigh.

The steaks they had won at the Fill the Boot fundraiser were delicious, and the beer was ice cold, and the afternoon carried on effortlessly. Reese sat back and watched everyone talking and laughing. She enjoyed seeing the smiles on everyone's faces but, it only made her miss her parents. She hadn't spoken to them since the day she moved out of Alex's house. *Maybe I should call them? I'm sure they would be thrilled to know I left Alex.* She pulled out her phone and held down the unlock key until the phone flashed to the home screen. The background picture was of Soph, her parents, and her posing in a silly way in front of their home in Texas, she stared at her screen, momentarily reminiscing. Gliding her thumb to her contacts she scrolled through and let her thumb hover over her parent's home phone number. Unable to swipe to allow for the call to go through, she let the screen go dim and finally off. She slid her phone back into her back pocket, arriving at the conclusion that the barbeque wasn't the best place to hash things out with her parents, especially, considering how the last conversation with her dad went. She wasn't sure if she was ready to talk to him yet, so she enjoyed the next several hours socializing with everyone at the party.

The barbeque slowly came to an end, and Reese said her good-byes to those who remained before pulling Jess off to the side. "See, I told you it would all turn out perfect!" She smiled.

"I know. I honestly don't know why I was freaking out. It all seems so stupid now." Jess laughed.

"It's because you love him," Reese gestured toward Nate, "and you wanted everythin' to be perfect. That ain't a crime, girl." Sweetly Reese nudged Jess' shoulder.

"This is why I love you!" She grabbed Reese. "You can effortlessly justify all my crazy!"

"That's what friends are for!" Reese giggled as she let go.

When the sun came up the next morning and Reese was on her way to work, she decided today was the day she would call her parents. Texas was three hours ahead of Washington and Rusty would definitely already be hard at work; Reese wanted to make sure she could talk to both of her parents. *I'll call this afternoon.* She set an alarm on her phone to remind her, since it was easy to lose track of time at work and make it easier to put off.

The day carried on as it usually did with a few calls sporadically throughout the shift. Nothing heart-pounding had happened in a few days but, Reese knew better than to say anything. The last time she mentioned it was quiet around the station their crew ended up with a thirty-car pile-up on highway eighteen. As they all settled in for what seemed to be an easy day the tones went off.

"Ambulance twenty-three, Engine twenty-three, Cardiac Arrest, one-zero-one-nine North Main Street, sixty-year-old male."

They jumped up from their seats and hastily made their way to the units.

"Sixty?" Reese asked. "That's young! My Dad is fifty-nine." She felt a billow of disbelief as she picked up the radio mic. "Ambulance twenty-three responding, can you confirm the age?"

"Copy Ambulance twenty-three responding, it's going to be a sixty, six-zero year-old male. CPR is in progress by family."

"Ambulance twenty-three, copy that."

Reese's mind subconsciously ran down possible factors causing a sixty year-old man to go into full cardiac arrest. She obviously knew that not all sixty year-olds were as active as her dad and some have significant health problems, but not all of them. She kept mapping Kyra to the address while as if on autopilot in the back of her head she continued to think of causes to help her be prepared. It was something she used to verbalize out loud when she was new but now it was automatic and she did it without realizing what she was doing.

They pulled up to the house and were greeted by family members frantically waving their arms in the air. The hardest part of this job sometimes for Reese was seeing people on the worst day of their life. Most family members were scared, confused, and even angry. They could get in your way and not allow you to do your job efficiently and a lot of times their panic could seep into you. In the beginning of her career it was harder to remain calm, and several times within her first year as a paramedic, the family members set the tone for the call. Reese learned pretty quickly that any call went better when she could find the balance between authoritative and compassionate. She was forced to remind herself on a regular basis in the first year that it was not her emergency.

"In here!" the older man on the curb yelled as he flailed his arms around. "Hurry, oh my god! He's not breathing! Hurry, please!"

Reese had only a few rules she lived by on the ambulance because everything else was too unpredictable. Rule number one: DON'T KILL ME! Rule number two: DON'T MAKE ME LOOK STUPID! Rule number three: WHAT HAPPENS IN THE BUS, STAYS IN THE BUS! And last but not least, rule number four: NEVER EVER DO WE RUN!

That last rule was added three years ago when Kyra did a trade with a rookie EMT six months out of school. He was only nineteen but looked no older than twelve, his boyish innocence clearly screamed, rookie. When he walked through the door

Reese rolled her eyes and thought, *I'm going to kill Kyra.* Later that day, they ran their first call together, for a fifty-six year-old woman who was vomiting blood. The woman had vomited around 1800 cc of blood, which was a lot by any standards, by the time they arrived at her house her husband was in a tailspin. Reese calmly knelt down next to the woman asking her how long she had been vomiting the bright red blood that half-filled the large bowl she had in her lap. Blood ran down the sides of her mouth and the smell stung Reese's nostrils; the smells of a gastro-intestinal bleed, or GI bleed, was very distinct.

Reese turned to the "small child" Kyra had left her with and kindly asked him to take the woman's blood pressure. Her partner stood there presumably petrified with fear; the woman did, in fact, resemble something out of a horror movie. She had to snap her fingers in his face to pull him from his petrified trance. He ran, literally, over to their bag where the equipment was to take a blood pressure and then once again ran back to the patient's side. He took her blood pressure by rapidly pumping up the cuff around her arm and then letting the air out so slow Reese was positive she could have re-painted the entire living room before he was done. He then had a look of panic take over his face when he once again had to pump the cuff back up. Reese watched his panic morph into complete fear as he once again released the air, even slower this time, he was noticeably shaking.

"What's the blood pressure?" she demanded.

"Um— This cuff must be broken or something," his voice was quivering and sweat began to bead on his forehead.

"Okay, listen to me, take a breath, what did you get?"

"I— I got... um, eight— um— no— seventy-eight over forty."

Reese knew she had to quickly get this woman out of the house and into the ambulance. She was actively bleeding somewhere in her stomach and her blood pressure was much too low—in short, she was decompensating. The husband re-entered the room with the woman's prescription medications and noticed her partner's panic-driven look.

"What's going on?" The calmness Reese instilled in him quickly vanished.

"Well, sir, your wife's blood pressure is a little lower than I would like it to be, so we're going to get her on the gurney and head over to the hospital." Meanwhile, as Reese calmly explained things to the husband, her partner was literally running all over the living room. "I'm going to take good care of your wife, sir, I promise," she said as she spotted her partner out of the corner of her eye. *What the hell?*

"What aren't you telling me?" the husband demanded as he shoved his coke bottle glasses up into place on his nose. "He's running around like a chicken with his head cut off!" the man pointed at her partner. "You people don't do that unless it's serious."

"He's new, sir, pay no attention to him. That boy is scared of his own shadow. I will make a deal with you, alright? When you see me panic, then you can panic, deal?"

"Deal," the man hesitantly agreed.

When that call was over, not only did Reese rip that kid a new one, but she tacked on rule number four to her previous rules.

"Running doesn't instill confidence, running makes you look incompetent, and running breaks rule number two!" she yelled at him.

Reese wasn't sure why that memory entered her mind as she stepped out of the ambulance on her way to a cardiac arrest, but it made her scoff as she talked to the man on the curb.

"We are coming, hon, do you know what happened?" she firmly asked while she pulled a backboard out of the ambulance and Kyra pulled the gurney.

"No, I don't know! We were all sitting around talking and all of a sudden Russ fell out of his chair!" He frantically replied.

"Okay, hon, thank you, we've got it from here."

"They're right inside the door!" he yelled.

Reese entered the house first with the backboard and their heart monitor in her hands. She saw a woman around her age kneeling over the top of a silver-haired man pumping on his chest. The guys from the engine were the last through the door behind Kyra, Stump immediately ordered Louie to take over compressions. The woman became hysterical once she was removed.

"Oh, Daddy, please! Daddy, please wake up! Dad, you can't die!" She then turned her focus to Reese, her amber eyes fierce. "Save him! What the hell are you doing? Save my dad! Please!"

Reese was squatted down next to the man's head preparing for intubation so they could obtain a secure airway. Everyone had their jobs to do. The heart monitor was connected and showed he was in fact flat-lined, no heart activity. *Damn it.* Turning onto her toes she looked up at Stump. No words were spoken, it was just a look, and Stump knew exactly what she wanted. He swiftly made his way over toward the man's daughter and kindly asked another family member to take her outside to get some air so Reese could work.

They worked hard, pumping his chest to circulate his blood. Reese secured the airway with a tube down his throat and quickly had good air exchange. She then moved on to obtain IV access in his vein and started pushing medications in hopes they would help jump start his heart. They did everything they could that day to save Russel Davis but, unfortunately, they called time of death in the emergency room. *I'm sorry, Russ, I tried,* she stood outside of the room in the ER. Reese was astonished that a man in wonderful physical shape and with no major medical history would just out of the blue die like that. She sat there, down the hallway, watching the daughter hysterically cry when the doctor broke the news to her and her family; dad was dead. It made Reese miss her dad even more.

She pulled her phone from her pocket and walked outside to make her phone call. The line rang several times before he picked up, she wondered if he saw the caller ID and was just as nervous as she was to talk.

"Hello?" Rusty answered.

"Hey, Dad, how are you?" Her voice was low.

"Are you okay, Reese?"

"Well, I'm not, to be honest. Look, Dad, I wanted you to know that I am sorry—"

"Why are you sorry? I should be the one to apologize, honey," he interrupted her. "I love you, Reesey, and I hope you know that no matter what you do, I'll always love you. I just want you to be happy, and frankly, Alex doesn't seem to make you happy."

"Dad, about Alex..." she sighed.

"Yeah?" She could hear a slight panic in his voice.

"I broke up with him." There was a brief silence between them before she continued. "I found out he was cheatin' on me with some girl at his station. I know I should've told you sooner, but I broke up with him shortly after we talked. I never meant to disappoint you, Dad." Her voice trembled. "I'm sorry."

"I'm proud of you, sweetheart." His voice sounded as though he was choking back tears.

"Well, I am officially all moved out of Alex's and I'm actually living with Kyra. You remember Kyra, right?"

"Oh yes, of course I do! Mom and I have always liked her. I'm happy that you are moved out of his house. God certainly answered my prayers by putting you with that crew at your firehouse. They're takin' good care of you, and that makes this old man happy, knowin' his little girl is not alone."

"They're pretty amazing. I have no idea where I would be without them."

Reese felt so much better patching things up with her dad. He was her favorite person in the whole world and she couldn't imagine life without him. They chatted for a while, Reese told him about the call she had just ran and how it broke her heart that, despite their best efforts, they lost the fight to bring him back. He comforted her, they laughed and joked, and Reese told him far more times than necessary, that she loved him. When they hung up, they returned back to their separate lives.

Their shift that day was finally coming to an end and everyone made plans to head out to Charlie's after work.

"Are you coming out to Charlie's tonight?" Reese asked Jess.

"Of course, are you?"

"Yeah, I don't know how long I will be out, though. For some reason I am just exhausted."

"Are you feeling alright?" Jess placed a warm hand on Reese's forehead, feeling no significant temperature difference she dropped her hand back onto her hip.

"Yeah, I'm just worn out. Not really sure why, but before I end up sick I should probably rest."

"Good call," Jess agreed.

They all headed over to the bar after their shift. Louie and Cole had found tables and pushed them together making one big table for everyone to sit at. Reese pulled up the empty seat next to Stump. She leaned over and rested her head on his shoulder. All she wanted to do was sleep.

"You okay, kid?" He asked.

"Yeah, I'm just tired."

"Sounds like you need a shot! Want a whiskey?"

"Make it a double. I'll get the next round."

"You've got yourself a deal!" Stump smiled and gave her a thumbs-up.

When Stump got back with their drinks Reese noticed that he had decided to do a double shot with her. Their glasses clinked together before they shot back the whiskey. She went to the bar moments later and got them a couple of beers. Walking back to the table the shot hit her, an overwhelming feeling of being intoxicated took over as her stomach slightly turned. *What the hell?* Doing her best to ignore the buzz, she sat down and began to nurse her beer.

As the night went on, she felt worse. The room would sporadically start spinning while she sat there. Stump turned to ask her, "Want another beer?"

The mere thought of drinking another beer caused her to feel nauseous.

"Uh— No thanks, I think I'm gonna jet here in a few. I really don't feel good." She pushed her half empty beer away from her.

"What's wrong?" he asked, placing a hand on her shoulder. "Are you sure you're okay?"

"I don't know. My stomach is feeling pretty... blah right now. I hope I'm not getting sick."

"Do you need a ride home?"

"Nah, I'm good. Thanks, though." Reese got up from the table. She quickly said her good-byes and headed out to her car to go home.

She felt dizzy and misplaced when she got into her car, she sat with her head on the steering wheel for a couple minutes. Fortunately, the dizziness finally subsided. She turned the key in the ignition and headed home. Once she was home she felt too exhausted to take a shower, she poured herself into her pajamas and crawled lazily into bed. Typically, she would take some time to wind down by playing games on her phone or just lay quietly thinking about the day but, that night she was asleep before her head hit the pillow.

She had slept so hard that when she forced her eyes opened the next morning, she hadn't moved all night. Glancing at the clock, it was ten in the morning. *Holy crap!* She sat up trying to gain her bearings. The dizziness returned as she got out of bed. Disoriented, she made her way down the hall slowly regaining her balance. The aroma of coffee filled the apartment, but when the smell hit her nostrils, it caused her stomach to roll. The smell became stronger when she turned the corner into the kitchen.

"Want some coffee?" Kyra cheeringly asked, holding out a cup.

"Uh, no thank you." She held her hand over her mouth and nose and quickly walked away.

Grabbing a blanket, she curled up on the couch. She was in a fog, still exhausted, as if she had been carrying around a ton of bricks. Her body ached all over and her nausea seemed to come in waves.

"Damn, are you okay, Reese?" Kyra came around the corner.

"I feel like poop!" lifting her chin to the ceiling to let her nostrils fill with air pushing down another wave of nausea.

"Not to be rude or anything, girl, but you look terrible!" Kyra was full of concern.

"Gee, thanks!" Reese cracked a small smile. "I think I'm sick. Finally have a few days off and looks like I'm going to spend it right here on my trusty couch."

"Maybe it's just a twenty-four-hour thing?" Kyra said, trying to be optimistic.

"God, I hope so."

Kyra sat down on the couch and turned on the television. A commercial was on for a local diner, advertising their famous breakfast. A stack of pancakes were shown with syrup running over the top of them. Reese sat avoiding eye contact with the TV. When she thought her stomach calmed enough, she glanced back at the TV only to see a picture of an egg, prepared over easy, with a fork cutting into the yolk. Her eyes widened as the yolk came running out of the egg, spilling over onto the plate. Her stomach turned and she was forced up off the couch and sent running down the hallway to the bathroom. She barely made it to the toilet before the vomit poured out of her like a volcano. She washed her mouth out and then her hands before walking back down the hallway.

"Well, that was fun," she said sarcastically before she sat down and covered herself up with a blanket. "Remind me not to watch food commercials until this is over."

Kyra chuckled. She tried to conceal her laughter with her hand over her mouth.

"I got you. Next time I'll tell you when it's over."

Reese stuck out her tongue at Kyra, before rolling over and snuggling up with her blanket.

Within minutes Reese was back asleep, out cold. She slept hard and long as her body tried to recoup from the sickness. She slept most of the day away, waking up for only brief periods of time. Kyra made her some chicken noodle soup, but Reese could only eat a small amount and vomited again shortly after. She felt miserable, but she was so thankful that Kyra was there to help her. That night she was in bed by seven, and slept solid for an additional sixteen hours.

When she woke up the next morning her stomach was still queasy, but thankfully it was better than yesterday. After slowly making her way into the kitchen she poured herself some water and grabbed a few crackers.

"How are you feeling?" Kyra asked when she came down the hallway.

"Eh, better, but definitely not great."

"I'll take better, better is good!"

"That is very true. I just feel like I have a blanket of exhaustion over me. I know that sounds weird. You know when you get sick and you just feel wiped out? Like, just walkin' down the hall is a chore."

"Yeah... sure, I guess." Kyra said while she looked at her skeptically as if trying to figure out how Reese got sick and she didn't.

"It feels kind of like that but a hundred times worse." Her voice was hoarse and her throat felt like someone had shoved a red hot branding iron down it.

Kyra sat down on the opposite couch from Reese in an apparent attempt to not catch whatever stomach virus she had, just in case Kyra had, indeed, gotten lucky, and hadn't caught the sickness yet.

"No offense, but I don't want whatever Ebola virus you have." Kyra laughed.

"None taken, you don't want this crap."

"Maybe you feel so tired because you're not eating and you're not able to keep much of anything down, including water. How many times have you thrown up?"

"Yea, maybe, let me think, I honestly lost count after five times." Reese said as she took a small sip of water, "maybe nine or ten?"

"Geez, girl, definitely stay away from me then." Kyra backed away as far as she could on her couch.

Reese was able to keep the water and crackers down all day. Food still didn't sound or smell good, but the crackers seemed to be her best option. She lounged around the house all day, watching movies and sleeping. Her entire four days off were spent recouping.

By the fourth day Reese was not sure why she wasn't feeling back to normal yet. She never ran a fever, she threw up only occasionally and her brain was still uncharacteristically foggy. Unsure of why she felt this way she decided to just grit her teeth and deal with it. Slowly, she started to move around more and accomplish minor tasks like doing laundry and getting her stuff ready for work the next day. With an early bedtime and some chicken soup she hoped that by the next morning everything would be back to normal.

Chapter 29

REESE WOKE UP starving. Usually, she would get ready and grab a quick bite to eat on her way out the door, but this morning her stomach was growling and she couldn't wait.

Rushing into the kitchen she poured herself a large bowl of cereal and devoured the whole thing within a few minutes. She had an irresistible craving for bacon and toast. *Mm, I could really go for a BLT!* She pulled out the ingredients from the fridge. Her mouth watered from the smell of sizzling bacon wafting through the air while she cut up the lettuce and tomato. The bread was lightly toasted, the bacon was extra crispy, and all was ready to prepare the exact sandwich her body craved. Kyra came into the kitchen as Reese finished the final touches on her masterpiece.

"Smells good, whatcha makin'?" Kyra asked.

Reese took a giant bite, relishing in how amazing her creation tasted. She felt incredibly satisfied that she almost didn't hear Kyra.

"A BLT," she muttered with a mouth full of food. "So damn good!"

"Someone is feeling better!" Kyra giggled, "Coffee?"

Reese felt her stomach turn at the smell of the cup that was already brewing in their Keurig.

"No thanks. Just smelling yours is making me sick to my stomach."

She took her sandwich into her room to finish eating. Pulling her uniform out of the closet she started to get dressed in between bites of her magnificent second breakfast. Her stomach was full and happy and completely satisfied. When she pulled on her uniform pants, she became very aware of how they pushed precisely on her bladder and made her urgently have to pee. She feared that if she tried to wait until she was fully dressed to pee she would end up having an accident. *That's odd, I've never felt that way before with these pants,* she thought, rushing off to the bathroom, thankful this time it was not to vomit. She brushed off how bizarre that moment was and went about her morning routine before her and Kyra left.

By the time she made it to work she already felt drained of energy. Dragging herself inside the station, the immediate smell of coffee once again filled her nostrils. *Oh God.* Covering her nose and mouth she immediately made a dash for the barracks in an attempt to escape the aroma. With slow deep breaths she was able to impede her overwhelming need to vomit.

"Morning briefing," Cole said as he poked his head into the barracks.

"Be right there," Reese said with a deep breath.

Walking into morning briefing the stench of coffee was unavoidable. She had never noticed how strong the smell was before. Standing at the back of the room, she decided to sit on the back table, right next to the door, just in case. Ray walked into the room; the smell of his cologne was overpowering, leaving Reese feeling like she could barely breathe. She coughed so hard the vomit crept up and sat at the back of her throat, causing her to run to the bathroom, where she vomited everything up that she had eaten that morning. *What the hell is going on?* She wondered, hunched over the toilet. Now just the thought of bacon caused her stomach to turn. Her mind wandered to how much she hated flimsy bacon; it had to be crispy or not at all. She pictured how her dad liked his bacon and was forced to hunch back over the toilet. Her stomach wrenched, constricting her muscles so hard they cramped, but nothing came out. The door to the bathroom opened when she came out from the stall.

"Hey, Reese, you okay?" Jess asked.

Reese came out of the stall and rinsed her mouth out before washing her hands. She quickly splashed water on her face in a small attempt to help calm her stomach down.

"I don't know, I got this stomach bug this weekend and it just won't let up. The smell of the coffee mixed with Ray's cologne just sent my stomach over the edge, I guess. I mean, I ate for the first time this morning but now it all got flushed down the toilet and I have zero desire to eat anything."

"Kyra told me that you've been sick. Are you going to be able to work?" Jess looked at Reese with uncertainty.

"I'm going to try."

They came out of the bathroom. Reese retreated back to the barracks with flashbacks in her head of how it used to be when she was with Alex.

"Are you not coming to the common room?" Jess asked.

"No, the smell of coffee is too much. I'm just going to go lie down."

"Alright, girl, I hope you feel better."

Reese faintly smiled before turning and walking away. She lay down on the bed and within seconds of her head hitting the pillow she was asleep once again.

She felt as if her body was made of lead as she sunk into the mattress. The world around her was black when she felt herself float into the abyss of sleep. It wasn't until heavy footed steps got louder that she even began to stir. A hand pushed into her numb body bringing her back to the surface of consciousness, immediately feeling agitated, Reese's eyes fluttered open.

"Reese?" Kyra was shaking her so hard the entire bed was moving. "Reese! Wake up!" she began yelling.

Reese groaned resisting the disturbance with every ounce of energy she had left.

"What's going on," she grumbled, barely able to articulate her words.

"Reese! We got a call! Get up!"

Her eyes popped open realizing exactly where she was. Everything was a haze when she stumbled out of the station and to the ambulance as fast as she could. She felt more than groggy. She was barely functioning.

"What's the call for?" she asked fixing her face and hair in the mirror on the visor of the ambulance.

"It's a choking of a two-month-old."

Reese froze, staring at herself in the mirror. The words two-month-old choking rang in her head. She knew she had to pull herself together, but how? The ambulance blasted down the street, the siren screaming at the other cars on the road, racing toward the residence.

"How long was I asleep?"

"Fifteen minutes, maybe twenty."

Reese rubbed her face, trying to wake up.

"That's it? It feels like I was asleep for hours!"

Kyra looked over at her, watching her struggle to wake up. Reese drank small sips of water, blinked her eyes really fast, and even gently slapping the sides of her face a few times.

"I know you feel like shit, Reese, and I'm sure this is a typical new baby, first time mom, and not really choking call. But, you've got to pull yourself together in case it's not."

"I know, I know. I got it, I'm good."

They rushed into the residence to find a young mom crying, holding her small baby up to her chest. The mother was visibly trembling with tears running down her face. Reese was unable to see the child underneath the pink fuzzy blanket she was wrapped up in.

"What's goin' on, sweetheart?" Reese asked with a calm voice.

"I'm not sure," her voice was shaky. "I was feeding her and she started coughing really hard. I think she stopped breathing because her lips turned blue." She sobbed

Reese gently grabbed the baby from her arms and pulled the blanket back to find a healthy two-month-old baby alert and looking around.

"Hey there, beautiful," A sense of relief rolled over Reese, and the infant gave a heathy cry as she took the blanket off of her. "I know, sweet pea, I need to take a look at you." Reese examined the little girl, checking her chest and lung sounds. She then pulled the baby to her chest and cuddled her gently. "Well, Mom, she looks fantastic. Her lungs are clear, she looks happy and healthy. She probably swallowed her milk wrong and some of it got stuck in her throat, but she was able to clear it on her own. Don't worry, it's actually very common. I have no doubt she'll be perfectly fine. We can take y'all down to the ER if you'd like, but I don't think it necessary. But it's up to you, hon."

The mother hesitated, trying to make a responsible decision. Reese turned her focus back to the now sleeping infant. A smell caught her attention—the diaper. The smell of urine and baby powder wafted into each breath. She tried to ignore it but her stomach rolled. Abruptly she handed the infant back to the mother. Reese inconspicuously took deep breaths after wisely backing away from the baby. She was able to choke back her need to vomit and the nausea eventually subsided.

The mother decided to keep the baby at home after calling her mom and asking her advice. In the end, the woman's mother decided to come and stay with her, and help keep an eye on her grand-daughter.

Kyra and Reese packed up their bags and took the gurney and their equipment back out to the ambulance. They put everything away before getting into the front seat of the ambulance.

"You looked a little green in there, are you sure you're, okay?" Kyra asked.

"I'm good." Reese said, not believing her own words.

Reese hoped that if she kept saying she was okay that it would eventually be true. Her nausea was coming at random times and didn't seem to go away. She felt hungry, yet sick to her stomach. None of this made sense to her.

Out of nowhere, as Reese was lost in thought, they hit a large pothole in the road. Reese grabbed her chest.

"What's wrong?"

"I don't know... my boobs are crazy sore."

It hurt again letting them go, and now every small bump in the road caused her breasts to throb.

"Why would they be so sore?" Kyra looked at Reese as if she had the answer but wasn't ready to say it out loud.

"I don't know. Maybe I'm getting ready to start my period and this stomach thing is making it worse?" Reese tried to play it off like it was nothing, although a sense of fear lingered in the possible reality she wasn't willing to admit.

"I guess that's possible..." Kyra hesitantly agreed.

Reese's head was spinning trying to wrap her thoughts around her new symptoms. In another attempt to not face the possible truth, she allowed her imagination to take over. She feared that something more was, in fact, wrong with her. *What if... that night with Alex... what if he hurt me when I was drunk and I just don't remember?*

Once back at the station, Reese took off toward the bathroom where she removed her uniform shirt and lifted her tank top underneath. Indulging in her fantasy, she scanned her body for any new bruising to indicate any kind of internal bleeding. Although, in the back of her head she was confident it had been too long for that scenario to be plausible, she continued to check anyway. Lightly running her hand across her milky skin, she found no marks or bruising of any sort. Feeling stumped, she pulled her tank top down and slowly put back on her uniform shirt. She racked her brain trying to come up with an explanation for what was now happening to her but, nothing outwardly came to mind. Once her shirt was tucked back into her pants she left the bathroom and headed back toward her bed.

"Hey, Reese, do you have a minute?" She turned around to see Stump standing in the hallway just outside of the common room. He had a giant smile on his face, his stance boasting with triumph and pride. "Can you come in here for a sec?" he asked while directing her with his hand out to the side pointing toward the entrance to the common room.

"I don't know, Stump, the coffee smell makes my stomach turn and then I throw up. This stomach bug sucks!" Her face was sullen as she dropped her head down, unsure if it was in fact a stomach virus.

"It's going to be okay, I promise. Can you please just come in here real quick?"

His smile was genuine and Reese felt pretty sure that she could trust him.

"Okay, but if the coffee smell makes me sick you are required to come hold my hair back for me!" she demanded giving Stump a fair warning of what was expected if this didn't go well.

"Alright, deal," he chuckled.

She walked in Stump's direction following him into the common room, holding her breath in hopes to avoid another spout of vomiting. She took short quick breaths. All eyes were on her when she realized the smell of coffee wasn't hitting her like it had before. A hint of curiosity arose. She continued to take slightly bigger breaths, slowly progressing toward a regular inhale and exhale. Still no stench of coffee hit her nose. Scanning the room she noticed everyone intensely watching her. The longer she stood there the more smiles emerged. Her eyes quickly glanced at the coffee station but, there was no coffee in the pots.

"What did you guys do?" Reese exclaimed with delight.

"Well," Stump began, "Jess told us that the smell of the coffee was making you throw up and then Kyra told us about how sick you were over the last four days, so we decided to eliminate the odor that's making you sick." Reese smiled, feeling thankful that her firehouse family would do that for her. "The common room isn't the same without you. So, take a big whiff and make sure it doesn't make you sick."

She did as he asked and enjoyed the faint citrus smell of the detergent they used to clean the coffee pots. When she exhaled a smile illuminated her face.

"It smells fantastic!" she said. "Thank y'all so much! I was *not* enjoying being closed off back in my room like old times."

"We didn't like it either!" Louie chimed in. "Like Stump said, it just ain't the same without you."

With bright eyes Reese pulled up a chair at the table and sat down to read the paper.

Chapter 30

ON HER SHIFT, Reese continued to fall asleep in between calls and even in the rig. Exhausted didn't even come close to describing how she felt. Her feet felt like cinder blocks were strapped to them and every time she moved it drained her even more. Unwilling to admit that the possibility of a stomach flu was becoming more and more unlikely, Reese went about her day trying to convince herself that it would go away. She was so distracted by her own issues she didn't even notice the whispers that the rest of the crew shared with each other about her so-called illness.

Thankfully, it had been an easy shift for them all. Reese's day was filled with either sleeping or puking with the occasional feeling of hunger. When the shift ended she drug herself out to her car and sluggishly loaded her belongings into the back before dumping herself in the driver seat and heading home. During her drive home her phone rang.

"Hey, Soph, it's been awhile!" Reese answered the phone, happy for the unexpected call.

"Hey, yea it has, Reese. How's it going?"

"Eh, I'm trying to get over this stomach thing."

"Oh, no, that sucks! What's wrong?"

"Oh, I don't know, I've been nauseated and throwing up off and on for days now. And I have discovered on this shift, for whatever reason, the smell of coffee makes my nausea worse. My boobs are incredibly sore, how weird is that? Pretty sure I'm going to start my period soon or something. I've just been feeling so exhausted lately like I'm dragging around a thousand pounds of bricks everywhere I go. All I want is to feel better. I'm over it already." As the words came out of her mouth Reese subconsciously put the pieces together. A small part of her has known for a few days now but, since stubbornness was one of her more undesirable qualities, she ignored what she knew deep down, and opted to "play dumb."

There was a pause.

Sophie said nothing except, "Hmm."

"What?" Reese worried.

"Well, when are you supposed to start your period? Are you late?"

Reese thought, but she couldn't remember.

"I think I'm supposed to start within this next week. I can't remember exactly when, though." Reese started counting in her head. "Wait, that can't be right." She recounted, again, and again.

Sophie finally broke her counting.

"All I'm sayin' is that is pretty close to how I felt before I found out I was pregnant with Piper. It won't hurt to at least take a test, Reese."

Reese thought for only a moment before turning her car around and headed to the store.

"Yea, you're right. I really don't think that's it though."

"Is it Ale–"

Reese cut her off before she could finish saying his name. "I'm not pregnant! I'm just going to get a test to shut you up!" Reese yelled defensively. Still not ready to admit that Sophie might be right.

"Okay..." Sophie giggled.

The girls hung up the phone when Reese pulled into the parking lot of CVS. She sat in the car, staring at the wall of the building. *She has to be wrong, there's no way.* Reese prayed, *Lord, please don't let this be happening. Please, please, I'm not ready for this.* She looked up from her plea with God, terrified.

Inside the store she weaved through the isles until she found the section filled with pregnancy tests. Standing like a statue, she could feel the anxiety building up within her. She vigorously shook her head, breaking her from her panicked state. She reached straight out in front of her and grabbed the first box her hand touched. She then proceeded to rush to the front of the store, all while still trying to convince herself this was a waste of time. After paying, she walked out of the glass doors with the test in hand.

During the drive home she turned her music up loud enough to drown out her own thoughts, changing every song that said the word baby, regardless of the origin. She pulled into her parking spot at the apartment, *should I tell Kyra...? Yes, of course I'll tell her, she'll probably laugh. There's no way I'm pregnant.* Brushing off the thought of motherhood, she walked in the door to find Kyra sitting at the table clutching a plastic bag.

"Hey! So on my way home from work Sophie called me, you're going to get a kick out of this! You'll never believe..."

Reese stopped when she noticed Kyra sitting at the table looking down at the bag in her hands with a look of guilt on her face. "Are you okay, girl?"

Kyra looked up at Reese, "Yea, I'm fine. I have something to tell you, but first tell me what Sophie said."

Reese looked at her skeptically before she continued to tell her about her conversation with Sophie.

"So I told her about how I've been stupid sick for the last five days and all the weird symptoms I've had and get this, she told me that's how she felt before finding out she was pregnant with my niece! Can you believe that? And then she tells me that I need to go get a pregnancy test ASAP! I mean, seriously, how ridiculous is that?" The look on Kyra's face was not a look of laughter, but a look of relief. She immediately tightened her grip on the bag in her lap. "That's crazy, right?" Reese said, trying to draw a response of agreement from her.

"Well, it's funny she would say that because that thought came into my head as well. Actually, it came into most of our heads today at the station. I hope you're not mad but, I decided to stop at the store on the way home and picked these up." Kyra dumped out the plastic bag and four different pregnancy tests fell onto the table. "I didn't know which one to get so I bought all the brands they had."

"Oh." Reese was shocked. *Am I the only one that finds this ridiculous?* "Well, I now think you both are crazy, there's no way I'm pregnant."

"The thing is, Jess and I figured it doesn't hurt to make sure. We can just rule this out first. If you aren't pregnant, then maybe you need to see your doctor because there is something definitely going on with your body."

"Alright, fine, if it'll get all y'all off my back, I'll go take it right now."

Reese grabbed one of the boxes off the table and stormed off down the hall to the bathroom, feeling more like she was walking toward her demise rather than her victory. *Aren't babies supposed to be a wonderful thing?* Her mind raced.

She opened the package and stared at the stick, thankful she had to pee again. *Come to think of it, I've been peeing a lot today, way more than normal. What if there is something wrong with my kidneys?* She huffed. *Okay, knock it off, just take the damn test, and rule this out before you begin diggin' your own grave.* She rolled her eyes at herself for even entertaining these crazy thoughts before taking a deep breath, pulling the cap off the test, and peeing on the stick.

She continued sitting on the toilet to make sure it absorbed enough to process correctly. The directions in the box said to wait two minutes before checking it, but Reese didn't need two minutes. She sat in utter disbelief as her eyes watched the stick intensely, it immediately revealed the answer. Two distinct lines, there was no question about it, the test was positive. She was pregnant. She set the stick down on the counter before getting off the toilet and pacing around the bathroom. *How— Well, we certainly know how, Reese, don't we? Oh my God! What the hell am I going to do?* She reluctantly came out of the bathroom with tears building up in her eyes and she held up the stick to Kyra.

"It's positive."

Kyra stood in front of Reese, who was holding the test in her hands, studying the lines as if she was waiting for the result to change. The tears that stung Reese's eyes spilled out and ran down her cheeks.

"Shit! Um, I, uh, I don't know what to say." Although Kyra had a feeling Reese was pregnant, now that she knew for sure, she was obviously shocked.

Reese stood with tears streaming from her face. She had always wanted a family but, definitely not like this. Her fantasy of being a mom wasn't a picture of her alone, and as of lately, not with Alex either. She pictured a loving husband by her side as they brought a child into this world. She fantasized about the Hallmark version of life where she and her husband would get through the first few months together and maybe she would be able to stay home and take care of her family the way her mother did. She stared at the two distinct lines in disbelief, her picture perfect family was crumbling. It was slipping through her fingers like water.

"What am I going to do? What if Alex finds out?" She covered her mouth, completely broken by the idea that Alex wasn't going to be out of her life like she had planned. "He'll hurt my child, he'll destroy it." She placed her hand on her stomach. "But he's the father. He deserves to know, right?" She looked at Kyra. "God, this is a mess! I don't even know how to take care of a baby!" Her breathing became increasingly erratic. "How am I going to do this alone? This isn't how this is supposed to be! My child is supposed to have a loving father, not a monster that I barely survived!"

Kyra placed her hands gently on her shoulders. "I'm not going to act like I even remotely know what you are feeling right now but, you are not alone and you never will be. Just promise me, when it comes to Alex and whether you tell him or not, you won't make any decisions until the dust settles."

"Okay, yeah, you're right." Reese took deep breaths. "I'll let the dust settle but, I don't expect you to sacrifice anything on account of me."

"I wouldn't be sacrificing anything, hon, I would be helping my sister raise my little niece or nephew. You know that you are family here, and at twenty-three. You're not alone Reese."

The word family resonated with Reese as she listened to Kyra ramble on about their crew and their help supporting a baby. It made her miss her parents, her sister, and even Uncle T. Her mind drifted off to think about her grandmother on her dad's side.

Esther Landon was a tough woman in a pint sized-package. Reese and Sophie called her Gran and she fit the description to a T. She was a small woman, barely able to see over the steering wheel of the car, and relatively petite. One would think she was frail and helpless by looking at her, however, she was tough as nails and Reese couldn't help but admire and look up to her. She was always in good spirits and relatively good health for her age by remaining active all of her life.

Remembering Gran, Reese was in disbelief thinking about how incredible she was, Gran never ceased to amaze her, she was strong and agile, and made it a point to put her family first. Gran had raised her dad and his three other siblings alone. Rusty's dad took off when he was still little and although, he would show up randomly in their lives, he never stayed very long. Esther was forced to stand on her own two feet and raise four children alone in an era where that was unheard of. She was looked down upon and ridiculed by those around her and yet, Esther rose to the occasion and went above and beyond for her family. She poured her heart and soul into her kids and raised them the best she could despite the hand she was dealt.

Reese never fully understood the magnitude of Gran's path until now. She stared at the pregnancy test, dwelling on how her life would mirror the woman she admired the most; if only Reese knew just how much she would draw from her and yearn for her guidance.

Even though Esther had her fair share of difficulties in life, she maintained a carefree and upbeat attitude. She always said, "It's not about what happens to a person but, how they're going to handle themselves in the midst of the ugly things life can throw their way." Reese was left wondering, *how could she just pick up and move on like that? How was she just okay with the life she was given?* Having more time to process the results of her test, Reese couldn't help but feel angry, scared, and, most of all, at a complete loss. *Maybe I should call Gran and ask her, where do I go from here?* Esther was now ninety-seven years old, still living in her own home with around-the-clock home health care. Somehow, Reese knew that her Gran was going to become the most important person in her life now that she was expecting.

"Reese, are you listening?" Kyra said bringing Reese back to the present conversation.

"Sorry, yes, I heard you and I truly appreciate everything but, I'm just tryin' to remember how to breathe right now."

Her phone lying on the dining room table began to make noise; it was a text from Sophie.

SOPHIE: *Did you take the test yet? I'm dying over here little sister! 1:30pm*

"Crap, I need to call Sophie," Reese said walking off to sit on the couch and dialed Sophie's number.

The phone barely rang before Sophie answered. "Hey, did you take the test? What's it say? Holy shit, I'm kinda freakin' out over here for you!"

"Yeah, I– um– I'm pregnant." There was a long moment of silence between them. Reese could feel the panic rise-up within her the longer the silence lasted. "Well, say something!" Reese finally shouted into the phone.

"Mom and Dad are going to kill you," Sophie said stifling her laughter.

"I know!" Reese cried. "Soph, I don't know what to do." Tears once again built in her eyes.

"Hey, now, it's going to be okay, Reese, we will figure this out. You know your family will always be there for you, no matter what."

"I know but y'all are two-freaking-thousand miles away! I mean how are all y'all going to really be able to help me?" Reese said, wiping her tears.

"I don't know, Ree, but we will figure this out, just breathe. When are you goin' to tell Mom and Dad?"

"Shit," once again Reese felt a tinge of panic. "I have to actually tell them! I was so busy freaking out I forgot to freak out about telling them too!"

"Breathe, sis, breathe!" Reese forced slow deep breaths as Sophie continued to talk. "I was thinking, maybe I could drive over to Mom and Dad's and be there with them while you tell them over FaceTime. I mean, I can't tell them for you, but I could, at the very least, help calm them down after you do."

"Yeah, that sounds good, I guess." Reese ran her hand over her face. "What am I going to say?"

"You'll figure it out, I'm sure, I need to let you go now, Piper is awake from her nap and will start cryin' soon if I don't go and get her."

They arranged for Reese to call her parents at eight o'clock, Texas time that night, they said their good-byes for now and ended their conversation. Kyra quietly came over and sat next to Reese on the couch.

"Your Station twenty-three family's here for you too, no matter what." She said in a soft and compassionate way, as if she were afraid Reese was going to leave to be closer to her biological family.

Reese smiled laying her head on Kyra's shoulder, happy to just sit in silence. No words could have been spoken that would make her feel better and no amount of reassurance would suffice. Reese just needed the silence to wrap around her weary and aching soul.

When five o'clock rolled around Reese could feel the nervous knot in her stomach; for once in the last five days her nausea wasn't caused by her baby. Reese clinched her phone in her hand, pacing around the living room. She decided to text Sophie to make sure she was holding up her end of the bargain. Reese couldn't do this alone.

REESE: Hey Soph, are you at Mom and Dad's? I'm freaking out! My stomach is in knots over here! 5:01pm

Sophie responded immediately.

SOPHIE: Just breathe, Ree! It's going to be OK and, yes, I'm here. Just pull off the Band-Aid. You'll feel better when you do. 5:02pm

Reese knew that Sophie was right, she was always right. Growing up, more times than not, her sister would warn her or give her words of wisdom as older sisters tend to do, and she, for the most part, was right. Well, except for the time they stole the car, Reese distinctly remembered her being very wrong about that, but in the spirit of "ripping off the Band-Aid" she picked up her phone and pushed the button to FaceTime her parents. The phone rang several times and Reese thought about how much she was about to change their lives with two little words.

"Hi, baby girl!" Maggie answered, her long blonde hair glistening in the kitchen lights. She waved her hand in front of her face. "How are you, honey?"

"I'm okay, Momma, just got off shift this mornin'."

"Sweetie, you look exhausted! Are you gettin' enough sleep?" Maggie's southern twang in her voice always became more noticeable when she was concerned. Her eyebrows furrowed as she drew her face closer to the screen, scrutinizing Reese's appearance to make sure she wasn't seeing things wrong.

"I'm okay. Look, Mom, is Dad there? I really need to talk to you both."

Maggie turned her face to the left and yelled over her shoulder for Rusty to come and talk to Reese. A few moments later Rusty appeared on the screen, while drying his hands off with a dish towel.

"Hey, Reesey!" He smiled into the camera, "how are you?"

"I'm okay, Pop," trying not to let her voice waver and make her parents have cause for immediate alarm.

"We sure do miss you! Sophie is here with Piper, they decided to swing by and visit. Paul's out of town until Friday workin' on a job in Oklahoma. I tried to get her to just stay with us tonight but she's stubborn, just like her mama," he joked.

Sophie started yelling off camera from another area of the house. "Daddy, I told you, I'm used to Paul bein' gone."

Although Reese couldn't see her she imagined her sitting on the couch rolling her eyes at their father.

Paul was the man who swept Sophie off her feet and became her husband shortly after meeting each other four years ago. They had Piper about five months ago when Sophie was rushed into emergency surgery for a C-section when her placenta tore away from the uterus wall, and had Piper six weeks prematurely. Reese used a few of her vacation days once Piper was able to go home. She had only held her niece a few times in the three days she was able to take off work.

While Sophie and Rusty argued about Paul being gone, Reese realized just how much she truly missed her family but, she was terrified to tell them she was pregnant. *Rip off the Band-Aid,* she thought, trying to ramp up the courage in her head.

"Hey, you guys!" Reese cut in waiting for a brief second of silence to interject. "Mom, Dad, I have something to tell you."

Both Rusty and Maggie abruptly stopped talking and turned their attention back to Reese with a look of concern on their faces.

"Sorry, sweetie," Maggie said "what's going on." She said, both Rusty and Maggie now patiently waiting for the news with smiles on their faces.

"Well, I want y'all to know that I love you and that I'm so very sorry. I didn't mean for this to happen, it just kinda did and, I hope that y'all can forgive me." Reese was starting to feel a little panicked.

"You're scaring us, kiddo," Rusty said, worry lines appeared on his face.

Reese looked down and took a deep breath. *Just rip the Band-Aid off.*

"I'm– Uh–Well, I'm pregnant..." Her parents sat on the other end of FaceTime, their smiles had faded and both of their mouths were hung slightly open. The only way Reese could tell FaceTime didn't freeze the connection was the emphatic blinking of disbelief in her parent's eyes. "I– Uh– I just found out today, I've been sick for like a week and Soph..." she tried to break the awkward silence.

"Sophie knew!" Maggie screamed, cutting her off. "You knew about this?" Maggie, still yelling, turned her focus back to Reese. "How could you have let this happen? What were you thinkin'?" Reese fought back the sweltering sting in her eyes. "Rusty, don't you have somethin' to say about how careless your daughter has been?"

Rusty turned his face off camera, he couldn't even look at Reese, and now the tears were streaming down her face.

"No," he said before getting up out of his chair and walking away.

Maggie was still yelling in shock and disbelief, she was yelling at Rusty for walking away, and yelling at Sophie for not telling her.

"I'm sorry," Reese whispered before putting her head down. "I never meant for any of this to happen."

"I was worried this was goin' to happen," Maggie confessed as if she didn't even hear Reese's apology. "I was worried he would suck you back in somehow."

Reese kept quiet as her mom vented out loud. There was still no sign of Rusty. Reese could hear the faint sound of the screen door open and close and figured he was outside asking God to show him how to still love her. Reese felt more knocked down by her father that day than anyone else. Maggie could yell until she was blue in the face, as much as that sucked, Reese felt okay because at least Maggie was saying something, however, the fact that Rusty said nothing made her feel much worse. The sheer disappointment on his face was enough to send Reese in a downward spiral of regretting ever making the call.

Maggie little by little started to calm down. Her yelling regressed to stern talking and then finally to normal. Reese mindlessly listened to her talk. *She looks as scared as I am.*

"Do you have any idea how hard this is goin' to be?" Maggie asked her as sincerely as she could. "How drastically your life is goin' to change? Have you even thought about any of this?"

"I have no doubt it'll be the hardest thing I've ever done, Momma, but this terrible situation is not this baby's fault."

Maggie lowered her head, as if she knew that Reese was right but, unwilling to accept it quite yet.

"I need to let you go," Maggie said.

"Um... okay... I love..." Maggie ended the call before Reese could finish, not getting the reassurance she needed from her parents, she plunged into depression causing her to sob drawing her knees to her chest and holding onto the only thing she could, herself.

Chapter 31

THE NEXT MORNING Reese woke up before her alarm. She had laid there most of the night tossing and turning, replaying last night's phone call in her head. Her father's undeniable discontent and rejection of her left yet another gaping hole in her heart, much like the one he had left when he yelled at her to leave Alex. Reese knew Maggie would need some time to calm down before they could talk and hash things out in a more productive manner. Reese also knew that it would probably be a long while before that would happen. She felt an overwhelming desire to speak to the one woman who just might be on her side, besides Sophie. Her phone brightened the dimly lit room from the street light that stood near her window. *It's 4 o'clock here, so that means it's 7 o'clock there,* she scrolled through her contacts for Gran's number.

The phone rang several times before she was kicked to voicemail. The automated message ran through the fact that Esther was not available and to leave a message after the beep.

"Hey, Gran, it's Reese. I really need to talk to you about somethin'. I kinda feel like you're the only person who'll actually understand what's happenin'. I miss you and I love you! Please call me back, even if Dad called you and you're mad at me too. Please, I'd like to hear from you. I Love you."

Reese hung up the phone and lay on her bed staring at the ceiling. *What if the test was wrong?* She sprang up and out of bed, grabbed all of the pregnancy tests off the dining room table, and rushed off down the hallway. Locking herself in the bathroom with a large glass of water she took all the tests, one after the other. Each test made the reality of her pregnancy more concreate.

"Reese?" Kyra pounded her hand against the bathroom door. "Are you okay?"

All of her hopeful glee must have woken up Kyra. Reese opened the door, holding all of the tests in her hand.

"I thought maybe it was a false positive and then things can go back to normal... My parents could stop hating me... and I could stop feeling like the biggest disappointment in their lives. But, it turns out five tests later," she put her head down, "I'm still pregnant."

Kyra wrapped her arms around her. "It's going to be okay, honey."

"Yeah, I guess."

Reese walked past Kyra and into her room, she sat down on the side of the bed feeling defeated and once again nauseated. While she sat staring at the wall her stomach turned and she took off running for the bathroom. Vomiting was becoming more and more a part of her daily routine. Now that she knew for sure she was pregnant it was time to embrace what that entails, vomit and all. She emerged from the bathroom after having to brush her teeth twice, vomiting once more because of the toothpaste; she headed back to her room. She lay in bed until 5:30 am and sent off a quick text to Gran, wondering why she had not called back yet, something not at all like her.

REESE: *Gran, its Reese. Please call me when you can. Love you. Xoxo 5:31am*

Now that Esther had in-home care, the ladies would help read texts to her and reply which made communication with her easier at times. Reese peeled herself out of bed for the fourth time that morning so she could pee.

"Ugh!" Reese grunted while walking into the bathroom. She heard the muffled sound of laughter coming from Kyra's room. "It's so not funny!" Reese whined.

Kyra poked her head out of her bedroom door. "Yeah, it kinda is!"

"I really wish I had something to throw at you right now." She sarcastically taunted. Reese was only half kidding; knowing damn well that had she actually had something to throw that it would have went flying straight at Kyra's head.

"You love me!" Kyra added, sticking out her tongue before quickly ducking back into her room.

Back out from the bathroom, Reese went into her room and pulled down her uniform from the closet. As she got dressed she decided to not tell anyone about her pregnancy, she needed her parents to talk to her first. She knew she could only handle fighting one battle at a time, and right now her focus was on how she was going to mend things with her parents. Buttoning her shirt, Reese already felt mentally and physically exhausted and she hadn't even left the apartment yet.

Walking into the station the smell of the coffee was strong and made her stomach turn. The crew from the shift before them must have made their morning brew, which consequently undid everything Stump had accomplished the shift before. A silence engulfed the common room as her shift examined her face when she walked by, and they promptly noticed, the coffee was still a problem. All she wanted to do was hang out with everyone, and now she couldn't stand the smell of coffee, one of her favorite things. It was the one thing that brought them all together in the common room and now she was repulsed by it. Sluggishly walking to the barracks, she sat on her bed, with her knees drawn up to her chest, trying to figure out her next move.

"Why are you sitting in here?" Jess asked as she sat down next to her.

"The smell of coffee apparently doesn't agree with me anymore." She turned and looked at Jess. "Have you ever had a plan, and then a giant wrench got thrown into the middle of it? Like you make this choice to be happy and move on and then *boom*, curveball! And now no one is speaking to you and everyone is angry."

Jess sat down next to her on the bed with a look of slight understanding on her face and a tight lip smile of concern.

"The boys are cleaning out the coffee pot so you can come back into the common room soon, and no one is mad at you, love."

"Oh yes they are. I took the plan that I had for my life and set it on fire. Have you ever done that?"

"Umm, well... I've had things not go according to plan but, nothing I couldn't handle." She reached over and swept the hair off Reese's face, before prying for information. "Do you want to talk about whatever's bothering you?"

"Why bother? Apparently, I'm just a disgrace and I really can't handle any more people mad at me at this point."

"Reese, I won't be mad at you, or scold you in any way. I just want to be here for you, we all do."

Reese lifted her head and looked at Jess. All she wanted was to tell them all what was going on and let them all gather around her and help hold her up, but she irrationally feared that they wouldn't.

"You can tell me, Reese, its okay. I'm on your side." Jess reassured her.

Rip off the Band-Aid Reese and just tell her. "Can you keep it a secret? I mean a major secret."

Jess's curiosity was evident in her excitement she could no longer hide.

"Of course I can, spill it."

"I– I'm pregnant." Reese lowered her head.

"Oh, my God, that's so exciting, congratulations, girl."

Reese looked at Jess, confused by her reaction. No one else had told her congratulations or praised this life-altering news in any way.

"Look, I know this isn't ideal, I get that but, let's focus on the good for just a second. You're going to be a mom! You're going to have this tiny, perfect human, and they are going to love you in a truly unconditional way! That's awesome!"

Reese smiled. She had not thought of it that way yet. She was too focused on her overwhelming fear of the unknown to remember that having a baby *is* exciting, no matter the origin, and that everything will work itself out in the end.

"Jess, I think you're absolutely right! I've been lookin' at this all wrong! Sure, this baby was unplanned but, it's definitely going to be a blessing!" Her excitement came to an abrupt halt as the thought of Alex crept into her head. "But what am I going to do about Alex?"

"I need you to listen to me very carefully." Jess turned to face Reese, her look unfaltering and stern. "For the sake of your child, Alex does not need to know. He will ruin this little one and do whatever he can to destroy you and a happy life!"

"I know." Reese said feeling overwhelmed and scared.

"It's simple. You had a one-night stand with someone and he doesn't want anything to do with the baby, so you're going to do it yourself. Alex doesn't need to know the baby is his."

Reese thought for a few minutes. The plan sounded good but, she started to feel extremely guilty. Alex was the father of this baby. *Doesn't he deserve to know?*

"I've gotta think about it. I'm not tryin' to make any major decisions right now. I'm so scared, I have no idea how to do this, especially alone."

"I know, it's smart to take your time and try to relax."

Jess got up and walked out of the barracks. Reese decided to head out to the rig and start her check off. She drifted through the equipment, bags, and cabinets in silence. Once she was done she stepped out of the back doors and onto the back step.

"I was coming to help you." Kyra said with an apologetic look on her face.

"No worries," Reese shrugged her shoulders stepping off the back step. "It's all done." Without stopping Reese flashed a quick smile and walked right on by.

She slowly made her way back inside the station. The stench of coffee was almost nonexistent. *Thank God!* She leaned up against the doorway of the common room, glancing over at Jess standing there smiling at her.

"Come on in, Reese, the guys just got done cleaning out the coffee pots for you."

Jess waved her hand toward the coffee maker as if she was Vanna White. It was cleaned out and turned off. They all nervously smiled at Reese who stood there with the biggest smile on her face.

"Thank y'all so much," she said with excitement but it quickly dissipated as she realized this was not going to go away in a few days. The guys had no idea that they would be giving up coffee for the next nine months. Her face turned grim at the realization that she would once again be banished to lying in her bed. She had successfully cut Alex out of her life, and yet a part of him was still controlling her. "I truly appreciate what all y'all do for me, but I don't know how long this'll go on for. Y'all shouldn't have to give up your coffee for me."

"Don't be silly, Reese," Jess said. "It's the least we can do for you right now." She winked at Reese.

Reese took a few more steps into the room, examining all the smiling faces awkwardly staring at her. She then turned her focus back to Jess who was fidgeting with her hands and standing there nervously. *Why are they all staring at me?* Her eyes narrowed, scrutinizing their faces. They all looked as if they knew something but were not allowed to say anything.

"Oh, my God Jess, you told them?" Reese scowled at Jess. "How could you?"

"Hey, before you get mad," Jess threw her hands out in front of her. "I simply said the smell of coffee is still making you sick with your stomach bug, and suggested we turn it off and clean it out again and everyone agreed. Then Cole said, 'Maybe she's knocked up, my sister couldn't handle the smell of coffee when she was pregnant.' And I said nothing. Before I knew it they were all commenting on how they thought the same thing since you got sick. When they all turned and looked at me, I guess the look on my face gave it away. That's when they all kind of ganged up on me. I'm really sorry, girl."

Reese suspiciously looked at Jess, unsure whether to believe her or not. Once she took her focus off Jess and looked at the others staring at her she noticed Stump nodding his head ever so slightly as if to back up what Jess was claiming.

"Okay, you suck but... I believe you." She turned to look at everyone. "I'm glad y'all know, but please, keep this in house. I can't stress that enough. I don't need Alex finding out."

Everyone agreed to keep her secret before they all stood up one by one congratulating her. She was showered with hugs and kisses on the cheek. The guys told her they would do all the heavy lifting for her from now on, and they refused to take no for an answer.

"I'm not a fragile glass doll, guys, I won't break. I might puke on you, but that would be out of pure love," she joked, unwilling to admit she feared they would look at her as weak.

Stump slowly came over to her and Reese caught a glimpse of him motioning her outside. Her stomach turned into knots worried that as her 'big brother,' he was going to be angry with her like her parents were. She nervously shoved her hands into her pockets before following him outside to the bay where the truck, engine, and ambulance sat in the garage of the station. Uneasy she stood there face to face with Stump and shifted her weight back and forth, unable to stand still.

"Are you feeling okay?" Stump asked while he reached his hand out and placed it on her shoulder.

"Huh?" she said, confused by his endearing behavior.

"Well, I figured this would be a lot emotionally for you to handle and I just wanted to make sure you're okay. When did you find out?"

Reese felt that all too familiar pain in her eyes. She was tired of crying and yet she constantly felt on the verge of breaking into a million pieces. She put her head down to break eye contact with Stump and gave herself a few seconds to regain her composure.

"I'm okay." She practically choked on the words as they left her mouth.

"Don't give me that generic bullshit." He removed his hand from her shoulder and crossed his arms. She lifted her head up, forcing herself to look at him. "I know you're not okay, Reese, and saying it over and over isn't going to just magically make everything good. Talk to me."

"Alright, Stump, you really wanna know? Well, I've thought I shed all the tears of sadness and fear out of me then I found out I was pregnant and I am pretty sure I've cried more in the last twenty-four hours than I have in my entire life. My sister helped me tell my parents last night and my dad couldn't even speak to me, let alone look at me, and now my mom on the other hand, screamed at me for about twenty minutes before she hung up on me as I was saying I love you. I tried calling Gran and she hasn't called me back either, so basically my whole family hates me except my sister and I'm carrying a child fathered by the devil himself, so no, Stump, I'm not fine." Reese instantly felt a sense of relief she hadn't felt since she learned she was pregnant. She was able to get out exactly what was happening and how she felt and, even more, admit out loud she was not fine. "Thank you," she said to Stump who stood there in front of her with a faint smile on his face.

"Feel better?"

"I do, actually," she said. "I didn't realize how much all of that was weighing on me."

"None of this is easy, Reese, but you have to be honest with those of us who love you. Big brothers are supposed to be there for their little sisters no matter what, and even more so, I will be there for my little nephew."

"What do you mean nephew?" Reese laughed. "What if it's a girl?"

"Nope, no way!" He placed his hand on her stomach. "This little guy is going to be the future Captain of Engine twenty-three, plus I have enough girl drama with my two daughters." He whispered to her belly, "Please don't make Uncle Stump go crazy!"

They both laughed, and before she knew it her tears of sadness that were building up behind her eyes were gone.

When they came back into the common room Reese looked around basking in the outpouring of love and support that surrounded her. She felt incredibly thankful for the men and women that she worked with; they gave her the support she didn't get from her family. Although she understood her parents' lack of enthusiasm and the overwhelming fear they must have felt about the situation, she just wished that they would have stopped and thought about what their daughter was going through and what she emotionally needed from them. She needed them to wrap their arms around her and love her in spite of her less than ideal situation.

Reese was now incredibly glad that her secret had been revealed to her station family but, what she didn't realize was, that secrets always have a way of coming out and spreading whether you want them to or not. All it takes is one person, the wrong person, to overhear a private conversation to unravel everything.

In the midst of her happiness she thought of Gran. *It's not like her to ignore my calls.* She pulled out her phone and found her name. Once again the phone rang and rang with no answer. When the voicemail came on Reese hung up but, within seconds her phone began to ring. She sat for a moment contemplating whether to answer it or not when her mother's name popped up.

"Mom, please, if you're going to yell at me again save it for later. I can't do this again right now."

"Reese." Maggie's voice was low and sorrowful. "I ain't callin' to yell at you, baby, but I ain't callin' with good news either." Fear crept up within Reese. "It's about Gran, sweetheart." Maggie tried to stifle her sniffling while Reese's heart began to race. "She was rushed to the hospital in the ambulance around three-thirty this mornin' with her heart actin' up."

"What do you mean her heart?" Reese's tone was urgent, and the commotion in the common room where she was standing abruptly stopped.

"Well, baby, the doctor said somethin' about congestive heart failure but I'm not sure what that means."

"Does she have fluid in her lungs?"

"I think so. They also gave her some sort of medication, and put a tube thing down her throat."

"They intubated her?" Reese's mind was now going a hundred miles an hour in a whirlwind of heartache and disbelief.

"Yes, they did. The doctor said somethin' about a DNR."

"It's a Do Not Resuscitate order; I know Gran filled one out when they put her pacemaker in three years ago. Did the doctor say what her DNR says?"

"I'm not sure. We got here about two hours ago and he told us some things but, I don't really understand all that medical talk like you do." There was a brief pause. "Oh wait, the doctor's comin' in right now."

"Mom, put me on speaker."

Reese could hear the movement of multiple people in her Gran's room and when the doctor walked into the room his presence was known by the silence that fell around them.

"Hi y'all I was told that y'all had questions."

He had a thick southern accent and yet confidence rang through his voice loud enough to hear through the phone. Reese swallowed her emotions and her overwhelming need to vomit before she spoke.

"Hey, yes, sorry, I'm the one with questions. I'm a paramedic but I live in Washington so obviously I can't be there at the moment. My mom just called me to tell me that my grandmother was brought into your facility around three-thirty this mornin', is that right?"

"Yes, ma'am."

"Alright, how long has she been in the medically induced coma?"

"Well, her breathin' was so shallow and she wasn't movin' much air. She started to panic which made things worse, as ya know. She was given the medications to sedate her around four o'clock."

"Okay, now her DNR, what are the specifications she has?"

"She wanted comfort measures only. We only intubated her to help keep her comfortable, but a chest x-ray revealed that her lungs are sixty percent filled with fluid and the tube has some pink froth comin' up. We've been suctioning her but without major interventions she has only a few hours left."

"Well, I know that if she signed a DNR for comfort measures only, she wouldn't want any major efforts made. What are the options about the tube? Do y'all pull it and just keep her comfortable then?" Reese felt her mind fill with grief but she shoved it down knowing that she would have to help make this decision.

"Yes, if y'all decide to honor her wishes she'll be extubated and placed on morphine to keep her comfortable."

"That's what she would've wanted. Can you give me a few minutes to talk to my parents and we will have an answer for you?"

"Of course, ma'am, for what it's worth I'm truly sorry."

"Thank you." Reese's voice fell to a whisper.

The doctor left the room when Rusty came on the phone.

"Do you think we should honor her wishes?"

"Daddy, as much as I hate to say it, I do, I think we should let her go, it's what she would want if she could talk. I know this is hard but she's lived a full life of ninety-seven years. The reality is that even if they do everything they can to save her, her body is tired and old. She has had a wonderful life but it's time to let her go."

Reese could hear sniffles coming from the other end of the phone and she sat in silence continuing to fight off her own tears of sorrow.

"Okay, sweetheart, we'll let the doctor know," Rusty said through his tears.

They hung up the phone and Reese felt her world begin to spin. The only woman who could possibly understand what she was feeling was unable to talk and would be dead within a few hours. Gran and all of her wisdom would be leaving Reese in her most immediate time of need. A feeling of guilt came over her. *I am worrying about me while she is the one dying.* The guys at

23 gathered around her and held her as she allowed her sorrow to swallow her whole.

About an hour later, Maggie called Reese and asked her if she wanted to say good-bye to Gran. When she agreed, Maggie told her to hang on so she could walk over to the bed and hold the phone next to Esther's head.

"Hey, Gran." Reese's voice was coarse. "I just wanted you to know that I love you so much. Thank you for bein' the most amazin' grandma a girl could ask for. I don't know if Dad told you, but I just found out that I'm pregnant. I wanted so badly to hear your voice and your incredible words of wisdom." Unable to hold back more tears within her, tears fell from her eyes. "I'm scared Gran, terrified to my core actually, and I don't know how to do this alone, I don't know how I am going to do this without you in my corner. Mom and Dad are so disappointed with me and I'm sure there's a part of you that feels the same way but I want you to know that no matter what, I promise to strive to follow in your graceful footsteps as a single mother. Thank you for all of the wonderful memories of potato pancakes at Thanksgiving and teaching me how a woman can be strong and beautiful all at the same time. You're a one in a million, Gran. Can I ask you one favor, okay? Can you please keep an eye on us all from heaven? I love you."

Reese was being held up by Stump and Louie when she broke down hysterically crying. Stump reached over and grabbed the phone from her hands. He hung up the call while Louie held Reese and her tears soaked his shirt. The minutes on the clock seemed to slow down as they passed. Reese held her phone in her lap waiting for the dreaded phone call. She not only mourned the loss of her gran, but she also mourned the loss of the alliance that she so desperately needed. She knew this day would come eventually, and that Gran could not live forever but, she yearned for her understanding and insight. Her stomach growled for Gran's potato pancakes and berry cobbler and although she knew Gran was not immortal, Reese was not ready to say good-bye.

Esther Landon passed away that afternoon at 2:13 pm.

Chapter 32

REESE WENT HOME early from work and decided to take the next couple of days off and fly home. She found a good price on a round-trip flight into Dallas. Purchasing the ticket, she felt grief choke in the back of her throat. She pulled her suitcase out from under her bed and unzipped the zipper, immediately feeling incredibly nervous to see her family, so nervous, in fact, that she contemplated canceling her flight three different times. Once her suitcase was packed and ready to go she placed it by the door and arranged for an Uber to pick her up and drive her to the airport.

While she waited, Reese called her doctor and made her first OB appointment for when she got home. Somehow, making that appointment made the reality set in more. She was going to be a mother. Looking to the heavens she talked to Gran.

"I hope I make you proud, Gran. I know you'll always have my back up there." Water welled up in her eyes. "God, I miss you so much already."

Her flight was set to leave at seven o'clock that night. She scheduled for the Uber driver to be there roughly two hours early to ensure that she would arrive with plenty of time before boarding. Once she heard the sharp honk of the horn, alerting her that the driver was there, she hastily made her way toward the car. During the drive she sat staring out the window, thinking about Gran and how much she missed her. When they arrived at the airport the driver helped her unload her small carry-on suitcase. She tipped him and headed off through the entrance of the airport.

People whirled around her as if she was moving in slow motion. Presumably, they were on their way to their business trips or their vacations. Reese blankly stared ahead feeling nauseated at the smell of people's feet as they removed their shoes to go through the metal detector. It took her only a few seconds to find her flight and gate. *Made it with forty-five minutes to spare*, she thought, wishing she could waste her time drinking overpriced beer at the lounge next to her gate. Instead she decided to find a seat and pulled out the book, What to Expect When You're Expecting, that Kyra bought her in the store that morning. Reese mindlessly flipped through the pages and scanned some words, charts, and diagrams. The time passed quickly once Reese decided to commit to actually reading the book rather than dancing around it like it was the plague.

She boarded the plane and resumed her intense reading. Her eyes widened as she read about possible side effects pregnancy can have on your body. Swelling was expected to happen pretty much everywhere. *Say good-bye to your ankles!* But the part that scared her the most was the possible complications. Even though she already knew about this stuff as a paramedic, she didn't know about this stuff as a mom. Reese quickly closed the book, resting the back of her head against the seat, not ready to dive into the many problems that could occur.

"First baby?" she heard a sweet voice say.

Reese turned her head to see a petite old woman sitting across the aisle from her. She had a small frame that resembled Gran in so many ways. Reese stared at her in shock at how much they looked a like. Her gaze lingered on the woman until the awkwardness became palpable, pulling Reese from her trance.

"Oh sorry, yes, I just found out that I'm pregnant," she said with a faint smile.

"How exciting!" the woman exclaimed. "You and your husband must be thrilled!"

Reese said nothing but a slight grimace flashed on her face at the word husband. No matter how much she tried to hide it, the woman noticed.

"Did I say something wrong honey?"

"It's not you," Reese tried to reassure her. "It's me. I'm not married. My ex was not the best person— he was pretty scary actually, so I ran. I just found out that I'm pregnant." Reese dropped her head.

"Oh honey, well, good for you!" the woman said catching Reese off guard. "It's not an easy thing to live through or heal from, but I also know it takes a strong woman to leave like you did, and an even stronger woman to not go runnin' back now that you're pregnant." The woman placed her hand on Reese's and continued. "My sister did what you're doing except she had one child, my nephew, who was only two years old at the time. She ran in the middle of the night. Her husband used to beat the snot out of her and I had written her so many letters encouraging her to run. He had moved them to Utah shortly after gettin' married and I was all the way in Texas. In my letters, I sent her small amounts of money and endlessly begged her to leave and she finally did. She saved all the money I had given her and bought two train tickets to Texas. About a month after they got here she found out she was once again pregnant. My husband and I helped her raise her kids while she worked her butt off, but you know what? She was one heck of a mother and her kids loved her so incredibly much."

Reese felt her jaw literally drop as the woman continued talking about how incredible her sister was and she felt beyond flattered that this woman would even remotely compare Reese to her sister. Reese didn't feel incredible or strong, in fact, she felt more broken and lost than ever. The next four hours passed quickly while Reese talked to her new friend. They talked about life and Reese's job, they laughed, and Reese fought back the occasional cluster of tears. When they exited the plane at Dallas airport they stood in the lobby of the gate and the woman turned to Reese, holding her in a long and much needed embrace.

"Lean on your family sweetheart, and everything else will work itself out. Our good Lord doesn't make mistakes, darlin'"

"Thank you." Reese wanted to say so much more to the woman but she was rendered speechless by how amazing it was to feel like Gran had sent her this wonderful stranger.

She pulled into the driveway of her parents' house in the small compact rental car. She sat in the car for a few minutes as the engine idled. Butterflies formed once again in her stomach and her nerves took over. Her hands were shaking and her heart raced, this was the last place she wanted to be. The last conversation she had with her parents, Maggie was yelling at her and Rusty couldn't hide the clear disappointment he felt.

"Reese? Is that you?" Maggie yelled from the front porch. "Rusty! Reese is here!" she exclaimed running down the steps to greet her. This was not the welcome Reese had anticipated but, she got out of the car and let Maggie throw her arms around her and hold her tightly. "I love you so much, sweetheart!" She lowered her gaze and placed her hand on Reese's stomach, pausing for a moment... "And I love you too, nugget."

Reese stood there in shock, unsure of what to make of her mom's reaction. *What's happening?* She had expected the cold shoulder, she was ready for Maggie to yell and lecture her on how incredibly stupid it was to get pregnant in this day and age by yourself. She kept trying to figure out who the woman was standing in front of her and what exactly she did with her mother. Rusty came strolling out of the house, his greeting was much less enthusiastic. He walked over, kissed Reese on the forehead, and grabbed her suitcase.

Once Reese got her things settled she came out of her room to find Sophie and Paul sitting on the couch in the living room with her niece Piper. Reese gave Sophie a quick hug before scooping Piper up in her arms and showered her with kisses. Piper was now a healthy weight. She was even chubby now and had a few rolls on each leg and beautifully plump cheeks that were simply irresistible. Reese held Piper in her lap while the five of them shared memories of Gran with laughter and wonderment.

The next morning Reese woke up and forced her exhausted body down the hallway and into the kitchen where Maggie was standing at the stove. She wore a white apron while stirring a large wooden spoon in a big pot that steam poured off the top of.

"Whatcha makin'?" Reese asked, astonished that food actually smelled delicious.

"Oatmeal," Maggie smiled. "It'll be done in about two minutes."

Reese pulled the orange juice from the fridge and gave her a Mom a quick kiss on the cheek before pulling two glasses and two bowls down from the cabinet. Reese poured the juice and grabbed spoons. It wasn't until she was scooping her oatmeal that Maggie broke the silence.

"I have to tell you something," she confessed.

"What's up?"

"I made an OB appointment for you today."

Reese looked at Maggie in disbelief, feeling pretty confused. Maggie clasped her hands together in excitement while Reese was left speechless.

"I wanted to be there for the first ultrasound appointment. I hope that's okay."

"Um– Wait, what?" Reese fumbled over her thoughts, trying to make sense of her mom.

"Look, sis," Maggie grabbed her hand, "I know your dad and I didn't handle things right when you first told us but, we're tryin' to handle them the right way now. We're just as scared as you are. Can you please forgive us?"

Relief overwhelmed Reese, she smiled up from her oatmeal, "Of course, Momma, I love you guys." Reese leaned over and hugged Maggie. "I'm just sorry that I've turned out to be such a disappointment to you both." Reese pulled away, lowering her head to the ground, forcing the words out.

"Don't you ever talk about yourself like that again, do you hear me!?" Maggie placed her hands on each side of Reese's face, lifting her head. "No matter what, we will always be proud of you and Sophie." Maggie smiled and hugged Reese again, even tighter this time.

Chapter 33

MAGGIE AND REESE showed up at her first doctor's appointment for the baby. They both sat nervously in the waiting room and Reese clenched her hands so tightly her fingers ached. She finally got used to the idea of having a baby and being a mom, just not the overwhelming nausea that seemed to take over her frequently. Reese felt nervous, unsure of what to expect. Mindlessly she clicked the button of the pen they gave her to fill out forms. Click, click, click, click, Maggie finally reached over and put her hand on Reese's leg that was shaking up and down like a jack hammer.

"Relax, sis, it's going to be okay," she said with a soft smile.

"Reese Landon," a high pitched southern voice announced her name.

Reese popped up out of her chair, her stomach in shambles, and her heart in her throat. She anxiously smiled at the nurse when she reached the door.

"Hey, my mom can come back with me, right?" Reese asked.

"Of course she can! Right this way, you two." The nurse took her weight, blood pressure, and pulse. "Everything looks fantastic. Do you know the date of your last period Ms. Landon?" Her squeaky and high pitched voice annoyed Reese, but ironically the irritation eased her nerves.

"Um, I think about... eight weeks ago, on the twelfth."

"Alright," She jotted the number down on her notepad before leading them down the hall and to the exam room. "We're going to have you change into the gown on the exam table. You'll need to get completely undressed from the waist down and then drape the sheet over your lap and the Doctor will be with y'all shortly." She exited with a warm smile.

"Thank you." Reese's voice trailed off as she focused on the exam table.

"I have butterflies in my stomach. I can't believe we're going to get to see our little nugget today!" Maggie said, taking a seat in an empty chair before turning away while Reese undressed and put the gown on. Once she was sitting on the exam table with the sheet draped over her Maggie turned back around. Reese was staring at the floor with a look of panic on her face. "What's wrong, sweetheart?"

"What if something is wrong with the baby? Or what if I'm one of those dumb girls thinkin' she's pregnant and she really isn't? I mean, this day is huge." With a long and drawn out exhale she continued. "I guess I'm kinda freaking out a little."

"Sis, if there's somethin' wrong with the baby then we'll deal with it, but let's just cross that bridge only if we have to, okay? Take some deep breaths. It's going to be fine."

"Okay, okay," she said between breaths.

Reese and Maggie sat in silence while Reese continued to take deep breaths for around ten minutes before there was a knock at the door. Reese double checked she was completely covered up, and when the door opened the first thing they saw was the ultrasound machine, followed by the doctor.

Dr. Morris was the head of the department. He was very tall, with a stalky muscular build. His thick and wavy hair was jet black with grey hairs speckled throughout the front, and the well-trimmed beard that covered up half of his face matched the color of his hair.

"Hey'a, Ms. Landon, how are you feelin'?" He asked with a smile.

"Well, I'm nervous and nauseated like crazy, but good." She nervously giggled.

"The nausea is pretty common. With any luck that'll go away by your second trimester. As for the nerves, I take it this is your first?"

"Yes." She smiled sheepishly.

"Well, in that case it's my duty to prepare you; the nerves never really go away. I have two daughters, fourteen and ten, and I still get nervous from time to time. It's a part of being a parent. I'm sure your momma can back me up on that." Dr. Morris motioned over to Maggie who was sitting with a smile on her face and nodding her head with delight. Reese really liked Dr. Morris. He was honest and witty and that made her feel comfortable. "You ready to see your little peanut for the first time?"

Reese's eyes widened with excitement, "Let's do this."

Dr. Morris positioned the ultrasound machine just right. Reese couldn't see the screen yet but out of nowhere she heard a sound. It was a rapid whooshing sound. Reese listened intensely trying to figure out what that sound was before realizing that it was her baby's heartbeat. Dr. Morris turned the monitor screen toward her, which was the exact moment that everything changed. She saw her tiny little baby, shaped more like a little bean and in the center of that bean was a rapid flashing that correlated with the whooshing sound. Tears filled her eyes and she knew that was it: that was her baby. She couldn't help but feel overjoyed. There was no room for fear or doubt; only immense love filled every last part of her soul.

"Oh my goodness," she whispered.

"Oh my, our little nugget is just perfect," Maggie exclaimed as she grabbed Reese's hand, squeezing it tightly with tears building up in her eyes as well.

"It's kind of amazing, right?" Dr. Morris said.

"Without a doubt, it's beautiful." Reese smiled.

"Well, everything looks fantastic. Baby is good, you're good. I would say you're about seven weeks along."

"Wow, okay." Reese calculated the math and sure enough that would put her with Alex the night she went home with him drunk from the bar. Putting aside any further thoughts about Alex, she asked, "Can I have an ultrasound picture?"

"Of course you can. Let me print a couple out for you. Go ahead and sit up." Dr. Morris handed her an ultrasound picture and booklet. "This booklet will explain the do's and don'ts of pregnancy, along with foods to stay away from, and tips for naturally helping with nausea."

"Perfect." She shook his hand. "Thank you so much, Dr. Morris."

"Yes, thank you for everything, doctor." Maggie shook his hand as well.

"Of course, my pleasure, I'll see you back here in four weeks."

Reese didn't bother telling him she wouldn't be back because she lived two thousand miles away. There was a feeling of regret that crept in when she realized that this wonderful and perfect doctor wouldn't be delivering her child. Within seconds he had put her at ease and with her mom by her side, in those few minutes she felt like she could conquer the world, but now that feeling was rapidly fading. Dr. Morris pushed the machine out of the room and left Reese to get dressed.

Later that day when they got home, Maggie took the ultrasound picture and showed it to Rusty and for the first time in what felt like forever Reese saw his face light up with delight. He took the ultrasound and hung it on the refrigerator with a magnet before walking down the hallway to wash up. Reese worked her way around the kitchen with Maggie preparing dinner. They chatted about baby names and how wonderful motherhood was. Once dinner was prepared, Reese set the table with plates, silverware, and napkins. The three of them gathered around and sat down at the table before Rusty said grace.

"Lord, we thank you for the food you've laid before us, may it nourish our bodies. We also want to thank you for my mother, Lord, she was an amazin' woman and we're blessed to have spent the time we did with her. I also pray for this little baby, Lord, I pray that Reese's baby remains healthy, Lord God. We're blessed beyond our means, and we thank you every day for your love and mercy, in Jesus name, Amen."

"Amen," Maggie and Reese said together.

There were several sniffs and boasts about how wonderful dinner looked and smelled by Rusty. He piled food on his plate with the eagerness of a small child having ice cream for dinner. Steak, potatoes, and barbequed zucchini was his favorite dinner and it showed with how excited he got with every bite.

"Isn't there somethin' you wanted to talk to Reese about, darlin'?" Maggie cut into his celebration.

"Oh! Yes, yes there is." Rusty wiped his face with a napkin and finished chewing the piece of steak in his mouth before continuing. "Reesey Piecey," he placed his hand on Reese's, "Mom and I have been talkin', and we really think... well, we really hope that you would maybe consider movin' back home." Reese sat frozen and confused. "You and the baby can live with us until you are able to move out on your own so we can be right here to help you."

Maggie chimed in, "Sis, I really hope you know how truly sorry we are for not being supportive before, we didn't know what to say or do but, we know we could have handled it better. So, please, just consider it. We'd love to have you come home."

"I promise I'll consider it," Reese pledged while feeling loved.

The rest of the week carried on wonderfully, she enjoyed catching up with old friends and spending as much time with her family as she could. Gran's body was cremated and they held a small family memorial at a lake just outside the city limits of Denton, Texas.

The morning of the funeral, Reese stood in front of the mirror in her black dress and red eyes. The tears would trickle out one by one as she thought of all the wonderful memories that she had with the woman they were laying to rest that day. Her mascara built up under her eyes. Grabbing a tissue from her dresser she fixed her makeup for the fourth time that morning. *How am I supposed to say good-bye to you Gran? How am I going to survive in a world where you aren't a part of anymore? You were always the rock Gran. Help give me the strength today for this.*

"You ready to go, sis?" Maggie asked when she came down the hallway.

"Yeah, I'm as ready as I'm goin' to be anyway."

"I know, honey." Maggie wrapped her arm around Reese. "This ain't easy on any of us, but we have to remember that Gran is in a place where she is no longer suffering."

Grapevine Lake was special to Gran. Reese never knew why before now, but standing there looking out at the water she felt at ease, as if Gran was standing right there with her. The sky was a bright blue with white puffy clouds that hung high overhead looking as if they were placed there by a professional artist. There was a gentle breeze that weaved its cool touch through the small group of people there to say good-bye to Esther.

Rusty was the last to speak. He stood with his back to the lake his mother loved and wrestled with his emotions. "I want to thank all y'all for comin' out today to pay respects to such an incredible woman. I remember as a kid how Mom would try to make even the worst of situations fun. A lot of you know that we grew up rather poor, being raised by a single Mom 'n all, but Mom never let the hard times in life get her down. I hope that if my brothers and I have learned anything from her, it's how to keep our happiness in tact when the world is trying to destroy it. Our mother has been the glue that has always held this family together and she will be dearly missed." Rusty's voice trembled, "I know that one day I'll see my mom again, so I know that this is not good-bye it's simply, I'll see ya later. I love you, Mom, and may you rest peacefully." Rusty blew a kiss to the sky before walking over to stand by Maggie who ever so slightly comforted her husband with a gentle caress of his arm.

Maggie sang amazing grace, and they spread Esther Landon's ashes next to her favorite bench overlooking the water. Reese tried her best to keep it together but she was unsuccessful. Uncle T stood next to her with his arm firmly placed around her. It was a beautiful day filled with love, laughter, and tears as they all said good-bye to the rock of their lives.

Back at Rusty and Maggie's house everyone shared stories of Gran while Maggie and Reese served up her famous blackberry cobbler. Esther was the last of her friends to pass away so all that remained at the house was her family and the in home nurses. Reese enjoyed talking to the nurses and hearing the countless stories they told. Gran brought joy and laughter everywhere she went and her old age never hindered that.

After a few more days at home her time in Denton came to an end, a tinge of regret broke through, she didn't want to leave. She had felt safe and at ease there more than she felt she ever could in Auburn. The morning she had to leave, she lazily packed her suitcase and gathered her things. When it was time to leave for the airport Maggie couldn't hide the tears in her eyes and the longing for her daughter to stay.

"I'm goin' to miss you, sissy." Maggie squeezed Reese tightly. "Please think about our offer."

"I will, Mom, I promise."

Rusty stood there patiently waiting for his turn to say good-bye while Reese and Maggie were locked in each other's arms. Once they let go Reese turned to Rusty and grabbed him. He held her even tighter than Maggie did in his strong and protective arms.

"Really think about our offer Ree, I love you, sweetheart, and we just want you and that precious baby to be safe."

"I know, Daddy. I will really think about it, I promise." She kissed him on the cheek before grabbing her things and heading out the door. She loaded her bag into the rental car and drove back to the airport.

The flight home was much quieter than the flight there. Reese refused to read her parenting book any more. Instead, she decided to think about her parents' offer to move back home. They did have a good point, moving back home would be easier and her momma could help her figure out how to be a momma herself. Reese felt deep down that was the smart choice to make but, she couldn't help but feel heartbroken at the thought of leaving Auburn and Firehouse 23—they were her family too.

The next day Reese showed up for work, ultrasound picture in hand. She showed off her little nugget proudly to everyone. She boasted about how the doctor said the baby was healthy and happy and all looked good. She caught them all up on her week in Texas, how she was able to catch up with old friends and also about her parents apologizing to her and were now being super supportive. She told them about how beautiful Gran's memorial was and how even now she missed standing on the shoreline of Grapevine Lake.

The guys caught her up on all that happened while she was gone and how miserable Kyra was being stuck working with a medic partner who had a god like complex. As they were explaining just how infuriating this guy was, the tones went off.

"Ambulance twenty-three, there's a car versus bicycle, possible broken leg."

"We'll continue this conversation later, I wanna hear all about this guy." Reese smiled as they rushed to the ambulance. Reese picked up the mic, "Ambulance twenty-three copy, in route."

"Copy, Ambulance twenty-three, you're in route." Dispatched acknowledged.

They raced down the road, Kyra beaming with a grin from ear to ear. "I'm so happy you're back."

They showed up on scene to see a man in his mid-twenties lying on the pavement holding his leg. It looked like a car had hit him while trying to make a turn into the grocery store parking lot. He had obvious deformities to the lower part of his leg and knee but no other major injuries that she could see. The man was short and very thin. His red hair was soaked in sweat under the helmet that was still strapped under his chin. He lay there on the ground crying out in pain.

"Hey, man, what happened?" Reese calmly asked.

"I was in the last stent of my ride, that asshole didn't even look!" He yelled out between his groans.

"Okay, hon, I know you're in a lot of pain but try to take a few deep breaths for me. We're gonna need to splint your leg before we move you. I know this is a silly question, and I'm sure I know the answer, but, on a scale from one to ten, what would you rate your pain?"

"Are you kidding me? It's ten!"

"Like I said, I know it's stupid but I have to ask. Kyra here is my partner and she brought over our equipment we'll need to help you out with your leg." Reese pointed to Kyra standing next to her. She was holding the leg splint and backboard next to their rescue bag that Reese had placed on the ground. "Before I can give you anything for the pain she is gonna get your blood pressure and a few other things. I've gotta go over and talk to the driver of the car. Remember, deep breaths."

"Tell that asshole he could of killed me!"

Reese placed her hand on the man's shoulder before getting up and heading over to talk to the driver of the vehicle. As she approached the car she saw a plump old man resembling Santa Claus sitting in the driver seat. He looked ghastly white and in pure shock. His hands visibly trembled and his breathing slightly labored. His thick bifocal glasses had slid down the bridge of his button-like nose. His hair was completely white and he had a scraggly and un-kept beard.

"Hey, sweetheart, were you driving this car?"

"Yes ma'am." His voice was shaky.

"Can you tell me how fast you think you were goin'?"

"Honestly it couldn't have been that fast, I was turning into the parking lot. I saw the guy on the bike, but I thought I had more time!" The man began sobbing. "Is he okay? Please tell me he's going to be okay!"

"He'll be okay. His leg is pretty messed up, but he'll live." Reese reassured him. "What's your name?"

"Albert, but you can call me Al."

"Alright, Al, are you okay?"

"Yes, yes I'm fine. Just a little shaken up, but I'll be fine. Please go help that poor man."

"Well, Al, we'll be here for a little bit longer, so if you change your mind, let me know."

"Will do," He said apologetically.

Reese quickly headed back over to the cyclist on the ground.

"Are you allergic to any medicine?" She asked as she wrapped a tourniquet around his arm and un-wrapped an IV needle.

"No."

"Okay, hold real still, I'm gonna start an IV on ya, this might hurt a little."

"It can't possibly hurt worse than my leg!"

"Good point." Reese softly giggled as she inserted the needle.

The IV was good and she secured the site with tape before pulling out her morphine and drawing up the medicine into the syringe. She slowly administered the pain medicine to avoid her patient from getting sick. Moments after giving the morphine she could see mild relief in his face.

"How are you feeling now?" she asked.

"It still hurts like hell, but that medicine helped a little."

"What's your name, hon?"

"Chris, Chris Hampton."

"Alright, Chris, we are going to place the splint on your leg, it's gonna hurt like hell, but we have to do it so there won't be more damage to the tissue in your leg, alright?"

"Okay." He said trying not to panic while anticipating the pain.

Reese and Kyra maneuvered around the pain and his screams of agony as they placed the splint and got him onto the backboard. Once he was seat belted in they moved him to the gurney and started the short transport to the hospital. When they got to the emergency room, Reese transferred over care to the trauma team before retreating outside for her paperwork.

Walking out the door she saw Engine 34 parked outside, and her stomach turned sour when Alex got out and quickly made his way to Reese.

"Reese, we need to talk," he demanded.

She instantly became very defensive almost as if her instincts were telling her she needed to be protective of herself and her baby. Just in this last week she had realized very quickly that her life was no longer just hers, her unborn child needed to be her number one priority for the rest of her life. Protecting it was all that mattered to her when she saw Alex and hearing his demand, she immediately felt threatened. It was not about her reputation, not the scrutiny she would surely endure, but it was about her baby's life and happiness.

"I'm pretty sure we don't," Reese said as she tried to walk past him.

Alex stepped in front of her, blocking her from walking any further.

"Yes, we do," he declared. "I heard that you're pregnant. If that baby's mine, I want to be a part of his life! I love you and I know we can make this work, for our baby's sake!"

Reese was surprised by the fact Alex knew about the baby at all. In hopes to not raise suspicion, she decided not grill him about how he found out, it would be a dead giveaway that the baby was, in fact, his too. She would get to the bottom of it another way. She stepped toward him, coming face to face with the man who used to relentlessly strike fear into her.

"Yes, Alex, I'm pregnant but, no, it's not yours. Now get the hell out of my way." Her voice was stern and absolute.

"What has gotten into you? How dare you talk to me like this?"

Her eyes narrowed and she grew enraged.

"I'm not the girl who rolls over and takes your crap anymore Alex. I'm not the girl who makes excuses for the bruises you gave me and I refuse to defend you, or spare your feelings. I'm the girl who's had enough of your shit, the girl who doesn't care what you think about her. So don't show up here and think that all of a sudden I'm going to allow you to push me around ever again! You can stand in front of me trying to intimidate me all you want, but your scare tactics no longer work on me. You want to run your fucking mouth about me? Go ahead! You wanna twist the story so you come out looking like a hero? Go ahead! I don't care! I realized that I would rather live the rest of my life with no one to love me than spend another moment with you. Now, not that it's any of your business," she was outwardly being condescending, knowing she was taunting him, "but I had a one-night stand, which resulted in this pregnancy. I don't need you, I don't want you, and my baby doesn't need you. So please, just go!" Reese shoved Alex out of her way and walked past him.

"That's a little harsh, don't you think, Reese?" His voice was a low growl, surely the thought of her being with someone else made his blood boil.

She stopped dead in her tracks, forcing down her fear that lingered under the surface and turned around.

"No, what would've been harsh is if I told you the truth of how I feel, so allow me to enlighten you. If you were on fire, Alex Cunningham, I would sit and watch you burn." Reese walked toward the passenger door and yelled, "Kyra, let's go!"

Kyra jumped out of the back of the ambulance, undoubtedly getting a front row seat to the latest fight between Alex and Reese.

"Yep, get in, I'll drive!" Kyra said as she looked at Alex, standing there baffled. "You pissed off the wrong girl, buddy!" Kyra suddenly yelled, before turning and walking over to get in the driver seat.

Reese got into the rig with her entire body trembling; her hands were shaking so badly she was unable to buckle her seat belt. Kyra reached over and placed her hand on top of Reese's.

"I am so incredibly proud of you! I know that wasn't easy but, you schooled that douche bag! Knuckle bomb!"

Reese looked up at her face and laughed out loud, feeling a sense of accomplishment, realizing she was proud of herself as well.

"Hell yeah I did!" she said as they bumped their fists together. "Let's roll, girl!"

Kyra put the rig in drive and took off past Engine 34 where Alex was sitting in the driver seat, intensely watching them as they drove by.

Back at the station Reese gathered everyone into the training room in hopes to get to the bottom of how Alex found out her secret.

"I just had a run-in with Alex over at the ER. Apparently he knows that I'm pregnant, and the only people that knew, as far as I know, are sitting right here. Does anyone know how he found out?" She sounded alarmed, she was afraid it wouldn't be long before Alex would try to come back around and call her on her bluff. She did her best to not sound too accusatory; she loved and trusted all her crew members but, was saddened by the idea that one of them may have slipped up.

Everyone looked around at each other completely befuddled by her news. Reese didn't want to believe that one of her brothers or sisters would betray her like that.

Jess interrupted the silence, "I texted my buddy out at thirty-four. He said that the supply delivery guy overheard us congratulating you on being pregnant. I guess he thought you and Alex were still together and innocently congratulated him on becoming a father."

Reese stared at Jess with a blank look on her face. *How could I've been so stupid? Secrets never stay secrets.*

"Kyra, do you think he bought the lie I told him?" Reese meekly asked, terrified more than ever that Alex wouldn't believe her.

"Hell, Reese, I almost bought it. You did good, girl. It'll all work out, just try to relax."

Reese wasn't sure that she could relax, not now that Alex knows she's pregnant. She knew she had to protect this baby, but the question that lingered in the back of her head was; what price was she willing to pay to ensure the safety of her child? Reese already knew that she would lay down her life for her little nugget, and no one will ever hurt it, not if she had anything to say about it. She placed her hand low on her stomach and smiled.

"You're right, Kyra, thank you." As she felt an overwhelming calm encompass her.

Chapter 34

OVER THE NEXT few days Alex wouldn't leave Reese alone. He called her all hours of the day and night. He even showed up at her apartment drunk on multiple occasions.

Reese knew she couldn't file a restraining order against him, because if she did, Alex would demand a paternity test and then she wouldn't be able to protect her child from him. She pulled out her phone and listened to the voicemails he left throughout the night.

"Reese," his words were slurred, and Reese swore she could smell the copious amounts of alcohol through the phone. "I miss you so much. I can't live without you anymore. I refuse to go on! Please, forgive me and let me be a father to that baby. I love you so much! I will be a good dad, I promise!"

Reese looked at the time of the voicemail, 1:17 am. She deleted it and moved on to the next one that was time stamped at 1:42 am.

"You're a fucking bitch, Reese! I fucking hate you! How dare you ignore me like that! I swear you're the most selfish and worthless bitch I've ever met!"

Reese hit delete to that voicemail and the seven others that followed it. After about a week of dealing with his harassment she woke up and called her phone company and changed her phone number. Next she deleted her email accounts and created entirely new ones and lastly she deleted all of her social media accounts. The only way left Alex knew how to contact her was showing up at her house or at Station 23 and at least in both places she was protected. At home she and Kyra had her Mossberg short barrel pistol grip 12-gauge shot gun and at work she had her brothers.

Although Reese felt safe, she couldn't one hundred percent ensure the safety of her child. *What if he breaks in the house and kicks me in the stomach, or breaks in and beats me until I lose the baby?* Placing her hand over the top of her unborn child, despite her desire to stay in Auburn, she came to the conclusion that moving home to Texas would be the better option for both of them.

Most people wouldn't agree with her choice to not tell Alex about his child but, most people hadn't walked in her shoes either. Reese didn't care about her reputation in Auburn anymore; the only thing she truly cared about was her baby and ensuring its safety. The safety she felt she needed seemed to live in Texas with her parents and not in the same city as her biggest threat.

Her mind drifted back to her time in Denton. She even fantasized about her and her child walking down the sidewalk hand and hand, happy, successful, and most importantly safe. She pictured her dad taking her daughter on little dates like he had with her and Sophie, or taking her son on fishing trips like he did with his brothers. Reese always had the most wonderful memories with her father and she knew this little one would need a man to look up to and although she was surrounded by wonderful men no one would ever compare to her dad.

The decision was made in her heart but, she kept going back and forth in her mind, toying with different options trying to make the idea of Auburn work. At the end of the day, it was time to make the choice she knew she had to make; she just needed to tell one person to make it real.

"Kyra, can I talk to you real quick?" Reese asked standing outside her closed bedroom door.

"Yeah, come on in."

Reese cautiously opened the bedroom door, walked over to the bed and sat down. Her head hung low, she interlaced her fingers while she searched for how to tell her best friend she was leaving.

"Is everything okay, is it the baby?" Kyra finally asked.

"No, no, the baby is fine, I um– well... I've been thinking a lot over the last week about how exactly this is going to work here in Auburn. How I'm going to create a safe place for my child to grow up." Reese shook her head realizing that was not where she should start. "Wait... let me back up for a second. When I was in Texas for Gran's service my parents and I talked... well, they talked and I listened."

Kyra was giving Reese her undivided attention in anticipation, as though she had a feeling of what Reese was trying to say but, she sat waiting to hear the inevitable words out loud. None of this would be real for Kyra or Reese until it was said out loud.

"Basically they asked me to move back home with them. They told me that I can have my old room and we could turn my sister's old room into the nursery for the baby. They also said they would help me figure out the whole Mom thing and be there for the baby and for me. I mean, even Sophie and my Uncle T offered to help out. I've felt torn and confused, and to be honest, I still do! And yet, on the other hand, I feel like deep in my heart I know what I have to do. So, for the safety of my child, I've decided to move back home. I have to get away from Alex. His harassment is not just affecting me anymore, it affects you, all the guys at twenty-three, and most importantly, it affects this baby. I don't want her or him growing up living in fear and I don't want to be afraid to take my baby somewhere as innocent as the park and have to worry about Alex showing up to ruin things, you know?"

A long silence lingered over the room, Kyra presumably tried to navigate a flood of emotions within her. Reese knew that Kyra didn't want to lose her best friend, she didn't want to say good-bye, and she most certainly wanted to be close for Reese to help support the baby. Reese hoped that Kyra would know in her heart that Reese was right, Alex would always be here in Auburn and Reese would never escape his grasp unless she completely vanished.

"I do know what you mean," Kyra finally said, "and as much as I don't want to lose you, I know that you're right. Your parents are amazing people, Reese, and this baby would be lucky to have them as part of its life." Kyra dropped her head. "God, I'm going to miss you."

"I'm going to miss you too!" They held each other tightly. "When I think about not being able to see you every day, when I think about losing everyone from twenty-three, it makes me want to not go. You are not just my best friend, Kyra, you're my sister!"

"And as your sister, I will support your decision to move home." Kyra squeezed her arms around Reese. "But I have to tell you, you'll never lose us from twenty-three."

"I know, but it won't be the same." Reese released from their embrace tears steadily flowing down her cheeks.

They both sat on the bed and wrapped their arms back around each other for several minutes. They cried and said repeatedly how much they loved each other and how much they were going to miss each other. Kyra continued to give her words of support, telling her that in that moment, it wasn't about her loss and pain, it was about Reese and her baby being safe.

The next day when Reese came on shift she muddled through the morning hellos with everyone, made a cup of decaffeinated tea, and walked over to Chief Gibbs' office. She silently stood in the doorway watching Gibbs on the phone when he motioned for her to come in. Slowly she headed to one of the chairs that sat in front of his desk and sat down while reminiscing on all of the memories she had in this office. The several good talks she had with her Chief and the countless concerning talks they had during her time with Alex. She felt happy that things at 23 were going to end for her on a good note. *End, things are going to end here...* just that realization alone seemed surreal.

"What can I do for you, Ms. Landon?"

"Well, I need to talk to you about something." Reese shifted in her chair and once again interlaced her fingers. "I need to talk to you about my resignation from AFD."

Reese sat staring at the floor in the midst of the silence. She could see Chief Gibbs' face out of the corner of her eye, he sat like a statue at his desk with his jaw literally open and his expression hung low with anguish.

"Reese, why are you doing this?" he softly wondered out loud.

"I guess I should've started with an explanation. I don't know if you were aware but Alex has been harassin' me since I got back. Apparently, he found out about me being pregnant. I decided for my child's safety to not tell him that the baby is his, I even told him to his face the baby wasn't his, and, unfortunately, that hasn't stopped him. He has been calling me non-stop for a week at all hours of the night. He's jammed my email full of drunken rage, shown up at the apartment demanding to talk to me..." As she heard herself speak she knew moving was the right choice. She paused for just a brief moment. "When I was home for my grandmother's funeral, my parents sat me down and asked me to consider movin' back home. I'm scared, Chief, I'm talking terrified, and I don't know that I can keep my child protected and safe here. Plus, my parents are going to help me, so I'm not doing this as alone, as I would be if I were here. I've gone back and forth, and I've tried to convince myself I can make this work in Auburn simply because I don't want to leave you and everyone here. But, I also know in my soul that going back home is in fact, the right decision."

"How can I argue with that?" Chief Gibbs dropped his shoulders in defeat. "Reese, you have a big heart, I just don't know how we're going to get past losing you." His voice lowered and Reese could see the water that built up in his eyes. "You've changed our lives here at twenty-three, Reese. You walked through those doors a doe-eyed southern girl and have transformed into one hell of a woman."

Reese wiped the tears that now fell from her eyes. She felt so honored to have been a part of this family, and she would always cherish the memories they made together the most.

"One more thing, Chief..."

"Yes?"

"I need this to be discrete. I need to basically just vanish. I have two-hundred and eighty hours of vacation time saved up and I have a plan if you're willing to help me with this."

"Of course, let's hear your plan."

"Obviously, I'll tell everyone here at Station twenty-three but, outside of this crew no one can know. My thought was I could use my two-hundred and eighty hours of vacation time which should cover me for a little over a month. You can do a temp fill of my slot but nothing permanent, and if anyone asks, I'm out of town on vacation but, you don't know where. That way I can still have money coming in while I drive back to Texas and get settled, I'm not rushing to get a job. I'll post-date a resignation letter for two weeks before my vacation runs out. That way I'm gone for a good amount of time, you don't know where I went and then I'm just gone for good."

"Sounds like you've thought this through."

"Well, overthinking is kind of my signature move, Chief." She smirked.

"I'm in, Reese, anything to help you out and make this easier."

"How soon can my last shift be?" she eagerly asked knowing that if she stayed for too much longer she wouldn't be able to make herself leave.

"We can do today as your last shift if you would like. That'll give you the next four days off before the next shift and you can pack and get ready to go."

"Oh man, I know that's the best option, but it really breaks my heart thinkin' this is my last shift." She took a look around soaking up all she could. "You have yourself a deal, today is my last shift."

She stuck her hand out and they shook on it. Gibbs stood up from his chair with sadness behind his eyes; he walked around his desk and wrapped his arms around her holding onto her tightly.

"Everything will work out the way it's supposed to." He released his embrace and looked her in the eye. "The man upstairs has a plan, Reese, maybe you can't see that at the moment, and maybe it doesn't feel that way right now, but he does."

"Honestly, I think the man upstairs forgot about me down here but, to be fair I have kinda forgotten about Him as well." Reese felt a strike of anger within her.

"Well, one day you just might feel differently. Now let's go bring everyone into the plan."

"Okay." She said letting Chief Gibbs lead the way.

They walked out of the office and called everyone into the training room where they held the morning briefings. Filing in one by one and seeing Reese in the front of the room with tears in her eyes, each person looked more confused than the one before them. Reese double checked the hallway before closing the door behind her. Chief Gibbs began sharing with everyone the decision Reese made and reminded them that it was their jobs as her brothers and sisters to stand behind her on this. He then explained her plan for leaving and how they agreed that today would be her last shift at Station 23. One by one, the looks of confusion dissipated and heads sunk low. No one wanted this to be real but, Reese hoped that they also knew this was truly what was best for her. She exchanged long, tear-filled embraces from everyone before they trickled back into the common room.

As Reese walked into the room everyone stopped and stared. They had moved from grief stricken back to confusion. They were exchanging looks with each other and yet, no one said a word for several minutes.

"Well, at least all y'all can have your coffee back after today," Reese joked trying to lighten the tension.

"You just made this decision yesterday!" Kyra declared. "And now that's it? You're just done?"

"Kyra, this ain't how I wanted it to go. I honestly thought I would have more time and I promise you that I hate this more than you do. After I leave, y'all are still gonna have each other but, I won't have any of you. Sure, we can talk and text on the phone and the occasional FaceTime but, in all reality here, guys, I'm the one who's losing the most in this scenario. I love each of you like family, yet, I'm being forced to walk away from it all, including all of you. I have to do this for this baby! I have to keep her safe! I have to put aside my feelings and my wants so that I can do right by my son or my daughter. Stayin' here just opens the door for Alex to cause problems for me and even worse for my kid. I cannot let that happen, I won't. I'm really sorry this has been sprung on everyone like this."

Reese could see the guilt that came over each and every one of them. They had all felt angry with Reese but, once she explained everything they realized this decision was in fact, much worse for her than any one of them.

"You're absolutely right, Reese," Stump said. "We support you."

"We got your back, Reese." Nate stood up from the table and placed his arm around Jess.

"I am going to miss the hell out of you, girl!" Jess uttered. "But, I know this is what's best for both of you," she said as she gestured toward Reese's stomach.

"I'll never be able to thank y'all enough for everything you've done for me. Y'all have changed my life and I'll never forget you. I'll be lying in bed with my kid a few years from now telling him or her about all y'all. I'm the person that I am today because of you, because of this firehouse, and because of your never-ending love. I wish y'all knew just how truly heartbroken I am over all of this."

"Okay, everyone listen up..." Kyra said standing on a chair. "We're the only ones who know about any of this but, that doesn't mean we can't throw her a Bon Voyage party. It's going to be tomorrow night, six o'clock at Charlie's."

Reese smiled amidst the cheers. The date and time were set to say good-bye and Reese decided it was best to leave on the fourth day so she could say a final good-bye to everyone. Stump had gathered the guys and they insisted she was not packing her things into the trailer alone before setting a time and day to come load her things.

Her last shift seemed to speed by, she spent a lot of time admiring the station and all the equipment they had, she would miss the exposed brick wall in the common room even though she hated the color of red brick. She would miss her lumpy mattress in the barracks where she slept but, most of all she would miss the energy of this place. The love they shared for each other filled the station. They were a team no matter what, and a family regardless of past mistakes. Reese tried to soak up every ounce of the love that illuminated the house.

"Ambulance twenty-three, fall victim at two-three-four-six west Cobble Street—elderly female, possible broken arm."

The tones went off for one final call and to Reese's delight it was Millie and once again she had not listened to her William. Reese felt happy that she would get to say good-bye to her favorite patient, and yet, concern lingered under the surface, hoping Millie was okay.

The sirens seemed to fade into the background of her mind driving toward Millie's house. She soaked up every minute of the very last ride she would ever take with Kyra. They exchanged giggles and smiles as the ambulance barreled down the road.

"I can't believe Millie is going to be my last patient here in Auburn, and with you." Reese turned to look at Kyra, tears building up in her eyes. "I'm just going to blame these tears on hormones."

"What about these tears?" Kyra laughed as she too wiped tears from her face.

"Um—" Reese thought for a moment. "Sympathy tears?" she joked.

"Yeah, sympathy tears, I like it."

They pulled up to the house and when they walked inside, Reese saw Millie sitting in a chair at her dining room table holding her right arm against her body. The girls quickly made it to her side and placed their equipment down on the floor.

"Millie, what happened?" Reese asked.

"Well, Reesey, I didn't listen to my William. I just had to grab my fork for my dinner real quick. I left it in the kitchen on the counter. I had already gotten my walker in position for me to sit down so I thought, it was only a few steps away and that I would be fine but, I was wrong. I lost my balance and fell. When I hit the ground I heard a pop sound and felt a blinding pain in my arm here. I'm afraid it looks broken." Millie pulled her hand away from her arm to reveal that her right lower arm had major deformities and it looked as if both bones in the lower arm, the radius and the ulna, were broken and her wrist dangled at a downward angle. "See?"

Reese quickly took note of the arm and glanced at Kyra sending her a telepathic look indicating they needed a splint. Millie's fingers still had good color and she was also able to move her fingers meaning there was still good blood flow to the hand.

"Did you pass out at all, Millie?"

"Oh no, sweetheart, I just get off balance sometimes. Other than my arm, I'm doing just fine."

"You didn't hit your head or anything?" Reese asked while she examined her head and neck and Kyra splinted the arm. "Millie, do you want me to give you some pain meds now or in the ambulance?"

"Oh honey, I'm usually pretty tough but this really hurts."

"No problem, sweetheart, give me just a few minutes and I'll have you feeling better in no time." Reese grabbed out her IV stuff and set it up. Kyra pulled out the morphine and an extra syringe. Once the IV was placed, Reese drew up morphine, and administered it to Millie. Within about a minute, the agony in her face faded. "Now, Millie, remember this isn't going to take your pain away completely, but it will help you not care about the pain as much."

"Oh yes, sweetheart, I can definitely see that now." Millie giggled.

The girls got Millie on the stretcher and into the ambulance. While they drove to the hospital Reese continued to check her arm, breaks with that much deformity could easily have loss of blood flow even if it's splinted with minimal movement. Color in her hand remained normal and the morphine seemed to make Millie even more chatty than normal.

"Reese dear, you look different. Why do you look different?" Millie reached up and ran her fingers down Reese's face.

"Um, well Millie, I'm pregnant," Reese said as she brought Millie's hand off her face.

"Oh my goodness, that's exciting, sweetheart! That must be it, you have that glow!" Millie slurred her words slightly from the pain medication.

"Uh yeah, I guess. I feel sick to my stomach more than I do anything else."

"Oh yes, I remember that. I was so sick with all of my pregnancies."

"Well, Millie, I'm very glad I got to see you today. I'm going to be out of town for a while, I'm taking some time off and I was hoping to see you before I left."

"Well, besides this thing," she held up her splinted arm, "I'm happy I got to see you too! And these meds you gave me are better than any wine I've ever drank!"

Reese laughed while she listened to Millie talk about how weird and amazing she felt for the remainder of the transport to the ER. Once they arrived at the hospital they moved her over into a bed and gave a report to the nurse. Reese was still standing in the room when Millie's voice trailed out of her room.

"I'm right here, Millie. What's up, love?" Reese asked, entering the room.

"Reese, I just want you to know that I have always adored you like a daughter. I care for you so very much and I want you to know that you'll be missed while you're gone. Come close," Millie said motioning Reese to come over so she could whisper in her ear. "I know that you're not just leaving town for a bit, dear, but God told me to tell you, He knows this is hard, but this is the right decision. Your family, especially your parents, will become more important to you than you can even realize right now. He's got you, Reesey, everything's going to be okay." Reese sat there stunned. She turned to look at Millie with shock and disbelief on her face. *How could she possibly know all of this?* "You're secret's safe with me, honey, now go, conquer greatness."

"Thank you, Millie. I'll never forget you," Reese whispered back before leaving the room.

It had been the perfect good-bye between Reese and her favorite patient. A small tear trickled down her face as she stood by the ambulance looking back at the Emergency Room. Reese was going to miss this place more than anyone would ever know and it killed her to not be able to say good-bye to so many amazing people but, this was for the best.

"This is the hardest thing I've ever had to do," Reese said to Kyra.

"I know girl, you have no idea how much you'll be missed around here."

"I can't even say good-bye to these people which is the hardest part. None of them even know they'll never see me again. I guess they might not care as much as I do."

"Of course they will, Reese, you're everyone's favorite paramedic."

"Yeah, I guess, if you say so." She returned Kyra's smile.

Reese watched people walking down the sidewalk and going about their business as they drove down the street back to the station for their final log-off as partners. Seven years of working with each other had come to an end and neither one of them were prepared for it. Reese grabbed the mic.

"Dispatch, this is Medic twenty-three, Log off EMT Vaughn and log off Paramedic Landon."

"Medic twenty-three, we show you logged off."

"It's been a hell of a ride," Reese said to Kyra putting out her fist for a fist bump. "I wish you knew how much I'm gonna miss sitting on your right."

"I'm gonna miss sitting to your left." Kyra bumped her fist into Reese's. "Seven years, and I can't believe it's over."

"Me either."

With a final deep breath, *this is it.* Her time at Auburn Fire Department was done. Only a handful of tears were able to fight their way out and down her face as she emerged from the rig.

Once inside the station, she decided to call Alex's brother, Lance before cleaning out her locker. She was hoping that he would let her set up a day she could go see Harper and Oliver one last time. Alex would, indeed, be furious if he found out, but Reese couldn't bring herself to leave without telling them one last time that she loved them. Although they were Alex's niece and nephew she loved them as if they were hers. She picked up the station phone and dialed his number.

"Hello?" Lance answered.

"Hey, Lance, it's Reese."

"Oh my God, hi, Reese...!" He pleasantly said, clearly excited to hear from her.

"I wanted to call to ask you a favor."

"Sure! What's up?"

"I know Alex would be furious if he knew I was callin' you but, I just wanted to know if it would be okay to stop by tomorrow and hang out with the kids for a bit."

"Of course you can! They've been asking for you, I tried calling, but your number says it's disconnected."

"Yeah, I know. Would it be alright if I stopped by around two-thirty?"

"That would be perfect! They'll be so happy to see you!"

"Thank you so much, Lance, see you then."

Reese hung up the phone and went into the barracks to gather up her things and to clean out her locker. She felt happy there was no one else around in the room while she cleared out her belongings because it gave her a few minutes to say good-bye to her career there, alone. Once she packed up her things and her bags were ready, she came out of the barracks expecting to find everyone waiting for her, but no one was there. She looked around the station trying to find anyone but, still no one was there. She knew that saying good-bye was going to be the difficult but, she knew she had to say good bye to everyone anyway.

"Hey Kyra, where is everyone?" Reese asked when Kyra walked by.

"I don't know. Here, let me help you. Let's take all of this stuff out to your car, and then we'll come back in to find them."

"Sure. Thank you," Reese said as Kyra took the box she had filled with her items out of her locker.

They walked outside and she saw the entire crew all lined up in formation just beyond the bay doors. The truck was pulled out of the garage and the American flag was hanging off the ladder that extended high into the sky. Reese wrestled down her tears when Kyra put down the box she held and ran to get into formation with them, and then Chief Gibbs stepped forward.

"Reese Landon, we all wanted you to know that we will miss you beyond what anyone can put into words. You're the light in the midst of our station, you're the joy that brings a smile to our faces, and you're the love we all feel within. It has been a true honor to work side by side with you. I hope the next medic that comes in understands they have some big shoes to fill." A deafening silence fell over the parking lot. "Attend, hut!" Gibbs yelled before they all raised their right arms in a salute.

Reese placed her pillow on top of her bag, stood upright, and raised her right arm in a salute.

"We know you have a lot to do," Cole said, "but don't forget to be at Charlie's at six o'clock tomorrow night, okay?"

Reese smiled and nodded her head yes.

Chapter 35

SHE LOADED UP her car and drove home feeling emotionally drained. Emptiness settled inside her. Reese knew she would never be the same without them. They held her up when she went through the hardest part of her life so far. She knew, without a doubt, that if it hadn't been for them she probably would have never had the strength to leave Alex.

On her way home she stopped and picked up all the boxes she could get from the local grocery store so she could head home and start packing, by pulling things from her closet she knew she wouldn't need. She then packed her travel suitcase with clothes for her trip home, and decided to keep only one pair of shoes out for driving and then packed the rest in boxes. One by one she filled the boxes with all of her non-essential items and stacked them at the door.

She worked alone. Reese assumed Kyra was out at Charlie's with the rest of the crew. She kept working. The only break she took was to eat a quick bite of food for dinner. That was until severe nausea kicked in and she spent the next several minutes throwing up in the bathroom. On that note, she decided to call it a night and head to bed.

Reese was sound asleep when she felt someone crawl into bed with her, startling her awake. She quickly turned her head to find Kyra.

"I'm sorry... I didn't mean to wake you. It's just... I'm really going to miss you." Kyra wrapped her arms around Reese squeezing her tightly. The smell of alcohol on her breath was strong, causing Reese's stomach to turn. "I love you."

"I love you too," Reese said putting her hand on Kyra's arm. "But if you don't get off me I'm going to throw up on you."

Kyra moved off of her as quickly as she could and Reese ran off to the bathroom for another vomiting session. The nausea was becoming more tolerable. The vomiting was almost second nature, but Reese hung over the toilet hoping that Dr. Morris was right and by the second trimester the nausea would go away. By the time Reese made it back to her bed, Kyra was sprawled out across the entire thing, sound asleep and snoring as loud as Rusty usually did. Shaking her head, Reese walked out of the room and slept in Kyra's bed.

The next morning Reese got up and made some decaffeinated black tea. She was stirring in some honey when Kyra came stumbling down the hallway. Her eyes were blood shot and the small amount of makeup she wore was smeared under her eyes. She was rubbing her temples and forehead when she came into the kitchen.

"How did I get in your room last night?" Kyra asked holding a coffee mug.

"Well, you kinda got into bed with me and told me how much you are going to miss me and then told me you love me. This was all, of course, before the smell of alcohol on your breath made me puke. By the time I came back you were sacked out." Reese giggled.

"Oh my God, I'm so sorry!" Kyra said, mortified.

"It was funny, don't worry about it, I just laughed at you and slept in your bed."

"But still, I'm sorry that I made you vomit." Kyra looked down at her cup and back at Reese. "Although, I know coffee makes you sick, I seriously need coffee."

"It's all good. I'll head into my room." Reese walked away before turning back to Kyra. "You have to remember to focus on the good things about all of this, like you can have coffee every morning again when I'm gone." Reese winked at Kyra.

That afternoon she went over to Lance and Helen's house. She took a quick moment and gathered her thoughts in the car before getting out and heading to the door. With one final deep breath she knocked. Within seconds the door flung open and Harper came running out and into Reese's arms.

"Reese!" she screamed. "You're here! You're really here!"

Her long auburn hair flowed freely as she grabbed Reese around the waist and squeezed tightly.

"Of course I am, sister! How are you?"

Next Oliver came sprinting around the corner jumping up into her arms. "Reese!" He wrapped his arms around her neck and squeezed as hard as he could.

They took her by the hands, dragging her inside and to the couch. Helen handed Reese a glass of water and joined them on the couch.

"Thank you." Reese smiled.

"You're welcome. How are you?" Helen asked.

"I'm doin' alright."

"That's good. I just have to say, I think you're so much better off." She softly smiled.

"Thank you, honestly the hardest part is this." She looked down at Harper and Oliver who sat right next to her on each side. "I miss them more than anything else."

"You're welcome to come by any time, Reese."

"I don't want to cause problems for everyone. As hard as it is, this is for the best." She looked down at Harper. "You know how much I love you, right?"

"Hmmm," she muttered. "This much?" she stretched her arms out to the sides as wide as they would go.

Reese leaned in and gently touched her nose to Harper's. "More," she smiled before wrapping her arms around her.

"How much do you love me, Auntie Ree?" Oliver asked tugging on her shirt.

She wrapped her arms around them both. "I love you both all the way to the moon and back!" She squeezed them both tightly. "But, sadly this is the last time I'll be able to see you guys."

"What do you mean Auntie Ree, why!?" Harper cried out, the happiness quickly vanished from their faces and tears instantly built up in Harper's eyes.

"Well, because your Uncle Alex and I are no longer together and to avoid any problems I have to bow out as gracefully as I can. I just wanted to see you both one last time so, I could say good-bye, and let you know that none of this is your fault. You two are amazin' and I love you so very much. I'm so sorry that I can't see y'all anymore."

"We're gonna miss you so much! You're our favorite Aunt!" Oliver whined as giant tears fell onto his cheeks.

"I wish things didn't have to be this way!" Harper had tears rushing down her face.

"I know, I wish it didn't either," A few steady tears seeped from Reese's eyes as well.

After several more strong and drawn out hugs and even more times of telling them how much she loved them, Reese gathered her things. She turned to Lance who looked just as heartbroken as the kids did.

"Thank you, again." She wrapped her arms tightly around him.

"Good luck with everything, Reese."

Helen walked over to Reese for one final embrace.

"Good-bye, Reese." Her voice at a whisper and a tear escaped her eye when she finally let her go.

Reese walked out the door feeling like she was leaving a piece of her heart behind. Those kids meant everything to her, and she vowed that no matter what she will forever love them with the same amount of strength that she did that day. She spent her entire drive home wiping tears from her face and neck as they poured out of her eyes like a faucet.

When she got back home she continued to pack and organize things throughout the day and she even rented the U-Haul trailer to attach to her car. The day moved along fairly quickly as she kept herself busy, trying to not think about leaving or the Bon Voyage party that night. Around four o'clock she stopped and took a shower before getting ready for her party. She left things simple and easy, straightened her hair and put on minimal makeup. She grabbed a pair of dark blue skinny jeans and an emerald green loose fit, off-the-shoulder shirt. With her converse on her feet and her keys in hand she was ready to head over to Charlie's.

At 5:55 she arrived at the bar, nervous about going inside. She didn't know what to expect. What if Alex found out about tonight and he put it all together, she knew she would be screwed. As the panic began to brew within her, Reese chose to take a breath and just relax. Tonight wasn't about Alex; it was about her saying good-bye. How am I going to say good-bye without giving my escape plan away? She feared.

"You comin' in?" A voice startled her from behind. She turned around to see Chad Platt walking toward the bar. "Isn't this whole thing for you, to send you off on your big trip?"

"Yeah, I guess," Reese said putting her head down.

"Where are you going?" he asked.

Panic rushed over her; she hadn't thought about what to tell people. Where was she going and why? The most basic question caused her to stand there frozen with fear.

"Reese?" he interrupted her frenzy.

"Um– Crap!" She paced back and forth. "I haven't even made it into the bar and I've already screwed everything up! I knew this party was a bad idea."

"What are you talking about?" he asked but she ignored him and continued talking out loud to herself. "Reese, slow down." He stopped her and forced her attention on to him. "Talk to me, what's wrong?"

Reese started to bite her nails, struggling with whether to just tell him or not. She knew the more people who knew her secret the more likely it was that Alex would find out but, she needed to talk to someone. She ended up breaking her own rule and spilled everything to Chad. He stood staring at her in amazement as she poured out everything to him.

"I'm sorry," she said "I just unloaded on you there and you didn't need to know all of that. I just– I'm freaking out a little bit, obviously. Where am I going for the next two months? That's the real mystery that needs to be solved here."

"You said your grandmother died, right?" He placed his hand on her shoulder. "Maybe you and your family are taking a trip across America to spread her ashes in all the places she wants them spread."

Her eyes looked up at him with astonishment.

"That's genius, Mr. Platt! You're a true lifesaver, you know that?" She stood upright and gave him a little peck on the lips.

"You're very welcome." He cracked a half smile and he pulled her close. They stood nose to nose both fighting the urge to kiss each other again. "I don't want to keep fighting this, Reese, and now that I know you're leaving that makes it an even stronger urge." He pulled her in closer and deeply kissed her. His tongue moved around hers with ease and she felt a tingle run down her spine. He was right. She was leaving and that would be it for the two of them, so why not have tonight? After several minutes of deep kissing he pulled away from her, leaving her in a trance of endorphins. "But first, the party," he grabbed her hand and walked her to the bar.

They walked into Charlie's hand in hand and when she looked up she noticed that the bar had been closed to the public and everyone that was there, was there for her. She smiled and felt very honored to have all of these people come out to see her off on her fake journey. Her smile was beaming from ear to ear as she weaved through the crowd of people. Nurses, doctors, police officers, firefighters, they were all here for her. Reese was surprised to see that so many people showed up to say good-bye.

That night she relaxed and enjoyed every last minute she had with them all, especially Chad. He stayed either by her side or with his fellow officers to give her some space but, Reese's eyes never wandered far from him. When he was across the bar, giving her space, her eyes would travel back to him every few minutes. They would exchange smiles across the room and Reese would flirtatiously bite her bottom lip. She spread the story Chad came up with to everyone there that night, in hopes that it would make its way back to Alex, buying her some time.

It was now time for her to say a few words, so she grabbed her glass of ice water and stood up in the middle of the crowd.

"First of all, I want to say thank you to each and every one of you for comin' out for this tonight. Seven years... seven years I've been here, and it seems like yesterday I was the new kid on the block. Each and every one of you changed my life for the better, and I love y'all so much. It seems impossible to live without all y'all for the next two and a half months!" She paused to look at her brothers and sisters from 23. "My crew, my amazin' crew, you've forever changed my life. Without your love and support, only God knows where I would be. I love y'all with all my heart." She raised her glass. "Well, it ain't whiskey, but cheers anyway!"

"Cheers!" everyone yelled.

She drank her water and enjoyed the laughter and the many stories that were told, some even at her expense. As the night came to a close, she found Chad at a table with his buddies.

"Hey there, handsome..." She smiled. "You ready to get outta here?"

"I'm ready when you are." He smiled before finishing the last gulp of his beer and placing his hand in hers, leading her out of the bar.

She stopped at the door and took one last look around, feeling overcome with happiness.

That night Reese and Chad spent their time together entangled in each other. They made love and it was sensual and meaningful. He made her feel wanted, beautiful, and very satisfied. They stayed awake talking about everything they could before falling asleep wrapped up in each other's arms. That was something Reese never thought she would want again but, with Chad it was different, she wanted to be there with her head on his chest and his arms around her. She felt safe and secure, not bound and trapped.

The next morning they woke up happily in each other's arms, happy to be with each other, they made love again. Shortly, after they were done, she threw her robe around herself and ran to the bathroom and threw up. She didn't get the door closed all the way and Chad came in and held her hair out of the way.

"You don't have to do that, I know this ain't pretty," she said, hunched over the toilet.

"I don't mind." he softly replied gently running his hand up and down her back.

About ten minutes later she was finally done and got up to brush her teeth.

"My teeth should be extra clean since I brush them multiple times a day now. This morning sickness is no joke."

"I see that! Are you okay?"

"Yeah I'm fine. Puking is like a new routine. I've gotten used to it for the most part."

He rubbed her back again before pulling her into his embrace and kissing her without hesitation.

Why can't I take him with me? Leaving Chad when it was just a kiss outside of the bar was easier than leaving him after last night and today. Chad must have felt the same way because he spent her last remaining days in Auburn with her making love in between times of packing and getting things ready to go.

"I wish I didn't have to leave you. I feel like we could've had a real shot if I stayed, you know?" she confessed.

"I wish you didn't have to leave either but I could never ask you to stay here where Alex is. It wouldn't be fair."

Reese put her head on his chest and let him hold her. She knew he was right and she knew leaving was the right choice but, nothing said she had to like it.

"Maybe once you get settled I'll come visit you. I've never been to Texas before."

"I would really like that." She pressed her lips against his.

The next day, Chad and the Firehouse 23 crew were there to help load her things into the trailer and see her off. After several trips back and forth her car was filled to the brim and the trailer looked like a complex game of Tetris. She said her final good-byes to everyone there and fought back the tears welling up within her eyes, this was it.

One by one her station 23 family filtered through to say their final good-byes. Ray was the first one to hug her and give her well wishes.

"I'm gonna miss you, Reese."

"I'm gonna miss you too, Ray. I gotta tell ya, I've always wondered about your hair, and since this is the last time I'll see you for a while, can I touch it?" she laughed. "I just gotta know what it feels like!"

Ray chuckled and leaned his head down. "Go ahead."

"Crunchy, I knew it!" Reese laughed before grabbing him one last time. "Good-bye, Ray, thank you again for everything."

"Reese," Cole said, "Twenty-three isn't gonna be the same without ya!" He wrapped his skinny arms around her.

"Cole, I'm gonna miss you but, please, for the love of Christ, shave that mustache off!" She laughed as she let him go.

"No way, man, this is how I get all the ladies!" He wiggled his hips and ran his fingers down each side of the mustache, twirling the ends.

"Whatever creeper," she laughed. "Nate, oh my, I have so many things to say to you." She smiled, wrapping her arms around him. "You'd better take good care of my girl, buddy. Don't you make me fly back up here just to kick your ass!" She joked before letting him go and wiping the tears from her face.

"I promise, I will," he smiled.

"Girl, how am I supposed to say good-bye to you?" Jess cried out throwing her arms around Reese.

"I know, love, I have no idea how I'm supposed to function without you around!" More tears streamed down her face. "We can't think of this as good-bye. I'll try to come back when I can, and you guys have to come down for my baby shower and when this kiddo is born! I don't know how but, we'll make this work. I love you too much to have this be good-bye forever!"

"You got yourself a deal!" Jess agreed.

"Kyra," Reese said hugging her tightly. "No partner will ever compare to you! I'm gonna miss you so much, I can't even begin to put it into words. The same goes for you! We have to find a way to make time for our friendship, because you matter so much to me, and I cannot stand the thought of losing you! I love you, my sister from another mister."

"I love you too!" Kyra cried as they stood in each other's embrace. "Yes, we'll make this work! Jess and I will definitely be at that baby shower, and the rest of us will come after this little one is born! You have our word!"

Reese and Chad had already said their heart-filled good-byes so she decided to save him for last. When she got to Stump she could no longer hold back her emotions. She flung her arms around him and held onto him.

"I'm so scared, Stump. What if I can't do this?"

"Sweetheart, you'll do fine. You know what you need, is hope sprinkled with a little bit of faith."

"What if I'm all out of hope?"

Stump released her and looked into her tear-filled eyes.

"Maybe hope has a way of finding you, if you just allow it."

"What am I going to do without you?"

"I'm always here, Reese, no matter the distance between us, no matter the time of day."

They held each other one last time. Tears fell from both of their eyes. Once they released their grasp she turned to Chad for their final good-bye.

"I can't even begin to tell you good-bye because if I try I'll never leave. I really think we could've been somethin' amazing and I'm so sorry that my drunken choices are going to rip that away from us. I could see myself falling in love with you, Chad Platt, and I hate that I have to leave."

She leaned in deeply kissing him one last time before having to tear herself away and get into her car. She waved with tears streaming from her eyes as she pulled out of the driveway.

The sun was setting while she drove out of town and onto the open road. She was almost three months pregnant and Texas bound. She wiped her tears and the faintest of smiles emerged on her face, for she knew her journey was just beginning. For a split second something fluttered in her lower abdomen... hope.

About the Author

JD Grace is new to the author scene. She has left audiences captivated with her debut novel, Rise From the Ashes, which is a fictionalized story based on her real life experiences. Rise From the Ashes, is the first book in the Reese Landon series where readers get to take a journey with Reese through the darkness that life deals her direction.

She found herself mixed up in an abusive relationship in her early twenties, and was forced to claw her way out, only to later struggle in putting herself back together while life continued to throw her under the bus.

She is a real life paramedic in a small county in the middle of California. She began her journey to being a paramedic in High School when she took classes towards becoming an EMT. She soon climbed the ladder in becoming a Paramedic where her skills and her strength have been tested time and time again.

She has always had a knack for writing, but never thought she could accomplish writing a book. When she was laid off work in 2017 she found the strength to overcome her fears and write her first book. Although she is now back working full-time on an ambulance as a Paramedic, she juggles her job, being a single mother of two beautiful girls, and her writing career. She also manages a blog called, From Lemons to Lemonade (website at the bottom), which is her real life story in all of its tragic glory and how she overcame the most unthinkable things with the strength of God, her girls, and her incredible family and friends.

Rise From the Ashes, is just the beginning for this new author. She's been able to relate to audiences with her raw and unapologetic descriptions of what an abusive relationship can look like. That light continues to shine in the second book in the Reese Landon series, Reborn Into Tragedy, which is scheduled to be released in early 2019.

Visit and subscribe to her blog at www.jdgrace.org

Acknowledgments

One would think I found happiness on my own, but they would be wrong. It was only WITH God, and through faith that we forged a new path together. We faced the unknown and found a passion that brings such joy to my life. So, my biggest thank you goes to the one and only, Almighty God. I took a chance on faith and found everything I've been searching for and so much more!

Thank you to my family who supported me in this new journey through thick and thin, I love you all more than you could possibly know.

My mom, who is my biggest fan, thank you for being real and never just telling me what I want to hear. You've been the pillar of strength behind my back from the beginning, and the words thank you doesn't seem to be enough.

My dad, oh, Pops, you've been the most amazing dad that any person could dream of. Thank you for believing in me, even if it was hard to come to. I hope you know just how much I love you.

My beautiful and amazing daughters, I love you both to the Milky Way and back. Thank you for putting up with my focus being in the computer writing and for never making me feel terrible about it, although I did. You two are my whole world and I'm thankful to be blessed with such incredible and strong willed girls. You both have forever changed my life and I'll love you with all that I am until my very last breath.

Bethany Faye Photography, you took my scatter brain vision and made it reality. As one of my favorite people in this world, I'm so thankful for you in my life. I can't wait to work with you on book two!

Miss Brittney Anderson, oh girl, you were an answer to my prayers! I 100% know that I was meant to find you. Thank you for putting up with my crazy brain that fire's like a machine gun. I'm so happy that we are not just two people who work together, but that we are friends. You took my story and helped me elevate it to the next level.

My EMS, Fire, PD, and ER family, you guys are a big part of my strength. Thank you for loving me in spite of my angry rants, my frustration, and those not so rare hangry moments. Always remember that you all mean so much more to this world than you are told. Our little county will always shine the brightest with you all in it. Thank you for the wonderful memories. I'm so thankful to have been able to work with such amazing people. It has been one hell of a journey that I will never forget. Thank you for friendships that became family, for reminding me that life truly is too short, and for the adrenaline rush of knowing what it feels like to save a life. Never stop taking care of each other, but most of all, stay beautifully weird amidst the chaos of this crazy life.

I love you all, and sincerely from the bottom of my heart, thank you.

CPSIA information can be obtained
at www.ICGtesting.com
Printed in the USA
FSHW010500160519
58191FS